THE UNIVERSITY OF THE STATE OF NEW YORK

CATHERINE STONE

DOCTOR OF MEDICINE

GEHM

A DOCTOR'S
SPLIT-SECOND DECISION

"Damn you! You said my wife could have a child. You told her not to worry. And now you're telling me she might die? I ought to—"

"Gordon, stop it!" Kim restrained him. "Even the best doctor in the world can't predict the outcome of a pregnancy. Catherine did the best she could." Kim put his hand on his friend's shoulder. "If it's any consolation, I couldn't have done any better."

"Mr. Graham," Catherine said, "there's still a chance we can save your wife and child."

Hope flared in his eyes. "How?"

"By performing a caesarian section."

"Catherine, no!" Kim cried.

"What is this caesarian section?" Gordon demanded. When it was explained, he blanched.

"I've done the operation several times in Paris," she said, "and I've never lost a patient. I can't promise that I won't lose Mrs. Graham or her baby, but it's the only chance we have of saving her."

"Do it," Gordon said.

"We'll need your help." Catherine told him what he had to do.

The next hour flew by in a blur. . . .

The OATH

LINDSAY CHASE

DIAMOND BOOKS, NEW YORK

Cover stethoscope courtesy of The Historical
Museum of Medicine and Dentistry in
Hartford, Connecticut.

THE OATH

A Diamond Book / published by arrangement with
the author

PRINTING HISTORY
Diamond edition / July 1991

ISBN: 1-55773-535-2

Diamond Books are published by The Berkley Publishing
Group, 200 Madison Avenue, New York, New York 10016.
The name ''DIAMOND'' and its logo are trademarks
belonging to Charter Communications, Inc.

PRINTED IN THE UNITED STATES OF AMERICA

10 9 8 7 6 5 4 3 2 1

To Zita Christian and Denise Gore,
friends and fellow writers, with thanks.
They know why.

The OATH

❧ CHAPTER ❧

ONE
___

CATHERINE dreamed of dead bodies again. The macabre images vanished when an insistent hand shook her shoulder and a shrill voice rang in her ear.

"Young lady, wake up!"

Her eyes flew open to find Mrs. Jenkins standing beside the bed, the feeble glow from a small kerosene lamp casting eerie shadows across the landlady's plump, lined face.

"What is it?" Catherine mumbled.

"Mr. Hunter's come for you. Why, the poor man pounded on the door so hard, I feared he would break it down."

Catherine sat up and rubbed the sleep from her eyes. "What time is it?"

"A little past one."

She groaned inwardly. "Tell him I'll be down as soon as I dress."

Mrs. Jenkins nodded as she waddled across the room. "I'd hurry, if I were you, before that man wears a hole in my hall carpet." When she reached the door, she stopped and turned. "It's a night fit for neither man nor beast, so you'd best bundle up with a good thick scarf and gloves." Her motherly advice given, she disappeared.

The shock of the cold floor against bare feet banished the last vestiges of sleep from Catherine's mind. Her teeth chattering, she dressed quickly as much for warmth as for the urgency of the situation. When she finished, she wrapped and secured her long nighttime braid around her head in a coronet, threw on a heavy wool cloak, and snatched up her black leather bag as she flew out.

She found Mr. Hunter still pacing back and forth in Mrs. Jenkins' foyer. He stopped and looked up when he heard hurried

1

footsteps on the stairs. The abject fear in his eyes made him appear even younger than his eighteen years.

"Dr. S—Stone?"

Catherine didn't tell him she was a third-year medical student at the Women's Medical College, not yet entitled to be addressed as "Dr." "Mr. Hunter . . . Shall we go? I expect you're in a hurry."

His head bobbed up and down. "I have a cab waiting."

February 9, 1888 was a terrible night for a baby to be born, Catherine decided when a ruthless blast of wind sliced through her cloak like a scalpel. The street was empty, save for the cab and the dark and uncaring rows of red brick houses. The only witness to their hurried departure was a small full moon hanging high in the clear, star-strewn sky, and even the moon appeared indifferent to the momentous occasion.

I'm going to deliver my first baby, Catherine thought. *There should be cheering throngs to wish me well.*

Half an hour later, after speeding in wordless silence through Philadelphia's deserted streets, they arrived at the Hunters' modest woodframe house in a neighborhood long past its prime.

Once inside the warm foyer, Catherine barely had time to take off her cloak before a scream of agony ripped the silence.

"Lucy! Dear God!" Peter Hunter cried, bolting up the stairs before Catherine could blink.

She wasn't far behind, racing up the stairs as quickly as her long skirts would allow. She located the bedchamber by following the muffled sounds of sobbing.

There she found Lucy wrapped in her husband's arms.

Catherine smiled as she entered the tiny room. "There's no need to cry, Lucy. Everything's going to be fine."

The girl looked up, her wide blue eyes glazed with pain. "I'm so scared, Miss Stone. It hurts something awful."

"Listen to me, Lucy. You must put such fears out of your mind this instant, do you understand?"

Lucy sniffed and nodded.

"That's my brave girl." Catherine walked over to the bed, which had been set with fresh sheets. A neat pile of extra folded sheets and several towels had been set on a chair beside the bed. "Did you boil them, as I instructed at the clinic?"

Lucy nodded.

Catherine turned to Peter. "Now I want you to boil me a big pot of water and bring me two basins."

The minute Peter dashed out of the room, his wife groaned, swayed, and clutched at a bureau for support. Catherine was at her side in an instant.

"How often are the pains coming?" she asked.

"Faster and faster now. This afternoon, I had one every hour or so, and tonight I got very wet. . . ." She blushed, unable to continue.

Catherine knew from Lucy's oblique reference that her waters had broken. "And do these pains feel different from the ones you had this afternoon?"

Lucy nodded.

"I think it's time for you to get into bed," Catherine said, taking her arm to help her.

Once Lucy settled in for her confinement, Catherine took one of the extra sheets from the chair, tied one end to the foot of the iron bed, and twisted the rest of it until it formed a long rope. She handed the puller to Lucy.

"When the pains come, I know you'll feel the urge to push with all your might, but it's too soon. When that feeling comes, I want you to pull on this instead." She handed the twisted sheet to Lucy. "Do you understand?"

The girl nodded, but there was no mistaking the terror in her eyes.

Catherine smiled and patted her hand, which was hot and damp. "You're going to do fine, just fine."

Just at that moment, another contraction hit Lucy, almost raising her from the bed, and a low moan escaped her lips.

At the door, Peter appeared with twin white enameled basins in one hand and a pot of boiling water in the other. Catherine had him set them down, then she banished him to the parlor.

After laying out the contents of her obstetrical bag on a sterile towel spread over a table, Catherine began the ritual of antisepsis. She set the forceps and speculum in a solution of boiling water and five-percent carbolic. After putting on an apron and hanging her stethoscope around her neck, Catherine palpated Lucy's abdomen to locate the baby's position in the womb and note its progress.

She stepped back with a smile. "Your labor is progressing very well, Lucy. Soon you'll be the mother of a fine, healthy baby and this will all be well worth it."

"It can't be soon enough for me, Miss Stone."

Catherine glanced at a small clock on the bedside table. It

said two o'clock. She hated to tell Lucy, but it would be several hours yet before her ordeal ended.

At five o'clock, just as a faint pink blush tinged the eastern horizon, Baby Hunter was about to be born.

Catherine rolled up her sleeves to the elbow, then washed her hands and arms in a carbolic solution, taking special care to scrub thoroughly with a small, soft brush for five minutes, until her flesh was rosy. Then she draped Lucy's bare legs with sterile sheets and prepared to deliver the baby.

From her place at the foot of the bed, Catherine said, "As soon as you feel the next pain, I want you to take a deep breath and press down as hard as you can."

"I can't bear it any more! I'll die!"

"Yes, you can, Lucy, and you won't die. It's almost over, but you have to help your baby. Take a deep breath and press down."

Catherine kept one eye on Lucy, whose purplish face was contorted with the effort. Sweat trickled down her cheeks and her hands were chafed and swollen from grasping the puller. She grunted and gasped as though she were being tortured on the rack.

But her efforts were rewarded: the baby's head crowned.

Catherine felt her own excitement rising. "Now, don't bear down any more. Open your mouth! Scream, if you have to, but don't bear down this time."

With Lucy's scream ringing in her eyes, Catherine watched in wonder as the baby's head rotated and the rest of the body, all wet and covered with white flecks of matter, came sliding out into her waiting hands.

Her first baby . . . Catherine felt tears of wonder well up in her eyes.

But her elation soon turned to panic when she saw that the small scrap of humanity wasn't moving or breathing.

She gently blew on the baby's face. No response. She then flicked a few drops of water at those still features. Still no gasp and lusty wail.

"Did I have a boy or a girl?" Lucy's weak voice came from the head of the bed.

Catherine grasped the baby by its heels, suspended it upside down, slapped its bottom smartly, and prayed.

The baby gave a little gasp followed by a wail of outrage.

Catherine breathed a sigh of relief and triumph as she saw a faint pink flush steal over the tiny body, followed by a flailing of arms and legs.

So tiny, Catherine thought. So perfect, with ten miniature fingers and toes, the little toes tipped with nails no bigger than pinheads.

She waited endless minutes until the umbilical cord stopped pulsating, then she quickly cut and tied it with fingers that were amazingly steady.

"Mrs. Hunter, you have a beautiful baby girl."

"A daughter? Oh, let me hold her. Please."

After checking the baby's pulse and respiration, Catherine wiped her dry, wrapped her in a soft blanket and handed the bundle to her beaming mother, who seemed to have forgotten her ordeal already.

Catherine smiled to herself as she washed off the dried blood stuck to her hands and watched for the expulsion of the afterbirth. She felt like a real doctor at last.

It was nearly ten o'clock before Catherine returned to the empty boarding house and flung herself down on her rumpled bed, a satisfied smile on her face.

Home at last, she slept and this time dreamed of babies with sweet dimpled smiles.

When Catherine awoke refreshed and alert, she took a few minutes to unbraid her thick chestnut hair, brushed it until it crackled and gleamed in a dark halo, and rearranged it in a neat chignon at the nape of her neck. She didn't need a mirror to tell her that her oval face and inquisitive pale blue eyes were quite ordinary, but she was not the type of woman to be overly concerned with her looks.

Then she walked down the hall to Sybilla's room. When she knocked, a faint voice replied, "Come in."

Catherine found her best friend and fellow student seated at her neat desk, poring over a dog-eared copy of Gray's *Anatomy*.

"Studying hard?" Catherine closed the door behind her.

Sybilla looked over her steel-rimmed spectacles. "Don't I always?"

She rose, went over to the only chair in the room, and carefully removed the human skeleton seated there. The bones clicked and rattled. "You must have a seat as soon as I put Bonette back where she belongs."

Once Bonette was hanging from a hook on the opposite wall,

Sybilla stared at Catherine with a critical eye. "What am I to do with you? You've left off your bustle again and your skirt's sweeping the floor."

Blonde, dainty Sybilla may have wanted to be a great surgeon, but she was always a lady, much more concerned with the outward trappings of femininity than Catherine. She would no sooner go out without her bustle than forget her scalpel and silk sutures.

"At the time, I had more important matters to consider," Catherine said. "Now, do you wish to continue talking of bustles, or do you wish to hear about the delivery?"

Sybilla grinned and sat down. "Don't be annoyed with me. The delivery, of course."

Catherine told her all about delivering Lucy Hunter's baby, and when she finished, Sybilla rose and hugged her. "I'm so proud of you."

"I didn't think I could do it." Catherine stood and paced the room, her blue eyes aglow with enthusiasm. "For the first time, I felt like a real doctor. Oh, I know we've studied medicine in the classroom and observed the other doctors, but it's different when someone entrusts her life to you and you're responsible for whether that person lives or dies."

"That's why we want to become doctors," Sybilla said. She then frowned, and rummaged through some papers on her desk. "By the way, a letter arrived for you today. It's from a Mr. Richard Fosse."

"Richard Fosse?" Catherine took the letter and eased herself into the chair.

"Who is he? I've never heard you mention him."

"He used to be one of my father's clients." Catherine tore open the envelope. "I met him at my stepmother's house when I went home to Cleveland for Christmas. He came to dinner several times and hardly said two words to me, so why is he writing?"

She soon found out when she read the letter. Catherine felt lightheaded and sick to her stomach—the same feeling she had experienced when she first saw and smelled a cadaver.

"What's wrong?" Sybilla asked when she saw her friend turn white and slump back in her chair. "Did somebody die?"

"Worse than that." Catherine swallowed hard. "He wants to marry me."

Sybilla stared at her. "What?"

Catherine couldn't trust herself to speak. She thrust the letter at Sybilla and pressed her fingers to her throbbing temples as her friend began reading.

Mr. Fosse was in the market for a wife. While he realized that he and Catherine had met only on several occasions, he was impressed with her ladylike bearing and quiet demeanor (Sybilla snickered at that) and wished her to return to Cleveland at once so he could court her properly. He then proceeded to enumerate his assets. A thirty-room mansion on prestigious Euclid Avenue with a coveted view of Lake Erie from the spacious backyard. Factories. A bank. Half of Cleveland.

But nowhere in the letter did he mention a medical practice for Catherine in the future.

A minute later, Sybilla raised her somber eyes. "Are you going to accept his proposal?"

Catherine sat up straight, her pale cheeks flushed with anger. "I will not withdraw from school to marry anyone, not with just four months left until I become a doctor! And how can I give up an internship at the New England Hospital?"

"But he says he has your stepmother's blessing, and that his wishes are hers as well."

Ruth had every reason to desire such a match for Catherine. At the time she married Catherine's lawyer father, whose own wife had died in childbirth, she was a young widow with four children from her previous marriage to support. Ten months later, she and her new husband had a daughter of their own, Liza Jane, now seven. Although the three eldest girls were married and lived in distant states and Jervis was self-supporting, that still left little Liza Jane to provide for.

Catherine shook her head and jumped to her feet. "Ruth doesn't control me. When Father died, he left me a small inheritance so I could be independent. I turned over part of it to appease Ruth, but I still had enough to finance my medical education if I weren't extravagant. I won't throw it all away now, no matter what my family wants. I won't!"

Sybilla scanned the letter again. "Fosse says that such a marriage would be quite advantageous to your family. Your stepbrother could choose which one of his companies he wanted to work for."

"Jervis would love that, I'm sure." Catherine crossed her arms to keep from exploding with resentment. "I wouldn't be surprised if this marriage was his idea."

"Why do you think that?"

"Because my charming stepbrother believes everyone on earth exists for the sole purpose of making his life easier. You should have seen him when I announced I was going to go to medical school. He hounded me day and night about how such study would make me unfeminine and that no man would want to marry me."

"Scrofulous swine." Sybilla was too much of a lady to swear, so she made up her own more colorful epithets.

"And it wasn't because of any deep concern for my welfare, either. He just wanted all my inheritance."

Sybilla shook her head.

Catherine crossed the room and seated herself. "They have always refused to believe that being a doctor is important to me." She drummed her fingertips against Sybilla's desk. "I won't deny that my family couldn't stand to use a bit of luck. Father's law practice was very successful, but money's been scarce since his death. And Ruth's extravagances haven't helped matters, either."

"So you've told me."

"It's exasperating when the bills pile up and Ruth looks as though she doesn't know where they came from and what needs to be done to make them go away."

Sybilla stared into space for a moment. "What if this Mr. Fosse were willing to wait until you graduated? Would you marry him then?"

"Not if he were the last man on earth." Catherine shuddered. "He's so old, Syb—fifty if he's a day, and I'm only twenty-two. And he's so huge, when he walks through the house, the floor shakes and all Ruth's geegaws rattle on their shelves. At dinner, he looked like a hog feeding at a trough."

"A bride wouldn't look forward to her wedding night with a husband like that."

Catherine grimaced in revulsion. "Believe me, that thought had crossed my mind."

"What type of man would you want to marry, Cat?" Sybilla asked.

Catherine hesitated for a moment. "Well, he'd have to be extraordinary. He'd have to realize how important being a doctor is to me. And he wouldn't treat me like some mindless ornament, who only thinks of clothes and balls."

"The antithesis of Mr. Fosse." Sybilla fell silent. Then she said, "So, my friend, what are you going to do?"

"I don't know. If it were only Ruth and Jervis, I wouldn't hesitate to refuse Mr. Fosse. But there's Liza Jane . . ." Her voice trailed off.

"Cat, some advice." Sybilla leaned over her desk and squeezed Catherine's hand. "In spite of all your bluster, I know you love your family very much. But I also know that you're dedicated to medicine and will make a fine doctor. Don't make a decision that you'll regret."

"Thanks, Syb." Catherine rose. "Well, I have some hard thinking to do, so if you'll excuse me . . ."

After supper, when Catherine returned to her room, she took down the silver-framed photograph from its place of honor on her chest of drawers and stared at her father's austere, unsmiling face.

"Oh, Father," she murmured, "I wish you were here to tell me what to do."

But she knew it was her decision and hers alone.

Catherine seated herself at her desk and began writing a letter to Mr. Richard Fosse.

The letter haunted Catherine.

Each morning, as she dressed, she vowed not to give Fosse and his marriage proposal a second thought. She had made her decision and would abide by it.

Once she was out of the house and on her way to a class or the college's hospital dispensary, the weighty responsibilities of medicine overshadowed her personal life. How insignificant her problems were when compared to the people she assisted treating day in and day out. She didn't have to have her right leg amputated after a carriage accident mangled the tibia into uselessness. She wasn't the six-year-old boy who would die a horrible death from hydrophobia after being bitten by a rabid dog. She could only imagine the heartache of a new bride diagnosed with breast cancer.

Two weeks later, on a cold Monday morning, an unsuspecting Catherine took her seat beside Sybilla in their Materia Medica and Therapeutics class.

Once everyone sat down and the class came to order, Dr. Clara Marshall, the instructor, began with, "Good morning, ladies. Today we will discuss the properties of mercury and its employment in the treatment of syphilis.''

Ten minutes later, just as Dr. Marshall was about to describe the symptoms of mercurialism to her enthralled students, a loud banging on the door made everyone jump in their seats.

Dr. Marshall scowled and turned to see who had dared to interrupt her class.

Before she could say, "Come in," the door swung open to reveal a veritable Apollo in a gray-checked traveling coat, his light brown hair attractively disheveled. Even a mustache and side-whiskers couldn't conceal the young man's beguiling looks.

Catherine stared, unable to believe her eyes. It was Jervis, and judging from his black frown and pursed lips, he was furious.

Dr. Marshall stepped forward. "Young man, I don't know who you are, but you had better have a good reason for interrupting my class."

Jervis's smile was sweet-cream smooth as he stepped into the classroom and bowed. "Begging your pardon, ma'am, but I'm here to see Catherine Stone. I'm her brother, and it's a matter of life and death.''

Mine, Catherine thought.

Sybilla leaned over and whispered, "So that's Jervis, here to make you change your mind."

"And drag me back to Cleveland," Catherine whispered back.

Dr. Marshall looked at her. "You are excused, Miss Stone."

Catherine rose reluctantly, conscious of curious stares boring into her back and Jervis's malevolent look daring her to contradict him as his gaze found hers and locked.

Catherine murmured, "I'm sorry for the interruption, Dr. Marshall.''

"Under the circumstances, you may use my office just down the hall.''

Jervis flashed the doctor his heartbreaking grin and Catherine could almost hear the flutter of feminine hearts. "Oh, thank you, ma'am. I appreciate your kindness during such a trying time."

Once they were out in the empty corridor and the door shut behind them, Catherine whirled on him. "Who in the hell do you think you are, interrupting my class like that?''

He shook his head, his brown eyes as cold as ether on bare skin. "Tsk, tsk, where are your manners? A real lady would have smiled pleasantly, asked how my trip was, and inquired after the family. And a real lady would keep her voice down.''

Catherine gritted her teeth and snapped, ''Dr. Marshall's office is this way.''

Once they were inside the quiet, empty office, Catherine crossed her arms to put a physical barrier between them. ''I'm assuming you have a reason for traveling all the way to Philadelphia from Cleveland.''

Jervis took off his coat with infuriating slowness, then leaned on the edge of Dr. Marshall's desk. ''You know why I'm here. And at great expense and inconvenience, I might add.''

''I assume it has something to do with the letter I wrote to Mr. Fosse in response to his offer of marriage.''

''Yes, it does.''

Catherine raised her brows. ''You didn't actually expect me to accept, did you?''

''Yes, Catherine, actually I did. So did Liza Jane and Mama. I must say, we're all very disappointed in you.''

Catherine dropped her arms, hands clenched at her sides. ''I'm not marrying him, Jervis.''

A flicker of genuine surprise passed across his bold features. ''What possible objections can you have to the man?''

Catherine patted her full skirts as if searching for something. ''If you'll wait one moment, I'll find my list.''

''Sarcasm is an unbecoming trait in a lady.'' He slid off the desk, jammed his hands into his pockets, and stalked around the office. When he stopped, he said, ''Damn it, Catherine! He's one of the wealthiest men in Cleveland.''

''That may be. But I don't know him, and I certainly don't love him. Besides, I have only four more months of schooling until I become a doctor. I fully intend to graduate and serve my internship in Boston.''

''Oh, that . . .'' Jervis dismissed her objection with a wave of his hand. ''You may think you want to be a doctor, Catherine, but what you really want is what every woman wants—a husband. Now that you'll have one, you can forget this foolish notion of yours.''

Nothing annoyed Catherine more than someone telling her what she thought or wanted. She forced herself to smile. ''I'm sure I will find a husband one day—and Richard Fosse won't be the man.''

Jervis's mouth turned up in a sneer. ''Beggars can't be choosers, my girl. What man is going to want a doctor for a wife, a woman who's at the beck and call of rabble? A woman who has to go out unprotected at night, constantly exposed to danger, not to mention the sickness she brings into her own home.''

"Then I shall remain a spinster for the rest of my days."

Jervis's face fell. "Have you stopped to consider what it would mean to the rest of us if you married Mr. Fosse?"

Catherine felt as though he were backing her into a corner. "That's not fair."

"No, you're not being fair. You're putting your own selfish desires before the good of your family. Will it be fair for Mama and poor Liza Jane to go without new clothes? Will it be fair for me to spend half my life working my way up at the newspaper when I can start at the top in Fosse's bank?"

"If your mother weren't so extravagant, the money my father left her would provide a comfortable living for all of you."

"How can you be so heartless to deny Mama her fripperies when they give her such pleasure?"

Catherine hardened herself against the guilt beginning to gnaw away at the edges of her conscience. "She'll just have to learn to do without twelve parasols and six pairs of opera slippers. As I have had to do without."

"She can't. Those of us who love her wouldn't ask her to."

"And as for you . . . there's nothing wrong with starting out at the bottom. Hard work builds character."

Jervis glared at her. "I deserve a chance. How can I ask Alice Blake to marry me if I don't make a decent wage?"

So it would also be her fault if Jervis lost the girl of his dreams.

"If Alice truly loved you, it wouldn't matter."

"But it matters to her Papa and I need his permission to marry her."

"Ah, I see," Catherine began, trying valiantly to keep her temper in check. "I have to give up my dream of becoming a doctor so the rest of you can live in the lap of luxury."

"Bitterness doesn't become you. A real lady never succumbs to such morally corrosive emotions."

Catherine exploded. "I am sick to death of hearing how unladylike and selfish I am!"

Jervis's face twisted as he brought his fist down on the desk top with a resounding crash. "And I am sick of trying to make you see reason!"

"You can't make me marry Fosse," Catherine said levelly, though her heart was pounding with the irrational fear that somehow he could do just that.

"Legally, I can't," Jervis agreed. His brown eyes narrowed, promising swift retribution. "But if you refuse, you will no longer be a part of our family."

Catherine felt as though he had just slammed his fist into her solar plexus. "What did you say?"

"You heard me."

She took a desperate step forward, her hands spread in supplication. "You can't mean that."

"Oh, but I do. You will no longer be welcome in our house. And you will never see Liza Jane again."

Never to see little Liza Jane's sweet smile again . . .

Jervis looked at her with a triumphant gleam in his eye, like a hound closing in for the kill. "Think about it carefully, Catherine. Very carefully."

"You rotten bastard."

"My, my, such language unbefitting a lady." Jervis put on his coat. "I'll come for you tomorrow morning at nine o'clock. If I have to return to Cleveland alone, you'll sever all ties with your family." He grinned. "See you tomorrow, dear sister."

And he sauntered out the door.

Once class was dismissed, Catherine and Sybilla returned to the boarding house.

Catherine told Sybilla everything Jervis had said, and then concluded, "If I don't marry Fosse, the family will have nothing to do with me. I'll never see Liza Jane again."

Sybilla just stood there, mouth agape, as helpless tears rolled down her friend's cheeks. "Surely he wasn't serious."

Catherine dabbed at her eyes with a handkerchief. "He meant every word. And he wants my answer by nine o'clock tomorrow morning."

"What are you going to tell him?"

"I don't know." She walked over to the window and stared out over the rooftops at nothing in particular, the harsh noon light making her look old and tired.

Sybilla muttered, "Why that greedy, selfish syphilitic snake! I wish he were here so I could strangle him with my bare hands for what he's doing to you."

Catherine didn't even smile.

"They're not worth it, Cat," Sybilla said. "None of them is worth a lifetime of being married to Richard Fosse. None of them is worth all the lives you could one day save as a doctor."

"How would you feel if you could never see your family again?"

Sybilla's parents and three younger brothers lived in Washington, D.C. and they were all very close.

"I would feel terrible," she admitted, "but not if they tried to force me to marry a man I didn't love."

A responsive flicker illuminated Catherine's eyes for a second, then died.

Sybilla pushed on. "Someday you'll have children of your own, maybe even a little girl like Liza Jane."

Catherine's shoulders slumped. "I know, but it's still hard to sever all ties with her."

"You're going to have to choose."

"I know. I just hope I have the strength to make the right choice."

When Jervis arrived at Catherine's boarding house promptly at nine o'clock the following morning, he thought it odd that there were no bags waiting in the hall.

"Where are your bags?" he demanded as Catherine showed him to the sitting room. "Do you expect me to lug them downstairs for you like some servant?"

Jervis stopped short and stared at her. As usual, Catherine's hair was in its untidy, unflattering coronet and the skirt of her plain brown dress trailed on the floor without a bustle to support it properly. But there was something different about her today.

"And good morning to you, too, Jervis," she said, her voice thick with sarcasm.

What was wrong with her? Her eyes should be red and swollen from crying, her face the picture of dejection and defeat. She should be drooping.

She smiled. "There are no bags in the foyer because I am not going with you."

"What did you say?"

"You heard me. I am not going back to Cleveland with you. I am not marrying Richard Fosse." Her face glowed with pride. "I am going to become a doctor."

"That's enough!" he bellowed. "I've been the head of the

family since your father died, and my word is law. And I say you're going to marry Richard Fosse.''

''What are you going to do, Jervis? Throw me over your shoulder and drag me back? Lock me in my room and feed me bread and water until I agree to do what you want?''

The sneering contempt in her voice was too much for Jervis. He raised his hand and took a step forward, fully intending to slap her to her knees and keep on slapping her until she came to her senses.

Then a cold, hard voice from the doorway said, ''Lay a hand on her, and you're a dead man.''

Jervis stopped in his tracks and stared at the door. There stood a dainty vision in rustling pale blue taffeta and ivory lace, a veritable green-eyed paragon of femininity that Catherine would do well to emulate. But there was nothing dainty about the wooden rolling pin she kept smacking against her palm. Behind her was a stout, gray-haired woman effortlessly wielding a large cast-iron frying pan. Jervis had no doubt in his mind that they would not hesitate to use those makeshift weapons against him.

Jervis dropped his hand and stepped back, breathing hard. ''My sister is coming back to Cleveland with me.''

''Not if she doesn't want to,'' Rolling Pin replied. ''Catherine, do you want to go with this—'' her lip curled ''—worthless piece of phlegm?''

''No, Sybilla, I don't.''

Frying Pan took a menacing step forward. ''Then you'd better get out before I ruin my good carpet with your worthless brains.''

Jervis glared at Catherine in helpless fury. ''You'll never see Liza Jane again. Is that what you want?''

''No, I don't. But you've forced me to make that choice.''

''Why, you heartless bitch!''

Rolling Pin spoke. ''Rest assured, Mr. Miller, if Mrs. Jenkins does hit you, you'll receive the best medical attention.''

''I think you'd better leave,'' Catherine said. ''We have nothing more to say to each other.''

Jervis whirled on his heel and stormed off, slamming the door behind him without so much as a goodbye.

When the three women were alone, Sybilla tucked the rolling pin under her arm and grinned. ''Good riddance.''

''We'll never see the likes of him around here again,'' Mrs. Jenkins declared with relish.

Catherine closed her eyes and sighed in relief. ''Thank you, ladies. If you hadn't been here, I think Jervis would have tried to force me to go back with him."

"I think so, too," Sybilla said. She shook her head. "How such a good-looking man can be such a viper . . ."

Later, when Catherine and Sybilla were walking to class together, Sybilla asked, "No regrets?"

Catherine shook her head. "I made my choice. If Ruth wants to see me so badly, she can thwart Jervis's orders."

Deep down inside, she was hoping against hope that her stepmother would do just that. But as the weeks turned into months without so much as a letter from Ruth, she realized that her family had disowned her.

After graduation that June, a tearful Sybilla entrusted Bonette the skeleton into Catherine's care while she studied surgery at the prestigious Ecole de Medicine in Paris. She promised to write, and the two friends agreed to open a practice together in New York City, once Catherine's internship in Boston was over.

❧ CHAPTER ❧

TWO
_____

CATHERINE stood on the sidewalk and sighed as she stared up at the brownstone with a "Rooms for Rent" sign in the first-floor window.

She refused to get her hopes up this time. In the two weeks she had been searching in New York City by elevated train and streetcar, Catherine hadn't found a suitable location for her practice that wasn't territory already claimed by some other doctor, usually male.

Undeterred, she took newspaper, map, and determination in hand and began every warm July morning with a search that usually ended in failure, disappointment, and hot, sore feet. But this time, she had a feeling that her efforts were about to be rewarded.

Squaring her shoulders to strengthen her resolve, she climbed the steep steps and rang the bell.

A minute later, a diminutive woman with old dark eyes set in a youthful, round face appeared at the door, "Yes?"

Catherine smiled. "I'd like to inquire about the rooms for rent."

Those sharp eyes flicked over her, then around, as though the woman were searching for something. "You got a husband?"

"No, I'm alone."

"Then what do you want these rooms for? You look like a decent, respectable sort, not the kind who needs rooms for herself. You should be living at home, with your family."

Catherine forced herself to keep smiling. "I'm a doctor. I'm looking for some rooms to rent so I can establish a practice."

When the woman just stared at her in wordless astonishment,

Catherine's hopes plummeted. Someone else was going to turn her away for the fourth time today.

To her surprise, the woman stepped back. "Come in. We can talk inside. I'm Mrs. Mason, by the way," she added over her shoulder.

"I'm Dr. Catherine Stone." As she followed the white-haired woman into a neat, clean parlor, Catherine noticed there was another room directly across from it. It would be perfect for her surgery, if she could just persuade Mrs. Mason to rent it to her.

"Sit down." Mrs. Mason indicated the worn horsehair sofa draped with delicate crocheted antimacassars. Once they sat down, she said, "So you're a lady doctor and you want to use my home for your office, is that it?"

"Yes." She glanced toward the other parlor. "I'd like to rent your other parlor and a room upstairs for myself, of course."

"I don't know if I want strangers coming into my home. I'm a widow who needs to take in boarders to make ends meet."

"Well, if you take in boarders, than you must be accustomed to having strangers in your house."

The unlined face remained expressionless. "It's not the same as having sick people coming and going all day. Why, I could get sick from them myself."

"They wouldn't be coming and going all day," Catherine pointed out patiently. "At least not at first, while I get my practice established. All we'd have to do is put a few chairs out in the hall where they could wait. And I'd make sure you don't contract anything from them."

"I don't know . . ."

Catherine tried to conceal her desperation. Mrs. Mason's West 10th Street neighborhood was perfect, solid and middle-class, so Catherine would have patients who could afford to pay their bills and on time. Although she felt it was her duty to treat charity cases, Catherine knew that a doctor just starting out couldn't base a practice on charity alone. She had her own bills to pay. She had to be practical.

She smiled. "I know it would be an inconvenience, Mrs. Mason, but I'd make it up to you."

"How?"

"I'd be willing to pay a little extra rent."

The woman shrugged. "I'm an old lady. When you reach my age, a little peace and quiet is more important than the money."

Catherine's spirits plummeted again. She rose and tried to

keep the disappointed quiver out of her voice. "Well, since we can't come to an agreement, I'll be on my way. Thank—"

"Now hold your horses and sit down."

Catherine paused, sat back down and held her breath.

Mrs. Mason rubbed her chin. "I'll consider renting you the rooms on one condition."

"And what is that?"

"That you be my doctor and don't charge me anything for it."

Catherine hesitated, suddenly suspicious. Even though the woman was in her early sixties, she appeared to be vigorous and in perfect health, so why was she willing to accept medical services for partial payment of the rent? She was certainly no invalid who demanded constant nursing.

"How often would you require my care?" Catherine asked.

"Just when I have a little ache or two."

"If you're looking for a nurse, Mrs. Mason—"

Dark eyes flashed. "I didn't say that! All I want is a little doctoring for my aches and pains, that's all, in exchange for the inconvenience of having my home turned into a doctor's office. And five dollars a week rent." She rose and folded her arms across her flat chest. "Take it, or leave it."

Catherine thought of additional days—weeks—of futilely roaming this strange city and knocking on countless doors, only to have them slammed in her face. And she'd never find a place this cheap.

"I'll take it."

Mrs. Mason grinned and extended her hand. "We have a deal."

Catherine shook hands. "A deal."

Later, when Catherine returned to her hotel room to collect her bags, her elation at finding such a perfect location overshadowed any niggling misgivings she might have had about Mrs. Mason's motives. The shrewd old woman had seen an opportunity to get something for nothing and drove a hard bargain; there was nothing more to it than that.

Catherine was going to start her medical practice, and nothing was going to stand in her way.

A week later, Catherine was standing at the foot of the steps and surveying the new sign of handsome black tin with her name in bold gold-raised letters attached to the door.

She smiled, then went back inside, glancing briefly at the motley assortment of straight-backed chairs lined against the foyer's wall. They were empty now, but soon . . .

Catherine was even satisfied with the way the parlor had become a surgery. They moved out most of Mrs. Mason's furniture, save for a desk, several comfortable chairs, and a curio cabinet with shelves and thick, locking glass doors that became her medicine cabinet. She longed for a proper padded leather examining table, but until she got some paying patients, a simple table with a mattress would have to do.

She sat at her desk and waited and listened all day for the doorbell to ring. But no one came.

Two weeks of waiting and listening passed, and still no patients rang her doorbell.

She spent her free time writing to Sybilla.

I know I should be patient. Dr. Bodley warned us that it usually takes two years to establish a practice, and here I am chafing at the bit after only two weeks. You'd think someone in this neighborhood would have noticed my sign by now and come for medical attention. I hope they're not avoiding me because I'm a woman.

It's especially puzzling because it's August, and there are sure to be babies suffering from cholera infantum. I saw a funeral procession for one yesterday, a poor little thing in its tiny white coffin. So sad. I wondered if I could have saved it, if only the mother had brought it to me in time. I don't mean to sound so despondent, but I can't help it. I am so impatient to practice medicine . . .

Catherine threw down her pen and rose. "If I am so impatient to practice medicine," she muttered aloud, "then I had better do something to help myself instead of just sitting here like a fool."

She marched past the row of empty chairs and across the hall, to where Mrs. Mason sat in front of the window. Mrs. Mason was one of those women who couldn't pass by a window without parting the curtains and peering out. If she wasn't at a window, she was standing outside, chatting with neighbors.

She knew everyone, and Catherine decided it was time she put her landlady's prodigious connections to good use.

"Mrs. Mason, I'd like to talk to you, if I may."

"Yes, Dr. Stone," she said without taking her eyes off the comings and goings in the street beyond, "what is it?"

"Do you know of any women who are going to have a baby?"

Mrs. Mason looked up reluctantly, her annoyed expression telling Catherine that she disliked being interrupted. "I'm afraid not. Why do you want to know?"

"It's a way for me to build up my practice," she explained. "If I deliver a woman's baby satisfactorily, she's likely to bring that baby to me when it's sick. Then other members of her family will come to me when they're sick, and she's likely to tell all her friends about me as well. And so on, until I have a thriving practice." She shrugged. "That's the theory anyway."

"Makes sense." Mrs. Mason rose quickly, for she was spry for her age. "Sorry I can't help you, but I don't know of anyone in the family way." She placed her hand on her waist and sucked in her breath. "But I've begun to feel poorly."

"Then let me examine you."

Mrs. Mason's face brightened and she followed Catherine into the surgery.

While Catherine unbuttoned the woman's dress, she asked, "What type of pains do you have?"

"Sharp pains real low, just above my private parts."

"In your pelvic area?"

"If that's what they call it, that's where they are." As the stiff black bombazine dress came rustling off, Mrs. Mason added, "I get headaches, too, and my stomach is queasy now and then."

Catherine removed her patient's tightly laced corset. "Well sit down on the examining table and let's see if we can find out what's wrong with you."

Once Mrs. Mason sat herself on the edge of the table, Catherine put on her stethoscope and began the examination, listening to the old lady's heart and lungs.

Minutes later, she stepped back, puzzled. "You seem to be as healthy as a horse, Mrs. Mason."

Dark eyes grew as cold as onyx. "I know there's something wrong with me. I get these headaches, I tell you, and pains in my . . . my pelvic area."

Catherine nodded soothingly. "Now if you'll just lift your petticoats and lie back, I'll continue my examination."

The moment Mrs. Mason reclined, Catherine noticed the incision scar on her lower abdomen.

"Mrs. Mason, when did you have surgery?"

"Almost twelve years ago or thereabouts."

"Do you remember what it was for?"

She shrugged. "The doctor didn't tell me what the name of the operation was, only that he was taking out some of my innards. He said it would make my aches and pains go away. It didn't, though."

But Catherine knew what it was for the minute she palpated the area and couldn't feel any ovaries: Mrs. Mason had had an ovariotomy. Could it have been to remove an ovarian cyst, or was it just a means of controlling hysteria?

"Who was your doctor?" she asked.

"Dr. Bliss was my last one, but he couldn't help me. None of them could. They cut me open, took out my innards, and I still get my aches and pains."

Half an hour later, Catherine straightened up and looked down at her patient helplessly. "I'm afraid I can't help you, either, Mrs. Mason. I can't find anything wrong with you."

Mrs. Mason jerked down her petticoats and sat up, her unlined face flushed and eyes snapping. "What do you mean you can't help me? You're supposed to be a doctor. Don't you know what you're doing?"

Catherine was so stunned she stepped back as though the old lady had struck her. "Mrs. Mason, I—"

"We had a deal, remember?" Mrs. Mason slid off the table and glared at Catherine. "You'd do all my doctoring if I rented you the extra room. Are you trying to get out of our deal by pretending there's nothing wrong with me? Is that it?"

Catherine felt her cheeks grow hot. "I am not trying to get out of our deal, Mrs. Mason. There is simply nothing wrong with you."

"That's what you say."

"Are you questioning my professional abilities, Mrs. Mason?"

"If you're as good as you say you are, you'd find something wrong with me." Then she turned away and began struggling into her dress.

And with those words, Catherine knew exactly what was wrong with Mrs. Mason. Her landlady suffered from imaginary illnesses. No doctor, no matter how skilled or proficient, could ever cure her.

Catherine saw herself being thrown out into the street by her disgruntled patient, and she knew what she had to do even though it violated every principle she believed in.

She sighed. "Perhaps I have been too hasty in my examination of you, Mrs. Mason. If you'll allow me to reexamine you. . . ."

Mrs. Mason lifted her dress back over her head and regarded Catherine out of suspicious eyes. Then she climbed back onto the table, those dark eyes watching Catherine's every move as though defying her to make a mistake.

Catherine percussed and palpated, occasionally muttering a vague, "Hmmm," and an "Aha!" or two before standing back.

"You have a nervous disorder," she said, "and I have just the medicine to help you."

A smile of delight split the woman's face. Evidently no other doctor had diagnosed her as having a nervous disorder before.

While Mrs. Mason dressed, Catherine went over to her desk, wrote a prescription for tincture of valerian with potassium bromide, and handed it to Mrs. Mason, who looked as though she had just received a particularly longed-for Christmas gift.

"I guess you do know what you're doing after all," she said before sweeping out of the surgery.

When Catherine heard the front door close and she knew she was alone, she sat down at her desk and buried her head in her shaking hands. For one shattering moment, that horrible woman had destroyed her confidence and made her doubt herself.

"I'm a good doctor," she said to Bonette, who hung silently in the corner. "I know I am."

While she hated herself for having pandered to Mrs. Mason, she knew it wouldn't serve any good purpose to argue with the woman. Catherine would lose her surgery and place to live and Mrs. Mason would only seek out yet another hapless doctor to cure her imaginary illnesses.

No, she decided she would keep on placating her landlady for as long as it took to establish her practice.

However, two weeks later, Mrs. Mason complained that the medicine Catherine had prescribed just wasn't working any more, so Catherine prescribed another placebo for Mrs. Mason's "aches and pains." That medicine too lost its potency after two weeks, and Mrs. Mason was back on the examining table, her gaze both scornful and accusatory.

Catherine wondered just how long she could keep on appeas-

ing her landlady with harmless bromides and sugar pills before
the wily old woman caught on and threw her out into the street.

Catherine stood at the window, watching passersby in the
street bow their heads into the wind and clutch their coats closed.

October was almost over. Catherine had been in New York
for almost four months, and still the row of chairs in the hall
remained unoccupied, gathering dust. The other boarders had
stopped asking her about her day. In addition, her bank balance
seemed to shrink with every passing week. If she didn't get some
patients before the onset of winter, she would be defeated.

She sighed dismally as she let the curtain fall and turned away
from the window. Perhaps she should consider opening a practice in some small town in Connecticut or Rhode Island, where
the competition wasn't as fierce. But then what would Sybilla
do?

Catherine decided that what she needed to do was get outside
for a while and think. So she put on her coat and left the house.

No sooner did Catherine walk halfway down the street than
she noticed a woman hurrying toward her. As the woman drew
closer, Catherine could see that she was carrying a child bundled
up in her arms. The child's helpless whimpers were heart-
rending.

Catherine noticed the flushed cheeks and dull eyes of a fever.

"Madam," she began, stopping the woman just as she was
about to bustle past. "I'm a doctor." She looked down at the
child, a little girl. "Perhaps I can help your daughter."

The woman stared at her out of suspicious eyes. "Are you the
lady doctor who's living with Mrs. Mason?"

Catherine smiled. "So you've heard of me."

"Oh, yes, we've heard about you all right." Her lip curled
into a sneer. "Mrs. Mason told us all about you, how you can't
even make her aches and pains better. You're not a *real* doctor,
and I wouldn't let you touch my baby if you was the last doctor
on earth!"

The woman hurried away, leaving a dumbfounded Catherine
staring after her.

As Catherine stood there, astonishment was soon replaced by
white-hot rage. She whirled on her heel and marched back to
the house.

The moment she stepped into the foyer, she called, "Mrs.

Mason!'' at the top of her lungs as she stripped off her gloves and strode into her office.

Seconds later, Mrs. Mason appeared, the picture of grandmotherly concern and innocence as she used her apron to wipe flour from her hands. ''Yes, Dr. Stone, what is it? You seem angry about something.''

''I am.'' Catherine was shaking so badly, she could hardly speak. ''I went outside a few moments ago for some fresh air. There I met a woman with her sick child in her arms.'' She balled her hands into fists to keep from wrapping them around the old woman's throat. ''When I offered to care for her child, do you know what she said to me?''

Mrs. Mason gave a guilty start, but recovered her composure almost at once. ''How would I know?''

''Oh, you know all right. You've been telling everyone in this neighborhood—anyone who will listen—that I'm not a good doctor, haven't you?''

''Why shouldn't I? It's the truth. You haven't been able to cure my aches and pains, so why shouldn't my neighbors know about it?''

''Why, you stupid, spiteful—'' Catherine was so furious she plunged on, her voice rising and becoming so loud she failed to hear the front door open and close. ''No doctor in the world can cure your aches and pains because they don't exist. They're all in your imagination.'' She laughed bitterly. ''Here I was, waiting for patients, and all these months you've been spreading malicious lies behind my back, ruining my reputation with your ignorance.''

Mrs. Mason's eyes narrowed as she bristled with rage. ''How dare you insult me in my own house! Well, I'm not going to stand for it, no sir. Starting today, I'm charging you double for these rooms, and if you don't pay the ten dollars, you can just get out!''

Then she was gone.

Mrs. Mason's threat was like a sobering dash of cold water. Catherine's hand flew to her mouth, but it was too late to call back the hasty, imprudent words.

Without someone like Mrs. Mason to laud her medical skills to others, Catherine hadn't a prayer of attracting patients from the neighborhood. Mrs. Mason had ruined her.

Eyes filling with frustrated tears, Catherine turned away, groping for her handkerchief.

"Excuse me."

The sound of an unfamiliar masculine voice caused Catherine to turn around and find a man standing in her surgery doorway. He was of average height and of average build, but there was nothing average about his looks. He was, quite simply, the handsomest man she had ever seen, a veritable golden-haired god capable of rendering a woman speechless.

Yet there was a disarming air of self-deprecation about him as well, almost as though he felt compelled to apologize for his physical perfection. Catherine warmed to him at once.

He must be a patient, and a wealthy one at that, judging from the impeccable cut of his black frock coat and the diamond stickpin winking in the center of his striped silk cravat.

Her heart sank. Why did her first patient have to be a young, good-looking man? She mustn't let him see how he dazzled and flustered her.

Catherine hastily dried her eyes and fought to compose herself. "How do you do?" She smiled and stepped forward, her hand extended. "I am Dr. Stone. I should warn you beforehand that I specialize in women's medical problems, but I'm fully capable of treating men as well." She blushed in spite of herself. "That is, if you don't mind a woman examining you."

Eyes the color of a hot summer sky sparkled. "I'm sure that would be a pleasure, Dr. Stone, but I'm not here as a patient. My name is Kimbel Flanders . . . Dr. Kim Flanders."

After her blush subsided, Catherine tried to hide her disappointment that he wasn't a patient after all. Then she wondered why another doctor was calling on her, and her suspicions made her anger return.

"Why have you come to call, Dr. Flanders?" she said coldly. "To assess the competition?" Catherine let her bitterness come pouring out. "As you may have overheard, I have no patients and am not likely to get any. And, as you can see, my surgery is poorly equipped. So you may return home to your grand Fifth Avenue practice and set your mind at ease."

The man stepped forward, managing to look both indignant and troubled. "Dr. Stone, I did not come here to gloat over your struggles to establish your practice. I came here to make you a proposition."

Catherine stared at him. "What sort of proposition?"

Dr. Flanders glanced toward the door. "Is there somewhere we could talk in private?"

"I'm afraid no place is safe from the prying eyes and ears of my landlady."

"Perhaps you'd join me at my house for luncheon? My carriage is right outside, and I give you my word to return you safe and sound."

Catherine hesitated. He was, after all, a stranger. But she was a doctor, used to going places with strangers.

"I'd be delighted to join you for luncheon and listen to this proposition of yours."

He smiled. "Splendid."

Catherine didn't say one word to Mrs. Mason about where she was going, even though she sensed the old woman peering at them through a crack in the hall door left purposely ajar.

Dr. Flanders retrieved his gold-headed cane and silk top hat, then held the door for her and they stepped out into the chilly air.

As she expected, Dr. Flanders' carriage was the embodiment of his prosperity, a magnificent black brougham a duke would envy, drawn by a pair of matching bays as well-kept as their master, with oiled hooves and glossy coats. Inside, the maroon leather seats were so soft, Catherine could have sunk down into them and never come up.

"I'm envious," she said as Dr. Flanders seated himself across from her.

"Don't be. It takes time to establish a profitable practice."

"For women like myself at any rate."

Reproach filled his eyes. "I'm not the enemy, Dr. Stone."

Chastened, Catherine looked down at her hands clasped in her lap. "I don't mean to sound bitter. I just learned that my landlady has been sabotaging my efforts to attract patients, and I'm still furious about it. But that's no reason for me to direct that anger at you." She looked up. "Please accept my apology."

"Apology accepted. I must confess that I eavesdropped on part of your conversation when I came in," he said, "and you have every right to be furious with her. What she did was unconscionable."

There was just something so sympathetic about Dr. Flanders' demeanor that Catherine found herself telling him all about what Mrs. Mason had done.

"That old hag has ruined my professional reputation." She sighed dismally. "I might as well pack my bags and return to Cleveland."

"That may not be necessary."

Catherine gave him a quizzical look. "What do you mean?"

"That proposition I mentioned earlier." He folded his gloved hands over his gold-topped cane. "Some of the wives of my patients are modest women who are uncomfortable having a male doctor treat them. Others would rather die than disrobe in front of a man other than their husband. And some of them will, if they don't get medical treatment soon." He hesitated. "I've been trying to find a woman doctor to treat them without offending their sensibilities. Would you consider accepting them as patients?"

Catherine stared at him in disbelief. "You would share your patients with me? But—but why? You don't even know me."

"Don't think I'm some sort of fairy godfather from some child's fable, dropping patients in your lap on a whim. To be frank, you would be in competition with two other women. I would watch you treat my patients for a day, and the woman I deem most qualified would receive my referrals."

Catherine couldn't believe her ears. To have the opportunity to establish her practice . . .

"Why did you choose me? There must be dozens of qualified women doctors practicing in this city."

He smoothed his mustache. "You live reasonably close by, as do the other two women. I happened to be walking down your street one afternoon and noticed your sign. After consulting with the county medical society, they told me that you had just opened your practice. I assumed that you'd welcome the patients."

"Considering what has just happened, they would be a godsend."

"Good. We'll discuss the details of our arrangement at my house."

As Catherine expected, Dr. Flanders' residence was an elegant but tasteful house on lower Fifth Avenue, smaller than she imagined, but just grand enough to proclaim its occupants as people of wealth and influence.

"Would you like to see the surgery first?" Dr. Flanders asked after he had taken her coat.

"Oh, yes, please."

Catherine's eyes grew as wide as a child's on Christmas morning when she entered her host's surgery and peered into a medicine cabinet that occupied almost half a wall. There were hundreds of stoppered glass bottles filled with powders, pills, and even tree barks.

"Morphine, conium, black wash for syphilis . . . you have a veritable pharmacy here."

"I like to have medications within arms' reach," he explained. "Beyond that door is my laboratory, complete with a microscope."

"Very progressive of you. I am impressed."

His smile was self-deprecating. "One must keep up with advances."

"I agree." Catherine walked over to the padded leather examining table and ran a covetous hand over it. "Someday . . ."

"In time," he agreed. "Well, I have a patient coming at two, so why don't we have our luncheon?"

Like Kim Flanders' clothes, carriage, and house, his dining room reflected his own exacting taste. As Catherine sat at one end of a mahogany table and glanced at her image in the polished surface, she sensed that the Limoges china and Tiffany silver were not there to impress or intimidate, but to please with their beauty.

"Where did you go to school?" she asked, helping herself to the cold roast beef, a welcome change from Mrs. Mason's usual tasteless cabbage soup.

"The University of Chicago." He gave a wry shrug. "I'm sure I've had a much easier time of it than you. The medical school accepted me right after college. Since my family is well-to-do, I built my practice through social contacts. A friend of the family, that sort of thing. No Mrs. Masons to worry about for me." He toyed with his beef. "I hope you won't hold it against me."

His gaze met Catherine's, and she was startled to find blatant masculine interest that had nothing whatsoever to do with their shared profession. She thought of all the appreciative stares she had received from Jervis's cronies and how they had made her flesh crawl. But it was different with Dr. Flanders. She liked the way he was looking at her.

Catherine suddenly became self-conscious. How did she look? Had any stray hairs escaped from their pins? Did he notice she was blushing?

"Is it too warm in here?" he asked.

Far too warm.

"Not at all," she replied, fighting to control herself. Finally, she said, "You've had a first-rate education, but are you a good doctor?"

"A damn good doctor."

"Then I won't hold your life of ease and privilege against you." She smiled. "Especially since you may be sending patients my way."

Dr. Flanders leaned back in his chair and burst out laughing—a warm, conspiratorial sound. "So, you have ulterior motives for forgiving me."

Catherine shrugged. "I don't resent my male colleagues just because they've had an easier time of it."

"Good. I'd hate to think I may be handing over my patients to someone who resents me." He hesitated. "Now it's your turn. Tell me about your life before you came to New York."

Catherine wanted to keep their conversation on a purely professional level, with no disturbing personal undercurrents, but Dr. Flanders was so easy to talk to and seemed so genuinely interested in her that she found herself telling him about her early years in Cleveland, her studies at the Women's College, and her internship at the New England Hospital.

When she finished, he said, "I'm sure you're an excellent doctor, but you understand that I have to see for myself before I entrust any of my patients' wives into your care."

"I would be just as cautious, if I were in your shoes. You have your own reputation to consider."

"How true. One candidate is coming tomorrow and another on Thursday, so why don't you come Friday morning? I'll send my carriage for you and we'll see what you can do."

"I'll look forward to it."

After luncheon was over, Dr. Flanders escorted her out to his waiting carriage and lingered with her for a few moments until the chill in the air set him to shivering.

"I should go back inside before I catch my death," he said, yet he remained standing there. Finally, he looked deeply into Catherine's eyes as he took her hand, and for a moment, she thought he was going to draw her fingers to his lips. "It's been a pleasure meeting you, Dr. Stone," he said softly. "I hope we'll have a long and fruitful association."

Catherine's heart raced at his touch, so firm and warm through her glove. "So do I, Dr. Flanders. Good day."

He handed her into the carriage and stood watching until she was out of sight.

All the way back to Mrs. Mason's, Catherine recalled every detail of her afternoon with Dr. Flanders, especially his great reluctance to part from her and the promise of seeing him again. Her hopes soared.

Perhaps her life was about to change.

Catherine expected to find her belongings piled up on the sidewalk when she returned to Mrs. Mason's, but everything remained just where she had left it. While she couldn't bring herself to apologize to the old woman, she managed to be civil and told her the extra rent would be forthcoming.

She would just have to be the one Dr. Flanders chose.

During the next two days, Catherine found herself experiencing niggling doubts that sent butterflies fluttering in her stomach and robbed her of sleep. What if she wasn't as good as she thought? What if she were only adequate after all?

She would soon learn how good she really was.

❧ CHAPTER ❧

THREE

WHEN the black brougham appeared outside on the third day at eight o'clock in the morning, Catherine felt as though it had come to transport her to her own funeral. But once she arrived at Dr. Flanders' house, Catherine's feeling of doom turned into excitement, especially when she found him in coat and hat, pacing the foyer.

"You're just in time to see your first patient," he said, tugging on black kidskin gloves. His blue eyes were deeply shadowed with weariness, but there was an infectious air of anticipation about him. As he grabbed his medical bag and ushered Catherine back out the door, he said, "Good morning, by the way. I trust you've had breakfast."

"Yes," she replied, though she doubted that weak tea and cold toast were what he meant.

"Good."

Once they sat across from each other inside the brougham, Catherine ached to ask him how her two competitors had fared, but she resisted the impulse. After all, the only person she should be competing against was herself.

Instead, she said, "Late night?"

He suppressed a yawn and nodded. "An elderly gentleman with pneumonia. I didn't get home until one a.m., but that's to be expected in our profession."

She suspected that her competitor didn't get home until one A.M. either, for Dr. Flanders would ask of her whatever he asked of himself—no more, no less. Well, Catherine could match whatever he asked of her.

"Whom are we going to see?" she asked, glancing out the window at the fine houses drifting past.

"Hortensia the Horrible."

Startled, Catherine looked at him. "Who in heaven's name is Hortensia the Horrible?"

Dr. Flanders grinned. "You'll see." And he would say no more about this mysterious patient.

Ten minutes later, the brougham stopped before an imposing mansion, and when Catherine followed Dr. Flanders inside, she found a young, harried-looking woman wringing her hands as she paced the foyer. She was too well-dressed to be the housekeeper or a maid, so Catherine suspected she was the lady of the house herself.

The moment she spied Dr. Flanders, she clasped her hands together and hurried over. "Oh, Dr. Flanders, thank God you've come! Hortensia has a horrible cough and won't let anyone near her."

Immediately Catherine envisioned an imperious, white-haired *grande dame* terrorizing her daughter and the servants with her querulous and unreasonable demands, earning her the soubriquet "Hortensia the Horrible."

"I came as soon as I received your message, Mrs. Peachtree," Dr. Flanders said in a soothing voice that visibly calmed the woman. "This is my colleague, Dr. Catherine Stone. Dr. Stone, I would like you to meet Mrs. Arnold Peachtree."

Catherine stepped forward. "How do you do, Mrs. Peachtree?"

To her credit, Mrs. Peachtree didn't stare at Catherine as if she were the bearded lady in a circus sideshow. She smiled distractedly and murmured a few pleasantries.

Dr. Flanders said, "If you don't mind, Bella, I'd like Dr. Stone to examine Hortensia."

"Perhaps she will succeed where others have failed. If you'll just follow me . . ." Mrs. Peachtree said, her worried frown returning.

Clutching her medical bag and breathing deeply to try to banish the butterflies in her stomach, Catherine followed Dr. Flanders and Mrs. Peachtree up a long flight of stairs that seemed to go on forever.

Finally, they came to a stop before a closed door. Mrs. Peachtree took a deep breath, gave Dr. Flanders a worried glance, then knocked. When a young woman in the uniform of a maid answered, Mrs. Peachtree whispered, "How is she?"

"The same, madam," the maid replied.

"You may go now. I'll ring if we need you."

The maid nodded and left.

"Hortensia," she called out sweetly as she entered, "that kind Dr. Flanders is here to see you."

Catherine followed them into the room and looked around, fully expecting to see a huge four-poster bed and a malevolent old lady propped up against a bank of lace-trimmed pillows.

What she saw was a rocking horse, several dolls having tea, and a large red ball that had rolled into a corner. The bed was no four-poster but a trundle bed, and its inhabitant quite different from what Catherine had envisioned.

Hortensia was not an old lady, but a little girl of perhaps four or five.

Catherine smiled as her doubts and nervousness melted away. Two seconds later, they returned tenfold as she learned why Dr. Flanders had dubbed this flaxen-haired cherub "Hortensia the Horrible."

"I don't want to see the doctor!" Hortensia screeched before succumbing to a coughing fit.

Her mother wrung her hands. "Hortensia, please. You must let the doctor make you all better. You know he won't hurt you."

"No!" Before anyone could stop her, the tyrant of the nursery moved with lightning speed and wrapped her blanket around her as tight as an Egyptian mummy.

"Hortensia!" her beleaguered mother wailed. "Come out of there at once or there will be no lemon custard for you tonight. And I won't allow you to ride your pony for a month."

Hortensia had no intention of complying, despite her mother's dire threats.

Finally, Mrs. Peachtree turned to them and shook her head, her eyes filling with frustrated tears. "I just never know what to do with her."

Dr. Flanders looked at Catherine. "Dr. Stone, perhaps you would like to try reasoning with the child?"

So this was to be her first test.

Catherine set down her medical bag and approached the lump on the trundle bed. "Hortensia, my name is Dr. Stone. I've been waiting to meet you for a long time so I can try to make you feel better, but I won't be able to if you don't come out."

Feeling two pair of eyes on her, Catherine leaned over and tried to unwind the blanket, but to her chagrin, the little terror had wrapped herself up so tightly, Catherine couldn't even find a place to get a fingerhold, let alone pull the child out.

Reason was not going to work, so Catherine decided to take more drastic measures. She looked around the nursery. That's when she noticed the doll.

This large, expensive-looking doll sat at the head of the tea table, its French bisque porcelain head crowned with human hair exactly the same color as Hortensia's. From the doll's exalted position in the toys' hierarchy, Catherine suspected that this doll was Hortensia's favorite.

"Well, Hortensia," Catherine said, her voice heavy with regret as she rose, "if you're not going to let me try to make you all better, I'm just going to have to leave and take your dolly with me."

The lump coughed once and grew very still.

Catherine walked over to the doll. "I bet this dolly with the golden hair is your favorite," she said, keeping one eye on the lump. She picked up the doll and slowly started for the door. "But it's my dolly now and I'm going to take it home with me."

"Mama, don't let her take my dolly!" Hortensia wailed from the depths of her blanket cocoon.

For one moment, Mrs. Peachtree looked as though she were going to side with her daughter. But she surprised Catherine by saying, "I'm sorry, Hortensia, but if you don't let Dr. Stone try to make you better, I am going to give her your dolly."

Silence.

"Goodbye, Hortensia," Catherine said. "Thank you for the dolly. I'll take very good care of it."

The blanket loosened and came away to reveal the subdued Hortensia, who glared at Catherine out of bright, angry eyes that held grudging respect for a superior opponent.

Catherine handed the doll to Mrs. Peachtree and knelt down by the bedside. "Thank you, Hortensia." She waited for the child to try to kick or bite, but the threat of losing her favorite doll was making her think twice.

Taking out her stethoscope, Catherine said, "Would you like to help me find your heart? All you have to do is put these in your ears and listen for the thump-thump, thump-thump. Would you do that for me?"

For one moment, she thought Hortensia was going to push the stethoscope away. Then she surprised Catherine by putting the tips of the binaurals into her ears.

Catherine smiled. First she placed the bell on the arch of Hortensia's bare right foot. "Is your heart here?"

Hortensia listened, then shook her head.

Catherine frowned in mock puzzlement as she put the stethoscope on Hortensia's knee, then her elbow. Each time, Hortensia shook her head and giggled at the doctor's exaggerated bafflement.

Finally, when Catherine did put the instrument over the little girl's heart, her eyes grew wide and she nodded.

"We found it!" Catherine glanced back over her shoulder and said, "Isn't that wonderful?" to Dr. Flanders and Mrs. Peachtree, who promptly applauded.

Having tamed Hortensia, Catherine examined the child's lungs without further resistance, and took her temperature.

"She's got a slight bit of congestion in her lungs," she said to the mother as Dr. Flanders examined the child himself. "It sounds worse than it is. I've written you a prescription for medicine she should inhale. Try to keep her warm and quiet. If her cough gets worse, just call—" She almost said "me," then added, "Dr. Flanders."

Mrs. Peachtree rang for the nursemaid, and when she reappeared to take charge, the mistress of the house led her guests out.

Once they were in the hall, Mrs. Peachtree turned to Catherine, relief written all over her face. "I don't know how to thank you, Dr. Stone. Hortensia is our only child, and she can be so difficult. I'm afraid I'm much too nervous to handle her properly."

"You must take a firmer hand with her, Mrs. Peachtree," Catherine said. "You are the parent, not Hortensia. If you can't control her when she's five, what are you going to do when she's ten and refuses to do her lessons, or kicks her governess?"

The woman sighed, her worried frown returning. "Easier said than done, Dr. Stone."

As they walked down the stairs, Catherine glanced at Dr. Flanders to gauge his reaction to her unorthodox handling of the child, her diagnosis, and advice to Mrs. Peachtree, but his face was an expressionless mask and revealed nothing.

Once they were back in his carriage after saying goodbye to the grateful Mrs. Peachtree, who thanked Dr. Flanders for bringing Catherine, he made his feelings known.

"I take off my hat to you, Dr. Stone. I never thought I'd see Hortensia the Horrible conquered in my lifetime. I've always dreaded treating her because I've tried everything, and she still fights me. Why I can't imagine, since I am such a charming fellow.''

Catherine smiled at that. ''She's not a bad child, merely spoiled.''

She wanted to ask him if her competitors had been sent to Hortensia and how they had fared, but she held her tongue.

''I agreed with your diagnosis as well.''

''That's reassuring, Dr. Flanders.''

His expression became more serious. ''However, one case does not a day make. We'll have to see how you do with my other patients before I make my decision.''

''That's only fair,'' Catherine agreed.

But as the carriage approached Dr. Flanders' house, Catherine found herself worrying less about her competitors and more about giving his patients the best medical care possible.

She found herself looking forward to more challenges as they walked through the door and saw his waiting area filled with a dozen patients.

Catherine stitched a scalp wound, scolded a young mother for almost killing her baby with overdoses of ''Mrs. Snyder's Soothing Syrup,'' and set a broken toe. Dr. Flanders observed her with a critical eye. Occasionally he would take her aside and challenge her diagnosis, but Catherine refused to be intimidated and held her ground. Ultimately, Dr. Flanders capitulated, showing Catherine that he was testing her.

Even during a quick lunch, Dr. Flanders made no mention of how Catherine was faring against her competitors. She suspected he was waiting for the end of the day to make his decision.

That afternoon, while Catherine treated a man with a virulent rash on the backs of his hands, Dr. Flanders was called away. He returned to the surgery just as Catherine's patient was walking out the door, a wide grin on his face.

''Another satisfied patient?'' Dr. Flanders asked.

Catherine nodded. ''In spite of the usual initial resistance to my being a woman.''

He paused. ''Would you come into my office? There's someone I want you to meet.''

''But we have three other patients to see.''

''Are their injuries serious, or can they wait?''

''They can wait, but—''

''Tell them to return later. I want you to meet an old and dear friend of mine named Gordon Graham. I'm hoping you can help him with a particularly delicate problem his wife is having.''

''What sort of problem?''

''Persistent miscarriages.''

After instructing the waiting patients to return later in the afternoon, Catherine followed Dr. Flanders out of the surgery and into his office, where a man stood looking out a window, his hands clasped behind his back. He turned when he heard them enter, and Catherine came face to face with a tall, imposing man. His long hair and beard gave him a leonine look. As his penetrating gaze lit on Catherine, his face twisted in anger.

''A woman? Flanders, what's the meaning of this? I thought I could trust you.''

''Mind your manners, Gordon,'' Dr. Flanders said, closing the door behind him. ''This is Dr. Catherine Stone, a colleague of mine, and you can trust her with any confidence you would entrust to me.''

Catherine stepped forward and extended her hand. ''How do you do, Mr. Graham.''

He shook it, though he was not pleased. Then he looked at his friend. ''She's still a woman. You can't expect me to discuss—'' he groped for the right word ''—that part of my marriage with her.''

''Gordon,'' Dr. Flanders said patiently, going to stand behind his desk, ''why don't you stop bellowing and sit down? Then you can tell Dr. Stone what ails your wife. I know she can help you.''

Catherine appreciated Dr. Flanders' confidence in her. She suspected that from the way Mr. Graham was acting, he feared his sexual relations with his wife would come under scrutiny in any discussion of her miscarriages. He needn't have worried; Catherine was just as nervous as he.

Graham sat in the chair next to her. ''Begging your pardon, Dr. Stone, but it makes me damned uncomfortable having you here.''

She turned toward him and looked him in the eye. ''Many men are uncomfortable talking frankly to a woman doctor, but we will be discussing your wife, not you. Dr. Flanders thinks I can help her, and all I ask is that you give me a fair chance.''

''Be that as it may, there are just some topics that should not be discussed in a lady's presence.''

Dr. Flanders said, "Even if she can help Genevra have the child you two want so desperately?"

"You're the best. If you can't help us, how can she?"

"Mr. Graham," Catherine said, "my specialty is obstetrics and gynecology—women's diseases and having babies. If your wife is having difficulty having a child, I could help."

Graham fell silent, his masculine outrage at the unconventionality of dealing with a woman doctor warring with his desire to get what he wanted.

To put him at ease, Catherine rose and went to stand before the window, where she stared up at the cold blue sky, her back to the men.

"My wife and I have been married for a little over a year," Graham finally said. "During that time, she has been in the family way twice." He took a deep shuddering breath. "She lost them both."

"I'm so sorry," Catherine said. "I know that must have been devastating for the both of you."

"I must have a child, Dr. Stone, preferably a son to carry on the Graham name and inherit my business when I'm gone. I was married once before, but my wife died childless. Genevra is my second wife and twenty years younger than I. My first wife's childlessness was a bitter blow. Now that it's happening to Genevra as well . . . it's beginning to strain my marriage."

Catherine looked over her shoulder and exchanged looks with Dr. Flanders. Here was a virile man in his early forties desperate for an heir. Perhaps he was putting too many demands on his young second wife.

"Mr. Graham, tell me about your wife's miscarriages."

"I don't understand it. One day she's blushing and telling me I'm going to be a papa, and two weeks later she's crying her eyes out and telling me I'm not anymore."

Catherine turned and walked back to her chair. "Does your wife have any reason to fear you?"

"Now just hold on one minute, Dr. Stone . . ."

"I don't want to offend you, Mr. Graham, but it's important."

He glowered at her. "I love my wife. She has nothing to fear from me."

"Does she want a child?"

"Of course she does! All women do. What kind of question is that?"

Dr. Flanders gave him a warning look.

Subdued, Graham said, "Yes, she wants a child as much as I do. She cries all the time and refuses to let Kim look at her. She says she can't bear the thought of losing another child and disappointing me." His expression was bleak. "I'm at my wit's end, Dr. Stone. I don't know what to do."

"Perhaps you would allow me to speak with her," Catherine said gently.

"Quite frankly, I'm skeptical. If Kim and I haven't been able to quell her fears, I don't know how you can expect to."

Dr. Flanders said, "You'd be surprised, Gordon. Sometimes a woman feels more at ease with another woman. And I can assure you that Dr. Stone will treat Genevra with the utmost delicacy and tact."

"I'm a desperate man." Graham groaned, running his hand through his hair, mussing it. He sighed heavily. "What have I got to lose at this point?"

"Nothing," Catherine assured him.

He rose, eager for action now that his decision had been made. "Shall we go, Dr. Stone?"

"I'll be right with you, but first, I'd like a few words with Dr. Flanders in private."

"Of course. I'll be waiting for you in the foyer." Then he left.

Catherine turned in her chair to face Dr. Flanders. "I am assuming you found no organic cause for Mrs. Graham's miscarriages."

"None whatsoever. She's the picture of health."

Catherine sat in thoughtful silence for a moment. Then she said, "Would she try to induce the miscarriages herself?"

Dr. Flanders' blue eyes widened. "Genevra? Never! She's the most loving—"

"I don't mean to malign her character, but you know that I must consider all possibilities."

"Your thoroughness is commendable, but I'd suspect my own mother of doing something like that before Genevra. Once you meet her, you'll see why. She loves her big bear of a husband to distraction. She would do anything for him, as he would for her."

Catherine rose. "Well, let's see if I can get to the bottom of this."

"Good luck."

She raised her brows. "Skill, not luck, is what I'll need."
But she had a feeling she was going to need both.

Catherine sat across from Graham in his carriage and tried to draw him into conversation, but failed. He was obviously worried about his wife and responded in monosyllables. Finally, Catherine gave up.

Moments later, Graham must have realized he was being rude, for the glazed look of worry vanished from his dark eyes and he looked at Catherine with keen appraisal.

"Why did a beautiful woman like you decide to become a doctor?"

She thought of her own mother's needless death. "I wanted to help other women and ease their suffering."

"A noble aspiration. But you should be home, tending a husband and children."

"Perhaps I shall. One day."

Graham shook his head. "The world is a cold, harsh place, Dr. Stone, not fit for the gentler sex. Men know this because we battle in it daily to support our families. I don't know of any man who would tolerate his wife subjecting herself to it. I know I wouldn't want it for my Gen."

"Then the man I marry will just have to be exceptional."

"Exceptional? Half mad is more like it."

Catherine refused to let him bait her. "Half mad will do nicely."

He regarded her in thoughtful silence. "You really don't mind not being like other women?"

"Oh, come now, Mr. Graham. You make it sound as if I have four arms or three legs."

"No insult intended, merely an observation."

"And I am like other women." She wanted a man to love her, and someday she would bear his children. "I just happen to be a doctor as well."

"Still, I wouldn't want my Gen to do what Flanders does all day, tending sick people. She belongs at home, safe and protected."

But if she is truly happy there, Catherine thought, *why does she keep miscarrying?*

Graham leaned forward, his dark eyes intense. "Dr. Stone, if you can help my wife, I'll give you anything you want. I am a very wealthy man."

And if she failed? She knew she would have no future in New York City.

"I can't promise anything, but I'll do my best."

The expression on Gordon Graham's face told her he expected more than her best.

The carriage drew to a halt and Graham flung open the door without waiting for the driver to do it.

"We're here."

Catherine had to pick up her skirts and hurry to keep up with Graham as he ignored his butler and strode through the foyer of his palatial Fifth Avenue home and started up the stairs, which she suspected he would have taken two at a time if she hadn't been with him to slow him down.

They hurried down an endless corridor, finally stopping before a closed door. Graham knocked softly, and when a voice bade them enter, he opened it and preceded Catherine in his haste to see his wife.

Her boudoir was all gilt, ivory lace, and pink ruffles that reminded Catherine of the inside of a candy box. She searched the room for Genevra Graham, and found her reclining on a chaise longue near the tall windows.

The moment Mrs. Graham saw her husband, she hid her handkerchief beneath a pillow and said, "Gordie, whatever are you doing home in the middle of the day?" as she rose from her chaise and glided toward them. "Is anything wrong?"

Redheaded Genevra Graham had to be all of nineteen, and Catherine was startled to find her as petite as her husband was large. Her hazel eyes, red from crying, were only for her husband as she extended her hands to him in greeting.

He gripped them and drew them to his lips. "Nothing is wrong, my darling. I'm just worried about you, that's all." He glanced over at Catherine. "And I've brought Dr. Stone with me. She's a lady doctor working with Kim, and she thinks she may be able to help us."

Fearful eyes fell on Catherine, and Mrs. Graham turned decidedly pale. "You've told her . . . everything?"

"Yes, my love. I had to."

She looked up at her husband, fresh tears beginning to gather. "Oh, Gordie, you shouldn't have . . ."

When Graham looked stricken at his wife's gentle reproach, Catherine stepped forward. "I can understand your reluctance to see me, but I think I can help you if you'll just give me a chance.''

The young woman turned away. ''But it's so . . . humiliating.''

''Please, Gen,'' her husband said. ''Just talk to Dr. Stone. Will you do that for me?''

''I'd do anything for you. You know that.''

There was such great intimacy and obvious passion between them that Catherine had to resist the urge to tiptoe out of the room and leave them alone. Instead, she said briskly, ''Very good. Now, if you'll just leave us, Mr. Graham . . .''

''I'll be downstairs in my study,'' he said with great reluctance, his eyes never leaving his young wife's tormented face.

Once her husband was gone, Genevra stood there stiffly, her arms at her sides and her head bowed, looking for all the world like a Christian martyr getting ready to face the Roman lions. She would have to be won over, and Catherine suspected she had her work cut out for her. But she had to succeed. Her future depended on it.

She smiled. ''You have such a beautiful home, Mrs. Graham. Would you mind showing it to me?''

Genevra raised her head and stared at her, obviously not expecting this. ''Why—why of course, if you'd like to see it.''

''I would.''

As Catherine suspected, Genevra was proud of her home— her sheltered world—and as they went from the endless upstairs bedrooms down to the parlor and dining room, the woman visibly relaxed and became more animated. She especially delighted in telling Catherine that ''Gordie bought this painting for me in Venice last year,'' and ''Gordie had Mr. Tiffany redecorate this room just for me.''

The woman obviously worshipped her husband.

When they finished, Catherine said, ''Would it be too much of an imposition to ask if we might have tea in the drawing room?''

''Not at all.''

Moments later, after a maid served tea and dainty French iced cakes, Catherine conversed easily with her hostess about growing up in Cleveland and tales of Sybilla and the Women's Medical College.

''And did you really have to cut up dead bodies?'' Genevra asked in a hushed voice, her eyes widening.

"Oh, yes," Catherine replied, sipping her tea. "How else could we learn how the human body works?"

"And did you have to cut up . . . men?" Genevra blushed prettily.

Catherine leaned forward as one imparting a secret. "The first time we had to dissect a male cadaver, I remember my professor saying, 'Now, ladies, I'll have no fainting or giggling, if you please,' since it was the first time any of us had ever seen an unclothed man. Of course, several of us did faint or giggle, but not Sybilla. She turned to us and said, as cool as can be, 'Well, I guess now we'll know what to expect on our wedding night.' "

Genevra blushed, but she also laughed until tears filled her eyes. She dabbed at them with a handkerchief. "Oh, Catherine, you are so funny. I feel as though I've known you all my life."

Which was exactly what Catherine had been counting on.

She placed her hand on the younger woman's. "I feel the same way, and as a newfound friend and a doctor, please let me try to help you."

Genevra was silent for what seemed like hours. Then she nodded and added in a resigned, frightened voice, "All right. I'll do whatever you ask."

"You won't regret it. Now, I understand that you think you're going to have a baby again."

Genevra plucked at her handkerchief. "I'm almost certain of it. I've been sick in the morning, you see."

"Then why don't we go to your bedchamber and examine you to make sure?"

Genevra turned pale, and her eyes darkened with fear. "Catherine, I—" She hesitated, then shook her head. "Never mind."

Catherine sensed that Genevra had been on the verge of confiding something of great importance. "What is it? You were about to tell me something."

"It—it's nothing. Come. Let's get this over with."

Before Catherine could question her further, Genevra headed for the door.

Once back in the bedroom, Catherine left Genevra to undress while she rolled up her sleeves and scrubbed her hands. When she was through, she found her patient, silent, stalwart, and red-faced as she lay in bed, covered by a sheet.

"Have you ceased to be unwell?" Catherine asked.

"Yes. Two months in a row."

Catherine examined her patient quickly to spare her further embarrassment. She found that the breasts' aureoli had darkened, one of the earliest physical manifestations of pregnancy. As Catherine progressed to the bimanual examination, she found the most conclusive evidence of all for pregnancy: definite alterations in the size, shape, and consistency of the uterus itself.

When she finished, she smiled down at Genevra. "Congratulations, Mrs. Graham. You're going to be a mother."

Genevra burst into tears.

Catherine sat on the edge of the bed and gathered the distraught woman into her arms. "There, there. It won't be the same this time, I promise. You'll have this baby."

Instead of comforting and reassuring Genevra, Catherine's words made her cry harder, great shuddering sobs that shook her small frame.

"Genevra, what's wrong? Won't you please tell me?"

Finally, she raised her head. "I—I'm afraid."

Catherine rubbed her patient's back. "I won't lie to you. All women fear the pain, but you'll have to endure it if you want a baby. And once it's over, you'll forget all about it, I promise."

If she survived, like Lucy Hunter. If she didn't have complications, like the fatal convulsions of eclampsia.

Genevra wiped her eyes with the back of her hand. "What if I die, Dr. Stone? What if Gordie's baby is so large that I can't give birth to it? He is such a . . . large man, and I am so small."

So that's what Genevra Graham feared most. And those fears and nervousness were so overwhelming, they were causing her to miscarry.

Catherine felt the heady rush of elation a detective must feel after solving a crime. Everyone was so concerned with finding a physical cause of Genevra's inability to carry a child to term, that they had overlooked her agitated mental state. She had not discussed her fears with her husband or her own doctor, but she had felt at ease discussing them with another woman.

You're a good doctor after all, Dr. Stone.

"Please get dressed," she said. "We have to talk."

Moments later, a red-eyed Genevra entered the parlor and sat down listlessly beside Catherine.

"While it's true that your husband is taller and larger than you," she began, "that doesn't mean that your baby will be so large that you can't give birth to it."

Genevra looked skeptical. "It doesn't?"

"No. The human body is a wondrous invention and makes provisions. While your pelvis is narrow, it's not narrow enough to prevent a birth. When the time comes, those bones will separate enough to allow your baby to be born, no matter how large."

"Do you mean that?"

"I won't lie to you. You may have a more difficult birth, but it won't be impossible, Genevra."

Tears filled her eyes. "I'm still so afraid." Before Catherine could comment, the woman rose and began pacing the room. "But I love Gordie so much, and I want to please him. I know he would be the happiest man in the world if I could give him a son."

"You must make a choice," Catherine said. "You must decide whether you're going to set your fears aside and give your husband this child, or give in to them and run the risk of a third miscarriage."

"I don't want Gordie to hate me."

"I doubt if he could ever hate you."

Genevra smiled at that. Then she said, "I'll do whatever you say to have this child, Dr. Stone. I won't be afraid."

Catherine smiled back. "Good. Now, I want to talk to your husband alone."

When Catherine told Gordon Graham she believed his wife's inordinate fears and nervousness were causing her miscarriages, he said, "But why didn't she tell me?"

Catherine shrugged. "Embarrassment, perhaps, or the fear that you would dismiss her fears as groundless."

"What can I do to help her?"

"You must set her fears to rest at every opportunity."

Then he thanked Catherine and sent her back to Dr. Flanders' office.

Dr. Flanders was astonished when Catherine told him what she had discovered.

"Genevra never said a word to me about her fears," he said. "I know excessive nervousness can cause a miscarriage, but I never dreamed . . ."

"Well, if she never said anything and presented a calm facade to the world, who would know?"

Dr. Flanders leaned back in his swivel chair. "Thank you. You've done well today. You were able to get Genevra to confide in you in a way that she wouldn't with me. I don't know how you did it, but I'm grateful, because I think the world of those two and want to see them happy."

Catherine felt her heart race. "Does that mean that I—"

"—will receive my referrals?" He grinned. "We still have patients waiting, doctor. You'll know my decision by the end of the day."

The end of their day finally came at eight o'clock at night, but Catherine was so tired, she decided to go into Dr. Flanders' library and contemplate her fate while he saw one last patient. Instead, she fell asleep.

Minutes later, Kim walked into the library and stared down at Catherine dozing in his favorite chair. Her thick brown hair looked golden in the shifting, flickering firelight and was just beginning to come undone from its pins after her strenuous day. She smelled faintly of carbolic, and droplets of blood were spattered on those parts of her bodice that hadn't been covered by the oiled silk apron.

She should be wearing a Worth gown, he said to himself, *and ropes of pale pearls.*

What are you thinking of? he chided himself as he took a step back. *You've known her for only two days.*

Yet he couldn't deny the unmistakable attraction he felt for Catherine.

And it had nothing to do with her beauty, for as a handsome man himself, Kim socialized with many beautiful women and had long ago learned not to trust beauty alone. No, it was her determination, dedication to medicine, and generosity of spirit that drew him. She was a veritable Pied Piper with her patients, beguiling them into trusting her with her sympathy and warm smile, then easing their pain with her formidable skills.

As he watched her sleep, he thought of the two other women he had been considering. While competent, they lacked Catherine's ability to inspire trust and build rapport. From the moment he had seen Catherine win over Hortensia with a mixture of firmness and gentleness, her competition ceased to exist. After working a miracle with the Grahams, Catherine won his boundless admiration. And something more.

She stirred and her eyes flew open. Kim felt lost in their blue depths.

"Dr. Flanders," she murmured, her musical voice rough with sleep. "Forgive me for dozing off like that."

"You were exhausted. After the day you've put in, I'd advise you to sleep for the rest of the week."

When she sat up, he handed her an envelope.

She stared at it. "What's this?"

"Your fee for treating my patients."

She stood up, her cheeks a faint pink. "But I can't accept this. They are your patients. I was treating them as a test. I didn't expect you to pay me."

She never disappointed him. "Take the money. You earned it. And my referrals as well."

That caused her eyes to sparkle in triumph. "You mean I—?"

"You're a fine doctor, Catherine," he said softly, unwittingly using her Christian name, "the best of the three. I know my patients—my former patients—will be in good hands."

"Dr. Flanders, I—"

"Kim. Please call me Kim."

"Kim, then. And you must call me Catherine."

He chuckled. "I believe I already have."

"I don't know what to say, except thank you."

"You deserve it."

She looked down at the envelope as though it contained a fortune. "Now I'll be able to pay Mrs. Mason's rent and establish my practice."

"There's something else I forgot to mention. If you should need any additional funds, the Women's Dispensary on Park Street is looking for a doctor to teach working girls proper hygiene."

Her lovely eyes grew bright with gratitude. "Thank you again, Kim. You've done so much for me already. I don't know how I'll ever repay you."

He was too much the gentleman to take advantage of that gratitude as he would have liked. Instead, he said, "By being the best doctor you can be. That will be payment enough." And the chance to see her again.

"I won't disappoint you."

He glanced at the clock on the side table. "Well, I think it's time I got you home. You'd better open your surgery bright and early from now on, because I'm sure all those empty chairs in Mrs. Mason's hallway will be filled in a week or two."

"Won't Mrs. Mason just like that," she added, laughing.

After driving Catherine home and seeing her to her door, Kim had his driver drive aimlessly around the city for a time, while he thought about Catherine.

❧ CHAPTER ❧

FOUR

WITHIN the next few months, Dr. Flanders' prediction came true: the chairs lining Mrs. Mason's hallway no longer stood empty. At first, most of Catherine's patients were Dr. Flanders' referrals, but as the neighborhood women noticed all the fine carriages waiting for fine ladies who were seeing Dr. Stone, they started going to her as well. If Dr. Stone was good enough for these elegant Fifth Avenue women, she was good enough for them.

As soon as Catherine's bank account swelled, she went to Bloomingdale's and bought several pretty wool French cashmere dresses in the conservative colors of black, brown, and dark blue for $16 apiece. She also invested in a thick, warm wool coat for the outrageous sum of $30. Catherine's purchase didn't seem so extravagant when she spent both Christmas and New Year's trudging through heavy snows blanketing the streets of New York to deliver babies.

Nowadays, she was so busy, she couldn't find time to spare for Kim. It seemed that whenever he invited her to dinner, she had a baby to deliver or she was seeing emergency patients well into the evening. The one time he had invited her to the theater, she refused because she didn't have an evening gown to wear.

Now January was coming to a close and Catherine had seen Kim only once since she had examined Genevra Graham, and that was in passing at their house. He had been politeness itself, but she could tell he was hurt and perplexed by her avoidance, however justified.

As her last patient bade her goodnight, Catherine promised herself that tomorrow she was going to find the time to call on Kim.

She locked up her surgery for the night, giving a lingering

look at the new padded leather examining table a grateful wealthy patient had given her, and started up the stairs so she could take a well-deserved nap before supper. Just as she was stifling a yawn, the doorbell rang.

There, standing on the top step, was Kim's driver.

He doffed his hat, wished her good evening, and handed her a note. "I'm to wait for your reply, doctor."

"Then do come in before you freeze to death," Catherine said, stepping back as a gust of frigid air swirled about her skirts. While the driver came in and shut the door behind himself, Catherine read Kim's note by the flickering gaslight.

Dear Catherine,
    You've been working too hard. Please come to dinner tonight.

                                            Regards,
                                            Kim Flanders

She knew he hadn't come for her himself because he wanted to give her the option of refusing, but tired or not, she couldn't. She had neglected their friendship far too long.

She told the driver to wait, got her new coat, and after telling Mrs. Mason that she was going out for the evening, left for Kim's house.

When she arrived, he answered the door himself, and the moment he saw Catherine, his face lit up with delight rather than the reproach she deserved. "Catherine . . . I'm so glad you could accept my invitation."

She smiled sheepishly. "Hello, Kim."

He stared at her for a moment, as though he couldn't believe she was standing in his foyer. Then he stepped forward. "Here, let me take your coat."

"I'm so ashamed of myself," she said, averting her eyes as she struggled with the buttons.

"Why?"

Catherine turned as he took her coat, his hands lingering on her shoulders for just a second longer than propriety dictated. "Because I haven't made time for you, and after all you've done for me. I feel like quite the ingrate."

"Catherine, Catherine . . . don't feel that way. I'm a doctor, too, remember? I know what it's like to have emergency cases force you to cancel invitations at the last minute."

"Still, that's no excuse."

"Let's have no more of such talk, shall we? You have nothing to feel ungrateful for. You've been busy, that's all, and I'm glad to hear it." He grinned. "Even if it does mean I've been deprived of your company."

His kind, sincere words and welcoming demeanor banished Catherine's awkwardness immediately, and she felt at ease in his presence once again.

He said, "Why don't we go into the library and have a sherry before dinner? We have much to talk about."

Once seated before the crackling fire in the quiet, book-lined library that smelled pleasantly of paper, morocco leather, and a touch of beeswax polish, Catherine truly relaxed for the first time that week.

Kim poured two sherries into cut crystal glasses and handed her one. He raised his in a toast. "To continued success."

She raised her glass. "To continued success."

Once Kim sat across from her, he said, "It looks as though Genevra will carry her baby to term, thanks to you."

"I'm very pleased with her progress. If she can just hang on for four more months and not give in to her fears . . ."

"I know Gordon is ecstatic. He thinks you can walk on water."

Catherine laughed. "Now that certainly is a change from the way he first felt about me."

"Gordon is a fair man. And if he has a son, he'll tell everyone he knows about the miracle you performed, and you'll find yourself with more patients than you'll know what to do with." His eyes danced with mischief. "Of course, you could always give some back to me."

"You can count on it." Catherine fell silent for a moment and stared into the fire as she sipped her sherry. "That's how it's done, isn't it? I perform a medical miracle for a wealthy, powerful person, he or she recommends me to their friends, who in turn all flock to my doorstep."

Kim waved his hand, encompassing the library and the house beyond. "That's how I got all this."

"But what about those who aren't wealthy and powerful?"

"Then you do dispensary work."

"I do. I took your advice and went to the Women's Dispensary. They hired me to teach hygiene classes, and soon I'll be visiting new mothers in the tenements to teach them how to care for their babies properly.''

Kim nodded in approval. ''I knew you'd be perfect for that job.'' He paused and studied her for a moment. ''Is that where your interest lies, in treating the poor?''

''Yes. That's what I did during my internship at the New England Hospital, and I found it very satisfying emotionally. Those women have nothing.''

''While charity work is certainly satisfying, you still need paying patients to pay your rent and your office upkeep.''

''Oh, I realize that.'' She smiled wanly. ''I suppose I do let idealism get in the way of practicality sometimes.''

''It's an endearing quality,'' Kim said, his voice becoming low and warm.

Catherine sensed his change in mood at once but ignored it. She wanted to keep their relationship purely professional. ''Well, I'm afraid practicality will have to win out at this point because I will soon be looking for a new office.''

''Oh? That surprises me. I thought you and Mrs. Mason had resolved your differences.''

''So did I, but it appears I am a victim of my own success. Now my landlady complains that there are too many people coming and going at all hours of the day, disturbing her and her boarders.''

''What did she expect? She knew you were a doctor when she rented to you.''

''I think that's just an excuse. Once the other women in the neighborhood started coming to me, Mrs. Mason lost face with them. Now she wants me out so she can regain her standing.''

Kim rolled his eyes.

''It's just as well,'' Catherine said, ''because in a month or two a friend of mine will be joining my practice and I'll need the extra room.''

Kim sat up a little straighter. ''Another woman?''

''Yes. Her name is Dr. Sybilla Wolcott and she's a surgeon. She's been studying at the Ecole de Medicine in Paris for the last year and is ready to come home and practice.''

''I'm impressed. The two of you should make the rest of us look to our laurels.''

''Unless I find new offices, we won't be impressing anyone.''

He set down his sherry glass, folded his hands, and stared out into space. Then he said, ''A friend of mine who lives in Washington Square is moving to California and looking for a tenant. Perhaps you could rent it from him, if I let him know you were interested.''

Catherine felt the heat rise to her cheeks. ''I'm so embarrassed. I didn't mean to suggest that you should find a new office for me.''

''Of course you didn't.''

''You've done far too much for me already.''

''Don't be silly. Friends can never do too much for each other.'' He rose from the chair in one easy, fluid movement and walked over to his desk, where he proceeded to scribble something on a piece of paper. Then he walked over and handed it to Catherine. ''This is my friend's name and address. I'll contact him tomorrow morning and tell him to be expecting you.''

She glanced at it and put it in her pocket. ''Once again, I don't know how to thank you, Kim.''

''How about by going ice skating with me on Sunday? The ponds in Central Park are frozen over.''

She smiled. ''How can I refuse?''

''You can't. And if you do, I'll sit on Mrs. Mason's doorstep all day until you come to your senses.''

Judging from the determined look in Kim's eye, Catherine believed he would do just that.

His housekeeper interrupted them to announce that dinner was served. Kim extended his hand to Catherine, and together they left the library for the dining room.

After dinner was over, he escorted Catherine home.

Sitting across from him in the dimly lit brougham, Catherine watched him without appearing to. His eyes were dark and hooded, his mouth pensive. She wondered what he was thinking.

All she knew was contentment. Kim made her feel contented and secure. He had done so much for her. It would be so easy to fall in love with such a kind, gracious man, but she was just beginning to embark on her medical career and romance would be an unwelcome distraction.

When they arrived at Mrs. Mason's and Kim had escorted Catherine to her door, he smiled. ''Thank you for coming to dinner tonight.''

''Thank you for inviting me.''

He looked as though he were about to say something, then changed his mind. ''I'll see you Sunday, then.''

''I'll be looking forward to it.''

Then they said goodnight, and Catherine watched him saunter down the steps, get into his carriage, and smile at her before driving away. He really was special, and being a colleague, he understood her dedication to medicine.

She found herself wishing that Sunday were already here.

Sunday dawned clear, cold, and still, the perfect day for ice skating.

At first, the glare of sunlight reflecting off the Central Park pond was so dazzling it blinded Catherine, but once her eyes grew accustomed to it, she found it refreshingly pure. There was no blood or pain here.

Kim, looking elegant as always in a charcoal-gray coat with astrakan collar and cuffs, said, "Let me help you with your skates."

Catherine sat down and raised her skirts to expose her booted foot. When Kim grasped her ankle, Catherine's face grew warm at his disconcerting touch, but she forced herself to concentrate instead on the skaters gliding back and forth across the pond's glassy surface.

Once her skates were on, Kim took her hands and helped her to her feet, where she wobbled for a moment like a newborn calf.

"Oh, dear . . ." she murmured, clinging to him.

He smiled as he tightened his grip on her hands. "You'll be fine once you find your sea legs."

"More like my skating ankles."

A moment later, Catherine gave Kim a confident nod. "I'm ready."

Kim started slowly, guiding the way as he matched his stride to hers and eased Catherine between skaters circling the pond.

"Am I going too fast for you?" he would ask every time Catherine faltered or swung too wide around a corner.

She would shake her head and smile.

Catherine discovered that Kim knew almost everyone out skating today, for he nodded and smiled at virtually everyone who passed. When she asked him who the person was, he invariably told her a well-known name she had read about in the newspapers—Astor, Vanderbilt, Sloane.

Finally, when her cheeks were rosy and stiff with cold and her lungs hurt, Catherine suggested they stop and rest for a while.

"I could use a breather myself," Kim said, guiding her back to the edge of the pond, where they found seats.

"That was so invigorating," Catherine said, "yet restful as well. Thank you for inviting me."

"You were working too hard. You needed a little time for yourself. Your patients aren't going anywhere."

They fell into companionable silence and watched the skaters.

Absorbed in the skaters gliding and twirling across the ice like figures on a music box lid, Catherine particularly noticed a tall man and his elegant partner as they skated toward them, for they were an arresting couple as perfectly matched as Kim's bay carriage horses. Broad-shouldered and solid, the man moved with lightness and grace. The woman, held as close as he could manage, matched his stride so well they moved as one in perfect harmony.

She was as ravishing as he was dashing, and they both had black hair, though the woman's was almost concealed by a large sable cossack hat that teased the man's cheek. A wide sable border trimmed her coat collar and hem, and she carried a huge muff of the same rare, expensive fur.

They knew their place in the world, and it was right up there with the sun, moon, and stars.

As the perfect couple sailed past with a sharp scraping of metal against ice, the man deigned to glance at Catherine. Eyes as gray and cold as the ice beneath his skates met hers for a split second, then drifted away without so much as a glimmer of interest, but she was left feeling strangely lightheaded, as if she had inhaled ether.

Catherine blinked and the couple was gone.

She turned to Kim. "Who was that?"

"Who?"

"That striking woman everyone is staring at, dripping in sable, with the dark-haired man by her side."

Kim squinted. "The woman is Francine Ballard, a well-known heiress, and the man with her is Damon Delancy."

Damon Delancy . . . the man with the cold gray eyes.

"I've never heard of him."

Kim looked surprised. "I thought everyone had heard of Damon Delancy. He's one of the Arizona copper kings. A very wealthy man."

"He looks it. So does she." Her curiosity satisfied, Catherine said, "Shall we take another turn around the pond?"

"Are you sure you've got the stamina for it?"

Catherine caught the teasing tone in his voice and managed an affronted sniff. "We'll just see who's got the stamina for it."

This time, before Kim could take her hand, Catherine darted out onto the ice ahead of him. "Come and catch me, if you can, Dr. Flanders," she taunted over her shoulder as she skated away.

Had she been looking where she was going, Catherine would have noticed the small strip of half-frozen grasses roughening the ice's smooth, glassy surface. The next thing she knew, one skate caught on the rough patch and stopped short, pitching her forward. Before she even had time to throw out her hands and break her fall, the ice was rushing up to meet her.

Catherine saw stars and felt a shooting pain as the ice cracked against her head. Then the rest of her body slammed down, knocking the breath out of her. She heard someone shout her name, and as she managed to struggle into a sitting position, she felt warm, sticky blood oozing onto her eyelid.

She was aware of someone kneeling beside her even before a deep, rough, masculine voice said, "Are you all right, miss?"

Catherine raised her head and looked into the cold gray eyes of Damon Delancy. "I—I think so."

"This should stop the bleeding," he said, pressing a white handkerchief into her hand.

Before Catherine could thank him, Kim was coming between them. "Please let me through. I'm a doctor."

White-faced, Kim was kneeling beside her, his arm around her. "Are you all right?"

She nodded weakly as she held the handkerchief against her bleeding cut. "That was silly of me. I should have been watching where I was going."

"Are you nauseous? Dizzy? Do you feel faint? Can you stand?"

Catherine noticed that people were beginning to gather round and gawk, but Damon Delancy was gone. "I feel fine, Kim. I think I'm more embarrassed than hurt."

"We'd better get you back to my office so I can take a look at that cut. Keep the handkerchief pressed against it while I help you up."

She managed an amused smile. "I am a doctor myself, you know. I do know what to do in an emergency."

"Sorry. I wasn't questioning your competence."

With one arm around Catherine's waist and the other grasping her free hand, Kim hauled her to her feet, where she stood swaying and leaning against him lest she collapse again. His strong, solid shoulder felt so good as he helped her to walk back to his carriage.

Once they were inside and the carriage moving, Kim sat down beside her and spread the heavy rug over her lap. "You're shaking."

Catherine rested her head back against the squabs and closed her eyes. "I'm just a little rattled, that's all."

"Rattled? I thought my heart was going to stop when I saw you go down. You could have broken your neck."

Still holding the handkerchief against her brow, Catherine turned to look at him. He had been terrified for her, a raw emotion that ran much deeper than mere concern of one friend for another.

Kim was sitting so close, Catherine could feel the warmth of his body through their coats, his quick breath against her cold cheek. And he was looking at her with a blatant yearning that had nothing to do with simple friendship.

"Let me examine that," he said, taking the handkerchief away. Kit tilted her face so he could look at the wound. "The bleeding's stopped. It's just a cut. It won't even need stitches."

"That's reassuring. I much prefer being a doctor to a patient."

He smiled briefly, then his smile died. He reached up and cradled her cheek with his palm, drawing her to him slowly, to give her time to pull away. But Catherine didn't want to. She gazed into eyes that were not cold gray, but hot blue, giving him permission.

Kim's lips were warm and smooth, sending a warm knot of pleasure uncurling deep within her. She held her breath to prolong the feeling as his lips parted and the kiss deepened expertly. When they finally parted, Catherine felt breathless and enveloped in a pleasant fog.

Kim smiled, raised her hand to his lips, and sat back. They rode back to his office in companionable silence—there was no need for words.

After Kim bandaged Catherine's cut, he took her home.

She thought of his kiss and smiled to herself as she rinsed the bloodstains out of Damon Delancy's fine lawn handkerchief and noticed it was monogrammed with white floss in an entwined double "D." When the handkerchief was dry, she folded it and placed it in a bureau drawer. She would have to find some way of returning it to its owner.

But the handkerchief was soon forgotten when Catherine moved into her new home and practice on Washington Square. The brownstone was so large and rambling that she had to hire a young housekeeper named Molly Cavanaugh to run the household and serve as her maid.

In the days to come, Catherine embarked on a course that would affect her for the rest of her life.

The brisk March wind almost tore Catherine's hat right off as she hurried up the steps to the Women's Dispensary.

The moment she walked into Dr. Hilda Steuben's office, the older woman greeted her with a brusque, "You sure you want to do this? It takes a strong stomach."

Catherine smiled. "And good afternoon to you, Hilda."

Dr. Steuben was a Valkyrie of a woman, as bristly as a porcupine, her pessimism warding off most of her colleagues, but Catherine sensed that Hilda's prickly demeanor protected her from being destroyed by the misery and squalor she dealt with every day.

Hilda grumbled something, causing Catherine to say, "Of course I want to do this. I volunteered for one day a week, didn't I?"

Hilda slipped on her coat. "I figure you'll last about a week. Maybe two. I can tell you're the soft-hearted type."

"Ever the optimist. I'll have you know I worked in the tenements in Philadelphia and Boston. I know what to expect."

"We'll just see about that. New York's tenements are worse than Boston or Philadelphia. They may even be worse than London's East End." She took her medical bag and she and Catherine left.

As they walked down the street, Hilda said, "You'll find the Germans are the cleanest and the Irish the dirtiest. The Italians refuse to learn English, so you'll need an interpreter. They're also hot-blooded and get into knife fights constantly, so be prepared to stitch wounds. I wouldn't know about the Jews because the Eastern Dispensary takes care of them."

Hilda's voice hardened in anger. "They're all dirty and irresponsible. No matter what we do for them, they're never grateful. They never try to get out of these hovels and better themselves. I always feel as though I'm fighting against the wind.''

Catherine stared at her. ''Hilda, I'm appalled. If you have no sympathy for immigrants here to make better lives for themselves, why do you treat them? Why aren't you in private practice?''

''Because there's nothing I love better than a good fight. If I keep coming at them, maybe one or two of them will pull themselves up by their bootstraps and make decent lives for themselves.'' Hilda sighed heavily. ''And I do it for the children, because they are the hope of the future.''

Catherine smiled and placed a hand on the other woman's arm. ''Why, you old fraud. I believe you're the soft-hearted type after all.''

Hilda bristled. ''That's a lie. I'm a crotchety middle-aged lady doctor who speaks her mind no matter who it hurts. Everyone knows that.''

Catherine said nothing, just smiled.

They walked down Cherry Street, and as they turned onto Mulberry Street, Catherine noticed a group of children playing together. They were all dressed in rags, with dirty faces, but one little girl of about seven caught Catherine's eye because she was as blonde and pretty as Hortensia Peachtree. But this little girl had no French doll with real hair and a bisque face to play with: she was nearly staggering under the weight of the baby in her arms.

Hilda swore softly under her breath. ''Children taking care of children . . .''

They walked down the street, and when they came to the corner, Hilda walked up to the policeman standing there and greeted him as she would an old friend. Then she introduced Catherine to Officer Shaugnessy and they continued on their way.

''Always introduce yourself to the policeman on the beat,'' Hilda said. ''He's the best friend you can have in this district.''

''I'll remember that.''

''See that you do. Your life could depend on it.''

Then Hilda stopped to buy a newspaper from a newsboy. ''And always buy a newspaper before you begin your visits,'' she said.

''But why? Do you expect to have time to read it, or are you going to give it to the tenants?''

''I can see you are a newcomer to New York. In most cases,

the women in labor don't have a bed with clean sheets. It's usually a pile of straw, if that. At least you can shred up a newspaper and use that to cover the straw and absorb the blood.''

Catherine boiled with righteous indignation. ''To treat women as if they're no better than—than farm animals . . . that's disgusting!''

Hilda gave her an ironic smile. ''Welcome to the East Side.''

Hilda consulted her list of patients they were to visit, then started walking between tenement buildings standing shoulder to shoulder, huddled together in their misery. The alley was dark, even at this time of day. Overhead, drooping swags of old clothes hanging from lines strung from one building to another strained to catch what little sun there was.

Catherine noticed bleak, blank faces staring at them from doorways and windows, but no one accosted them.

Hilda looked up. ''See those fire escapes, the ones filled with junk?''

''Yes.''

''The tenants sleep out there in the summer because it gets as hot as inside a volcano in those flats. And sometimes a baby falls between the bars. Last summer, I lost fifteen of them to fractured skulls.''

Catherine shivered.

''And in the summer, there are the cholera infantum epidemics. At least I can save some of those.'' She gave Catherine a cynical look. ''Still want to do this?''

''More than ever.''

Despite her stout assurance, Catherine felt the first stirrings of doubt. She was a doctor, dedicated to healing the sick. Yet how long could she endure the sight of so much human misery before she herself became as hard and cynical as Hilda Steuben?

Just as she and Hilda came out of the alley and rounded a corner, a boy came catapulting out of a doorway, screaming something in a foreign language.

Hilda stepped forward, halted his flight by grasping his shoulder, and said something in his native tongue. The boy babbled something in return, grabbed Hilda's hand, and began pulling her toward the doorway.

''The children are the messengers,'' Hilda said to Catherine. ''This one says that his mother is sick.''

They followed the boy into a dank, dark foyer and up some rickety stairs that creaked and groaned under their weight.

Catherine held her breath—the stairway stank of urine and garbage—and she watched her footing, for the boards were worn and loose.

Finally, they came to a door and the boy ushered them into a large room that received its only illumination from a solitary window. The room smelled of unwashed bodies and stale cooking, and cockroaches scurried off to hide as Catherine and Hilda approached.

A woman was lying face down in the middle of the room. A small brown bottle lay a foot away from her outstretched hand.

Hilda knelt beside the unconscious woman and rolled her over. She had been beautiful once, but poverty and hunger had ravaged her, leaving nothing but waxen skin drawn as tightly as a drum over sharp facial bones. Hilda felt her neck for a pulse. Nothing. She looked up at Catherine and shook her head.

Catherine picked up the bottle and smelled it. "Carbolic acid?"

Hilda lowered her head and sniffed the dead woman's lips. "She killed herself with it. It's a common way of committing suicide in the tenements. Cheap and effective."

Catherine just stared at her. Then she snapped, "Isn't there someone who can take these children away? Do they have to see this?"

"They've seen worse." Hilda spoke to the boy who had brought them here, and he herded his brothers and sisters out. One of them started crying as he closed the door behind them. Hilda rose to her feet.

Catherine looked around the room for a sheet, a curtain, a rag—anything to cover the dead woman, but the room was bare. Finally, she snatched Hilda's newspaper and arranged it over the dead woman's face.

Seeing Hilda's peculiar expression, Catherine said, "At least let her have a little dignity in death."

"I'll get Shaugnessy. He'll call an ambulance and get someone to tell the husband."

"And the children? What will happen to them?"

"Don't even ask."

Later, after the policeman took charge and Catherine and Hilda resumed their rounds, Hilda turned to her and said, "Had enough?"

"I'll be fine. Where are we going next?"

Hilda smiled. "Maybe you will last longer than two weeks after all."

Later that afternoon, when Catherine returned home, the first thing she did was strip off her clothes and take a long, hot bath to wash the filth and odors of the tenements from her body. After seeing a few patients, she changed for dinner and waited for Kim's carriage to call for her.

During the past several weeks, Catherine had felt herself drawing closer to Kim, feeling deep emotions she had never felt for a man before. She wondered if she were falling in love.

When she arrived at Kim's house, he greeted her at the door, as always, and discerned her mood at once.

"Catherine, what's wrong?" he asked, taking her coat. "You look tired and upset."

"I am. I spent my first day in the tenements." She shivered in revulsion. "I've never seen such squalor and human misery."

"It's not for the faint of heart or stomach. Would you like a sherry before dinner?"

"Yes, thank you."

Once she sat down in Kim's library, surrounded by fine books and furnishings, Catherine felt herself unwind. She sipped her sherry and closed her eyes. "This is very pleasant."

"Tell me about your day."

So while Kim listened, Catherine told him all about the dark, damp cellars she had trudged through and the rickety stairways she had climbed. She told him of the cases of measles she had seen and the baby she had helped Hilda deliver. And she told him of the suicide.

His eyes darkened in sympathy. "That must have been appalling."

"Death is a part of medicine. I'm used to it." Catherine rubbed her forehead. "But when it happens to people like this, who have so little, it seems especially unfair. They haunt me afterward, Kim."

"Then perhaps you should forgo dispensary work and concentrate on your other patients."

Catherine looked at him. "You don't do dispensary work, do you?"

"To be honest, I find it too depressing," he replied. "Besides, people like the Peachtrees and the Grahams deserve medical care as much as anyone else."

"But they can afford any doctor they choose. People in the tenements can't.''

Kim's expression turned defensive. "Are you insinuating that I'm somehow less of a doctor because I choose to treat the wealthy?''

"Of course not. I'm just trying to explain how I feel."

The warmth returned to his demeanor. "You're too kind-hearted for your own good, Catherine."

"That's what Dr. Steuben says, and I'm beginning to think she's right."

"But in spite of that, you will succeed."

She smiled. "You have such faith in me."

"Oh, it's justified." Kim glanced at the door. "I think I hear my housekeeper coming. Dinner must be ready. Shall we go?''

They rose and left the library to dine.

After a relaxing meal in elegant surroundings that did much to dispel Catherine's depressed mood, they returned to the library. In this quiet room, with no one to see and censure, they sat close together on the Chesterfield sofa.

Kim gazed deeply into Catherine's eyes, then slipped one arm around her corseted waist.

Catherine closed her eyes and leaned back against the sofa, waiting for his kiss. At first his mouth was soft and gentle, brushing against her lips, preparing them for further intimacies. She responded by running her hands along his back, pressing him closer.

She came to her senses when she felt him undo the top button of her shirtwaist.

Catherine stayed his hand. "Please, Kim, not that."

His blue eyes filled with chagrin and he murmured, "Sorry." But that didn't stop him from continuing to kiss her.

Finally, Kim pulled away, breathing heavily. "One of these days," he said, his voice husky, "I'm going to want you to stay."

"One of these days, I won't want to leave."

He drew his thumb along her lower lip. "What about tonight?''

"I'm sorry, Kim. I'm just starting my medical practice, and to take a lover would be too distracting." She smiled to soften her rejection. "Especially a man like you."

He drew away, rose, and turned his back toward her. "You're

right. Forgive me for even suggesting it. To embark down that road would only lead to disaster.''

Catherine rose and put her hand on his arm. "It's not that I don't want to. You know you've come to mean a great deal to me, and it would be so easy for me to stay with you tonight. But I am a woman and have the most to lose. I must consider the ramifications carefully. Please understand.''

He turned to face her. "Of course I do.''

"I knew you would. You're always so understanding.''

"Sometimes I wish I weren't.''

Catherine glanced at the clock on the mantel. "It's late. I should be going.''

Kim kissed her goodnight and took her home.

Later that night, as Catherine lay in bed and stared up at the ceiling, she thought about Kim's fervent embraces. She knew that certain experts claimed that women didn't experience sexual feelings, yet she always felt the most voluptuous stirrings whenever Kim kissed her. Her body responded like dry tinder to a match, filling her with disturbing, wanton thoughts of lying naked with Kim and letting him do whatever he wanted to her.

But she couldn't bring herself to become his lover. An unmarried woman who slept with a man was considered fallen and immoral, and if Catherine's patients ever found out, the scandal would ruin her reputation and all she had fought for. Yet whenever she was in Kim's arms, she was tempted to give herself to him, no matter what the price.

She drifted off to sleep wondering just how long she could go on fighting her own desires.

Thoughts of Kim lingered in the back of Catherine's mind the following morning, but she managed to keep them from affecting her work. He was all but forgotten when she received an unexpected visitor.

Catherine was just putting some bottles away in her medicine cabinet when a voice behind her said, "Where is my Bonette? Did you throw her to the dogs?''

She whirled around and a bottle of morphine crashed to the floor. Catherine ignored it. *"Sybilla!"*

Sybilla stood in the doorway, a wide smile on her face, as she hurried toward her friend. "Hello, Cat. Did I surprise you? That Molly person insisted on announcing me, but I told her that I was an old friend and wanted to surprise you.''

"Surprise me?" Catherine ran to meet her and they hugged like long-lost sisters. When they parted, she said, "Sybilla, it's so wonderful to see you. You look wonderful!"

Outwardly, Sybilla hadn't changed. She was still the epitome of delicate femininity, even more so now that she had spent time in Paris. But there was something different about her that Catherine couldn't quite identify.

Sybilla held her at arm's length. "And look at the fashion plate you've become! French cashmere . . . I am impressed. And you've finally stopped putting your hair up into that dowdy coronet."

"Ah, but I did triumph over the bustle."

Sybilla laughed as she unpinned her bonnet and removed it. "Bustles do have their uses," she said cryptically.

"But why didn't you tell me you were arriving today?" Catherine said. "I would have gone to meet your ship."

"I didn't want to take you away from your patients," she replied. "Besides, I wanted to surprise you."

"You certainly did that."

Sybilla looked around the surgery. "I must say you've done very well for yourself. A brownstone on Washington Square, a housekeeper . . ."

"I had help."

"That Dr. Flanders you told me about in your last letter?"

Catherine thought of Kim and smiled. "The same."

"I feel awkward about sharing your practice now. You've done all the work, and I just come in to reap the benefits."

"Sybilla Wolcott, I'll not have you talking that way, do you hear me? I want you here. Not only are you my friend, I can use your surgical skills."

"Are you sure?"

"I am positive. And I don't want to hear another word about it."

Sybilla hugged her again. "You are a true friend."

Catherine glanced at the door. "I'm also a doctor, and I'm afraid if I don't tend to my patients we won't have a practice to worry about. Why don't I have Molly get you settled, and we can talk later?"

"We have a whole year to catch up on."

"I can't wait."

Catherine had to wait until three o'clock before her last patient left. She prayed she would have no emergencies for the rest of the day—there was so much she had to share with Sybilla that they hadn't been able to say in their letters. This was one time she wasn't going to put her patients first.

Catherine and Sybilla sat together in the parlor and talked randomly, going off on tangents when the mood struck them, interrupting each other when they needed to. Paris, New York, dispensary work, surgical procedures . . .

"Did Ruth ever try to reconcile with you?" Sybilla asked.

Catherine smiled ruefully. "I'm afraid not. I'm probably an embarrassment to my family."

"No loss."

Catherine shrugged. "As much as I hate to admit it, I do miss them sometimes, especially Liza Jane." Then she added, "Enough about me. Tell me all about Paris."

"Well, it wasn't all work and no play."

Sybilla went on to tell her about Saturday nights in the Left Bank cafes and leisurely Sunday picnics in the Bois du Boulogne. She described the new Eiffel Tower, Notre Dame cathedral, and grand houses of the boulevards so vividly that Catherine felt as though she were there.

Suddenly a shadow passed across Sybilla's face. "And I met a man."

"A man?" Catherine studied her friend for a moment. "I can tell he is important to you."

"Was. Was important to me." She shrugged. "He came from a fine old French family that wanted him to marry a woman from another fine old French family, not a—*mon Dieu!*—lady doctor. In the end, he did as his *maman* wanted."

Catherine's heart went out to her. "Oh, Sybilla, why didn't you tell me? You shouldn't have had to endure such a disappointment alone."

"Because I knew you were struggling with your practice and I didn't want to burden you."

"You aren't a burden. You never will be."

"It hurt at first, because I thought he truly loved me. But now . . ." She managed a brave smile. "I will console myself with my surgical career."

Catherine could tell that her friend didn't want to say any more about her lost love, so she kept silent.

Sybilla said, "I must say that I've learned so much at the Ecole de Medicine. Did I tell you that I've done three successful caesarian sections?"

Catherine's eyes widened in astonishment, for she knew full well that very few women survived a caesarian section; that was why doctors preferred to perform a fetal craniotomy and sacrifice the life of the child.

"You didn't lose a patient?" she asked.

"Not one. It's still risky, but if the surgeon is scrupulous about antisepsis and meticulous about the uterine and abdominal sutures, the operation is often successful."

"I don't know if any hospitals here would allow you to do the procedure."

"Fatheaded fools."

Catherine smiled. "Merely cautious."

Sybilla muttered something under her breath, then said, "Come upstairs and see what I brought from France."

Once upstairs, Sybilla went to her bed where her braided wire bustle sat.

Catherine frowned. "Sybilla, there's something in your bustle."

"Just wait until you see what." She turned the bustle over, removed a cloth covering affixed to the bottom, and held out the bustle for Catherine's inspection.

Inside were hundreds of small rubber cups that could fit over Catherine's thumb.

She picked one up and turned pale as comprehension dawned. "Sybilla, these are pessaries."

Sybilla grinned. "Anticonception devices."

"They're illegal."

"I know. That's why I smuggled them in my bustle. The inspectors in Customs didn't suspect a thing."

"What do you intend to do with them?"

"Cat, I'm astonished that you would even ask such a question. I intend to give them to those patients who don't want any more children."

"Sybilla, you can't! They'll arrest us if anyone finds out. We'll never be able to practice medicine again."

"Don't get so upset. I don't intend to give them out to anyone who asks. We'll have to make sure they can be discreet."

Catherine felt overwhelmed by panic, as though she were drowning. "We can't risk it. There's too much at stake."

"But I thought you were dedicated to bettering women's lives. How can a woman's lot improve if she keeps having children year after year like—like a broodmare?"

Catherine thought of the women in the tenements with their many children crowded into one room.

"I'll concede that you have a point, but I'm not comfortable with breaking the law. We have to discuss this further, Syb."

Sybilla sighed. "I can understand your hesitation. You've worked hard to establish this practice. I don't want to jeopardize it." She looked down at her bustle full of pessaries. "Where shall we hide these?"

Catherine smiled in relief. "Somewhere where the curious Molly can't find them and wonder what they are."

Later that night, long after an exhausted Sybilla retired, Catherine sat in the parlor and listened to the night wind rushing through the square.

She thought of Sybilla's smuggled goods and broke out in a cold sweat. What if her friend ignored her wishes and distributed the pessaries without her knowledge?

Catherine rose and went to turn off the gaslight. She had been looking forward to having Sybilla join her, but now she wasn't so sure. She hoped the disagreement wouldn't mean the end of their close friendship.

She went upstairs to bed.

CHAPTER

FIVE

AS the warm weather arrived, Catherine found herself occasionally recalling that cold winter day she had slipped on the ice and had come face to face with Damon Delancy. She dismissed such thoughts as pointless daydreaming, for she doubted she would ever see him again. After all, she wasn't one of the exalted who dwelt among the sun, moon, and stars.

This fine May morning her existence was far from celestial. She had just come from stitching knife wounds, treating a burn, and telling a new mother that her baby was going to die, so she was not in the best of moods when she started to cross Bleecker Street.

As she looked to her left for an opening in the traffic, several small boys caught her eye because they had the look of deviltry about them as they put their heads together in a huddle. Catherine scowled, wondering what mischief they were contemplating.

Suddenly one of the boys drew his arm back and threw with all his might. His target was evident when a large black horse walking down the street started, then exploded, screaming in terror before bolting as though shot from a cannon.

Catherine watched in horror as the startled rider tried to rein in his witless mount while weaving among other riders, carriages and lumbering wagons. Without warning, a water wagon made an abrupt right-hand turn, blocking the runaway's path. For one heart-stopping second, it looked as though the frenzied horse was gathering himself to try to jump the wagon, but at the last minute, the animal swerved, veering sharply to the left.

His rider must have been anticipating such a move for he managed to stay in the saddle as his horse swerved. But when the animal stumbled, the man went flying through the air and landed hard.

Clutching her medical bag, Catherine picked up her skirts and ran toward the hapless man now lying so still in the middle of the street.

Chaos reigned. Curious pedestrians surged forward while carriages and hansoms swerved to avoid the man. No one dared to stop the horse as he regained his footing and charged down the street, sending people scattering like autumn leaves as his empty stirrups beat against his ribs, goading him to run even faster.

"Please let me through!" Catherine cried as she tried to fight her way through the crowd. "I'm a doctor."

They parted for her, but not without startled looks and murmured comments.

By the time Catherine fought her way through, the fallen rider was sitting up, propped against a burly man kneeling on one knee beside him. His left arm hung uselessly at his side and his dark head was bowed, indicating that he had probably fainted.

"I'm a doctor," Catherine said, setting down her medical bag and kneeling in the street.

She ignored the incredulous mutterings going on around her, and reached out to gently lift the man's head so she could examine him for signs of concussion or fractured skull. At her touch, the man stirred. When he raised his head of his own volition, Catherine found herself looking into the cold gray eyes of Damon Delancy.

She stared for what seemed like an eternity, unable to speak.

He winced. "Who in the hell are you? And where is my horse?"

So he didn't remember her from their brief meeting in Central Park. Irrational disappointment stung her as her hands fell away.

"I am Dr. Catherine Stone. And I suspect your horse is halfway to the Statue of Liberty by now."

A mocking smile tightened his mouth. "A lady doctor . . . Just my luck."

The burly man supporting him chuckled.

"You are lucky that I happened by," Catherine replied coldly, turning his head to see if he was bleeding from the ears, "because I'll have you know that I'm a damn fine doctor, Mr.—?"

"Delancy. Damon Delancy." If he expected her to recognize his illustrious name, he didn't show it.

"Count yourself lucky, Mr. Delancy. You don't have a fractured skull." But he did have a scrape along his cheek.

"Thick-headed one, ain't he?" the burly man said.

Catherine touched Damon Delancy's left shoulder gently, and when he flinched, swore, and shot her a murderous look, she added, "But I suspect you have broken or fractured your collarbone."

"All I know is that it hurts like hell, and I don't appreciate having it poked and prodded."

Catherine bristled, but bit back the retort forming on the tip of her tongue.

Suddenly someone from the crowd shouted, "Hey, lady! You're blocking traffic. Call an ambulance and get him outta here."

"Well, Mr. Delancy," Catherine said, "we can either have the police call an ambulance to take you to the nearest hospital, or—"

"No hospitals."

Catherine didn't blame him. Hospitals were for the poor or the seriously ill.

"Very well. My office is just around the corner. But if you don't wish a 'lady doctor' to treat you, I can put you in a cab and send you to your own physician."

"You'll do. I don't expect you'll kill me."

Right at that moment, Catherine could have cheerfully done just that, but she reminded herself that he was a man in pain who wasn't responsible for his actions.

She rose and said to the burly man, "Would you be able to help him to my office?"

The man nodded and helped Delancy to his feet, where he turned white and swayed for a moment.

"Will you be able to walk?" Catherine asked.

He nodded as he grasped his left arm beneath the elbow to keep every step from jarring it.

The three of them started for Catherine's office.

By the time they arrived, Damon Delancy looked on the verge of collapse. He was as white as arsenic powder and the skin around his mouth had a greenish tinge. Beads of sweat dotted his forehead and streaked his taut, lean cheeks.

Molly answered the door and hurried ahead to ready the surgery. Since Sybilla was nowhere to be seen, Catherine assumed she was in her own surgery down the hall with a patient.

Catherine didn't relax until her patient was sitting on the examining table. She was just about to thank the burly man for his help and send him on his way, when Damon Delancy offered him his card and the opportunity to return the favor for helping him.

Once the burly man left, Catherine took command. "We'll have to take off your coat and shirt if I'm to examine you."

A smile tugged at the corners of his mouth. "And have you examined many men, Dr. Stone?"

Catherine gave him a cool, level look. "Hundreds, Mr. Delancy. Nay, thousands. I assure you that I'm quite beyond letting the sight of an unclothed man fluster me. But I rather doubt that you've ever been examined by a woman doctor."

"No, I haven't."

"Well, just think of me as you would your mother, healing some childhood scrape."

"That," he said, his eyes darting over her in quick appraisal, "is out of the question."

Catherine felt her cheeks grow warm at the rough intimacy in his voice, and she took refuge in anger. "Mr. Delancy, you try my patience. If you don't wish me to examine you, I'll call an ambulance and have you taken to the hospital. What's it to be?"

He sighed in surrender and began unbuttoning his riding jacket, but when he tried to shrug out of it, the pain stopped him cold. He swore as his hand fell away.

"Let me." Catherine managed to get his right arm out of the sleeve. "I'll be as gentle as I can, but if I hurt you, please tell me."

"If you hurt me, you'll know it," he growled.

Somehow, she managed to ease the left sleeve off his injured arm with only a short gasp and shudder on Damon Delancy's part. As Catherine folded the smooth worsted riding jacket and set it aside, she noticed it was expensive and impeccably tailored.

"Now the shirt," she said.

When the shirt came off, Catherine tried to examine him with a critical, professional eye and failed. His torso was as perfectly sculpted as the classical Greek statues Ruth had strewn around the Cleveland house to impress visitors, and much to Catherine's chagrin, she was not immune to the sensuous masculine power of rippling muscle.

She forced her wandering gaze back to his injured shoulder

and noticed the pale, thick scar on his upper arm. "Knife wound?"

His eyes widened briefly in surprise. "Bullet."

"The doctor who treated you didn't stitch it, did he?"

"There wasn't time."

"That's unfortunate. That scar would be less noticeable if he had."

"It doesn't matter to me what it looks like. Not many people see it."

Catherine wondered if the woman in sable was a member of the privileged ones who had.

"I'm sorry for digressing." Catherine turned her attention to his shoulder and made her diagnosis. "You have a fractured clavicle. When you fell, did you hit the ground with your palm?"

He nodded.

"Well, I'm going to have to set the bone, then put your arm in a splint to position it so it will heal correctly. I'm warning you that it will be quite painful."

"I've endured worse."

"I can give you morphine for the pain."

"No!" he snapped. "I've seen what morphine addiction can do to a man."

Catherine stiffened. "I wouldn't give you enough to addict you, merely ease your pain."

"Thank you, but I'd rather not."

"Suit yourself."

Catherine went to work to set the fractured bone so that it would heal properly, without deformity. She realized her patient was in great pain, for he turned as gray as potted paste and his jaw clenched, but Catherine couldn't do slipshod work just to spare him. Above all, she was a doctor.

"Done!" she announced with a triumphant smile when she finished. "Now all I have to do is—"

With an odd wheezing sigh, Damon Delancy slumped forward in a faint.

Catherine caught him around the waist, staggering under his weight as she broke his fall. She eased him down on his back, then managed to swing his legs up after him. After pausing for a moment to catch her breath, Catherine went to work, bringing the man's left hand to his right shoulder and applying Sayer's dressing.

When she finished, she leaned against the medicine cabinet

and took another deep breath. Damon Delancy was still unconscious, looking less forbidding than he did when awake and
glowering with anger. Catherine filled a basin with cold water,
wrung out a cloth and began bathing his face.

His eyelids fluttered open. For once, his gray eyes seemed
warm as they regarded her in confusion.

"You fainted," Catherine said. "But I've set your arm and
bandaged it. You should be as good as new."

He scowled at the bandage. "How long do I have to stay with
my arm strapped to my chest?"

"Four weeks, then keep your arm in a sling for two weeks.
Your own doctor can advise you."

"You can be sure of that."

Catherine didn't take offense at his implied criticism of her
medical skills because she was confident his own outrageously
priced Fifth Avenue doctor couldn't have done any better, as Mr.
Delancy was sure to discover.

He sat up. "I'd like you to find a messenger boy to take a
note to a friend."

"Does your friend have a telephone?"

"Of course," Delancy replied, his tone of voice adding an
unspoken, "Doesn't everyone?"

Catherine went to her desk and took out a piece of paper.
"There's a pay telephone station at the tobacconist's down the
street. If you write your number and message, I'll have my
housekeeper make the call."

Delancy scribbled his message on the paper Catherine offered,
and when he finished, he reached into his coat pocket with his
free hand, took out some coins, and handed both message and
money to her.

"His name is Nevada LaRouche . . ."

Half an hour later, Catherine was sitting in her office when a
breathless Sybilla came running in.

"You won't believe what's in our waiting area," she said.

"An elephant? A python?"

"Something even better." Sybilla paused for effect. "A real
live . . . cowboy!"

Catherine stared at her. "A what?"

"A cowboy straight out of a dime novel. 'Rider of the Range,'
'King of the Pecos.' I couldn't believe it either when Molly told
me, so I just had to peek. You should see him, Cat. He's actually

wearing spurs and carrying a ten-gallon hat, right here in New York City!''

"He's probably Nevada LaRouche, Mr. Delancy's friend. The name would fit a cowboy.''

"Nevada LaRouche . . .'' Sybilla murmured dreamily. She rushed over to the window, took off her spectacles, squinted at her reflection, then patted an imaginary stray curl into place. "How do I look?''

"Beautiful, as always.''

"Good, because I think I've just met the love of my life and I want to impress him.''

Catherine gaped at her. "Sybilla, I've never seen you so—so twitterpated over a man before.''

Her friend shook out her skirt. "You didn't see me in Paris. I learned there's more to life than cysts and sutures.''

Then Catherine recalled Sybilla saying something about a tragic love affair. "But even so, you don't know this Mr. LaRouche.''

"Cat, any man who can dress like that in New York City has got to be sure of himself.'' She smiled slowly. "And I do so love a man who is sure of himself.''

Catherine shook her head as she rose from her desk. "Well, if that's how you feel, let's meet Mr. LaRouche.''

The moment Catherine saw Nevada LaRouche standing at the window of the waiting area, away from the other patients, she thought she had never seen a man look more out of place. It wasn't just the wide-brimmed Stetson he carried, or the tooled leather cowboy boots and silver spurs he wore. And it wasn't that his sun-streaked hair brushed the nape of his neck and his mustache dropped to his chin in defiance of prevailing fashion for short hair and neat mustaches. No, it was that air of caged restlessness that set him apart, an undefinable quality demanding wide-open spaces and endless sky.

He turned when he heard them enter, and Catherine found herself looking into a pair of wary blue eyes. "Mr. LaRouche?''

He grinned as he crossed the room. "Yes, ma'am.'' His voice was a deep and lazy drawl.

"I am Dr. Catherine Stone.''

"Pleased to meet you, ma'am . . . er, doc.'' His eyes drifted toward Sybilla and sparkled with frank admiration.

Catherine added, "And this is my colleague, Dr. Sybilla Wolcott.''

"How do you do, Mr. LaRouche?" Sybilla said, a heartbeat away from simpering.

"The pleasure's mine, Dr. Wolcott." Then he said to Catherine, "Where's my partner? I'll bet he's as ornery as a rattlesnake that's just been stepped on."

Catherine smiled at that. "An apt description. He's resting in the examining room, so if you'll just follow me . . ."

Sybilla, who had patients of her own to see, said, "It was a pleasure meeting you, Mr. LaRouche," a little breathlessly.

"Likewise, and I hope we'll be meetin' again real soon, Dr. Wolcott," he replied, sounding as if he meant it.

They walked to the examining room accompanied by the jingle of the cowboy's spurs, and when they walked in, they found Damon Delancy trying to struggle into his shirt.

He stopped. "Nevada . . . it's about time. What'd you do? Walk here?"

The cowboy turned to Catherine. "You'll have to excuse my friend here, doc. He always sounds as sweet as vinegar when life don't go his way."

"So I've noticed," she muttered.

Nevada said, "So what in the hell happened to you?"

"Raincloud bolted. I fell off. Simple as that."

Catherine stepped forward to help him with his shirt. "Actually, some boys threw a rock at the horse. That's why he bolted."

Nevada shook his head. "I warned you that Cayuse was loco."

"He's a good horse, just spirited, and I'll spare no expense to find him."

As Catherine reached for his jacket, Delancy said, "I'll carry it. I just want to get out of here."

As he took his jacket and started for the door, Catherine said, "Just a moment, Mr. Delancy."

He turned, an irritated scowl on his face. "What is it?"

"The small matter of my fee."

He reached in his jacket and pulled out a money clip and wad of bank notes. "How much?"

"One hundred dollars."

The two men gaped at her. Then Damon Delancy's face turned a furious dark red.

"A hundred? That's thievery! My own doctor wouldn't charge me more than thirty, and he's the best in New York."

"I don't care what other doctors charge. I told you my fee is one hundred dollars,'' Catherine said. What she didn't tell him was that she planned to donate seventy of it to the Women's Dispensary. Damon Delancy was wealthy. He could afford to help those less fortunate than himself.

He peeled off several bank notes and stuffed them into her hand. ''Here's thirty dollars, exactly what I'd pay my own doctor, no more, no less.''

He headed for the door, and with an apologetic shrug, the cowboy followed him.

Catherine stormed after them. ''Come back here! You still owe me seventy dollars.''

''I owe you nothing,'' he retorted over his shoulder, ''and there's not a court in this country that wouldn't agree.'' He stopped at the door and turned. ''Good day to you, Dr. Stone. If my own doctor finds you've butchered my shoulder, I'll see to it that you never practice medicine again.''

The men left.

''Why that arrogant bastard . . .'' Catherine muttered to herself.

Then she whirled on her heel and returned to her waiting patients.

Later that evening, after listening to Sybilla extol Nevada LaRouche's attributes to the skies, Catherine retired to her room to read her medical journals in peace, but thoughts of Damon Delancy kept distracting her.

''Arrogant, insufferable man . . .'' she muttered, setting aside her journal.

Oh, how he hated being helpless! She could still see the steely glint of determination in his eyes as he fought against the pain. No, Mr. High-and-Mighty Delancy certainly liked to have his own way, and woe be to anyone who tried to stop him, even a loco Cayuse named Raincloud and an uppity lady doctor who had the temerity to demand one hundred dollars.

Catherine sighed. Whatever possessed her to charge him so much? His arrogance had angered her, and his not recognizing her from Central Park hurt more than she cared to admit. Still, her method of retaliation had been unprofessional and unworthy of her.

Stifling a yawn, Catherine decided it was time for bed. She was sure to have a busy day tomorrow.

The following morning, Molly awakened her to say that a message from Gordon Graham had just arrived.

Genevra had gone into labor, and her husband wanted Catherine to come to the house right away.

Catherine feared that Genevra was going to die.

She stood by the bedside and watched helplessly. Genevra lay there, her fingers twisting the sheet covering her swollen abdomen as if she could somehow wring out the pain. Another low moan of desperation escaped her lips, and Catherine's heart went out to her.

Genevra had been in labor for twenty-four hours already, and she still hadn't dilated fully. But now she was so exhausted from the incessant, grinding pain of her struggle, Catherine doubted that she would have the strength to endure any more.

"Judas!" Genevra hissed between dry, cracked lips. "You lied to me! You told me I'd have this baby, but I'm not, am I? I'm going to die." She averted her face and tears of helplessness trailed down her flushed cheeks.

"Genevra, I—" Catherine sought words of comfort, but failed.

She walked out of the bedroom, closed the door behind her, and leaned heavily against it as another scream rent the air. Genevra was right. Catherine had betrayed her. She never should have encouraged her to have this child. She should have warned Genevra more forcefully about the dangers and let her decide what to do. But she was so confident of her medical skills that she had assumed she would be able to handle any crisis that arose.

And now Genevra was to pay the supreme price for Catherine's arrogance.

Catherine sighed deeply and closed her eyes, truly frightened now. How she wished she could turn back the clock. Her advice to Genevra would be so different.

"Cat?"

She opened her eyes to find Sybilla coming down the hall toward her. Catherine was glad Sybilla had asked to come along. "How's Mrs. Graham?"

Catherine's eyes filled with tears. "I think I'm going to lose her or the baby or both, Syb. She hasn't dilated enough for me to try the forceps yet, and already she's exhausted." She shook her head in defeat. "I should have listened when Genevra told me how much she feared having a child."

Sybilla grasped her arm and squeezed hard. "Don't you dare

give up now, Catherine Stone. There's still something we can do for her.''

Catherine felt the blood drain from her face. ''You don't mean—''

''A caesarian section.'' Before Catherine could comment, Sybilla moistened her lips and plunged on. ''I know you're going to tell me it's risky, but I know I can do it. All we have to do is get her to a hospital. You can assist me and I'll do the rest.''

''We'll never find a hospital in time.''

Sybilla shook her head. ''Don't underestimate the power of wealth. Surely her husband must sit on one or two hospital boards. I'm sure he can get us into one quickly enough if it means saving his wife's life.''

Another scream came from behind the closed door.

''What have we got to lose?'' Catherine said, her mind suddenly clearing of regret and her heart filling with hope. ''Let's have a talk with Gordon. And if he doesn't murder me, perhaps we'll have a chance to save his wife's life.''

Sybilla grinned. ''Now that sounds more like the Cat I know.''

They hurried downstairs to Gordon's study.

Catherine's courage almost deserted her when they walked in, for the minute Gordon saw them, he bellowed, ''When in the name of God Almighty is this baby going to be born? Hasn't my wife suffered enough?''

Kim, who had arrived an hour ago to provide additional consultation, attempted to place a soothing hand on his arm, but Gordon shook it off.

Facing Genevra's frantic husband was like standing at the foot of a volcano, waiting for it to erupt. Catherine took a deep breath and squared her shoulders.

''There are complications,'' she began, her heart hammering against her ribs. ''I'm afraid we may lose your wife, the baby or both.''

''Are you telling me my wife is going to die?''

Kim grabbed Gordon's arm as if anticipating violence and Sybilla took a step closer to Catherine.

''She could,'' Catherine said.

The volcano erupted. ''Damn you! You said she could have a child. You told her not to worry. And now you're doing an about-face and telling me she might die? I ought to—''

''Gordon, stop it!'' Kim restrained him. ''Even the best doctor in the world can't predict the outcome of a pregnancy. A woman risks her life every time she becomes pregnant. Catherine did the best she could.''

Gordon flung him off and grasped the edges of his desk as if the furniture could keep him from throttling Catherine. "I never should have listened to you, Flanders. I never should have trusted her.''

Kim put his hand on his friend's shoulder. "If it's any consolation, I couldn't have done any better.''

"Mr. Graham," Catherine said, "there's still a chance we can save your wife and child.''

Hope flared in his eyes. "How?''

"By performing a caesarian section.''

"Catherine, no!'' Kim cried.

"What is this caesarian section?'' Gordon demanded. When Sybilla explained, he blanched.

"I've done the operation several times in Paris," she said, "and I've never lost a patient. I can't promise that I won't lose Mrs. Graham or her baby, but at this point, it's the only chance we have of saving her.''

"Do it,'' Gordon said.

"We'll need your help.'' Catherine told him what he had to do.

The next hour flew by in a blur.

After Gordon revealed that he was a heavy contributor to St. Paul's Hospital, he, Sybilla, and Kim rushed to convince its manager that they required an operating room and assistance immediately. As soon as they left, Catherine went upstairs to ready Genevra for the ride of her life in the horse ambulance.

Genevra was still struggling, but at least she was alive. She was past the point of blaming Catherine or even curious about where she was going and what was going to happen to her.

As she rode on the back of the speeding ambulance, its warning bell clanging for everyone to get out of the way, Catherine prayed that both Genevra and the baby would survive the operation, because if they didn't . . .

She shuddered and put the thought out of her mind.

When they arrived, they found Kim waiting, his handsome face creased with worry.

Catherine asked if they had secured an operating room.

Kim spoke as men were unloading Genevra from the ambulance. "Gordon forcefully reminded them of his generous contributions to this institution, and how they would stop immediately if we weren't given everything we needed to save his wife and child.''

"Do they know we're doing a caesarian section?"

"Yes, and they aren't too pleased."

"If it saves her life . . .''

"And if it doesn't?''

Catherine swallowed hard. "I daresay my career will be in jeopardy once again.''

"Worse than that. Gordon will probably kill you.''

Catherine looked at him sharply, expecting to see a twinkle of laughter in Kim's eye to ease her tension. But he was deadly serious.

They hurried as Genevra was wheeled into the operating room.

They were ready to begin.

Tension and disapproval hung as thickly as old-time carbolic spray in the operating room. The nurse and two assisting physicians the hospital had provided said nothing, but Catherine could read the bitter resentment smoldering in their eyes.

Only Sybilla appeared confident. First she covered Genevra's swollen abdomen with two sterile towels, leaving an opening for the incision. Her fingers were steady on the scalpel as she made the first foot-long cut.

The two assistant physicians stepped forward to quickly tie off severed blood vessels and swab excess blood with sponges. Sybilla then cut the peritoneum, reached in, pulled out the uterus as calmly as if she were picking strawberries and rested the organ on the towels. It was as purplish as a ripe plum, and a collective gasp of awe rippled through the operating room.

Sybilla cut the uterus. Blood spurted halfway to the ceiling, startling and spraying everyone. She ignored the blood on her face and frowned in concentration as she reached in and withdrew both baby and placenta.

"You take care of the baby, Dr. Stone," she said, handing the slippery bundle to Catherine. "I still have work to do.''

Catherine stared down at Genevra's child in wonder, for its features were perfectly formed, not distorted by the rigors of passage down the birth canal.

"It's a boy," she said. "And he must weigh at least ten pounds.''

"Well, at least Graham has his son," Sybilla muttered, preoccupied with suturing the uterus.

The baby stirred and took his first gasp of breath, followed by a lusty wail.

"And the mother?" Catherine asked, not daring to hope.

"Still alive," someone answered.

Catherine watched as Sybilla quickly finished suturing the uterus, then closed the abdomen with deft stitches. Perhaps if Genevra died, the child would be of some comfort to Gordon. She could only hope.

She cleaned the baby and carried him out of the operating room, down to the room where Gordon and Kim were waiting.

"You have a son," Catherine said.

Gordon rushed up to her, not even sparing a glance for the baby. "How is my wife? Is she—?"

"Dr. Wolcott is finishing the operation. But your son is fine."

Gordon turned away. "What good is he if I lose my wife?"

Catherine exchanged looks with Kim.

He came up to her and whispered, "Why don't you take the baby back to the Grahams? There's a nurse waiting. Then go home and get some sleep. You look dead on your feet. There's nothing else you can do here."

Catherine nodded and left with the baby.

Several hours later, after seeing Baby Graham safely settled in his new nurse's care and returning home to Washington Square for a nap, Catherine was awakened by a knock on her bedroom door.

It was a pale, bleary-eyed Sybilla.

Catherine sat up. "How's Genevra?"

"She survived the surgery itself, thank God." She sagged into the nearest chair. "Her uterus contracted and there was no additional hemorrhaging. I'm confident my sutures will hold. Now we just have to wait and hope septicemia doesn't set in."

They waited for five nerve-wracking days while Genevra battled for her life. On the afternoon of the sixth day, Catherine returned from the Women's Dispensary to find Gordon waiting for her.

The big man was sitting in the chair before her desk, elbows resting on his knees, his leonine head in his hands.

She feared for the worst.

"Gordon?"

He rose, his cheeks hollow and dark eyes bright with tears. "She's going to live."

Catherine felt giddy with relief. Sybilla had done the impossible. "Thank God!"

Gordon cleared his throat and stared at his shoes like a schoolboy who had been caught breaking a window. "I just want to apologize to you and Dr. Wolcott for the terrible things I said. If it weren't for the two of you, my wife and son wouldn't be alive today."

Catherine smiled. "Apology accepted. I'm glad Genevra is going to be all right."

He reached into his pocket and withdrew an envelope. "This is something to show my appreciation."

"Thank you."

"No, thank you, Dr. Stone. If you'll excuse me, I'm going to get home to my wife and son."

"Give my best to Genevra, and tell her I'll be calling on her soon."

Just as he reached the door, he turned. "We've decided on a name for him by the way."

"What is it?"

"Stone Wolcott Graham."

Catherine flushed with pleasure. "I'm honored, but it's such a big name for such a tiny baby."

"I've got big plans for him. He'll grow into it."

After they said goodbye and Gordon left, Catherine stood there for a moment and uttered a silent prayer of thanks.

Stone Wolcott Graham . . .

When she looked inside the envelope, fully expecting to find her usual fee, she was startled to find a check for five hundred dollars.

Kim raised his glass of champagne. "To Stone Wolcott Graham."

Seated in Kim's library, Catherine and Sybilla raised their glasses and echoed his toast.

"There were moments when I thought both of them were lost," Sybilla admitted.

"It's a tribute to your skills as physicians," Kim said.

"Were there any repercussions from the hospital?" Catherine asked.

"Let's just say they hope this was their first, and last, caesarian section," Kim replied.

"Pus and gangrene!" Sybilla snapped. "Don't they realize

they could save so many lives if they worked to perfect the procedure?''

''Change always comes slowly, especially in the medical
profession,'' Kim said.

He set down his champagne glass. ''Enough about our es-
teemed profession. How would you two ladies like to go to a
ball with me?''

''A ball?'' Sybilla's face brightened. ''We'd love to, wouldn't
we, Cat?''

''Who's giving it?''

''Bella Peachtree,'' Kim replied. ''It's to be her last social
event before her family goes to Newport for the summer. Since
you treated Hortensia, she specifically asked that you be there,
Catherine.''

Catherine set down her champagne glass and rose. ''I'm afraid
I shall have to refuse.''

''Why?'' Sybilla wailed.

''Simple. I don't have anything suitable to wear.''

Her friend gave her a disgusted look. ''Of all the silly excuses . . . With that check Gordon Graham gave us, we can
certainly afford ballgowns.''

Catherine stared at her in shock. ''That money should go back
into the practice.''

''Well, you can put your share of the money back into the
practice, but I'm going to use mine to buy ballgowns for the
both of us.''

''You're going to be stubborn about this, I can tell,'' Catherine said.

''I want to go to that ball. I've worked my fingers to the bone.
I think I deserve to have a little fun.''

Kim held up his hands. ''Why don't the two of you discuss it
and tell me what you decide to do?''

They agreed, but privately, Catherine had no intention of going to the ball.

Later that evening, when they were back home and sharing
hot milk in their kitchen, Sybilla turned to Catherine and said,
''All right. Now what's the real reason you don't want to go to
this ball?''

Catherine drummed the table with her fingertips. ''I just know
I'll feel out of place, that's all. The wealthiest people in New
York City will be there in their silks and diamonds. We'll look
like poor relations. People will stare at us.''

"Catherine Stone," Sybilla said in exasperation, "you and I have defied convention to become doctors, and you sit there and tell me that you're afraid of people staring at you?"

"Yes!" She rose and pulled her wrapper more closely about herself as if for protection. "Ruth always used to make me go to those affairs in Cleveland, and on the way home, she would list all the social gaffes I had made that evening, ostensibly to help me. But her criticisms just made me feel gauche."

"I see."

"I suspect you do."

Sybilla rose and placed her hand on Catherine's arm. "That would discourage anyone from ever setting foot in a ballroom again, but it wouldn't be like that this time. Ruth isn't around to criticize you, and no one is going to make you feel awkward."

"I still get butterflies in my stomach just thinking about it."

Sybilla's hand fell away. "If you won't go for yourself, then go for Kim."

"What do you mean?"

"I think Kim really wants you to go. He tried to hide it, but he looked disappointed when you said you wouldn't go."

Catherine returned to the table with a sigh and sat there in silence.

"Kim would be there to protect you," Sybilla pointed out. "And I'd be there for moral support."

Catherine managed a smile. "And besides, you want a new ballgown."

"Am I that obvious?"

"Only to someone who knows you as well as I." Catherine rose. "Very well. I'll go. But you have to find a seamstress and make all the arrangements. And I'm warning you, I don't want it sized for a tight corset."

Sybilla smiled excitedly. "I'll make all the arrangements. And thank you, Cat."

"You're welcome. I just hope I don't live to regret this," she muttered.

❧ CHAPTER ❧

SIX

THE moment Catherine felt her new gown slide down her upraised arms and caress her body as softly as a whisper, she was glad Sybilla had convinced her to splurge on luxurious *mousseline de soie* rather than a cheaper fabric.

As Molly began tugging and adjusting the bodice, she said, "Oh, Dr. Catherine, you do look beautiful!"

"It's the gown."

It was a deceptively simple design with short sleeves and a gathered bodice ending in a cluster of soft pink silk rosebuds off to the side at the waist. The full skirt and short train rustled in a seductive swish with every step because of the stiff taffeta lining.

"Oh, no, miss," Molly insisted as she began buttoning the tiny covered buttons running up the back. "It's more than the gown."

Catherine flushed with pleasure as she inspected herself in the full-length mirror. She had to admit that even the dark burgundy silk couldn't be totally responsible for her glowing ivory skin and blue eyes that appeared especially dark and mysterious tonight. It was the anticipation of taking a well-deserved respite from work and waltzing the night away.

"Don't you think the bodice is indecently low?" she asked. She could see the tops of her full breasts thrust upward from the corset's tight lacing that enabled the gown to fit properly.

Molly chuckled. "That's because you're always buttoned up to your chin." Then she stepped back and gave Catherine a critical once-over. "You need jewelry."

"I don't have any." Then she remembered. "Of course I do. One moment." She went to her dresser and rummaged around in the top drawer until she found what she was looking for in a box way in the back. "My mother's cameo."

Once Molly tied the grosgrain ribbon around Catherine's neck, she began dressing her hair in a simple Psyche knot, adding several pink silk rosebuds to complete the coiffeur.

"I'll bet you could put Ruth to shame," came Sybilla's voice from the doorway.

Catherine rose and gasped in astonishment at the sight of her friend.

If Catherine's gown was elegant simplicity, Sybilla's was high drama intended to attract attention. Made of ivory crepe de Chine and black brocade, it was liberally trimmed with swags of polished jet beads on the sleeves and bodice so that they danced and shimmered with Sybilla's slightest movement. Her pale golden hair provided the perfect backdrop for a black aigret feather and jet bead loops that brushed her left earlobe.

"What do you think?" Sybilla purred, throwing back her head and extending her arms in a theatrical pose.

"I think Nevada LaRouche will die with his boots on when he sees you."

Both Sybilla and Molly giggled.

"It's the least he could do after all the trouble I've gone to," Sybilla agreed.

Then she examined Catherine with a critical eye. "And you . . . where is the Dr. Stone I know? All I see is a ravishing society belle poised on the verge of breaking hearts."

"Now stop it this instant! I don't look that much different."

"Oh yes, you do."

Catherine glanced at herself in the mirror once again as she tugged on her long white kid gloves and smoothed them up past her elbows. She smiled sheepishly. "I do look rather elegant, don't I."

Sybilla handed her a fan to complete the toilette. "Kim will be flabbergasted when he sees you."

Moments later, Catherine was more than satisfied with Kim's reaction when she came sweeping down the stairs in her new finery. He had been standing in front of the hall mirror, adjusting his white tie. Then he turned at the sound of footsteps and looked up. The moment he saw her, he stopped and stared, blatant desire igniting his gaze as it roved over her.

"Catherine, you are breathtaking," he said, stepping forward to take her hands and clasp them to his heart. "You will be the loveliest woman there tonight, and I will be the envy of every man.''

Catherine blushed. "And you, Dr. Flanders, will make me the envy of every woman.''

Seeing Kim look so poised and polished in the formal white tie and tails made Catherine think of something her father had once said about no man ever being truly comfortable in formal attire. Kim, however, had to be the exception, for he appeared as relaxed as if he were wearing a smoking jacket.

And tonight he was all hers.

Sybilla, who had purposely waited to allow Catherine time to make her entrance, now glided down the stairs.

"Don't use up all your compliments on Catherine," she said. "Save some for me.''

Kim grinned at her audacity. "Compliments don't do justice to how beautiful you look, Dr. Wolcott.''

"Thank you.'' When Sybilla reached the foot of the stairs, her gaze lingered appreciatively on Kim. "And don't we look dashing ourselves tonight. If Catherine weren't my best friend . . .''

"You'll just have to share me," Kim said, offering his arm to each of them.

Laughing together, they left for the ball.

The moment Catherine walked into the Peachtree's ballroom, she sensed that something magical was going to happen to her tonight. The room glittered, from the two huge crystal chandeliers to the beads and diamonds on the women's gowns, while music and conversation ebbed and flowed around her.

She breathed deeply. "Don't the flowers smell divine?'' she said to Sybilla, trying to make herself heard above the music and conversation. "I've never seen so many Gloire de Paris roses and orchids in one place in my life. Even Ruth never decorated this lavishly.''

"Ruth didn't have the Peachtrees' fortune," Sybilla said, her eyes wide with awe.

Kim glanced at the card the butler had given him in the entrance hall. He smiled in approval. "Splendid. I'm to be your dinner partner, Catherine.''

Sybilla looked at him hopefully. "And who is to be mine?''

"Nevada LaRouche," he replied, "if Bella Peachtree keeps her word.''

"Kimbel Flanders, I could just hug you for arranging this!''

He raised one hand as if to ward her off. "Please control yourself, Dr. Wolcott," he said with mock severity. "A simple thank you will do."

"Thank you, thank you, thank you!" She stood on tiptoes and craned her neck. "Now, where is that rugged range rider?"

Catherine was the first to spot him in the crush. "Over there, by the alcove, talking with that redheaded man."

Sybilla grabbed Catherine's arm. "Oh, Cat, I could just swoon! He's wearing white tie and tails."

"What did you expect? His boots and a Stetson?"

"Of course not. But even in this crowd, he still looks alone somehow. Aloof. Unapproachable."

"I suspect Nevada LaRouche is the type of man who always looks that way," Catherine mused, thinking of wide-open spaces and the unending sky.

"Not for long," Sybilla said.

Kim restrained her. "Before you go running off to trap your prey, Dr. Wolcott, at least grant me a dance."

"Just one." Sybilla handed him her dance card and waited for him to pencil in his name somewhere, then she excused herself and headed toward her quarry.

Catherine watched her go. "I hope he doesn't hurt her."

"I wouldn't worry about Sybilla," Kim said. "From what I've heard, this LaRouche fellow is a decent sort in spite of his reputation. If he's not interested in her, he'll let her know long before her heart has a chance to be broken."

Catherine watched as Sybilla walked up to the cowboy and greeted him with a smile. Judging from the grin Sybilla got in return, Catherine felt reassured that Kim was right.

"Come," Kim said, placing his hand in the small of her back to guide her. "There are some people I'd like you to meet."

If Catherine was nervous in such august company, Kim was in his element. He knew everyone, greeting the men with a hearty handshake and the women with a charming smile and a compliment. Only Catherine noticed how some smiles froze when he introduced her as "Dr. Stone."

You've endured worse, Catherine said to herself as they moved on.

But there were others who greeted her warmly and said, "You must be one of the doctors who saved Genevra Graham's life. What a pleasure it is to meet you."

Finally they returned to the sidelines, where rows of gilt chairs stood.

No sooner did Catherine sit down than a man came up to them and said, "Dr. Flanders, may I take you away from this lovely young lady for a moment?"

Kim gave Catherine an inquiring look. "Would you mind being left alone for a few minutes?"

"Of course not. Go ahead. I'll be fine."

When she was alone, Catherine looked around the crowded ballroom hoping to catch a glimpse of Sybilla, but she and the cowboy were nowhere in sight. Instead she found Damon Delancy.

He was standing in the middle of the ballroom, as much at ease in this milieu as Kim. His severe black evening attire and snowy white shirtfront made the perfect foil for his saturnine good looks, and with his left arm in the raffish black sling, he resembled a warrior wounded in battle, eliciting feminine sympathy from the women clustered around him.

Catherine was momentarily distracted when she heard an unfamiliar female voice behind her say, "Have any of you met the young woman Dr. Flanders has been keeping company with?"

She was just about to turn in her chair, smile, and introduce herself when another woman's response stopped her cold: "No, and I don't wish to. Not only does she work for a living, she's nothing more than some insignificant social climber from Indiana or Idaho or somewhere out there."

Catherine flinched as though someone had struck her across the face.

Get up and leave before you hear any more, she told herself.

But something kept her sitting there, listening to those cruel, cutting voices.

"She's most unsuitable. Kimbel comes from such a fine family."

"If he should marry her, society will never accept her."

"You don't think he'd go that far, do you? Why, she'd ruin his career!"

Catherine rose then, her cheeks burning with humiliation. Just at that moment, Damon Delancy looked up and stared right at her, the hypnotic power in those compelling winter eyes touching her from halfway across the room. She watched with rising panic as he excused himself and started toward her with all the deliberation of a stalking wolf.

Catherine's heart suddenly began to pound, and she searched frantically for a hiding place. She couldn't find one. She couldn't find Kim either. Damon Delancy was the last person she wanted to talk to right now.

She had to escape. She picked up her skirts and hurried toward the ballroom entrance, ignoring curious stares.

She breathed a sigh of relief when she reached the dimly lit hallway, but she was still not safe here, for couples lingered in the shadows. She hurried down a darker corridor and tried one of the doors. It led to the library.

She would be safe here.

Catherine closed the door behind her and stood in the sudden silence. She looked around. A small lamp burning on a nearby reading table provided just enough illumination to make the room a warm and inviting refuge.

But not for long.

No sooner did she walk over to one of the long windows than she heard the sound of the knob turning. The door swung open, filling the library with the faint strains of music and the commanding presence of Damon Delancy.

He stood there for a moment, his tall frame outlined by the doorjamb and those winter eyes alight with speculation.

"So here's where you've run to," he said.

"I haven't run anywhere. I came in here for a breath of fresh air. The ballroom is stifling. Now, if you'll excuse me . . ."

She started for the door, fully expecting Delancy to step aside so she could pass. He didn't. He closed the door behind himself and left his hand resting on the knob, barring her way.

She was trapped.

"If the ballroom is so stifling," he said softly, "why are you so eager to return to it?"

The library was so quiet, it was as though the books were listening. Catherine fancied he could hear her heart's wild pounding.

"Mr. Delancy, please let me pass."

"Not yet. I wish to talk to you."

Catherine glared at him. "Well, I don't wish to talk to you. You were unspeakably rude to me the day of your accident, and I have no wish to subject myself to your churlishness again."

He surprised her by saying, "I quite agree. That's what I wish to speak to you about."

Catherine hesitated. There was something different about Delancy tonight. Where he had once been a roiling sea, he was now a still pond. She found herself wondering which was more dangerous.

She let out the breath she had been holding and stepped away from his disconcerting nearness. "All right. I'll listen."

He released the doorknob and came to stand before her.

"I wish to apologize for my behavior that day. As my cowboy friend so aptly put it, I become as sweet as vinegar when life doesn't go my way, but I was furious over losing my horse and in pain. I realize that's no excuse, but—" he raised his right shoulder in an apologetic shrug "—it's the only one I have to offer you."

"It will be sufficient. I accept your apology."

"Thank you."

Before Catherine realized what he was doing, he took her hand and brought it to his lips, while his gray eyes imprisoned hers. His lips were warm through her kid glove, and Catherine felt a shiver that left her breathless ripple across her shoulders. She stood there as if mesmerized, unable to pull her hand away.

Finally, Delancy lowered her hand, but still held it. "Once again, thank you for helping me that day."

"You're welcome." When an awkward silence ensued, Catherine wildly thought of something to say. "Speaking of your accident, did you ever find your horse?"

"Yes. Some men caught him and brought him to one of the public stables. The owner recognized Raincloud and contacted me."

"And how is your clavicle—your collarbone?"

He finally released her hand and smiled. "Much better."

"You had your own doctor examine it?"

"Yes. And as much as he hated to admit it, he said he couldn't have done any better."

"I'm not surprised. I told you I was a capable doctor."

A wry smile tugged at his mouth. "And modest as well, I see."

"Truthful," Catherine retorted. "What would you have me do, blush behind my fan and simper, 'Oh, no, it was nothing, nothing at all'?"

"Most of the women in that ballroom would have done just that."

Those other women in their Worth gowns and diamonds and frozen smiles . . . Catherine sighed. Another reminder of how different she was. How often she had to go against the wind. Not that she would trade being a doctor for all the Worth gowns in Paris, but—

"What's wrong?" Delancy interrupted her thoughts.

"Why—why nothing."

"I beg to differ, Dr. Stone. Any fool can see that you're upset about something. Am I responsible?"

"You flatter yourself."

"Well, something must have happened to send you bolting out of the ballroom like that."

"As I said, I was merely trying to avoid you and your terrible temper, sir."

"Then you went to extreme lengths." His eyes narrowed. "Oh, no, I sense there is something else amiss."

Damn the man! Those cold gray eyes could see too much. Catherine slapped her palm with her fan. "Very well. I was just thinking how different I am from those other women in the ballroom."

Delancy studied her in disconcerting silence. "How so? You are just as lovely."

He thought she was lovely? She felt the warmth of embarrassment shoot up her cheeks.

"We are different in other ways. They prefer attending balls and I prefer setting fractured collarbones. They discuss their trips to Europe, while I discuss staying in the city and trying to save tenement babies from cholera infantum." She added silently, *and they think I'm an insignificant social climber.*

"You made your choice, didn't you? Are you regretting it?"

"Of course not!"

"I should think you've learned by now that we can't have everything we want in life, Dr. Stone, so stop feeling sorry for yourself."

Catherine wondered what he had wanted in his life that he couldn't have. "Why, thank you for that enlightening bit of philosophy, Mr. Delancy. It makes me feel so much better."

Her sarcasm wasn't lost on him, for he grinned.

"You may be a doctor, but I daresay you have more in common with those women than you care to admit," he said, his voice turning low and silky.

How had he come to be standing so close to her? Catherine could see the facets on his diamond shirt studs. But she would not be the first to step back.

"Do tell me, Mr. Delancy. I am most curious."

His gaze fell boldly to her lips. "You all want to love and be loved in return."

This was one discussion Catherine didn't want to have with this particular man. She stepped around him. "We should be getting back to the ballroom. We've been away too long."

He didn't press her. "How true. They'll be announcing our engagement before we know it."

Catherine colored hotly. Being alone with a bachelor gentleman for any length of time could cause a scandal for an unmarried woman.

Then he surprised her by saying, "May I see your dance card?"

Catherine stared at him in surprise. He wanted to dance with her? The few times they had met, he had acted as though he wanted to strangle her. "My—my dance card?"

He smiled. "Yes. I'd like to request the honor of a waltz, if I may."

"Yes, I—you can dance with only one arm?"

"I can do many things with only one arm."

Catherine didn't dare ask him to elaborate.

He took her dance card, steadied it on the reading table and scribbled his name for the second waltz. Then he handed it back to her. "Shall we go?"

Catherine hesitated. "Mr. Delancy, I have an apology of my own to make to you as well."

Delancy raised his dark flaring brows. "Oh?"

"My fee for setting a fractured collarbone is only thirty dollars, which you paid in full." She stared down at her fan. "The other seventy dollars was intended as a donation to the Women's Dispensary."

She expected him to explode at her audacity, but to her surprise, he burst out laughing, a hearty rumble that nearly shook the books on their shelves. "Dr. Stone, I think you have the instincts of a pirate."

"Or a Wall Street financier?"

"Touché."

They headed back to the ballroom.

No sooner did they walk in the door than Kim walked up to Catherine with a proprietary glint in his eye that plainly said that he didn't think her an insignificant social climber.

"Kim," she said, "I trust you've met Damon Delancy?"

Kim extended his hand. "Of course."

"Dr. Flanders," Delancy replied, shaking Kim's hand.

"Is your arm better?"

"Much better. It should be as good as new in a few weeks, thanks to your capable colleague here."

Catherine found it difficult to believe that this charming man was the same one who had threatened to ruin her medical career if she butchered his shoulder.

He was interrupted by the dinner bell.

"Well, if you'll excuse me, I've got to find my dinner partner. Doctors . . ." And with a disarming smile, he left.

Kim was too much of a gentleman to take Catherine to task for wandering off with another man. He smiled and offered her his arm. "Shall we dine?"

As she took his arm, she debated whether to tell him what she had overheard, then decided against it.

Instead she said, "He only wanted to apologize to me and ask for a dance."

"You don't owe me any explanations, Catherine."

"I know, but I wanted to give you one anyway."

"As long as you didn't grant him the last waltz."

"No, that one is yours."

He beamed and they joined the others deserting the ballroom for the dining room and the lavish buffet supper awaiting them there.

Damon had long ago perfected the art of pretending to listen attentively to his dinner partner while engaging his interest elsewhere, and it served him in good stead tonight. He was able to dine with Francine Ballard while watching Dr. Stone surreptitiously.

He hadn't realized it at the time of his accident, when all he could do was lash out in anger and pain, but Dr. Catherine Stone was a beautiful woman.

He focused on her for a moment over Francine's left shoulder. In a room full of sleek women in thousand-dollar Worth gowns and hundred-thousand-dollar diamond parures, Dr. Stone stood out like a rose among orchids. Her uncluttered dress of burgundy silk must have cost one-tenth the price of Francine's beaded confection, and her only adornment was a sweetly old-fashioned cameo on a grosgrain ribbon around her neck.

Damon's Aunt Hattie had owned such a cameo, the only piece

of jewelry she had ever owned in her hardscrabble life, worn only once a year on her wedding anniversary. She was gone now, the cameo buried with her.

Damon shook his head and the poignant memory vanished.

"Isn't this lobster delicious?" Francine said.

"Delicious," Damon agreed, but he was not thinking of the food on the plate he was balancing on his lap.

He risked another look at Dr. Stone. Her thick glossy brown hair was swept up into a knot, accentuating her long, slender neck, the white slope of her shoulders and the creamy swell of her bosom, parts of her primly hidden the day of his accident. But what really made her stand out was that—judging by her animated expression—she was genuinely enjoying her partner's company.

Suddenly he realized that Francine had said something and was waiting for a response.

Francine Ballard was the perfect lady. She never talked loudly or gesticulated; she never contradicted a man's superior opinion or showed anger; she made a man feel strong and capable by her very helplessness.

She would make the perfect wife for a man of thirty who had made his considerable fortune and decided it was high time he settled down. Then why had he been avoiding her lately?

"I beg your pardon?" he asked with a dazzling smile few women could resist.

If he annoyed her, she wasn't so unladylike to show her displeasure. "I said I'm not looking forward to spending the summer at Sea Winds this year."

Sea Winds was the name of her family's thirty-room English Tudor summer "cottage" in Newport.

"Why not?" As if he didn't know.

She lowered her lashes demurely. "Because you won't be there, of course."

"Oh, I shall spend some weekends there."

"But I thought you go to your Hudson Valley estate in the summer. What is it called?"

Catherine Stone was leaning forward to say something to Flanders. Damon strained to hear, but there was just too much chatter going on all around them.

"Coppermine," he said before Francine could suspect he wasn't listening to her.

Her dark eyes sparkled flirtatiously. "Surely Newport has some attraction for you." Meaning herself, of course.

Damon played her game. "Some attractions, yes."

Francine looked pleased, while Damon wished the dinner would end and the favors distributed for the cotillion that would start the dancing. He wondered how he could avoid dancing with her.

She said, "Who is that woman with Mr. LaRouche? I've never seen her before."

Damon glanced across the dining room. "Her name is Sybilla Wolcott, I believe, and she's a doctor."

"A doctor? You mean she takes care of sick people?"

"Yes, Francine, that is what doctors usually do."

A shudder of distaste rippled across her alabaster shoulders, causing the rubies and diamonds in her necklace to shiver and twinkle. "How perfectly dreadful."

"Not only is she a doctor, she's a surgeon."

Now Francine's dark eyes widened, showing true emotion for the first time tonight. "She cuts up people as if they were roast beef? How disgusting. Whatever was Bella thinking of to invite such a person into her home? It's almost as bad as inviting an artist or a writer."

"I believe she's a friend of Dr. Flanders. You know Kim Flanders, don't you?"

"Of course. He's a prominent physician. All the best families go to him."

"Well, Bella invited him and two lady doctors."

"I can see inviting Dr. Flanders. He's a man, after all, and being a doctor is an honorable profession for a man. But two lady doctors . . ." Francine was truly scandalized, the most passionate Damon had ever seen her since they were introduced a year ago. It was a refreshing change from her usual cool, imperturbable facade.

Suddenly a frown cluttered Francine's smooth brow. "She must be the lady doctor who saved Genevra Graham's life and her baby's."

"Oh?"

"You didn't hear about that?" Francine took another forkful of lobster and chewed. "I'm surprised. All society was agog with the story of how these two lady doctors performed some rare, dangerous operation and saved not only Mrs. Graham, but also her baby son. Both would have died."

Damon looked at Catherine. "How fortunate for the Grahams."

"Still, but for a woman to cut up people . . ." Francine shuddered again.

"Didn't I mention that a lady doctor set my fractured collarbone?"

Francine's fork stopped halfway to her lips. "You most certainly did not!"

"Yes, and she did a fine job of it, I must admit." He rotated his shoulder. "Doesn't hurt a bit now."

"You mean she—" Francine set down her fork and picked up her ivory fan, snapping it open with a decisive click "—she saw you . . ." Her voice trailed off and she looked away.

"Without my shirt," Damon whispered.

Francine's eyes widened and her delicate nostrils flared. Damon couldn't tell if the prospect of him shirtless excited or appalled her.

"How—how utterly shocking and—and indecent for a woman to—to . . ."

Damon reached out and placed his hand on hers. "Dear Francine, I can see I've offended your delicate sensibilities with such frank talk. Do forgive me."

His contrite tone mollified her, for she turned into the flirt once again. "Only if you promise to visit me in Newport this summer."

"Of course," he said, even as his gaze wandered over her shoulder to Dr. Stone.

This time, Francine caught him at it. She turned in her chair to see who dared take his attention away from her. When she turned back, she said, "Why, that's the woman who fell down on the ice in Central Park."

Damon's attention snapped back. "What?"

"You helped her, remember? You gave her your handkerchief because she was bleeding from a cut on her forehead."

Catherine Stone was the fallen skater?

Damon studied her carefully, envisioning her with a wool hat concealing her hair and one hand hiding half of her face as she desperately tried to stop the bleeding from a cut over her eye. The picture fit. It was the same woman.

Damon sat back in his chair and finished his supper, his thoughts in a turmoil. Why hadn't she said anything to him about meeting him that day? All the time they were together after his accident, she had acted as though she had never seen him before.

He wondered why. And he was going to find out.

When the cotillion and the first waltz ended, Catherine went back to her seat and fanned her warm face while Kim wandered off in search of punch. For once, she was glad Ruth had instructed her so rigorously in the social graces, for Catherine had given a creditable accounting of herself during the long, intricate opening dance.

She wondered why Mr. Delancy had not danced in the cotillion.

Catherine smiled when Kim returned with two cups of punch, and she tried not to think of those malicious women as she drank the refreshing liquid.

When she saw Damon Delancy approach, Catherine knew he was coming to claim her for the second waltz.

"Dr. Stone," he said, bowing low and extending his hand. "I believe the next dance is mine."

Catherine placed her hand in his and followed him out onto the dance floor, while Kim went in search of his partner.

She faced him and placed her left hand on his good right shoulder and he rested his right hand in the small of her back. But where could she put her right hand since his left one was in its sling?

He saw her problem at once. "Perhaps I could take my arm out of the sling for a while . . ."

"Don't you dare! You could cause irreparable damage."

A devilish glint warmed his eyes. "Why don't you just place your hand on my shoulder and I'll do my best to lead? Perhaps we'll invent a new dance tonight, the One-Armed Waltz."

Catherine did as he suggested, but this position drew her indecently close to him, so close that she could smell the citrus tang of his shaving soap and see the dark flecks in the irises of his eyes.

"You—you are holding me too closely, Mr. Delancy," she stammered, blushing as she tried to step back out of his arms.

His hand tightened on the small of her back. "You have seen me half-naked, yet you object to my holding you closely for a waltz? And I thought you were a woman of courage, Dr. Stone."

Catherine stiffened with indignation. "The situations are hardly the same!"

The music started and Catherine found herself whirled away in spite of her reluctance. If she didn't follow his lead, she would create a scene, so she acquiesced.

"You dance very well with one arm," she said.

He smiled down at her. "I told you I do many things well with one arm." The smile died. "Why didn't you tell me that we had met before?"

Catherine knew at once that he was referring to her skating accident in Central Park. "I didn't mention it because I was sure you wouldn't remember me and didn't want to subject myself to the embarrassment. And since you didn't recognize me or mention the incident until now, I can see that I was wise to keep silent."

He exhaled audibly. "You certainly know how to put a fellow in his place. But in my own defense, you were wearing a wool hat and scarf, and you had your hand up to your face. How could anyone recognize you?"

"Point well taken," Catherine conceded.

Then he surprised her by peering down at her eye. "Were you badly hurt?"

"No. The cut didn't even need stitches."

"I'm glad to hear it."

They went around the dance floor in silence, then the waltz ended. Delancy escorted Catherine back to her seat, bowed, and returned to the dark-haired beauty Catherine remembered all too well from that day in Central Park.

The ball ended at two o'clock the following morning.

Damon seated himself in his carriage and rapped on the roof with his cane. When the driver's window slid open, he said, "Ivory's."

As Nevada took the opposite seat, he grinned and said, "You read my mind." He looked at Damon's sling. "You sure you're up to it?"

"I'm sure, or I wouldn't be going."

Nevada's smile faded and he grew silent and pensive.

"What's on your mind?"

"If Miss Francine weren't such a lady, she'd have your hide tacked to her parlor wall."

"For what?"

Nevada shook his head. "My friend, you only danced once with her tonight and once with the doctor lady."

Damon stretched out his legs and tried to get comfortable. "What of it? Francine Ballard doesn't own me."

"No, but she'd like to. And everyone assumes she will, since you've been seeing so much of her."

"Well, everyone assumes wrong. I've taken her skating once or twice and danced with her at several balls. Her father is a business associate of mine and has invited me to dinner, but I've never formally declared my intentions toward his daughter. No one has a right to assume anything."

Damon leaned his head back against the squabs and closed his eyes, a signal that he wished to be left alone. His relaxed air was deceptive, however, because inside he was anything but calm.

He kept thinking of Francine and how she would be the perfect wife for a wealthy, powerful man. She would manage his household with all the logistics of a general, making it a peaceful, welcoming oasis for him to come home to at night. She knew enough not to discuss such controversial topics as art, music, or literature at the dinner table, yet she could converse about food and wine for the duration of a three-hour meal. And Francine Ballard never did anything out of the ordinary, like become a doctor.

Then why not marry the woman? Even he didn't understand the reason for his own reluctance.

Damon opened his eyes and looked at Nevada. "You sure seem taken with Dr. Wolcott."

A look of satisfaction lit up the cowboy's face. "She's as pretty as a snowdrop, ain't she? Smart, too. Never could abide a stupid woman."

"She seems taken with you, too."

"I can't see why. I'm just a homely, cold-hearted gunslinger who happened to see the error of his ways just in time."

Damon snorted in derision. "You're also a man with a sizable fortune."

"Thanks to you." Nevada's expression grew serious. "I'd like to think a woman would marry me for the man that I am, not the size of my bankroll."

Damon shrugged. "Don't delude yourself. A sizable bankroll can be a powerful inducement to love."

He was too much of a cynic not to believe that his own fifty-six-million-dollar fortune had something to do with his own desirability.

"I wonder if Sybilla would take me if I just had the clothes on my back," Nevada mused.

"Only if you left on your spurs."

Nevada burst out laughing, and Damon joined him.

Fifteen minutes later, the carriage stopped and they disembarked before what looked like a large, elegant private home.

When they entered the foyer, they found Ivory herself waiting to receive them. In her lace gown of mocking white, she resembled a virginal bride rather than the notorious madam she was.

"Good evening, gentlemen," she said, inclining her head regally. Her shrewd glance flicked over Damon's injured arm. "I trust your injury isn't serious enough to keep you from enjoying yourself this evening?"

"Not at all," he replied with a wink.

She said, "Danse is waiting, as you instructed. And what will be your pleasure tonight, Mr. LaRouche?"

Nevada grinned. "I think I'll just take my pick, ma'am." And he went sauntering off toward the parlor where there was raucous laughter underscored by the energetic tinkle of piano music.

The house's facade may have been stylish, but inside, it had a sinful heart.

Damon started up the stairs curving to his left. He preferred taking his pleasure in a brothel rather than keeping a "petite amie" as many of his colleagues did. Such an arrangement avoided the emotional entanglements that went along with keeping a mistress.

Once upstairs, he walked quickly down the long gaslit corridor of closed doors. He heard a light trill of laughter, then a deep masculine groan of pain. He shook his head in disgust and walked faster, stopping before Danse's room.

It took her a moment to answer the door, telling Damon that she must have fallen asleep waiting for him. When he wanted her, he reserved her services for an entire night, preferring not to smell another man on her sweet skin.

The door opened, revealing the dark-haired prostitute in all her voluptuous glory. Tonight she wore a tightly laced black satin corset without chemise or pantaloons beneath it, so that all Damon focused on were her bare breasts and wide hips.

"Damon," she murmured, her husky voice touched with sleep, as she stepped aside to allow him to enter. When she saw his sling, her doe's eyes widened. "What happened to your arm?"

"An accident," he replied as he grabbed her around the waist and pulled her against him for a hard, deep kiss.

She helped undress him, taking special care not to hurt his shoulder, but once they were in bed together, passion overrode caution. Danse kept Damon floating in a haze of sexual torment for what seemed like hours, until she finally granted him the release he needed.

Much later, after he returned the favor with his free hand, she kissed his forehead, murmuring, "Damon," before rolling away and falling asleep.

He tried to sleep, but couldn't. While lovemaking sated his body, it didn't relax his mind. He kept thinking of Francine, wondering what she would do in their marriage bed. Like the lady she was, Damon suspected she would close her eyes and endure his animalistic urges stoically.

Was it so unrealistic of him to expect passion in his own wife? Judging from what other men said, he supposed it was.

Then he thought of Dr. Stone and her outspokenness. He smiled to himself. He had enjoyed her company tonight. She was like a swig of whiskey after a diet of milk.

Imagine her audacity at trying to fleece him out of money for her Women's Dispensary!

He closed his eyes and smiled in anticipation. He knew just the way to repay her.

Catherine rose a little after noon, and when she went to the kitchen for their informal breakfast, she found Sybilla there ahead of her.

"Good morning, sleepyhead," Sybilla said. "Did you sleep well?"

Catherine nodded and she yawned and shuffled over to the stove for her morning coffee. When she sat down at the table, she said, "And did you enjoy Mr. LaRouche's company last night? You were very quiet in the carriage on the way home."

"Well, Kim was with us."

Catherine raised her brows. "And just what is it that you couldn't say in front of Kim?"

"I wanted to tell you some things about Damon Delancy that Nevada told me, and I didn't think Kim would appreciate hearing them, that's all."

"And why not?"

Sybilla ran her finger around the rim of her coffee cup. "Because I think he's jealous of Mr. Delancy."

Catherine laughed in astonishment. "That's preposterous! Why should Kim be jealous? I hardly know Mr. Delancy. Besides, Kim doesn't have a jealous bone in his body."

"I beg to differ. He didn't take his eyes off you when you and Delancy were waltzing together."

"That's nonsense, Syb, utter nonsense."

"Call it what you like, but I know the green monster of envy when I see it."

"Let's change the subject, shall we? You spent so much time with Nevada that I'm sure he told you his life story."

Sybilla frowned. "Now that I think about it, he had me telling him all about my interesting, unconventional life, but he revealed very little about himself. But he did tell me how he met Mr. Delancy." She paused. "He saved Nevada's life."

"How?"

"It seems that some men—'bushwhackers' he called them— were lying in wait for Nevada along some mountain trail, ready to kill him. They almost did, but Delancy came along and sided with Nevada." Sybilla's gaze fell away. "They killed the three men."

Catherine drained her coffee cup, suddenly wide awake. "They killed them?"

Sybilla nodded.

Catherine rose and went to the stove for another cup of coffee. The man she had waltzed with last night had helped kill three men. Damon Delancy seemed different now. Unprincipled. Dangerous.

Behind her, Sybilla said, "Don't judge them too harshly, Cat. We both know how uncivilized the West is."

"I'm not judging them," she replied, returning to the table. "I'm sure they did what they had to do to survive." She reached across the table and grasped Sybilla's hand. "This doesn't change your opinion of Nevada, does it? You're not afraid of him now, are you?"

"Of course not. Regardless of what he did in the past, he's one of the kindest, gentlest men I've ever met. But somehow I don't think Kim would share my opinion. That's why I didn't tell you this in the carriage."

Catherine smiled ruefully. "You're right. I daresay Kim would disapprove."

Sybilla crossed her arms on the table. "What about Kim? Do you love him? Intend to marry him? Come, don't keep your best friend in suspense."

Catherine stared into her cup. "I honestly don't know. Oh, I enjoy his company well enough." And his embraces—she enjoyed those all too well. "But do I love him?" She looked up at her friend. "I've been too busy practicing medicine to give it much thought."

It was true. With her own practice, volunteering at the dispensary, and working in the tenements, Catherine had less time to spend with Kim, much to her regret. And ever since Sybilla had come to live with her, she had no time alone with the man because he felt honor-bound to include Sybilla in his invitations.

"Has he ever told you he loves you?"

"No."

"Any mention of marriage?"

Catherine's smile died as she thought of what those women had said about her being unsuitable for a man of Kim's social standing. As much as she had tried to shrug off their hateful words, they still stung.

"What's the matter?" Sybilla demanded.

Catherine reluctantly told her what she had overheard at the ball.

"Why those dreadful, spiteful old snobs!" Sybilla sputtered. She reached out and squeezed Catherine's hand. "I hope you didn't take their venom to heart." Then she sighed. "Oh, dear, I can see that you have."

"That's his world, Syb, and those people are part of it. If Kim ever asked me to marry him and I accepted, I just wonder if I would ever fit in."

"If Kim agreed with their shallow opinions, he wouldn't have anything to do with you. Give the man a little credit, Catherine."

She sighed. "You're right."

"Of course I am."

Catherine just smiled and shook her head.

Without warning, Molly appeared in the doorway carrying a long white box tied with a wide red ribbon. "This just arrived for you, Dr. Catherine." And she set the box on the table.

"What can this be?" Catherine asked.

"Looks like flowers to me," Sybilla said. "I'll bet they're from Kim. Hurry up and open it before I die of curiosity."

"Here's a card." Catherine opened the envelope and read the message. She looked up at Sybilla. "It's not from Kim. It's from Damon Delancy."

Sybilla's eyes grew as round as saucers. "Damon Delancy? What does it say?"

" 'If you wanted a donation to your Women's Dispensary, why didn't you just ask for one?' " Frowning in puzzlement, Catherine opened the box to reveal a dozen long-stemmed American Beauty roses.

"Sweet sutures!" Sybilla exclaimed.

"Those are roses, Dr. Sybilla," Molly said, "not sutures."

"Just a medical figure of speech, Molly." Sybilla removed one of the flowers, frowned at it, and said, "But these are very special roses indeed. Take a look."

Catherine watched in astonishment as Sybilla unrolled what looked like a bank note from around the stem. When she held it up, Catherine's jaw dropped.

"A one-hundred-dollar bank note?"

Sybilla nodded and picked another flower. "Here's another one. And another." She paused. "Cat, each of these roses comes with its own hundred-dollar bank note. If my arithmetic serves me correctly, there's over a thousand dollars here."

Catherine sat back, dumbfounded.

Sybilla said, "You wanted a donation to the Women's Dispensary, and I guess Damon Delancy gave you one. And then some. The man has style, I'll say that for him."

"I can't accept this!"

"And why not? The money isn't for you; it's a donation to the dispensary."

"I just feel odd about accepting it."

"You'll get over it." Sybilla blithely started unrolling the rest of the wrinkled money and setting the bills in a little pile to the left of her plate.

"Shall I put the flowers in water, doctor?" Molly asked.

"After I finish removing the money," Sybilla said.

Flustered, Catherine put her hands to her cheeks. She had never expected he would do something like this.

"Why don't you write him a note and thank him?" Sybilla said gently.

Catherine rose. "Yes. I should thank him."

Later, when she telephoned Delancy's home from the tobacconist's pay phone, someone told her that the master was out,
so she left a message thanking him for his generous donation to
the Women's Dispensary. Then she sat down and wrote him a
note, since she didn't know when she would be seeing him again.

❧ CHAPTER ❧

SEVEN

DURING the next few weeks, Catherine was too absorbed in her work to spare a thought for Damon Delancy. Her heart went out to Sybilla, however, who had not heard one word from Nevada LaRouche since the night of the Peachtrees' ball.

Catherine wished he would at least send a message. Sybilla was becoming as irritable as a colicky baby, snapping at Molly for the most innocent provocations and complaining to Catherine constantly about her incompetent co-workers at Bellevue, where she had been hired as a staff surgeon.

Catherine was ready to call on Nevada LaRouche herself and demand to know his intentions, when a Mrs. Hathaway walked into her office with a challenging medical problem that claimed all of Catherine's attention.

"I don't think you can help me" were the first words out of Mrs. Hathaway's mouth as she seated herself before Catherine's desk. "But my husband insisted that I come."

Mrs. Hathaway was a tall, thin woman with a sad, colorless face and an air of resignation common to those who lived with constant pain. She also appeared exhausted, drooping in her chair as if her body lacked a skeleton to support it.

"I can't promise miracles, but I hope I can help you," Catherine said.

"I've been to five doctors and three hospitals. No one has been able to help me. Why should you be any different?"

"At least give me a chance, Mrs. Hathaway."

"Fair enough."

Catherine sat back. "Now, please describe your symptoms."

"I'm so tired all the time, doctor," she mumbled, as if speaking normally took too much effort. "The minute I wake up, I just want to get right back into bed. And I usually do. Sometimes I stay there all day. I have headaches, and pains in my womb.''

''You don't go out at all?''

''I don't get five steps outside the door before I'm exhausted. I have to turn around and go back. It took all my strength to come here today.''

''And what about your family?''

''They have to get along the best they can. My husband owns a successful printing business, and we have servants, so the children have someone to care for them when I can't. Which is most of the time since I became ill two years ago.''

''How many children do you have?''

''Ten. The oldest is ten, the youngest two.''

How could such young children possibly get along with their mother bedridden? Catherine thought.

Mrs. Hathaway sighed. ''I don't care about my children. I don't care about running the household. I don't care about anything.''

Catherine shook her head sympathetically. ''You look much too young to have lost interest in life.''

''I'm thirty-two.'' Mrs. Hathaway supported her lolling head with one hand. ''My husband doesn't know what to do with me. The poor man keeps sending me to doctors, but they all say the same thing.''

''And what is that?''

A flash of anger started to cross her face, then faded with the effort. ''That they can't find anything physically wrong with me. If there's nothing wrong with me, doctor, why do I always feel so sick and tired?'' She sniffed quietly into her handkerchief.

Catherine rose and placed a comforting hand on the woman's shoulder. ''There, there, Mrs. Hathaway. Let me examine you and see what I can find.''

Catherine examined the woman from head to toe, and like her five predecessors, could find nothing physically wrong with her.

She stepped back, puzzled. ''I must be honest with you. I can't find any physical reason for your exhaustion either. I suspect it's caused by a nervous disorder called neurasthenia.''

Mrs. Hathaway nodded. ''That's what some of the other doctors said I had.''

''How did they propose to cure you?''

''One advised me to take a nerve tonic made from—'' she wrinkled her nose ''—goat glands. Another had me wear a galvanic belt. A third wanted me to go to a sanitarium for a rest cure. I tried them all, doctor, even that goat gland tonic, and none of them worked.''

Catherine said, ''Perhaps you have been lacing your corset too tightly. I would suggest you give up your corset for a month or two and see how you feel.''

''Give up my corset? Never! Everyone will think I'm a loose woman or one of those crazy dress reform people. Besides, the clothes I have wouldn't fit and my stomach would bulge if I stopped wearing my corset.''

''But if you're bedridden, who's to see you?''

''At least it makes me feel good.''

Catherine couldn't chastise her, for she knew it was impossible to convince members of her own sex to loosen their stays or discard them altogether, even for their health's sake. She helped the exhausted woman to sit up on the examining table.

''Don't look so disheartened, Dr. Stone,'' Mrs. Hathaway said. ''It's not your fault that you can't help me.''

''If you had a broken arm or a uterine tumor, I could help you. But since neurasthenia is a nervous condition and none of the cures have worked for you . . .'' She shook her head.

''I understand.''

Catherine helped her to dress, then took her arm and escorted her back to her waiting carriage. As she watched it drive away, she never felt more frustrated or more helpless.

Later that afternoon, Sybilla returned growling and snapping from the hospital.

''Rusty retractors!'' she sputtered, as she swept into the parlor where Catherine had tea waiting. ''How can members of my own sex be so—so stupid!''

''What happened?'' Catherine asked.

''This actress came to me and wanted to know if I would remove some ribs so she could have a smaller waist. The woman was willing to risk surgery just for vanity.''

''You refused, of course.''

''Most emphatically.''

Once Sybilla calmed down and poured herself a cup of tea, Catherine said, ''I had an interesting patient today.''

She told her about the neurasthenic Mrs. Hathaway, including the woman's debilitating exhaustion and lack of interest in life.

''It's so frustrating because I can't do anything for her,'' Catherine said. "I don't believe in goat gland tonics and galvanic belts."

Sybilla scowled and rose. "You can help Mrs. Hathaway and women like her. We all can."

"What are you talking about? If there's nothing physically wrong with the woman, how—?"

"Cat, it's obvious. You said the woman is thirty-two years old and has ten children. She's been pregnant or nursing for most of her adult life, and she's probably sick and tired of—of feeling like a cow!"

"But motherhood is a noble calling for most women."

"I won't dispute that. I hope to be a mother myself some day. But I also think a woman can experience its joys just as much with three or four children as a dozen."

Catherine had an uneasy feeling about where this discussion was headed, and she didn't like it.

Sybilla walked over to the window and looked out into the street. "We both know women's lives would be improved immeasurably if they didn't have so many children. Look at the women in the tenements, having babies they can't even afford to feed and clothe."

"I agree."

Sybilla turned and regarded her quizzically. "Then why won't you help your patients practice anticonception? I still have my bustle full of pessaries. And I know where to get more."

"I've told you why," Catherine said, willing herself to remain calm. "It's illegal."

Sybilla dismissed her protest with a wave of her hand. "Who would know? I'm sure our patients would be so grateful they wouldn't tell a soul what they were doing."

"Perhaps. But it's still too risky."

"Oh, to hell with the risk!" Sybilla cried, bristling. "I thought you were a woman of courage and principle, Catherine Stone, but you're just as bad as the men. You don't care if your patients suffer needlessly. You only care about your damned practice."

Trembling, Catherine rose. "That's not fair! I care about my patients just as much as any other doctor I know, yourself included. But I also don't believe in breaking the law."

"The law is idiotic! They should change it."

"I agree. But until they do, I'll abide by it. And as far as caring about my 'damned practice,' I've worked too hard not to! And so have you, Sybilla Wolcott."

"And what are you going to do when you get married? Aren't you going to practice anticonception, or are you going to have a child every year?" Without waiting for Catherine's reply, Sybilla added, "Of course you won't. How could you practice medicine if you're perpetually pregnant?"

She's not angry with me, Catherine told herself, *she's really angry with Nevada LaRouche.*

"And if you'll use anticonception devices, why won't you give them to your patients who ask for them?" Sybilla demanded. "That's hypocritical, don't you think?"

A knock on the door interrupted Sybilla, and when Catherine bade them enter, Molly timidly stepped in, looking from one to the other as if trying to gauge who was in the better mood.

"A telegram for Dr. Sybilla," she said, handing the paper to Sybilla then hurrying out of the parlor.

Sybilla opened the telegram, read it, and turned ashen.

"What is it?" Catherine demanded, rushing to her side, their argument forgotten.

"It's my father. He's had a stroke, but he's still alive, thank God. My brothers want me to come home immediately."

Catherine put her arm around Sybilla's shoulders. "I'm so sorry."

The telegram fell from her hand. "Father! A stroke . . . I'm stunned. He's always been the picture of health."

"You'll have to go at once," Catherine said. "I'll help you pack, then we'll get you to Grand Central."

An hour later, Catherine was standing on the platform, saying goodbye to a forlorn Sybilla.

"Stay as long as you need to," she said, clasping her friend's cold hands. "And don't worry about your patients. I'll tell the hospital what's happened."

"You're the best friend a woman could have."

As Sybilla boarded the train, Catherine said, "I'll miss you. Hurry back."

"I will."

The warning whistle shrieked, and Sybilla disappeared in a hiss of steam and chugging of wheels.

In the hansom cab returning to Washington Square, Catherine couldn't stop thinking of her argument with Sybilla before the telegram's arrival.

Was Sybilla right? Was she doing a disservice to her patients

by refusing to supply them with anticonception information and
devices in spite of the risk to herself?

Troubled, she stopped at Kim's house to tell him what had
happened to Sybilla's father and to ask his advice.

"Catherine," he said, coming out of his surgery to greet her
with a smile and a peck on the cheek. "What a pleasant surprise."

"I wish I could say that this is a social call, but I'm afraid
I've some bad news."

His smile died and he ushered her into the library. "Nothing
serious, I hope."

As she seated herself, she told him about Sybilla's hasty departure for Washington, D.C. and the reason behind it.

Kim shook his head as he poured her a sherry. "How terrible.
I hope the poor man recovers. How long will Sybilla be gone?"

"I don't know. She did promise to return as quickly as possible, though."

Kim handed her the sherry and sat down beside her. "You
look as though you've just lost a patient. What else is troubling
you?"

*Dear Kim, always so adept at sensing what lurked beneath
the surface.* "Sybilla and I had an argument before she left."

He reached out and ran the backs of his fingers along her
cheek. "About what?"

"Anticonception."

He choked on his sherry. When he stopped coughing, he said,
"For herself?"

Catherine blushed. "Of course not! She wants to distribute
such information to our patients."

She rose and paced the room. "While I agree with Sybilla in
principle, what she's advocating is illegal." She stopped. "Oh,
Kim, I just don't know what to do. Sybilla is like a sister to me.
I don't want to cause a rift between us. But I don't want to
jeopardize what I've worked so hard for."

Kim rose, took her in his arms, and held her. "Poor Catherine. What a dilemma."

She closed her eyes and let herself become lost in his strength
and comfort for a moment.

Kim released her and stepped back. "Don't become involved
in Sybilla's scheme," he said sternly. He paused. "Do you know
who Anthony Comstock is?"

"Of course. He was instrumental in getting Congress to pass

the Comstock Act. He's also the head of the New York Society for the Suppression of Vice.''

''Yes.'' Kim's handsome features hardened. ''He's the self-proclaimed guardian of the public's morals, and you should fear him.''

Kim sipped his sherry. ''Do you know what he does? He rides the trains and searches for any anticonception devices being sent through the mails. If he finds any, he confiscates them and has both the sender and receiver prosecuted and sent to prison.

''Or he and one of his cronies will visit a doctor's office and pretend that he and his wife want to prevent more births. When the poor doctor feels sorry for him and gives him the information, Comstock has him arrested for distributing obscene materials.''

Catherine exploded with righteous indignation. ''That's appalling!''

''I quite agree, but our hands are tied. How are we to know if a patient asking for such information isn't a member of Comstock's purity brigade? That's why we advise abstinence rather than any mechanical means of preventing conception.''

Catherine just shook her head.

''So when Sybilla returns, I would strongly caution her against having anything to do with distributing anticonception information. Unless, of course, she wants to risk going to prison for five or ten years.''

Catherine shuddered at the thought.

Kim took her hand. ''Enough of this unpleasant talk. Come sit next to me. I have something to tell you.''

Curious, Catherine joined him on the sofa, sitting close enough so he could put his arm around her if he so desired.

He turned his body so he could face her and draped his arm across the back of the sofa. ''Genevra has invited us to spend the weekend with her and Gordon in Newport.''

''I've never been there.'' It was too exclusive for Catherine's blood.

''She thought we'd all enjoy a respite from the city.'' When Catherine hesitated, he said, ''Please say you'll come. Newport is lovely, and even though there will be a houseful of people, we'd still have some time to be alone.''

''How would we get there?''

''By Gordon's private railway car late Friday afternoon. We'd stay the weekend and return to the city late Sunday night.''

"But what about my patients?"

"Have Molly send them to the Women's Dispensary." Kim's voice grew soft and persuasive. "You've been working like a slave, Catherine. Surely you're entitled to one weekend free."

She sighed. Two whole days of clean, fresh air and endless ocean, where the only sounds would be the raucous cries of seagulls wheeling overhead and the crashing of foam-capped waves against rocks . . .

"Well, I haven't seen Genevra since she went to Newport for the summer, and I do miss my little namesake."

"You won't be sorry."

He reached out, placed his palm against her cheek and drew her toward him for a kiss. Catherine reached for his mouth hungrily, seeking to erase all tension in the warm, sweet bliss of his embrace.

When they parted, Kim pressed his hard cheek to hers. "I've missed you so much," he whispered. "We haven't had a moment alone since Sybilla joined you."

"I know it's been difficult."

He drew away and gazed deeply into her eyes. "It's been hell." He hesitated. "Will you stay for dinner tonight?" *And longer*, was the implication in his voice.

She grimaced. "I have patients waiting."

"I see."

But Catherine could tell from the sudden coolness that crept into his tone that this time, he did not understand at all.

She rose. "I should be going."

"Of course." The words were flat and clipped, without warmth. "I'll have my carriage take you home."

Once they were in the foyer, Catherine said, "I'm looking forward to Newport this weekend." It was all she could offer him for now.

It must have been enough, for he relented and smiled. "So am I."

After they said their goodbyes and Catherine was inside the carriage, she leaned back against the squabs and closed her eyes. Why was she so hesitant to commit herself to Kim? He was fast becoming impatient with her, and she couldn't blame him. She couldn't keep him at arm's length forever.

Perhaps this weekend at Newport would resolve her feelings.

• • •

"So what do you think of the summer cottage Gordie built for me?" Genevra asked Catherine as they strolled across the wide green lawn that swept away toward the steep cliffs.

The wide brim of Catherine's straw hat shielding her eyes against the blazing July sun, she looked back at the magnificent mansion set against a backdrop of stately copper beech trees rustling gently with the sea breeze.

"Cottage! Genevra, Briarleigh is a veritable palace! I've never seen anything like it."

Of the many grand French chateaux and English manor houses that Catherine had seen lining either side of Bellevue Avenue, none rivaled Briarleigh. This Italian villa preened like a beautiful woman displaying her jewels—the red-tiled roof, the long veranda running the length of the house, the graceful arched porticoes facing the blue-green sea.

Genevra smiled as she twirled her ivory-handled sunshade that matched the pale green dress she wore. "It is rather grand, isn't it? But Gordie and I love summering here. It's so cool and quiet. I can't bear the heat and stench of New York City in the summer."

"Yes, it is like sleeping in a furnace," Catherine agreed, thinking of all the oppressive summer nights she had almost gone mad from the heat.

Genevra flashed her a guilty glance. "How thoughtless of me . . . You couldn't get away for the summer?"

"I can't leave my patients for that length of time." She turned to Genevra. "And how have you been feeling?"

"Oh, sometimes I feel tired, but all in all, I'm much better." Genevra hesitated. "Catherine, I must apologize for all those horrid things I said to you when I went into labor."

"No, it is I who should apologize to you. Your fears weren't groundless; the baby was too large for a safe delivery. I should have been more emphatic about the dangers you faced."

Genevra shuddered. "Everything worked out for the best. I'm alive, and I have my beautiful baby boy. He is worth it."

"I'm glad you feel that way."

"When I see Gordie's face light up with pride every time the nurse brings little Stone to us at tea time . . ." She paused and muttered, "Still, I wouldn't want to repeat the experience," under her breath.

Kim and Gordon walked toward them through the sunken garden.

"Isn't this magnificent?" Kim asked. As usual, he looked as

though he belonged here in his cool white flannel suit and straw boater.

"It's beautiful," Catherine agreed.

"We thought you ladies would enjoy bathing at Bailey's Beach this afternoon," Gordon said, staring at his young wife in adoration.

"But I don't have a bathing costume," Catherine protested.

"We have plenty of extras," Genevra told her. "I'm sure we can find one that fits you."

Gordon added, "Then at five o'clock, we'll go for a carriage ride down Bellevue Avenue. It's something of a ritual here."

"It gives us a chance to show off," Genevra said.

Catherine's heart sank. She had only her burgundy silk gown and cameo with her. When compared with Genevra's nine changes of clothing a day, Catherine's wardrobe was something of an embarrassment.

Gordon continued with, "And tonight we're having a few people over for dinner."

"Anyone we know?" Kim asked.

"Oh, some people from Boston and a surprise or two," Genevra said mysteriously. Then she turned to Catherine. "Shall we get ready for Bailey's Beach?"

The two women hurried back to the house.

Later, as Catherine slid up to her shivering shoulders in the chilly waters of the Atlantic, she decided that Bailey's Beach was less a place for swimming than yet another means of excluding the socially unacceptable. The Grahams were part of the Newport elite, so Genevra and her guests were welcome, but Catherine noticed that the guard turned away more than one carriage. Somehow, it diminished her own enjoyment of such a rare treat as bathing in the sea.

As she listened to the splashing and cries of delight around her, Catherine wished the day were already over.

"Did Genevra say any more about who's coming to dinner?" Catherine asked Kim as he escorted her down the sweeping staircase of yellow Siena marble.

"No Astors, Vanderbilts, or Belmonts," he replied. "That's all she would say." He squeezed her hand reassuringly. "You needn't worry, Catherine. You could hold your own with the Queen of England herself."

She fleetingly thought of the malicious harpies at the Peach-trees' ball, then dismissed them from her mind once and for all.

"Dear Kim. You always know just what to say."

He leaned over to brush a quick kiss across her cheek. "You will be the loveliest woman here tonight."

When they entered the parlor, a room with more gold leaf than comfortable chairs, they found that several guests had already arrived. Catherine warmed to Mr. and Mrs. Arbuthnot of Boston right away, but felt a distinct chill race up her spine when introduced to their nephew, Ezra Pease—a sullen young man who informed her that he was a student at Harvard University, as he stared unblinking at Catherine's breasts in an offensive manner reminiscent of Jervis.

Kim drew Catherine aside and turned her attention to the parlor entrance. "Look who's here."

There, standing in the doorway, was Damon Delancy.

What is he doing here? Catherine thought in panic.

It was as though she had spoken aloud. Delancy looked across the room. When their eyes met, he held her gaze as though she were the only person there. Catherine tried to look away, but couldn't. Then he inclined his head in acknowledgment and the spell was broken.

"Miss Ballard is with him," Kim said at her elbow. "He and LaRouche must be staying with her family at Sea Winds, the Ballard summer home." He looked at her. "Would you like some champagne?"

"Yes, please."

Catherine tried not to stare as Francine Ballard, exquisite in a frothy confection of blush pink gauze, fluttered around Gordon and Genevra.

Nevada LaRouche patiently waited his turn to greet his host and hostess, but the moment he saw Catherine, he strode across the room to her.

" 'Evening, Dr. Stone."

"Good evening, Mr. LaRouche. How good to see you again."

His eyes darted around the room. "I don't see Dr. Wolcott here."

"Oh, she couldn't come," Catherine replied. "Her father was taken ill suddenly, and she went home to Washington to be with her family."

He frowned. "I'm sorry to hear that. I was looking forward to seeing her again."

Catherine gave him a look of wide-eyed innocence. "Then why did you disappear after the Peachtrees' ball?"

His gaze slid away sheepishly. "Commerce, ma'am. It does keep a man busy."

"Ah, I see."

"I sure hope Dr. Wolcott is as understanding as you when I see her again."

"She won't be, Mr. LaRouche. Take my word for it."

That took the cowboy aback. Catherine suspected he was more adept at handling six-guns than a headstrong woman like Sybilla.

"But she will be coming back to New York?" he persisted.

"I suspect so. While Sybilla is close to her family, her medical practice is here."

"I'd be obliged if you let me know the minute she comes back."

"I will."

"Thanks."

Just at that moment, Kim returned with the champagne and exchanged a few pleasantries with LaRouche before Delancy and Francine reached them.

He is not going to rile me, Catherine reminded herself, sipping her champagne.

After greeting everyone, Delancy said, "Dr. Stone, I don't think you've met Miss Ballard." And he introduced them.

Catherine felt those dark eyes flick over her and dismiss her as someone of no importance. Francine said aloud, "I don't think I've ever met a lady doctor before. How . . . interesting."

About as interesting as brushing one's teeth, she implied by her bored expression.

"I find it so," Catherine replied. Then she turned to Delancy. "I see you're not wearing your arm in a sling, Mr. Delancy. Your fracture has healed then?"

"Perfectly," he replied, "thanks to you."

From the vicinity of the divan came a sneering, "Women should stay home where they belong. They have no right becoming doctors—they can't do the job as well as men."

Dead silence. Everyone turned to look at Ezra Pease sitting there with an empty glass of champagne in his hand and staring balefully at Catherine.

"I take issue with that," Gordon said, crossing the room to join them. "If it weren't for Dr. Stone here, my wife and son wouldn't be alive today."

Delancy's lip curled as he looked down at the young man. "You won't find anyone in this room with a disparaging word to say about lady doctors."

The warning was lost on Mr. Pease, fortified with champagne. "Harvard Medical has never admitted women to study medicine and never will. And it's for a good reason: while women are morally superior to men, they are physically and intellectually inferior."

Catherine stepped forward. "Thank you for defending me, gentlemen, but I am more than capable of defending myself."

Pease leaned back in his seat and folded his arms smugly. "You can try."

"Your first statement that women belong in the home intrigues me. Why?"

"Because women are the moral guardians of society. Through their influence in the home, they raise their children and curb man's most bestial tendencies. They are responsible for civilizing the human race. But to do that, they've got to stay at home." He snickered at his own wit.

Catherine raised her brows. "Civilizing the human race? That sounds like an awesome responsibility for anyone. But since women are physically and intellectually inferior, it's a wonder we succeed at all."

Pease turned red.

"And do you think women should become nurses?"

"Of course. That's because nursing is more suited to women's sympathetic, nurturing natures."

"I see. So you praise a woman's ability to nurse, but think she couldn't succeed as a doctor." She smiled. "By the very virtue of my existence, I can prove you wrong on that count, sir."

Laughter filled the room, causing the young man to turn an even deeper crimson.

He shook his head stubbornly. "Women have delicate sensibilities and shouldn't be exposed to dead bodies and such. It coarsens them."

Catherine laughed. "You have obviously never been in an anatomy class with a group of female medical students." When the laughter subsided, she added, "If women have such delicate sensibilities, why do male physicians treat them at all? If anything, your assertion makes a strong case for women doctoring

other women, because disrobing before a strange man is sure to
offend any woman's sensibilities.''

"Point well taken," Damon Delancy said, chuckling.

"She's got you there, Ezra," Gordon added.

Finally, Pease had nothing to say and sank deeper into his
seat.

Mrs. Arbuthnot sighed as she exchanged glances with her
husband. "For all his education, I fear my nephew has made an
ass of himself once again, and it's time for us to depart."

"Aunt Agatha—!"

She silenced him with a withering stare, and Catherine suspected Ezra depended on his aunt's good will for more than
lavish weekends in Newport.

"But you haven't had dinner," Genevra protested.

"Some other time, my dear," Mrs. Arbuthnot said with an
apologetic smile. "You don't really want to watch Ezra sulking
all evening because a woman has bested him, do you?"

Damon was finding it difficult to concentrate on course after
lavish course being set before him, because he was too busy
speculating about Dr. Stone and her relationship with Dr. Flanders.

He wondered if they were a couple. Whenever he encountered
Dr. Stone, Dr. Flanders was usually not far behind, like a faith-
ful lap dog. Yet they lacked the air of exclusivity usually shared
by two people in love.

Damon appeared to be engrossed in Francine's discussion of
selecting privet hedges for a country estate, but was really studying Kim Flanders behind the pyramid of oranges at the other
end of the table.

He didn't like him. The man was just too perfect with his
golden good looks and air of being born with a silver spoon in
his mouth. He probably never had to work hard for anything
in his life, including his medical career.

What could an intelligent woman like Catherine Stone see in
a man like that? Damon wondered.

He was determined to find out.

When the long, lavish meal finally ended and Damon and
Francine were on the way back to Sea Winds at midnight, all
she could talk about was Dr. Stone's disgraceful behavior.

"And how was her behavior disgraceful, pray tell?"

"Why, she contradicted that charming Mr. Pease in public!"

She fanned herself as if weakened physically by the emotion of their exchange.

Damon chuckled. "She did make that arrogant pup look like a fool, I'll say that for her."

Francine looked at him, aghast. "Damon, you sound like you admire her for ranting like a fishwife."

"She didn't rant. She merely defended herself quite rationally. And quite ably."

"Well, even if she was in the right, a lady should never flaunt her intelligence in public."

Damon sighed. Why should he bother explaining when Francine would never understand?

"If you don't mind, I'm going to escort you to the door and return to Briarleigh," Damon said. "Gordon and the other men are going to play cards tonight, and I'd like to join them."

And because Francine was the perfect lady, she told him to go right ahead.

It was one o'clock in the morning, and Catherine felt as though she could stay awake forever.

She set down the book she had been reading and went to the window where the shimmering, moonlit sea beckoned. She might never have another enchanted night like this one, so she quickly dressed herself in her shirtwaist and skirt and crept through the darkened house.

The men were playing cards in the game room, while Genevra and the servants were abed, so no one accosted Catherine as she let herself out and glided down to the sunken garden.

She seated herself on one of the low stone balustrades still warm from the summer sun, and ran her bare toes through the cold silky grass, not yet wet with dew. The cloudless night sky was strewn with stars, and a full moon gave its benediction overhead. Catherine closed her eyes and let the warm night breeze brush against her cheeks, teasing her with the soft, sweet scents of rosa rugosa and hydrangea almost overpowered by the tang of brine.

As she had imagined, the only sounds were the whisper of the wind and the waves crashing steadily against rocks. No hoofbeats, no rattling wheels, no screams of pain.

With a contented sigh, she removed her hairpins one by one, then shook her head until her silken hair fell heavily against the back of her neck.

"Do you mind if I join you?"

Catherine nearly jumped out of her skin, her hand flying to her chest to keep her heart in place. She twisted around, but she already knew the intruder's identity.

"Mr. Delancy! You scared me half to death."

"Sorry. I didn't mean to."

He set down the bottle of champagne and two empty glasses he carried, stepped over the balustrade with the grace and agility of a cat, and sat down next to Catherine. She noticed his white tie hung loose and unknotted about his neck and his black jacket smelled faintly of cigars.

"Why did you come back?" she asked. "I thought you had returned to Miss Ballard's house."

"I did." He uncorked the champagne bottle deftly and handed Catherine a crystal glass. "But I was feeling restless and thought I'd come back for a game of cards. And you?"

"It's too beautiful a night to spend sleeping." She watched the moonlight change her champagne to liquid silver. Her first sip tasted like enchanted nectar.

"I agree."

Catherine took a deep breath, aware as always of this man's presence. Usually, it disturbed her enough to make her move away, but tonight, after her victory over Pease, she was filled with a sense of her own power and refused to let Damon Delancy intimidate her.

"Do you like Newport?" he asked, his voice as quiet as the breeze.

"I like the sea and the natural beauty of it," she replied. She would let him infer what he wished concerning her opinion of the lavish mansions and exclusivity.

"But not these ostentatious piles of stone."

"I didn't say that."

"You didn't have to." He gave her a frank, assessing look. "Do you disapprove of wealth, Dr. Stone?"

"If I did, I wouldn't be here, accepting the Grahams' lavish hospitality. No, I just abhor vulgar display and waste. One can do great good with money, as you did with your donation to the Women's Dispensary. It was greatly appreciated, by the way."

He smiled slowly. "I'm glad you liked the roses."

"It was a most ingenious way of making a donation, I must admit." She hesitated. "And what of you, Mr. Delancy? Do you plan to build a cottage here soon?"

"No, Dr. Stone, I'm afraid the sea holds little appeal for me. I built my summer getaway in the Hudson River highlands, where there is some semblance of mountains."

"Like out west, where you were born?"

He looked at her in astonishment. "Wherever did you get the notion I was born out west? I was born in New York City."

"You were? But I thought—"

"Then you thought wrong." He sipped his champagne and stared out to sea. "Do you know those street arabs you see everywhere in the city?"

"The homeless ones who sleep with their feet in boxes and on steam grates in the winter? Oh, yes, I know them well."

"I was one of them once."

Catherine's head whipped around and her jaw dropped. "You? How—how horrible."

His mouth hardened. "Save your pity for someone who needs it, Dr. Stone."

"I wasn't feeling sorry for you. I was just trying to reconcile the Wolf of Wall Street with a destitute street arab."

He smiled at her use of his nickname. "I'd probably be dead today if it hadn't been for the Church of God Rejoicing. They rounded up a bunch of us young hooligans and sent us out west on an orphan train."

Catherine knew that various religious organizations sought to settle homeless children with families in the midwest and west in an effort to bring them a better life.

"Where did they finally leave you?" she asked.

"With a couple in Nebraska who ran a general store. I stayed with them until I was eighteen. My foster mother Aunt Hattie taught me my manners and cleaned up my language. After she died, her husband and I had a falling out, so I left to seek my fortune.

"I traveled around here and there, doing odd jobs. When I wandered down to Arizona, I discovered that the miners working the copper and silver mines had no tobacco. Being raised by shopkeepers, I decided I'd try to fill that demand. I looked around and found tobacco in a neighboring state, shipped it back by mule, and sold it for a small fortune."

"That's where you met Mr. LaRouche and discovered your copper mine."

He nodded. "That's also where I learned to do what I do best."

"And what is that?"

"Make money." He saw her glass was half-empty and refilled it. "And what about you? What made you want to become a doctor? Did you rescue injured birds and squirrels and nurse them back to health?"

Catherine ignored his teasing tone. "No, I became a doctor because of my mother." She took several swallows of champagne for the courage to continue. "When I was twelve years old, she died in childbirth. And do you know why, Mr. Delancy?" When he didn't respond, she added, "Years later, my former governess told me that the doctor—a man—was in a hurry to get to the opera that night.

"And because he was in a hurry, he wasn't there when she began to bleed to death."

The breeze stopped. Even the roaring of the ocean sounded far away.

Catherine looked over at the man sitting so still next to her. His head was bowed as he stared into his champagne, and she couldn't tell what he was thinking.

"Do you know what appalled me the most about my mother's death?" she asked, turning her face back to the sea.

"Tell me."

"This man had the power of life and death over her."

She rose. The sea tilted to one side in a spray of sparks, then righted itself as she regained her equilibrium.

"That's when I decided I would become a doctor, so no woman would have to suffer what my mother did at the hands of that man, or any other like him."

Catherine started walking. The champagne made her feel as weightless as a ghost skimming over the grass. If she reached up, she could pluck the moon from the sky and hold it in her hand.

From far away she heard someone call her name.

She walked faster. She had to get to the sea and wrap herself in the diamonds sparkling on its surface. Then she would be the envy of all the women at the Peachtrees' ball.

She almost reached the end of the lawn when a band of steel wrapped itself around her waist, lifted her off her feet, and spun her around. She staggered and reached out to steady herself.

When the world stopped spinning, Catherine found herself standing before Damon Delancy, her hands clutching his broad shoulders.

"Why, you're drunk," he said.

She giggled. "No. Yes. I don't know."

He raised his hands to her face, his palms like fire against her cheeks. His eyes were silvery in the moonlight, and even Catherine could read the silent yearning in their depths.

She should have pulled away, but couldn't.

"Tonight you don't look like a prim lady doctor who fights death every day," he whispered, his voice as dark and promising as the night. "You are a siren, with moonlight in your hair and starlight in your eyes."

Even as she said, "You're drunk," she wished every lying word were true.

"Oh, no," he replied, smiling. "Not drunk. Something else."

When he lowered his head, she swayed to meet his lips with her own. His mouth was warm and commanding, tasting of champagne and just as potent. His lips parted, the tip of his tongue demanding entrance.

Catherine felt a jolt of desire rock her back on her heels, but Damon wouldn't let her fall. The deep intimacy of his kiss made her dizzier than the champagne, igniting her senses with a shameful, blazing hunger.

Her hands slid down the smooth fabric of his shirtfront to wind around his narrow waist. As she pressed her breasts against his unyielding chest, and she felt her nipples harden of their own volition, she dimly realized she was wearing nothing but her chemise beneath her shirtwaist.

She groaned against his mouth and pulled him closer to her, reveling in the hard maleness of him. She wanted him to unbutton her shirtwaist and slide his long fingers beneath her chemise so he could cup her silken flesh, but she dared not ask.

When they finally parted, breathless and astonished, he held her clasped in his arms, her head against his shoulder as he stroked her hair with one hand.

Catherine closed her eyes, letting his strength steady her. Kim's kisses had never shaken her like this. Never.

Thoughts of Kim made Catherine pull away. "Why did you kiss me?"

"Because I wanted to. Why did you kiss me back?"

She had no answer, so she turned away, guilt at her own complicity making her scan the darkened windows of Briarleigh, hoping that no one had seen them standing on the cliff's edge, locked in an embrace.

"It's late," she said. "I have to go inside."

He sighed. "And I have to return to Sea Winds."

Catherine hurried ahead, and he followed several paces behind.

❧ CHAPTER ❧

EIGHT

SYBILLA dabbed the sweat from her brow with her handkerchief as she trudged alongside Catherine up the brownstone's steep steps. Ever since she had returned from Washington three days ago, she sensed something was troubling Catherine.

Oh, she appeared well enough as they stayed up as late as they dared, talking of Sybilla's family and all that had happened in her absence. But Sybilla sensed a preoccupation behind Catherine's outward air of contentment.

Now, as she and Catherine entered the dark, cool foyer that was empty of patients on this turgid August afternoon, Sybilla said, "I would like a cold glass of lemonade before I melt."

Catherine set down her medical bag with a weary sigh. "So would I."

Molly appeared out of nowhere. "Would anyone like something cold to drink?"

"Molly, you're a godsend. Lemonade would be welcome," Sybilla said, going over to the mirror to remove her bonnet and tuck in any stray wisps of blonde hair.

After spending a heartbreaking day in the tenements, trying and failing to keep dozens of babies from dying of cholera infantum—the dreaded "summer sickness"—all Sybilla wanted to do was fall into the nearest chair, close her eyes, and forget those suffering little faces.

Once she and Catherine went into the parlor and gulped their lemonade, Sybilla said, "All right, my friend, what's wrong?"

Catherine smiled wryly. "You must be a mind reader, Syb."

"I've known you too long not to tell when something's troubling you, so out with it."

"It's Kim," she said, looking down into her glass.

"Kim? You two suit each other like hand and glove. What could he have possibly done that's troubling you?"

"He's one of the few doctors in New York City who isn't helping with this cholera infantum epidemic in the East Side."

As Sybilla knew, the summer cholera epidemics were so severe that the department of health put out an urgent call for doctors throughout the city to volunteer time to treat the sick babies.

Sybilla watched as her friend set down her glass and walked over to a window, her distress evident in her bowed head and slumped shoulders. She waited while Catherine looked out into Washington Square and collected her thoughts.

Finally, she turned and said, "Kim's been so good to me that I hate to find fault with anything he does, but . . ." She shrugged helplessly.

"But you think he's shirking his responsibilities as a doctor by not helping with the epidemic."

Sybilla knew Catherine was loyal to those she cared about, but she was also very idealistic. She believed passionately that a doctor's first responsibility was to his patients.

Catherine raised her head defiantly. "Yes, I do. As much as I hate to admit it, I fear Kim is more concerned with society than he is with medicine."

Sybilla rose. "You astonish me. I've never heard you say a negative word about Kim, and quite frankly, I can't understand why his being a society doctor upsets you so much. Just because he prefers treating the wealthy doesn't mean he's less dedicated to medicine than you or I."

"He said the same thing to me once," Catherine admitted. "It's just upsetting to me that he would choose to spend a carefree week in the Berkshires with his wealthy friends rather than help the rest of us save babies."

Sybilla joined her by the window. "Well, it would seem that the two of you have philosophical differences you'll have to resolve."

Catherine looked at her oddly. "There's something else." She took a deep breath and blurted, "Damon Delancy kissed me."

Sybilla's eyes widened and she staggered back. "What?" Then she bounded forward, grasped Catherine by the shoulders and shook her. "Sweet sutures, Cat! When did this happen? And why didn't you tell me?"

When Sybilla released her, Catherine said, "It happened while

Kim and I went to visit Genevra in Newport for a weekend. You were in Washington at the time. I went for a late-night stroll and Mr. Delancy happened to be there as well.'' She made a dismissive movement with her hand. ''We both had too much champagne to drink and he kissed me. I don't know what came over me, but I kissed him back. The moonlight must have addled my brain.''

Sybilla slid down into the nearest chair. ''I'm in shock. So what happened after he kissed you?''

''Why, nothing. He went back to Francine Ballard's house and I haven't seen him since. Not that I expect to,'' she added, a little too hastily, Sybilla thought. ''It was meaningless, something done in the heat of the moment. He's no doubt forgotten about it, as have I.''

I wouldn't be so sure about that, Sybilla thought. ''And where was Kim when all this was going on?''

''Why, playing cards in the house, I hope,'' Catherine replied.

''Damon Delancy, of all people,'' Sybilla murmured with a shake of her head. ''I didn't think you liked him, even after he sent you those roses.''

''I didn't. That is, until we had a chance to talk some more that night in Newport. He's had a hard life, yet he triumphed over adversity.''

Sybilla listened while Catherine told her about Delancy's harrowing childhood on the streets of New York, being sent west on an orphan train, and making a fortune selling tobacco to the copper and silver miners.

''Very interesting,'' she said.

Just then Molly appeared in the doorway. ''Excuse me, Dr. Sybilla, but there's another message from Mr. LaRouche.''

Sybilla's pulse quickened at the sound of the cowboy's name. It had been so long since she had seen him—too long.

''I'm too busy to reply,'' she said.

''But this is the third message he has sent today.''

''I'm still too busy.''

When Molly left, Sybilla frowned and said, ''I wonder how he knew I was back.''

''I told him,'' Catherine replied. ''He was at Newport with Mr. Delancy and asked for you. I told him what happened to your father, and he asked if I would let him know when you got back. So I did.''

Sybilla smiled, absurdly pleased. So he cared after all.

Catherine said, "I just don't understand you. When that man didn't call you after the Peachtrees' ball, I thought you were never going to get out of the doldrums. Now that he wants to see you, you say you're busy."

Sybilla tossed her head. "It never hurts to keep a man dangling. Remember that."

A loud pounding on the front door interrupted her, and when she and Catherine raced to answer it, they found two men standing there, one supporting the other.

"My friend here just collapsed," the one holding the other gasped.

"Bring him in here," Catherine said. "Quickly!"

Sybilla followed. It was time to get back to work.

Later, after she and Catherine had treated the man for sunstroke, Sybilla sat alone in her office, thinking about her conversation with Catherine.

She looked over at Bonette. "I think the lady doth protest too much about Damon Delancy, don't you?"

The skeleton grinned in agreement.

Sybilla sat back in her swivel chair. She thought it odd that Catherine now criticized Kim for being "too society," when she had accepted it before. Could it be that she was comparing him to Damon Delancy and finding him lacking?

The sound of measured footsteps punctuated by the jingling of spurs caused her to start and look up.

There standing in the open doorway was Nevada LaRouche, looking none too pleased.

"Good afternoon, Sybilla," he said without smiling. "You don't look that busy to me."

Sybilla's heart started pounding so fast she could barely breathe. But she forced herself to reply calmly. "Good afternoon, Mr. LaRouche. Appearances can be deceiving. I am quite busy."

As he came toward her desk quietly and inexorably, Sybilla had to fight down the urge to flee. She could imagine the fear those men must have felt when facing Nevada LaRouche in a gunfight.

He stopped before her desk and looked down at her, his blue eyes cold. "I've sent you three messages today and you wouldn't answer any of 'em. Mind tellin' me why?"

She rose and faced him. "As Molly told you, I've been very busy. And I'm still busy, even if I don't look it to you, so if you'll excuse me . . ."

He sighed. "Woman, you do try a man's patience."

As quick as lightning, the cowboy lunged. Before Sybilla had time to divine his intentions, she found herself clasped in his arms and slung over his shoulder like a burlap bag of horse feed.

"Put me down this instant!" she screeched, trying to kick him in the ribs while she pounded on his back with her fists.

"Not until you and I have a little talk," Nevada replied, striding out of her office.

She might as well have been pounding a brick wall for all the good it did, but Sybilla was so furious at the man's audacity that she kept fighting him as he carried her down the hall.

"Catherine!" she screamed. "He's kidnapping me. Call the police."

Nevada LaRouche just chuckled.

Catherine came running out of her office, but when she saw who was doing the kidnapping, all she said was, "Why, Mr. LaRouche, whatever are you doing to poor Sybilla?"

"Don't worry, doc. I'll bring her back safe and sound. That is, if I don't skin her alive first."

"Catherine," she wailed, "don't just stand there smirking. Do something!"

"That's what you get for keeping a man dangling, Syb," she said before disappearing into her office.

Sybilla muttered an incoherent sound of rage, battered the cowboy's back one last time, then gave up as he carried her through the door and down the steps. She wasn't going to give the insufferable man the satisfaction of making a spectacle of her. As it was, not only was her hair coming loose from its pins, she had to endure the stares and snickers of several passersby before Nevada set her down beside his carriage.

"Get in," he said.

"Over my dead body." And she kicked him in the shins—but not too hard.

The man barely grimaced. "I said, get in."

Sybilla glared at him, then started to walk away, only to find her left wrist grasped in an unyielding hold. She spun around and snarled, "Let go of me this instant!"

"You don't get inside this carriage, I'm going to take you over my knee right here in front of everybody. Now what's it to be?"

One look at his face told her he wasn't making idle threats.

Without a word, Sybilla got inside the carriage, wedged herself in the farthest corner, and debated fleeing through the other door.

"I'd only catch you and bring you back," Nevada said to her unspoken question.

She glared at him, shoved her spectacles in place, and stayed put.

When her abductor got inside, he seated himself across from her, then signaled for the driver to drive on.

Sybilla sat there in stony silence, glowering at him.

LaRouche grinned. "You sure fight like a wildcat, I'll say that for you."

His words didn't mollify her. "How dare you treat me as though I were some—some saloon girl you can manhandle and ridicule!"

His smile died. "You wouldn't talk to me, so I had to do something. I didn't hurt you, did I?"

Sybilla considered telling him that he had broken her ribs and she was in agony, but decided that she didn't want to be on the receiving end of his wrath when he discovered she was lying. "Don't be an idiot. Of course you didn't hurt me."

"Good, 'cause I wouldn't want to. But we do have to talk."

"Talk away, Mr. LaRouche. You've taken me hostage against my will, so I'm not going anywhere."

He leaned back against the squabs and stretched out his long legs perilously close to Sybilla's skirt. "Why you been avoiding me, Sybilla?"

Trembling with indignation, she said, "I've been avoiding you? You've been avoiding me since the Peachtrees' ball, so I merely assumed you never wanted to see me again."

"So that's it." His voice became soft and rough, sending a shiver along Sybilla's arms. "You know that's not true."

"I know no such thing," she retorted, determined not to give an inch.

His brow furrowed in puzzlement, he slowly stroked his drooping mustache. "I had my reasons."

"Oh? And what were they, pray tell?"

"Commerce. Men's business on Wall Street. It had nothing to do with you."

"I see."

"No, I don't expect you do," he said gravely, studying her,

"but I did miss you. And I think you're as pretty as a snowdrop on a mountainside, especially with your yellow hair coming down like that, all soft and loose."

His simple, sincere words made her recall Jean-Claude, her Parisian lover. He had wooed her with stanzas of French poetry and passionate declarations of love that left her dizzy. He had claimed that he loved her, yet he betrayed her and broke her heart. Nevada's words may have been simpler but they were no less eloquent, and Sybilla knew with a deep, abiding certainty that this man would not betray her.

"And if I hadn't missed you so much," she said softly, "I never would have gotten so angry with you."

She rose and brazenly sat next to him, feeling a wash of pleasure as those wary eyes warmed as they roved over her face.

"There's something you should know," she said. "I loved another man once, a lifetime ago. We were lovers."

He shrugged. "I figured as much."

"You did?"

"A woman like you wouldn't roam loose for too long before getting roped. But I don't hold with living in the past."

"Neither do I."

When he reached out to cup her cheek, she turned her face to kiss his rough, callused palm.

"Don't waste your kisses there," he muttered, drawing her into his arms.

He kissed her as though she was a woman who had once had a lover, his mouth heavy and hungry. Sybilla didn't coyly pull away when she felt his tongue take possession of her mouth. She thought fleetingly that he tasted sweet as she welcomed the blissful invasion eagerly. When his hand touched her breast, she acquiesced by placing her own hand over his to stay it.

They parted reluctantly some moments later.

"Is there somewhere we can go?" Sybilla asked, then held her breath waiting for his reply. Would he think her too forward for asking? A woman of loose morals more interested in carnal pleasure than propriety? Would he lose all respect for her? She had to take the risk.

"I know a place . . . if you want to."

Sybilla exhaled softly. "Oh, I want to. But it wouldn't be your rooms in Damon's house, would it? I wouldn't feel comfortable going there."

He shook his head.

She thought of the bustle packed away in her closet. "I have to go home to get something first."

"Then why don't we meet tonight?"

"That would be better. I can tell Catherine I'm going out to see a patient." She would confide in her friend when the time was right, but not while everything was too new and so fragile.

After Nevada ordered his driver to take them back to Washington Square, they held hands in silence.

Then he said, "Someday I want you to tell me all about that other feller. Not right now, but someday."

"Someday I will," she agreed.

Damon stood at one of the many tall windows in the Peach-trees' parlor, parted the heavy velvet curtains and stared out into the street. A warm September rain was falling steadily, glazing Fifth Avenue like a mirror. He watched as cabs drove by, the drivers hunched against the rain, but none of them stopped at the Peachtrees' front door.

Where was she? he wondered. It was almost time for dinner and there was still no sign of Catherine.

He had called in a favor and seen to it that the invitation was for her alone, not her shadow Dr. Flanders, and according to Bella Peachtree, Dr. Stone had accepted the invitation.

He couldn't get Catherine out of his mind, and it infuriated him. What was so special about her? He had known women more beautiful. Her outspokenness was often irritating, and the mere fact that she worked for a living was an affront to the male sex.

Damon smiled at his reflection in the night-black glass. Much as he hated to admit it, he relished her candor. When he recalled the way she verbally demolished that Pease idiot in Newport . . .

Then he remembered what had happened afterward on the front lawn, when the moonlight turned her unbound hair to silver and she went so willingly into his arms.

A voice at his elbow said, "What's so interesting out there, Damon? You've been standing here for hours."

He released the curtain and looked down at Francine. "I was just looking to see if the rain stopped, that's all."

"If it doesn't, it will ruin my new slippers."

Bella Peachtree claimed the room's attention, sparing Damon from commenting.

"I don't know what's keeping our last guest Dr. Stone," she

said, "but I'm afraid I can't hold supper any longer—my chef insists it will be ruined. So please adjourn to the dining room."

The eleven guests rose and followed their hostess out of the parlor.

"Where is Mr. LaRouche tonight?" Francine asked.

"He said he had a previous engagement," Damon replied. Lately Nevada had been going out alone at night without a word of explanation to anyone. But he was a grown man, free to come and go as he pleased.

No sooner was everyone seated at the long mahogany table, than the butler hurried to Mrs. Peachtree's side and whispered something to her.

Bella listened, then announced to her guests, "I'm afraid Dr. Stone won't be able to join us after all. She just telephoned to tell us she's been called away on an emergency."

Polite murmurs of sympathy rippled up and down the table, then talk turned to other matters as the butler served the soup course.

Damon looked at the empty chair directly across from him and wanted to get up and leave. What was the point in staying if she wasn't going to be here?

"Can you imagine if a lady doctor were your wife?" Francine asked. "You'd be right in the midst of an important dinner party like this one, and she'd have to leave to tend some sick person."

"Why, I suppose she would," Damon replied.

"I don't know any man who would tolerate that, except another doctor." Francine turned and looked at him. "Do you suppose that's why she and Dr. Flanders are keeping company?"

Damon clenched his teeth. "I don't know, Francine. You might try asking them."

"Oh, Damon, I couldn't do that. It would be rude."

"I'm sure they keep company for other than professional reasons."

"I can see why he would attract her. He is so handsome and well-connected socially. But I can't understand what he sees in her."

Not wanting to listen to a litany of Catherine's faults from Francine, Damon turned to the elderly lady on his left and began discussing this year's horse show at Madison Square Garden.

He managed to keep the conversation away from Catherine

and her profession for the rest of the evening, and was never so happy to leave a gathering as he was that one.

By the time he said his goodbyes and got into his carriage, it was nearly midnight. Rain was still falling, but it had eased off. Even the city's foul air smelled clean and fresh, as if the falling rain had scrubbed it.

Instead of having his driver take him home, Damon told him to drive down to Washington Square. When they arrived, they parked a short way up the street from Catherine's house. Except for a light on outside the door, the house was dark. No one was home—yet.

Damon listened to the rain pattering softly against the carriage roof as he watched and waited. He was a patient man when he had to be.

Twenty minutes later, his patience was rewarded.

By the glow of the streetlights, he could see two figures hurrying down the street, a woman holding an umbrella tilted at an angle in one hand and a bag in the other. A man strode by her side.

Damon froze. Had Catherine lied to Bella? Did she miss the Peachtrees' dinner just so she could keep an assignation with Flanders?

He recalled what Francine had said at dinner about them being so well suited. They understood the demands of their profession, and that could create a special bond.

As the couple drew closer to Catherine's front stoop, Damon saw that the man he had mistaken for Flanders was really a uniformed policeman escorting her home. He accompanied her up the stairs, took her proffered hand and shook it. When she disappeared inside, he walked back the way he came, swinging his billyclub.

Damon waited until the policeman rounded a corner, then he got out of his carriage and strode across the street through the rain, taking care to avoid the puddles.

He twisted Catherine's doorbell once. No answer. He twisted it again. This time he heard hurried footsteps, followed by her startled face peering out at him through the sidelight.

She opened the door, and he noticed she was wearing a simple shirtwaist, not a formal gown. "Why, Mr. Delancy. Is something wrong? Are you ill?"

"No. I was at the Peachtrees' tonight, and when you didn't arrive, I thought something might have happened to you."

She smiled. "Thank you for your concern, but I'm fine. I was called away on an emergency."

"I see." A cold drop of rain ran off the brim of his top hat and slithered down his neck, making him shiver.

"You look cold," she said, opening the door wide. "Come in."

He thought of her reputation and hesitated. "Your neighbors—"

"My neighbors know this is a doctor's office, and they're used to seeing people coming and going at all hours."

He thanked her and stepped inside the dimly lit corridor, removed his hat, and stood there stiffly, not knowing what to do next.

Catherine smiled. "Why did you come here tonight? It's very late." Deep circles may have shadowed her eyes and her skin was inordinately pale from fatigue, but she held herself together as if her will were steel.

"I wanted to talk."

"Then let me take your coat." When he removed it, she hung it up on a coat tree in the corner, then said, "I'm having my supper in the kitchen. Why don't you join me for a cup of tea and a piece of Molly's poppyseed cake?"

"In the kitchen?"

Her face glowed with amusement. "You remember the kitchen, don't you? The place where the cook prepares meals?"

He smiled sheepishly. "I must confess I haven't been in one since I acquired a cook."

"You're dressed a bit too formally for it, but we'll allow you in anyway. Follow me."

As he followed her down the hall, Damon thought her behavior odd. After what had happened in Newport, he expected her to be a little awkward in his presence, perhaps even embarrassed to face him, or at least hurt that he hadn't seen her since. But she was acting as though the incident had never occurred.

He felt chagrin at this affront to his masculine pride, but he maintained his composure as they entered the kitchen—a warm, immaculate room smelling faintly of soap and cinnamon.

He smiled when he saw the cast-iron stove against one wall and a scarred oak table and chairs right in the middle of the room. "It reminds me of my aunt's kitchen in Nebraska."

His comparison must have pleased her, for she beamed. "Have a seat while I put the kettle on."

He seated himself across from her meager supper of cold

chicken and salad, and immediately wished he had brought her some of the hot lobster and pâté he had eaten tonight. Feeling out of place in his formal attire, he undid his white tie and left it draped around his neck.

"Please excuse me while I finish my supper," she said, seating herself, "but I'm famished."

"Why were you called away?" he asked.

"One of my patients went into premature labor. Her baby died."

He scowled in distaste. "You say that so matter of factly, as if you're discussing the weather."

She didn't bridle in offense. "I know it may seem callous to you, but death is a part of my profession. My patients do die. I can't save them all. If a doctor couldn't accept death as part of life, he—or she—would go insane."

"I've never thought of it that way, but you have a point."

Catherine ate in silence for a moment. When she finished, she said, "I will tell you this. When someone old who has lived a full life dies, I don't feel as bad as when a baby or a child dies. To have their lives end before they even have a chance to begin . . ." She shook her head.

Damon tried to recall what Francine had talked about tonight, but found that he couldn't remember. Yet he was sure what Catherine had just said about death would linger in his mind for a long time.

The kettle started screeching, so Catherine rose and brewed the tea. As Damon watched her, he noticed that her hands were long-fingered and strong, capable of both setting bones and doing something as mundane as making tea. She accomplished the task with economy and grace, and he wondered how adept those hands would be at arousing a man.

He swallowed hard and willed his thoughts elsewhere, fast.

Once Damon had a cup of steaming tea and a generous piece of cake in front of him, Catherine said, "Now, what did you come here to talk to me about?"

He sipped his tea. "I'd like you to spend this weekend at Coppermine, my country house in the Hudson River Valley."

Catherine started, her expression one of surprise and shock. "Mr. Delancy, I—"

"Not alone. Other guests would be there, of course. In fact, if Nevada hasn't invited Dr. Wolcott already, I'm sure he will soon." Damon would see to it.

That seemed to placate her. "What about Miss Ballard?"

He shook his head.

"And Kim Flanders?"

"No."

"I see."

"I enjoy your company, Dr. Stone," he said softly. "I would like us to become better acquainted, and I could not do that with either Flanders or Francine monopolizing us."

At last he had succeeded in flustering her. Her pale cheeks turned a delicate pink and her lower lip trembled ever so slightly.

She hastily rose under the pretext of clearing away her plate, but Damon suspected she was finally remembering Newport and needed to put distance between them. He decided he liked her flustered. She became soft and vulnerable, without her usual physician's cool armor of detachment.

Finally, she said, "If Sybilla agrees to go, than I shall accept your kind invitation as well."

He grinned. "Splendid. You'll have a wonderful time, I promise you."

"I'm sure we will—Sybilla and I, that is."

Damon told her about the Peachtrees' dinner as he ate his cake, and when he finished, he lavished compliments on Molly's baking, then rose to leave.

At the door, after he put on his coat, he took Catherine's hand and drew it to his lips.

"No, please don't," she protested. "My hands still smell of idoform."

She tried to pull away, but he just tightened his grasp and brushed her knuckles with his lips. "The scent is not unpleasant to me."

Her breathing quickened. "How gallant of you to say so, Mr. Delancy."

"Damon, please."

"Then you must call me Catherine."

"With pleasure." He smiled. "Goodnight, Catherine."

"Goodnight, Mr.—er, Damon." She showed him to the door and looked out. "It's stopped raining."

"Why, so it has." He turned to her, wished her goodnight again, and slowly crossed the street, savoring the feel of her eyes on him.

When he got into his carriage he saw she was still standing in the doorway, watching him.

He smiled as he sat back against the squabs. So, she was not immune to him after all.

Four days later, Catherine stood on the deck of Delancy's steam yacht the *Copper Queen* as it sailed up the Hudson River. But she couldn't concentrate on the majestic hills guarding the winding river on either side. She kept thinking of yesterday's confrontation with Kim.

When she went to his house and told him where she and Sybilla were going for the weekend, he turned livid.

His fair brows came together in a scowl, his patrician mouth hardening into a thin line of displeasure. "You're going where?"

"To Damon Delancy's country house."

"Are you aware that he didn't invite me?"

"Mr. Delancy did mention it."

"And you are still going?"

"Well, Sybilla won't go without me, and she wants to go very much." She regarded him in exasperation. "Kim, you are a dear friend and I realize we have been going to these social events together, but I wasn't aware that I'm not allowed to accept invitations that don't include you."

He threw up his hands. "You're right. I don't have any claim on you. I have no right to ask you not to go. It's just that—damn it, Catherine!—I hate to see you going off with another man, especially one as ruthless as Delancy."

Then say something to make me stay, she thought.

"You make it sound as though I'm eloping with him, and that's not the case at all. I'm only doing this for Sybilla." She walked over to him and placed her hand on his arm. "Don't be angry with me, Kim. Please."

She waited, hoping he would take her in his arms and beg her not to go because he loved her and wanted her. She waited for him to stake his claim and fight for her.

But all he did was pat her hand in a brotherly fashion and say, "I could never stay angry with you, Catherine. Go to Delancy's if it will make you happy."

Who could not be happy here? Catherine decided, standing on the deck of a yacht while the mountains loomed blue in the early morning light.

Catherine watched as Damon crossed the spotless deck toward her. Dressed as he was in a casual brown tweed jacket, with a brisk breeze rifling his black hair, he looked less forbidding but no less in command.

"What do you think of the *Queen*?" He stood beside her and leaned his arms against the rail.

"I don't know what's more magnificent," she said, "your yacht or the scenery."

He smiled. "The *Queen* could sail across the Atlantic if she had to, but even I wouldn't claim she's superior to God's artistry." He ran his hand along the shiny brass rail with the delight of a child. "When I was so poor I couldn't even afford a ride on the ferry, I used to spend hours watching the ships sail into New York harbor, dreaming of the exotic places they had seen. I promised myself I would own one some day."

His admission tugged at Catherine's heart. "And now you do."

Just then the captain signaled to Damon, who excused himself and went striding back down the deck.

Sybilla joined her. "This is going to be a glorious weekend, I can just tell."

"I'm surprised you can bear to leave Nevada's side for a second."

"Oh, I'll have him all to myself soon enough." She sighed as her adoring gaze slid back to the lanky cowboy talking with the other guests. "I'll never forget the day he abducted me."

Catherine smiled at the recollection. "Neither will I. You didn't look too pleased with him at the time, hanging over his shoulder and screeching like a banshee."

"He made me see reason." She was silent for a moment. "A woman can't respect a man who won't fight for her, and Nevada proved that he would always fight for me, even against myself."

Catherine thought of Kim. Would he fight for her as Nevada had fought for Sybilla? He hadn't so far.

Sybilla turned her head toward the four people clustered together at the other end of the yacht. "What do you think of the other guests?"

"We just met them this morning. I don't know them well enough to offer an opinion."

"But what are your first impressions? Come, come, I know you have some. You always do," Sybilla pressed.

Catherine looked over at her fellow guests talking with Nevada. A tall, willowy woman stood out.

"Dahlia Talmadge—the banker's wife?—is stunning, but she's

very reticent and remote. I can't explain it, but there's something very strange about her."

"She's dead inside," Sybilla said flatly. "You look into her eyes and nothing looks back out at you. And as for her husband . . ." She shuddered. "He reminds me of those old paintings of satyrs, with their thick leering lips and lecherous eyes."

"And if he slicks down his hair with any more macassar oil . . . The Bonningtons seem harmless though," Catherine added, referring to a middle-aged couple who looked so much alike they resembled brother and sister rather than husband and wife.

Sybilla chuckled. "They're such a pair of tabbies it's hard to believe he runs a successful dry goods business."

Catherine held her straw boater down against a sudden gust of wind off the water. "I wonder why Damon invited them? I've never seen them at the Peachtrees' or Genevra's."

"Nevada told me that Damon wants to borrow money from Talmadge's bank to invest in Bonnington's business or buy it." She yawned. "I don't know. All that talk of financing and stocks puts me to sleep."

Just then the rest of the party drifted over and joined them at the bow.

Damon said, "We're approaching Coppermine to our right. Once we reach the house, we'll drop anchor and a launch will take us to my dock."

Catherine turned her attention to the shore, conscious of Damon standing at her elbow. As the *Copper Queen* glided through the water, the shore appeared to draw closer.

Coppermine stood atop a high hill overlooking the river, and Catherine had to tilt her head back to see it nestled in its grove of stately oak and elm trees, their leaves just beginning to turn vibrant shades of red and gold. To her surprise, it was not an imposing English country home like Briarleigh in Newport, but a small Georgian style house built of white granite.

"This the only place you own, Delancy?" Mr. Talmadge, the banker, asked.

"For now," Damon replied.

Mrs. Bonnington, the businessman's plump wife, said, "I think it's lovely."

"What do you think?" Damon murmured in Catherine's ear.

She turned her head to find those winter eyes regarding her expectantly. "I find it warm, welcoming, and refreshingly unpretentious."

Her answer must have pleased him, for he smiled.

A launch transported them to the dock where two carriages, a brougham and an open victoria, were waiting to take them up to the house.

Once they arrived, went inside and walked around, Catherine felt Damon's eyes on her as if he were watching for her reaction. She didn't need to feign approval as she stepped into the central court atrium that soared past the second floor and ended in a stained glass skylight. Her delight was obvious as she peered into the drawing room and library, small well-proportioned rooms off the atrium.

"No ballroom, Delancy?" Talmadge said, licking his thick lips as he looked around. His wife followed him as silently as a spirit.

"No." Damon's reply was edged with annoyance. "I don't entertain on a large scale here. Coppermine is where I come when I want to get away from people. I don't share it with just anyone."

It must have flattered the banker for Damon to consider him among a select few, for he closed his mouth and didn't find fault with his host's house again.

After Catherine and the other guests were shown to their rooms upstairs, Damon gave them a tour of the house and extensive grounds, including a dairy farm and vast orchards. He didn't leave her side the whole time, and Catherine got the surprising impression that he wished the other guests weren't there.

Once they returned to the house, they ate lunch, then everyone was left to their own devices. Sybilla and Nevada disappeared. Mr. Talmadge insisted the rest of the men go shooting that afternoon, much to Damon's evident annoyance. With Mrs. Bonnington and the banker's wife off to their bedrooms for naps, Catherine decided to sit on the terrace and listen to the leaves rustling in the warm September breeze.

That evening at dinner, Catherine discovered that Damon preferred lively conversation and encouraged everyone—the women included—to discuss anything they wished on topics ranging from the deluge of immigrants to Edwin Booth's last appearance in *Hamlet*. His guests were hesitant at first, but with Damon leading the way, opinions were soon flying right and left.

Later Dahlia played the piano with more technical excellence than passion, and soon it was time to retire.

Just as Catherine was about to climb the staircase leading

upstairs, Damon stopped her. "Come out onto the terrace. I haven't been alone with you all day."

Catherine's pulse quickened as he escorted her through the French doors, then closed them behind him. She hid her nervousness at being alone with him by going over to the balustrade and looking down at the silver river.

"Glad you came?" he asked softly, coming up behind her.

She turned and smiled. "Yes. I hadn't realized how much I needed a change of scene until I came here. Coppermine is beautiful."

He stood beside her. The moonlight filtering through the trees cut dark, brooding hollows into his lean face. "I thought you'd appreciate it."

"Dinner was a novel experience," she said, placing her hands on the cool stone balustrade.

Damon grinned, a wide white flash. "Most dinners are so damned boring. All that talk of privet hedges and Miss Minnie Mumble's trip to Rome is enough to make me fall asleep in my soup. So in my home, I demand at least a little stimulating conversation from my guests. It's one of my many eccentricities."

Catherine smiled. "I'm afraid most women aren't adept at making stimulating conversation. No one encourages us to do so."

"Oh, you always hold your own, but Sybilla—" Damon shook his head in wonder. "She gives new meaning to the term 'plain speaking.'"

Catherine laughed at that. "She is opinionated, but Nevada doesn't seem to mind."

"Yes, he's quite smitten."

"And she with him."

She felt those compelling eyes on her, and she shivered.

"Cold?"

"A little. I should have worn my shawl."

He looked at her. "Would you like to go riding with me tomorrow before breakfast?"

"Riding? On a horse?"

He raised his thick brows. "What else?"

"I—I don't ride. I don't like horses. They're big and I'm afraid of them."

He gaped at her. "Dr. Stone afraid of horses? I don't believe it."

"Well, it's true. Ask Sybilla."

"You don't have to be afraid. I'll mount you on a horse so gentle a baby could ride her."

Catherine stood there for a moment considering his request. Finally she capitulated. "All right, I'll go. But if I break my neck, it will be your fault."

"Don't worry. I wouldn't let anything happen to your beautiful neck."

The rough intimacy in his voice made her shiver again. Damon was standing so close his sleeve was almost touching her bare arm.

"We should go in," he said almost reluctantly.

Once inside, he bade her goodnight and told her he would meet her in the atrium at eight o'clock sharp.

Damon found Catherine waiting for him the following morning. She wore a dark blue jacket that accentuated her full bosom and narrow waist, and no hat to hide her upswept brown hair that danced with golden lights. "Good morning."

When she noticed he was wearing top boots and riding breeches, her face fell in dismay. "I'm afraid I don't have a riding habit."

"Your skirt looks sturdy enough. Besides, we're rather informal up here unless we're riding with the Dutchess Hunt Club."

When they walked out the front door, he saw a groom holding the horses he had requested, a tall chestnut gelding for him and a small black mare wearing a sidesaddle for Catherine.

She approached the mare warily.

"Don't be afraid to pet old Star here," Damon said. "She won't bite."

She put out a tentative hand and patted the small white star on the mare's forehead. "I wonder why you named her that?"

He smiled. "It was either that or Blackie. Now let's get you up in the saddle."

Catherine swallowed hard and gamely stepped forward. When she put her left foot into the stirrup, Damon grasped her around the waist disappointingly armored by her corset and lifted her into the sidesaddle, where she sat stiff with nervousness.

"Relax," he said gently as he handed her the reins. "You're not going to your execution."

"It's a long way down to the ground from up here. And the ground is hard."

"Then don't look down," he said, effortlessly mounting his own horse. Then they started off.

"Sit up straight," he said. "You're slouching."

"I'm just trying to keep my balance. What if I fall off?"

"If you feel yourself falling, bring your left knee up against the horn. You'll stick to that sidesaddle like glue."

As they rode through the wooded park, Damon kept an eye on Catherine, but the farther they rode, the more she relaxed.

"It's so beautiful here in the morning," she said in a hushed voice, "so different from New York City."

Damon readily agreed. Except for the muffled clopping of their horses' hooves and the occasional raucous crowing of fractious crows, the park was silent. Sunlight slanted through the trees, turning dewdrops into diamonds scattered in the grass. Traces of fog still hung like ghostly wraiths down along the river's edge, and the air was as bracing as gin.

"I'm surprised you left your patients to come here," he said.

"Oh, even a doctor is entitled to a day or two off," she replied, reaching out to pat Star's neck. She looked over at him. "You ride very well. Did you learn when you were out west?"

He nodded. "The horses weren't as elegant or well-mannered as this blue-blooded beast, but they taught me what I needed to know."

"I'm a city girl myself. I never had much of an opportunity to ride in Cleveland, just the odd pony now and then."

"We'll have to see to it that you get more practice in Central Park."

"Thank you, but I'm afraid I don't have the time for riding in Central Park."

"Not even if I promise to make another sizable donation to the Women's Dispensary?"

She tried hard not to smile. "You would resort to bribery?"

"Yes."

"Well, perhaps that could persuade me."

He burst out laughing at that.

They rode out of the park, crossed the road and headed for an open field bounded by low stone walls that had been there for over a century.

Damon wasn't expecting the rabbit that bounded out from beneath a shrub and streaked across Star's path. The mare threw up her head, squealed in surprise and was galloping across the field with more speed than Damon believed she had in her. His heart in his mouth, he kicked his gelding and went tearing after the runaway.

As he raced after them, he prayed Catherine wouldn't panic and fall off before he could reach her. But she must have remembered what he told her about the sidesaddle horn because she was still in the saddle.

The chase was over before it began. Star must have decided that running away was too strenuous. She slowed down of her own volition, and when she finally came to a stop at the edge of the woods, she lowered her head and began grazing nonchalantly.

Damon was out of the saddle and running before his horse came to a full stop. "Catherine!"

Her face was ashen, her blue eyes wide with shock. When he reached up for her, she tumbled out of the saddle and into his arms. He could feel her trembling, hear her breath coming in ragged gasps.

"Easy," he murmured, enfolding her in his arms and resting his cheek against the top of her head. "You're all right. It's all over and you're safe. Hush."

He expected her to burst into tears, but wasn't surprised when she didn't. She simply sagged against him, and when she regained her composure and her breathing returned to some semblance of normalcy, she drew away, her eyes filled with accusation.

"You swore that horse was gentle enough for a baby to ride. I could have been killed!"

"But you weren't."

A surge of relief so overwhelmed him that Damon reached for her again, grasping her by the shoulders to hold her still while he sought her mouth with his own. The moment his lips touched hers, Catherine caught her breath, then let it out with a sigh of surrender as her arms slid around his waist, pulling him toward her. She was safe. His hands slid down her arms and across her back just to make sure. Then he sifted his fingers through her hair, reveling in its heavy, silken texture.

Without warning, Catherine stiffened and pulled away. "What am I thinking of?" she cried. Then she glared at him. "Is that why you invited me here, so you could take such liberties with me?"

"You didn't think I took such liberties that night in Newport.

In fact, you seemed to enjoy kissing me then, just as you did now.''

Her fury evaporated. ''We both had too much champagne, then. And now, I'm just too overwrought to think clearly.''

He walked up to her, placed his fingers beneath her chin and forced her to look at him. ''Don't blame the champagne or this near accident. You wanted me to kiss you. Admit it.''

She looked away. ''If I did, it was a mistake.''

That stung him. His hand fell to his side. ''Why was it a mistake?'' he asked gently.

Disarmed, she sighed. ''I—I'm sorry if I've offended you. It's just that I don't wish to encourage any . . . romantic notions, if that is what you are harboring.''

Damon rocked back on his heels. Francine and half the women in New York would do anything to encourage such romantic notions in him, and here the most fascinating woman he had ever met was rejecting him.

He raised one brow. ''I thought you enjoyed my company. Why are you suddenly keeping me at arm's length?''

''Because medicine is such an exacting taskmaster. It leaves no room in a doctor's life for anything else.''

Damon studied her thoughtfully as she stood there with her arms crossed, looking as determined as Joan of Arc. ''Or anyone?''

''Only as a friend, nothing more.''

''Is it because of Flanders?''

''Of course not. Kim has no claim on me. We're good friends and colleagues, that's all.''

He extended his hand. ''Well, if friendship is all you can offer me, Catherine, than I shall count myself proud to be your friend.'' Damon grinned slowly. ''But I intend to change your mind about romantic notions.''

She looked at him with a strange assessing look, then extended her hand. ''You can try.''

''I never can resist a challenge.'' Her fingers were warm and strong against his, and he had to resist the urge to pull her into his arms again. He was going to have to go slowly with this one.

''Shall we go back to the house for breakfast?'' he said. ''I'm starved.''

Catherine regarded the grazing mare reluctantly. ''Can I walk?''

"No. If you don't get back on, you'll always be afraid to ride again, so up you go."

She made a face, but she bravely let him lift her into the saddle.

As Damon mounted his own horse and they rode side by side back to the house, he considered her words carefully. She had been more than honest with him. She had made it clear that medicine came first in her life.

He wasn't used to being second best in anything he attempted, and the experience was a novel one. It just made him more determined than ever to win her.

NINE

FOUR weeks later, Catherine was busy restocking her medical cabinet when Sybilla appeared in the doorway.

"Are you going to go horseback riding with us this afternoon?" she asked. "It's such a perfect sunny day, and the air is brisk."

Catherine shook her head. "Genevra asked if I would stop by to examine little Stone, so as soon as I finish putting these away, I'll be off."

Sybilla came in, took several bottles and started helping. "She sends for you every time that poor child sneezes."

"After all she went through to give birth to him, she's afraid of losing him, and I can't say that I blame her."

"Perhaps when you're through there, you can join us."

"I don't think so. I'm not in the mood for riding today."

Sybilla sighed dreamily. "I'm always in the mood for spending time with Nevada. I love watching the children's faces when they see him come riding by on his painted pony with that western saddle and lariat of his."

Catherine smiled as she recalled the awestruck stares. "He is a magnificent sight."

"You really should come. Your riding has improved, and you want to get some use out of that new riding habit you bought, don't you?"

Catherine knelt down to put several bottles on the lower shelf. "There will be other opportunities."

"But Damon will be so disappointed if you don't come."

Catherine rose and brushed her skirt. "Oh, I doubt that. The four of us went riding just last Sunday and out to dinner at Delmonico's two nights ago. He knows my medical practice puts constraints on my time."

Sybilla looked as though she were about to say something, then changed her mind. She fit in one last bottle, then closed the door. "Well, we'll just have to go without you, then. I'm off to change. Give my regards to Genevra and little Stone."

"I will."

Catherine smiled as she watched Sybilla sail out of the room, then she turned her attention back to the remaining bottles.

Damon will be so disappointed . . .

She set down a bottle of laudanum and seated herself at her desk. She had to stop seeing Damon so often to put some distance between them before she became entangled in an emotional web. But then she remembered the morning Star ran away with her, the gut-wrenching panic at losing control, the fear of falling under those iron-shod hooves. And she remembered the relief when she tumbled into Damons' waiting arms, the feeling of safety and security.

She remembered his kiss all too well. Worse yet, she had enjoyed it.

She forced that disturbing thought out of her mind, locked the laudanum in the cabinet, and got ready to leave for Genevra's.

When she arrived at the Grahams' half an hour later, she was surprised the butler showed her into the Tiffany drawing room rather than the nursery.

Genevra, looking elegant in a teagown of rust-colored velvet trimmed with a waterfall of ecru lace spilling down the bodice, rose to greet her. "Catherine . . ."

Catherine set down her bag and looked around in puzzlement. "Good afternoon, Genevra. Where is Stone?"

"My dear little son is in the nursery," she replied, "but before you see him, I thought we might have a little talk. Please, do sit down."

Once Catherine sat down, Genevra plucked at the lace of her bodice. "Is it true what I've heard?"

Catherine blinked in confusion. "What have you heard?"

"That you are keeping company with Damon Delancy."

She regarded Genevra in dismay. "Damon and I have not been 'keeping company.' I spent a weekend at his country house along with five other guests. I occasionally go horseback riding or to the theater with him, but Sybilla and Nevada are always with us. We are never alone." *Almost never,* she amended.

"I thought you should know that everyone in society is talking about you two. They want to know who you are and where you come from. I've heard that Francine Ballard has taken to her bed, and every mama who has ever flung an eligible daughter in Damon's path wants to know if he's going to marry you.''

''Marry! That is preposterous. We are good friends, nothing more.''

Genevra sighed. ''I thought so. But he does speak highly of you. He thinks you're intelligent, beautiful, and charming. Gordie heard him say you were the most intriguing woman he's ever met.''

Catherine blushed. ''Oh, come now, Genevra.''

''It's true.'' She sighed. ''I wish men found me intriguing instead of beautiful. Gordie does, of course, but it's not the same.''

''I admire Damon, but I don't have romantic feelings for him. And being the object of gossip upsets me.''

''I know. That's why I wanted to tell you what people were saying.''

''Thank you. You're a good friend. Now, shall I go up and check little Stone?''

''Please do. He's been sneezing all morning.''

By the time Catherine finished examining the baby, who had nothing more serious than a mild case of sniffles, her annoyance with being the brunt of gossip had dissipated.

As she sat back in the hansom for the return trip to Washington Square, Catherine felt like a pawn on a chessboard, with society making the moves. Well, they would soon learn they couldn't manipulate her.

So Damon thought her intelligent and beautiful, ''the most intriguing woman he's ever met''? She smiled, pleased in spite of herself. But it didn't change anything. She had warned him about harboring any romantic notions, and if he persisted, he would only get rebuffed.

No sooner did Catherine arrive home than Molly told her Dr. Hilda Steuben wanted her at the dispensary, so she turned around and rushed back out again. She didn't manage to drag herself home until eight o'clock that evening.

Sybilla was in the parlor, her spectacles sliding down her nose as she read the *New York Herald*. She looked up as Catherine entered. ''Another emergency?''

Catherine rubbed the back of her stiff neck. ''More like five. Two premature births, one beating, one knifing, and one broken leg—that's all.'' She sat down and put her feet up. ''How was your ride?''

''Just wonderful. But Damon missed you.'' When Catherine made no comment, Sybilla said, ''Have you read about his latest exploits in the paper?''

''Damon? What has he done this time?''

''He's taken over a large steamship line. Here, read it for yourself.''

As she took the paper from Sybilla, Catherine thought of the penniless orphan who had watched the ships sail into New York harbor and swore that he would own one someday. Now he owned a whole fleet of them.

Catherine just scanned the article, as the jargon of commerce was as incomprehensible to her as the mysteries of medicine were to others.

She said, ''It would appear that the battle to acquire this shipping line was a long and bitter one.''

''That's what Damon said, but he looked ecstatic that he had finally won it, like a Norman knight conquering the Saxons.'' Sybilla leaned forward, her eyes shining. ''He's going to give a ball in two weeks to celebrate, and we're invited, of course. And we'll need new gowns. If you wear your burgundy silk one more time . . .''

Catherine set down the paper and sniffed. ''Is that all you can think of, balls and ballgowns? I thought we were supposed to be doctors, not society belles.''

Sybilla reared back in her chair. ''Now just one minute, Cat. I resent your implication that I am somehow less dedicated than you just because I enjoy getting dressed up and having a good time now and then!''

''I—''

''I go to Bellevue every morning to perform surgery, and I see to my patients here when I come home. I work in the tenements more than Kim Flanders does, so I think I'm entitled to enjoy myself now and then.''

Having spoken her mind, Sybilla crossed her arms and glared tight-lipped at her friend.

Catherine rubbed her aching forehead. ''I'm sorry, Syb. I didn't mean to imply anything of the sort. Genevra said something that upset me, that's all, and I apologize for taking it out on you.''

The apology placated Sybilla in an instant. "What did she say?"

Catherine told her, then rose and began pacing the parlor. "I have no use for society, Syb, and I don't want to get drawn into its petty intrigues and manipulations. I had enough of it being brought up by Ruth, thank you very much. It's too rigid and confining."

"So what are you going to do, stop caring for Stone and Hortensia because their parents are members of society? Are you going to stop seeing Kim and Damon because they occupy that same social circle?"

"Damon and Nevada are different. They don't belong in that world any more than I do."

Sybilla sighed. "Cat, you are fretting over nothing. No one is going to force you to conform to society's rules if you don't want to. You haven't yet, and neither have I."

"I detest gossip, especially when it's unfounded, and it seems to thrive among the wealthy."

Sybilla fell into a thoughtful silence. "What are your feelings for Damon?"

Catherine thought of how his cold gray eyes warmed with laughter whenever something she said amused him. "He's a friend, like Kim."

"You're not answering my question."

"I like him well enough," she retorted in exasperation.

"I always thought you wanted to get married."

"Oh, I don't know. I'm beginning to think that men are just too much of a distraction."

"The more time I spend with Damon," Sybilla said, "the more I like him, even more so than Kim. Damon's the kind of man who can go to a ball and charm a duchess out of her tiara, then go down to a bar and drink the stevedores under the table without compromising who he is."

Catherine was silent for a moment as she pondered Sybilla's assessment. "Considering his background, it's not surprising."

"Not that he can match Nevada, of course."

Catherine smiled. Sybilla would think that, being in love with the man. "Well, if we're going to attend Damon's victory ball, I think we had better notify the dressmaker, don't you?"

"I'll do that the first thing tomorrow morning," Sybilla said. "I think you'd look lovely in blue velvet with perhaps a touch of brocade."

"You're the expert."

• • •

Catherine nervously fingered the plush midnight-blue velvet evening cape Sybilla had talked her into buying, and stared out the window of Damon's carriage.

"I hope it doesn't snow," she said.

"It's November," Sybilla replied. "The weather is always so unpredictable. But it wouldn't dare snow on the night of Damon's ball."

Catherine smiled. "I doubt that even Damon would claim to control the weather."

Moments later, they arrived at Damon's house, a mansion on "Millionaire's Row" at the upper end of Fifth Avenue near Central Park. While not as huge as Cornelius Vanderbilt's 57th Street mansion—a replica of Fontainebleu made of red pressed brick with limestone trim—Damon's English manor house was no less impressive.

Damon and Nevada were at the door to meet them.

"You look beautiful," Damon said, his eyes sparkling as he handed Catherine out of the carriage and tucked her hand in the crook of his arm.

"Thank you. And you look handsome, as always."

"So you think me handsome after all," he murmured as he escorted her inside, followed by Nevada and Sybilla. "I was beginning to wonder."

Catherine felt her cheeks grow warm as she realized this was the first time she had ever complimented Damon on his looks.

As they entered the foyer, a liveried footman stepped forward to claim their wraps, but Damon removed Catherine's cape himself, letting his hands linger for just a moment on her shoulders as he slid the garment off.

When he saw her gown, he bowed low over her hand. "You should always dress this way."

That annoyed her. "Ah, yes, bound in velvet and brocade, unable to set a collarbone or deliver a baby."

Damon scowled. "You needn't be so touchy. I meant it as a compliment, nothing more."

Sybilla, who looked stunning in a gown of seafoam-green stamped velvet, interrupted them. "Damon, you've outdone yourself. You've created spring in here while it's winter outside."

And he had. The profusion of hothouse roses, pansies, carnations, and azaleas delicately perfumed the air and gave the illusion of springtime in November.

Then Sybilla said, "Nevada, why don't we try out the dance floor before the other guests arrive?"

"Suits me." He took her hand and they walked off.

Damon turned to Catherine. "I have a favor to ask of you."

"Oh?"

"Would you receive my guests with me?"

Her hand flew to her chest in panic. "I—I couldn't. People would assume we were . . . more than friends."

He raised one brow. "Do you mean to tell me that the un-conventional Dr. Stone cares what other people think? You disappoint me."

Catherine stared at him in chagrin. "Of course I don't care what other people think."

"Then you'll join me?"

She sighed. "All right. I'll do it as a favor to you."

His cold gray eyes warmed. "This means a great deal to me, Catherine."

"But what about Francine Ballard?"

"What about her?"

"Won't she feel slighted that you didn't ask her?"

"Probably. But both you and Francine make too many false assumptions about my feelings for her."

She looked around the foyer in resignation. "Where shall I stand to receive your guests?"

They stood in the vestibule off the foyer when the first guests started to trickle in ten minutes later. In half an hour, the trickle turned into an endless stream of elegant, bejeweled people. Catherine ignored the speculative looks, whispers and false smiles, and greeted Damon's guests as graciously as if she were his wife, even when Francine passed through and gave her a cold, hard stare.

She was so relieved to see Genevra's friendly face that she didn't notice a frantic man in a dark gray coat elbowing his way through the receiving line.

As the man stepped up to them, Catherine felt Damon tense up at her side and say, "Rollins, what in the hell are you doing here?"

People stepped back as if sensing something was amiss. An eerie silence filled the vestibule.

Catherine looked at the man Damon had just addressed, and her blood ran cold at the desperation in his eyes.

"Damn it, Delancy!" Rollins cried, his shrill voice rising. "Why'd you have to do it? Why'd you have to take it all?"

His shaking hand dipped into his coat pocket and he drew out a gun, its blue-black barrel glinting ominously in the flickering gaslight. A collective horrified gasp rose from the guests. Before Catherine had a chance to blink, Damon flung out his arm and pushed her behind him.

Over Damon's shoulder, Catherine watched as several of the men divined Rollins' intent and lunged for him, but it was too late. With a twisted leer of triumph, Rollins put the gun to his temple and fired. Women screamed as the crack split the air. Rollins' body jerked once from the bullet's impact, showering bystanders with blood and brains. Then he sank to the white marble floor as if he were a puppet whose strings had just been cut.

Damon surged forward while guests came pouring out of the ballroom like a herd of stampeding cattle. Pandemonium reigned as men and women milled about. Catherine had to fight her way to Damon's side, where he was down on one knee beside the man whose shattered head was resting in a pool of blood. Gathering the hem of her gown out of the way, she reached down and felt the man's neck for a pulse. There was nothing.

"I'm afraid he's dead," she said.

Damon's ashen face mirrored his devastation. "Damn him. It didn't have to end this way."

Catherine looked up and saw that Francine was lying not far off in a swoon. "You," she snapped to the man cradling her. "I'll need her shawl."

Too stunned to refuse, the man gave it to her, and Catherine draped it over Rollins' head.

She grasped Damon's shoulder, hard. "You'll have to call the police, and I'd suggest that you send your guests home. At least those that aren't witnesses."

He nodded, but when he didn't move, Catherine wondered if he had really understood her. Nevada, however, did.

"Ball's over, folks," he said.

It was after midnight before Catherine could think clearly. By listening to the police question Damon, she learned that

Oscar Rollins had been president of the shipping company Damon acquired. Damon had dismissed him just two days ago.

Finally, when the footmen removed the body and the last policeman left, a haggard Damon came into the parlor where Catherine and Sybilla were sitting and waiting.

"That's the last of them," he said, rubbing his bloodshot eyes. "I think you should leave before the newspaper reporters start descending on me once they get a whiff of this."

Catherine rose. "I'd like to stay." When she saw Damon's questioning look, she amended, "For a little while longer. If you don't mind."

"Mind?" He reached out and caressed her cheek. "If you hadn't offered, I would have asked you to stay."

Sybilla looked from Catherine to Damon, stifled an exaggerated yawn and rose. "I'll have Nevada take me home. I'll see you there, Cat." She wished them goodnight and left.

Catherine took one look at Damon and her heart went out to him. His disheveled black hair stood on end as if he had been raking it repeatedly with his fingers, and his face looked haggard and drawn with shock, the beginnings of a beard shadowing his jaw. Droplets of dried blood spattered his white shirtfront, a potent reminder of the tragedy.

"Let's go into your study," she said gently. As strong as he was, Damon needed her.

He nodded and led the way down the hall.

When they entered the room, Catherine closed the door behind them. "Sit down. You look as though you're ready to drop."

With a groan, he sank down in the nearest chair, propped his elbows on his knees, and cradled his head in his hands. "I'm sorry you had to witness that, Catherine. A man blowing his brains out isn't a pretty sight."

She knelt before him and grasped his cold hands. "You're forgetting that I'm a doctor. I've seen much worse." Her voice trembled slightly when she said, "I'm glad he didn't shoot you."

He squeezed her hands in return. "By the time this is over, I'll probably wish he had."

"Don't even say that in jest," she snapped. Then she looked around the cozy study. "Do you have any brandy?"

He nodded toward a cabinet. Catherine rose and found a bottle of bourbon and several glasses. She filled one almost to the top and set it before him. "Drink it. You'll feel better."

"Doctor's orders?"

"Doctor's orders."

He drained the glass in one obedient swallow, leaned back in the chair and closed his eyes. "Lord, what a nightmare. I can't wait to read the newspapers tomorrow."

She took the chair across from him, her mind roiling with questions. "May I ask you something?"

"Anything."

"Why was Rollins so despondent that he felt the need to kill himself in front of you?"

"Because I ruined him."

The bald words shocked her. "I can't believe you'd do something like that."

Damon's eyes flew open. "Ah, sweet, loyal Catherine, always seeing the best in everyone. Alas, I'm afraid it's true. You heard what I told the police. I took over Rollins' shipping company, then dismissed him so my own people could run it." He rested his head back again and watched her out of narrowed eyes.

Something told Catherine not to press it, but she had to. "I don't understand. Was it necessary to ruin him? That's so—so calculated."

Damon shrugged. "I had nothing personal against the man. I just wanted his company and did what was necessary to acquire it. He didn't play the game as well as I, so he lost."

"One's life seems a high price to pay for losing a game."

"I didn't put that gun to his head or pull the trigger. Other men lose their positions, their entire fortunes, yet they go on. But Rollins was weak, and only the strong survive."

"But what happens to the people who work for a company that you acquire?"

"Some keep their jobs and others lose them. My main concern is a company's growth and profitability."

"You shock me, Damon. Your employees are human beings just like you or I, with wives and children and dreams of their own." Her voice rose incredulously. "And you say that money is more important?"

"I'm a capitalist, not a socialist. I'm concerned with making a profit."

"And I'm a doctor concerned with helping those people you scorn, so it would appear we're working at cross purposes."

She rose, walked over to one of the windows and pushed aside the heavy velvet drape. It was beginning to snow, huge flakes hiding in the darkness until they strayed into the light of the streetlamp.

"You're a powerful man, aren't you?" she mused aloud, trying to fight the growing disillusionment that saddened her. "You can create springtime in November. Take away a man's livelihood and self-respect. Perhaps even drive him to his death."

"Catherine, Catherine . . ." he murmured reproachfully.

She heard him rise and watched his reflection materialize in the dark window glass. When she felt his hands rest lightly on her bare shoulders, she shrugged him off.

"I've upset you, haven't I?" His breath was warm against her neck. "I can sense you withdrawing from me."

She turned. "I'm seeing another side to you, Damon, a ruthless, heartless side I never dreamed existed. A side I don't find attractive."

A muscle worked in his jaw. "So you think me heartless? Was I heartless the day you fell on the ice? Was I so heartless when Star ran away with you?"

His deep, persuasive voice conjured memories of the man who made her laugh and offered such sweet comfort, and his compelling eyes dared her to look away.

When Catherine said nothing, he murmured, "Answer me."

"You've never shown me anything but kindness."

"I would never hurt you, Catherine." He traced the line of her jaw with his thumb. "But I'm far from perfect. I have more than my share of faults."

"I'm not asking for perfection. But quite frankly, this side of you frightens me."

"Frightens you? I don't want you to fear me." Then he reached for her before she could step away, crushing her to his chest, his cheek unyielding against her own. "Dear God, you know that's not what I want!"

She squeezed her eyes shut and almost succumbed to his hunger for her, but all she could see was Oscar Rollins lying lifeless in his own blood.

Catherine steeled herself and pulled away. "I—I think I had best be going. It's very late and it's beginning to snow."

Damon's left arm shot out, barring her way. "I can't let you go. Not when this lies unsettled between us."

"Let me go or I swear you'll never see me again."

He studied her for a moment with burning eyes, then dropped

his arm in resignation. "You're free to go. I won't keep you here against your will."

Judging by Damon's determined expression, Catherine suspected he would do just that if he could get away with it.

She said nothing as she started for the door.

After they left the study and Damon fetched her wrap, they walked in strained silence to the door, where another carriage waited.

As he assisted Catherine up the steps, he said, "I will call on you tomorrow afternoon."

"That's too soon. I need time alone to think."

His eyes appeared black and implacable in the snowy darkness. "Very well, but don't think you can avoid me forever. We will settle this, I promise you."

Then he shut the door and the carriage rolled off.

From the doorway, Damon watched the carriage until the swirling snow swallowed it, then he went inside. The foyer was silent except for the sound of one of the maids scrubbing what was left of Rollins off the shiny marble floor.

He returned to his study, poured himself another shot of bourbon, and sat down to think.

Catherine had inadvertently shown him her weakness tonight: she had a soft heart for anyone who was sick or distressed.

Damon smiled. When she had seen him stunned and shaken by Rollins' death, she came to his side, taking control, sharing her comfort and strength. And she had stayed with him.

Damon sat back and steepled his fingers. He agreed with Catherine's assessment that he was calculating. With a few well-placed comments here and there, he had fueled rumors linking his name with hers, so she would get used to the idea. Now he had to win back her trust.

He needed to find a way to use tonight's scandal to his advantage.

Damon found the numbers of several newspaper reporters he knew who owed him favors, went over to the telephone and put his plan into action.

"Have you seen today's *Sun* and *World*?" Kim demanded late the following afternoon, the moment Catherine walked into her foyer.

"No," she replied, pulling off her mittens and unwinding her blue knit scarf. "I've been at the dispensary all day, amputating an eleven-year-old girl's toes. She had frostbite."

And all the while thinking of her bitter parting from Damon.

"What's in the papers that warranted your coming over here?" she asked, removing her coat and hanging it up.

"I'm surprised you haven't heard. The whole town's talking about the man who shot himself at Delancy's ball last night."

"I saw it, Kim. I was there."

"I suspected as much. Delancy didn't invite me. I think he doesn't want any competition in his pursuit of you."

"He is not pursuing me." She rubbed her cold hands together briskly. "Would you like some tea?"

"No, thank you."

"Molly?" Catherine called out. "Tea, please?" Then she turned to Kim. "What do the papers say?"

Kim followed her into the parlor. "Nothing complimentary. Excoriating, in fact," he added with relish. "Robbing a man of his livelihood. Driving him to suicide. Leaving his widow and six children destitute. Read them for yourself."

Catherine took the papers, seated herself and began to read the *Sun*.

"Public opinion isn't on his side. They're calling the 'Wolf of Wall Street' the 'Widowmaker' now," Kim went on. "Outraged citizens have been gathering outside his house and harassing him."

Catherine's head jerked up. "What?"

"Jeering at him, throwing snowballs at his carriage. It's no less than he deserves."

She frowned. "You are exceedingly charitable today, Dr. Flanders."

"You don't mean to say you feel sympathy for a man like that? Catherine, Damon Delancy drove another man to his death! Surely you can't defend what he did."

"Of course not. But neither do I believe in gloating over someone else's misfortunes."

Molly bustled in with the large tea tray, set it down, then left. Catherine poured herself a cup in silence, then returned to the papers while Kim stared at her in chagrin.

After reading for a few minutes, Catherine threw down the papers in disgust. "They make him sound like a monster!"

"He is," Kim replied coolly. "And I'm mystified by your defense of him."

She felt her cheeks grow warm. Why was she defending Damon to Kim? Just last night she had said much the same thing to Damon himself and would have agreed with Kim's assessment wholeheartedly—Damon Delancy was a ruthless, unscrupulous man.

Just then the front door opened and Sybilla's voice came floating in from the foyer. "Br-r-r! It's cold out there. If I don't get a cup of tea at once, my blood will freeze."

She popped into the parlor doorway. "So there you are. And Kim, too. This is a surprise."

He said, "We're just discussing the Delancy debacle. Perhaps you can explain why Catherine feels compelled to defend him."

Sybilla looked from Kim to Catherine as she shook snow from the hem of her coat. "I would never presume to explain Catherine to anyone."

After hanging up her coat and joining them, Sybilla said, "Now, what is all this about Damon? I caught a few snippets of rumor in the hospital, but didn't pay much attention to them."

"Read for yourself," Catherine said, handing her several newspapers.

Sybilla scanned the headlines, then shot Catherine an alarmed look. "Kim," she began with a sweetly apologetic smile, "would you be so kind as to excuse us? There's something I've got to discuss with Cat in private."

He rose reluctantly. "Of course. I must be going anyway. I just stopped by to see if Catherine had heard about Delancy."

After Kim left, Catherine turned to Sybilla with a grateful smile. "Thank you. I was beginning to wonder if he would ever leave."

Sybilla shut the parlor door. "Came to gloat, did he?"

"Oh, yes. He displayed a side that's not very admirable, I'm afraid."

"That's because he's in love with you. But it's more than Kim, isn't it? I can tell you're upset, and I suspect it has something to do with Damon and what happened last night after Nevada and I left."

Catherine sighed wearily as she sat down on the divan. "I wanted to talk to you about it this morning, but you had already left for the hospital."

Sybilla sat down next to her. "Talk about what?"

Catherine told her what she and Damon had discussed. "He was like someone I didn't know, Syb—cold and calculating and unscrupulous. When I left his house last night, I felt so appalled that I wasn't sure I ever wanted to see him again. Yet just now, after reading the terrible things they've written about him in the papers, I want to rush right over there.'' She rose and began pacing the parlor. "I feel like a bouncing ball—up, down, up, down.''

"That's because you like Damon's good side, but now you've discovered another side to him, one you can't admire at all. So each side is pulling you back and forth.''

Catherine pondered that for a moment. "That's plausible.''

"Nevada isn't perfect either,'' Sybilla began. "I don't like the idea that he's killed men in gun fights. But I have to decide if I'm going to accept his imperfections, or never see him again.''

"You don't have to tell me what you've decided.''

Sybilla grinned. "You know me too well.'' Then her smile died. "Think about Damon's situation for a moment, and I think you'll find that there's more to admire than condemn. Besides, do you really want to stop seeing him? Forever?''

Catherine thought of his teasing smile and the way his cold gray eyes lit up whenever they met her gaze. When she recalled his tenderness and concern, the thought of never seeing him again felt like a blow.

"No,'' she admitted. "I don't want to stop seeing him. The very thought kept me awake half the night.''

"I know. I heard you pacing the floor.''

Catherine set down her teacup. "I think I'll go over there. I'm sure he'd like seeing a friendly face, especially after today.''

Sybilla smiled. "I'm sure he would.''

As she sat in a hansom cab weaving its way through the snowy, slushy street, Catherine considered Sybilla's advice and thought of Damon. No one could blame Damon for seeking to insulate himself with wealth, having spent his childhood in such poverty. He had contributed generously to the dispensary and remained loyal to friends like Nevada. Catherine didn't doubt for an instant that if she ever needed him, he would be at her side without her even asking.

Damon was also one of the most attractive men Catherine had ever met.

She shivered as she watched the winter afternoon slide into twilight along Fifth Avenue. When Damon held her in his arms and kissed her, he made her feel wanton and desirable on some primitive level she didn't profess to understand. And she knew instinctively that he desired her.

She felt her pulse quicken as Damon's mansion came into view. It may have been in the middle of a city, but it looked as solitary and shunned as some gothic estate on the edge of a desolate, windswept moor. The hecklers had all gone home to their warm houses and suppers.

She would be alone with Damon.

The moment she disembarked from the cab and stepped into the foyer, she sensed the rightness of her coming here. No flowers perfumed the air, no thick puddle of blood stained the floor. Only a subdued silence remained.

Catherine gave her name to the butler, who disappeared down the corridor leading to Damon's study.

"Catherine?"

She looked up to find Damon standing at the top of the curved marble staircase. "Good afternoon, Damon."

Catherine studied him as he walked down the stairs, his step slow and measured as if he were uncertain how she would receive him. Damon looked weary but unbowed, like a fallen angel.

When he reached the foot of the stairs, he stopped and regarded her warily. "After last night, I wasn't sure I'd ever see you again."

"I thought about what you said, then decided that you were right. None of us is perfect."

He smiled. "Let's go into the parlor."

As Damon turned, Catherine got a close look at the right side of his face. She gasped and reached out. "Dear God in heaven—!"

He stayed her hand. "Don't fuss. It's nothing, really."

"Nothing! Has a doctor seen this?" With her free hand she turned his face. High on his cheekbone was a dark, raw bruise. "Damon, what happened?" she asked softly. "Were you in a fight?"

"Someone threw a snowball and it hit me in the face, that's all. And yes, a doctor has seen it."

"That's all? If it had hit you in the eye, it could have blinded you."

"But it didn't, so don't worry about me."

Catherine fell silent as he drew her arm through his and led her across the foyer to the parlor.

Once inside, Damon closed the door and leaned back against it. "Why did you come tonight?"

"With everyone attacking you, I thought you might welcome a friendly face."

"If it's yours, yes." He walked up to her and took her hands in his. "It's been hell for me today."

"Come sit on the divan and tell me about it."

Catherine sat down and watched as Damon seated himself close to her and stretched out his long legs. He looked battered and exhausted, with dark circles beneath his eyes.

"The press has vilified me before, but never like this," he said. "As soon as the newsboys hawked the papers, irate citizens gathered outside my house, throwing stones, snowballs, anything they could get their hands on. I finally had to call the police."

"I'm sure the fervor will die down once another scandal replaces Rollins' death."

He looked at her with such intensity that Catherine caught her breath. "A tragedy like this shows a man who his true friends are."

"You have many friends, Damon."

"Business associates and acquaintances perhaps, but few true friends." He took her hand and absently rubbed the back of it with his thumb. "Why did you change your mind about me? When you left last night, you regarded me as Satan incarnate."

"Not quite in so black a light." Catherine clasped his hand as tightly as she could, for she needed the courage to admit that her feelings for him had changed. "I found I couldn't bear the thought of not seeing you again no matter what you had done."

Damon grew very still, his expression intent. "Do you mean that?"

"Yes, God help me." Catherine placed her hand gently against his bruised cheek. "Years ago, people threw stones at the first women medical students, you know. But that didn't stop us."

Damon turned his face so he could kiss her palm. "I would kill anyone who tried to do that to you."

Would Kim ever protect her so fiercely? she wondered.

"You know, you and I are alike in many respects," he said.

"How? I didn't think we were alike at all."

"Oh, but we are. We both don't run with the herd, though your motives are higher and nobler than mine. We do what we have to in order to get what we want."

Catherine sat back and studied him for a moment. Damon Delancy was such a complex man, full of unexpected insight. She was being drawn closer and closer to him, and was helpless to resist.

She turned toward him, moving closer until her breast brushed his shirtsleeve, her gaze lingering on the chiseled lips she wanted to kiss. Damon's left arm slid around her shoulders, and he tilted her chin to give her what she wanted.

The moment Damon's smooth, warm lips met hers, Catherine knew this kiss was different. It wasn't a kiss born of champagne indulgence or shared danger, but one of mutual attraction and growing desire.

Damon's mouth was blissfully heavy, sending little shocks through Catherine as a knot of pleasure uncurled deep in her abdomen. She became the aggressor. Her hand slid up his shirtfront and curled around the nape of his neck, holding him while she opened her mouth and claimed his with her tongue.

She felt him shudder in surprise at her boldness, and his response only inflamed her passions further. As she deepened her kiss, the aching response of her own body nearly shattered her. She wanted him to slide his hand beneath her skirts and soothe her with his fingers.

He drew away, gasping, and when he was finally able to speak, he teased, "Brazen wench . . . Aren't you afraid such behavior will encourage romantic notions?"

"Has it?"

Damon chuckled as he kissed her chin, his lips trailing along her jaw. When his hand boldly cupped her breast, Catherine gasped and her eyes flew open as sweet fire ignited her. She had never let Kim take such liberties, but with Damon, it seemed so right. Her last coherent thought was that all her textbook learning about the human body did not prepare her for this erotic onslaught.

Damon watched her intently as he rubbed his thumb against the fabric of her shirtwaist, slowly teasing her nipple into hardness. He whispered, "Do you like my touch?"

Catherine gathered her last shreds of self-control. "I know I shouldn't, so we had better stop."

He drew away and looked down at her, his gray eyes like fathomless pools. "But you know you don't want to."

"No," she replied raggedly, even as she yearned for his burning touch again, "but there are consequences to consider."

"Ah, consequences . . . I suspect that under that veneer of sober responsibility lurks a heart of reckless abandon. One day you're going to give into it and never be the same again."

Catherine regarded him in astonished silence. No one had ever pictured her as reckless about anything. That this man could see her in such an unaccustomed light tantalized her. Still, she felt compelled to deny it.

"I'm never reckless," she insisted. "I always weigh the consequences of my actions very carefully."

He smiled lazily as his hand grazed her breast again as if testing her resolve. "Did you think of the consequences of coming here alone tonight, to a bachelor gentleman's home? They could be dire indeed."

His soft, seductive words and arousing touch made Catherine's heart hammer faster. "I must be going."

Damon leaned forward and nuzzled her ear. "Isn't there anything I can do to persuade you to stay a little longer?"

If she stayed any longer, she suspected she and Damon would become lovers, with dire consequences arriving in nine months' time. That prospect was like a dash of cold water.

"I'm afraid not." To break the spell, she forced herself to move away from him and rise.

In one fluid motion, Damon was on his feet beside her. "I'll let you go, but on one condition."

"And what's that?"

"That you promise to see me again. As often as I like."

"As often as I have time."

He smiled. "You drive a hard bargain, Dr. Stone, but I suppose I'll have to be satisfied with it."

Then he drew her arm through his and they left the parlor. In the foyer, Damon told the butler to have his carriage brought around, then he helped Catherine with her coat.

When the carriage came, Catherine turned to Damon and said, "Goodnight, Damon."

"Goodnight, Catherine."

As she started for the carriage, she felt her wrist grabbed and she spun around right into Damon's outstretched arms. She gasped in surprise when he crushed her against him and kissed her so passionately, he arched her back.

When he finally released her, breathless and shaking, he grinned wickedly. "That's what I mean by reckless abandon."

Her lips still bruised from his kiss, a dazed Catherine accepted his outstretched hand and let him assist her into the carriage.

Damon watched the carriage disappear into the night, then he went inside.

He absently touched his bruised cheek and smiled slowly as he strolled to his study. Catherine had taken the bait. She came to him as he knew she would, her trusting heart brimming with sympathy.

He sat at his desk, put his feet up and clasped his hands behind his head. He wanted her as he had never wanted another woman—not just as a mistress for a few weeks or a few months. He wanted more than physical satisfaction. He wanted to spend the rest of his life waking up in the morning not knowing what to expect of his woman. Perhaps that's why he hadn't patronized Ivory's in several months. Beyond her voluptuous body and erotic skills, Danse possessed nothing that enticed him. Francine possessed even less.

If he wanted Catherine for a lifetime, he would just have to marry her.

CHAPTER

TEN

A week before Christmas, Catherine was surprised to see Genevra walk into her office. Two spots of pink stained her high cheekbones, and her red-rimmed eyes glittered with tears.

"Genevra, what's wrong?"

"Catherine, you've got to help me." Her hands trembled as she unwound her luxurious fox fur wrap and draped it across the back of a chair. She nervously smoothed the skirt of her bottle-green ensemble, but didn't remove the fox toque.

Catherine rose from behind her desk and placed a comforting hand on her friend's arm. "Come, tell me what's wrong. It can't be as bad as all that."

"But it is." Genevra clasped her hands together and closed her eyes as if gathering strength. "Dear God, I'm *enceinte* again."

"Why, that's wonderful. Congratulations."

Genevra's hazel eyes flew open and she stared at Catherine as if she had lost her mind. "It's not wonderful at all. It's the worst calamity that could ever befall me."

She collapsed into a chair and burst into tears, her narrow shoulders shaking.

Catherine recalled the first time just over a year ago when she had first met Genevra. At that time, she had been distraught over her second miscarriage. She had that same air of desolation about her now.

"Don't cry," she soothed. "You're upset."

Genevra dabbed at her eyes with a handkerchief. "Of course I'm upset. I don't want this baby. After what I went through just to have little Stone, I don't want to risk my life again. I'm too young to die."

Her fierce declaration shocked Catherine. "Last year you were willing to do anything to have a baby."

"That's because I was so naive. I didn't realize how horrible it would be. I know better now."

"Why are you here, Genevra?" Catherine had her suspicions, but she asked anyway.

Determination steeled Genevra's voice. "I've heard other women say that doctors can get rid of it somehow. I don't care what you give me or what you do, I just want you to get rid of it and make sure I never have another one."

"You're asking me to perform an abortion."

Genevra leaned forward expectantly. "Can you do it?"

There was no question that Catherine could. Behind her, in the medicine cabinet, were glass bottles of ergot, apiol, and other strong drugs capable of inducing an abortion. She could also use instruments to scrape the embryo out of the womb.

"I'm sorry, Genevra, but I won't. Not only are abortions illegal, they destroy human life. I have taken an oath to protect human life."

Genevra's face crumpled in dismay. "But you're my friend! You must do this for me. You must!"

"How do you know you're even pregnant?"

"I've ceased to be unwell for two months in a row, and I feel horrible, the same way I did when I was having little Stone." She pressed her fingers to her forehead. "I know I'm *enceinte* again, Catherine, I can sense it."

"Why don't I examine you just to make sure?"

Genevra twisted her handkerchief. "And if I am, will you get rid of it at once? Today?"

Catherine sat back in frustration. "Does Gordon know that you're here and why?"

Genevra looked guilty as her gaze slid away. "Of course not."

"I can't believe you're doing this behind your husband's back, Genevra. I've never seen two people so much in love. How do you think he would feel if he knew you were carrying his child and had aborted it? This child is his as well."

Genevra raised her chin, and her voice was both cold and hot with passion. "I love Gordie, but I almost died giving birth to the son he wanted so desperately, the son you all conspired to make me bear. I think I've more than proven my love for him. No one can expect me to go through that again, and *I won't*!"

"I know you're frightened, but—"

"You don't know anything about the torture I went through and yet you sit there so piously and preach to me about destroying another life. You're not even married, for pity's sake. What do you know about it?"

Chastised, Catherine sat there in silence.

"What about my life? What if having another child destroys my life? Doesn't that matter to any of you?" Genevra continued.

"Of course it does. But childbirth is one of the risks of marriage. You know that. Besides, if you're as nervous and fearful now as you were after your miscarriage last year, you'll probably have another miscarriage."

"Can you promise me that will happen?"

"I can't promise you anything."

"Then I want to get rid of it and make sure I don't have another."

"I'm sorry, but I just can't do it."

Tears of betrayal filled Genevra's eyes. "I thought you were my friend, Catherine."

"I am." She spread her hands in supplication. "We could perform another operation to save you and this baby, if we had to."

Genevra gave her an accusatory look. "If you really cared about me, you would do this."

Catherine shook her head in frustration. "There are laws that transcend friendship, and I'm afraid this is one of them. I'm sorry."

"But it's not even a baby yet, is it? Not really." Genevra rose, her eyes dark with desperation. "Please, Catherine, I'm begging you. I'll never tell anyone as long as I live. I'll give you anything you want—money, clothes, jewelry—*anything*, if you'll do this one favor for me."

"I just can't."

Genevra stepped back, trembling in rage. "Well, thank you for nothing, Dr. Stone."

"Genevra—"

"You've taken sides against me and I won't forget it." Genevra reached for her wrap and draped it around her shoulders with the aplomb of a woman twice her age. "If you won't do this favor for me, I'll find someone who will." Head held as regally as a queen, she strode away. When she reached the door, she turned. "And don't bother to call at the house any more. I'll be finding a new doctor for little Stone as well."

Then she left, slamming the door behind her.

Catherine sat at her desk, listening to the echo, then she rose and went to the window. She pulled back the curtain and watched as Genevra got into her waiting carriage and drove away. She wished Sybilla were here to talk to, but she and Nevada had gone to Washington, D.C. to spend Christmas and New Year's with Sybilla's family. Still, she knew exactly what Sybilla would say if she were here: *You should do it, Cat. Another pregnancy would jeopardize Genevra's life, and if she should die, Gordon loses a wife and little Stone loses a mother.*

Catherine sighed and returned to her desk. The argument made sense, but she still couldn't bring herself to comply with Genevra's wishes. To Catherine, abortion was murder.

But you've performed fetal craniotomies, Sybilla's spirit said. *I would call dismembering a baby murder.*

"It's not the same," Catherine said aloud. "Abortion is so premeditated, but a fetal craniotomy is done without premeditation. We do it as the situation arises, to save the mother's life."

Sybilla's spirit had more to say about that argument, but Catherine closed her mind to it. She had made her decision and she would stand behind it.

There would be a price to pay, of course. The thought of losing Genevra's friendship saddened her more than losing her, and possibly her friends, as patients. And she would miss her namesake little Stone as well.

"Oh, Genevra . . ." Catherine muttered as she turned away from the window and summoned her next patient.

Genevra's distraught mental state preyed on Catherine's mind, however, so two days later, she went to the Grahams' house to see if Genevra was ready to listen to reason.

Catherine waited in the foyer while the butler went to tell Genevra that Dr. Stone was here. Catherine looked around at the spicy evergreen garlands twisted around the staircase banister and the Chinese *famille verte* bowl overflowing with freshly cut holly on the narrow foyer table, and she thought it ironic that in the season celebrating Christ's birth, Genevra wanted an abortion. Five minutes later, the butler returned.

"I'm sorry, Dr. Stone," he said, looking decidedly uncomfortable, "but Mrs. Graham conveys her regrets that she no longer wishes to receive you. She also wished me to tell you that the task you had discussed several days ago has been completed.''

So Genevra had found someone else to perform her abortion. And Catherine knew who.

Feeling hollow and numb inside, she thanked the butler and after turning for one final look, left the Grahams' house for good.

When she arrived at Kim's house, Catherine had to wait while he treated a patient, so she was able to rehearse exactly what she wanted to say to him. Ten minutes later, the surgery door opened and a well-dressed woman came out, glanced at Catherine, and left.

Kim stood in the doorway, grinning in delight as he rolled down his shirtsleeves. ''Catherine, what a pleasant surprise. I'm glad you're here, because there is something I want to ask you. Why don't we go into the library? It's so much cozier than my office.''

''And there's something I want to ask you,'' she said, following him. She glanced at the tall Christmas tree standing in one corner, its full boughs lavishly trimmed with wide gold velvet ribbons and white candles waiting to be lit.

He sat on the sofa and patted the seat next to him. ''Ladies first.''

Catherine remained standing. ''What is it you had to ask me, Kim?''

''Why are you so serious? I wanted to invite you to spend Christmas Eve with me, that's all.''

''I'm sorry, but I've agreed to spend Christmas Eve with Damon.''

Kim's handsome face darkened and he jumped to his feet, jammed his hands into his pockets and strode across the room to the fireplace. ''Delancy, always Delancy. Didn't it ever occur to you that I might want you to spend Christmas Eve with me?''

''I want to spend Christmas Eve with Damon,'' she said. ''He asked me a few weeks ago, and agreed because I enjoy his company.''

''More than mine, obviously.''

Catherine sighed. ''I didn't come here to hurt you or argue about Damon. I came here to ask you a question.''

''What is it?'' he snapped.

Catherine took a deep breath. ''Did you abort Genevra's baby?''

Kim raised his head defiantly. "Yes. And why shouldn't I? That poor child almost died bearing Stone."

Catherine felt sick inside. "Oh, Kim, how could you? To deliberately take a life . . ."

He glared at her as he went to the sideboard and poured himself a generous brandy. "Don't preach to me, Catherine. We've all deliberately taken lives at one time or another."

She shook her head. "After you lectured me about Anthony Comstock and the perils of distributing anticonception devices, you risk your own career to perform an abortion?"

Kim tossed down his drink and shrugged. "Genevra is a dear friend of mine. It was the least I could do."

"Is it because she's a dear friend, or a prominent member of society who can further your career?"

His pale face turned beet red. "I resent what you're implying!"

"What about Gordon? He's your friend, too. That was his child as well. Didn't he have a say in what happened to it?"

"Gordon has his son. He shouldn't ask his wife to put her own life in danger for another child."

"But isn't that for him to decide? You didn't even give him the chance!"

Kim swallowed some brandy and studied her out of slitted eyes. "Do you remember when we met last year, how you competed with two other doctors for my patients?"

"Of course."

"I chose you because I admired your ability to inspire trust and build rapport with your patients. I thought you had the makings of a great doctor." He shook his head. "I was wrong."

His admission stunned her momentarily. When she recovered herself, she bristled. "Pardon me if I disagree with you. I think I'm a damn fine doctor!"

"Technically, yes. You can deliver a baby with the best of us. But a great doctor concerns himself with his patients' lives as well as their aches and pains. You see every situation in terms of black and white, with no shades of gray. You place idealism before the reality of your patients' lives."

Stung, Catherine retorted, "That's not true! You're just making excuses for performing Genevra's abortion."

"The reality of Genevra's life is that she would probably die if she bears another child. That is my main concern, not your impractical idealism."

Catherine shook her head. "I don't recognize you any more, Kim. What happened to the kind, generous man who wanted to help a struggling doctor establish herself in New York?"

He set down his glass and strode toward her, his arms open as if to embrace her. "He's still here, Catherine, waiting for you to forget Delancy and come back to him."

She neatly sidestepped him. "I'm sorry, Kim. After this, I'll never feel the same way about you again."

As she turned to leave, he grabbed her arm, his fingers biting into her flesh with unexpected force. "It's Delancy, isn't it? He's poisoned your mind against me."

Catherine turned and regarded him coldly. "You've done that without anyone else's help."

His hand fell away in defeat. "I've lost you, haven't I?"

"I don't think you ever really had me."

He glanced at the Chesterfield sofa, where they had shared many a passionate embrace. "That's not true." He hesitated. "I love you, you know. I think I've loved you from the first moment we met."

Catherine took a deep breath, feeling regret for all they had once shared. "I'm afraid I can't return that love. Too much has changed between us."

"I don't believe that."

Best to make the cut clean and quick. "I'm sorry, Kim. Goodbye." She didn't wish him a Merry Christmas, just turned and walked away.

"Catherine, don't go!"

This time she didn't turn back for one last look.

In the hansom cab, Catherine rested her head back and closed her eyes, trying not to let Kim's accusations and feelings of bitter disillusionment overwhelm her, but failed. He was wrong about her placing idealism before her patients' lives. She would never feel the same way about Kim again. Not only had he betrayed his profession, he had betrayed a friend as well, all to advance himself. In his own way, he was just as ruthless and calculating as Damon, but less honest about it.

She thought of Damon and the bitterness eased. She had almost refused his invitation to spend Christmas Eve at his house, but Catherine's family had disowned her, and with both Sybilla and Molly away, she felt especially lonely. The loss of both Genevra and Kim saddened her deeply as well. There could be no harm in spending Christmas Eve with Damon, who would also be alone.

She smiled in anticipation as the cab stopped before her house.

At five o'clock on Christmas Eve, just as Catherine was rushing out the door toward Damon's waiting carriage, she almost collided with the tobacconist's messenger boy running up the steps.

Go away, she said to herself with a sinking heart. *This is Christmas Eve.*

"Message for Dr. Stone," the lad said crisply, handing Catherine a slip of paper.

After tipping the boy and wishing him a Merry Christmas, Catherine read the telephone message by the flickering gaslight of her hallway. As she feared, the note was from Hilda Steuben, informing her that a building had collapsed on Third Street and they were bringing the injured to the Women's Dispensary. Catherine was needed immediately.

But tonight was Christmas Eve, and she was supposed to spend it with Damon. For the first time since Catherine had become a doctor, she resented that yet another emergency was about to devour her personal life.

She turned and went upstairs to change out of her blue velvet dress, so it wouldn't get ruined by sweat and blood. When she came back downstairs again, she hesitated. Damon would no doubt be furious with her for canceling their plans, no matter how valid the reason, so she hastily scribbled a note. When she got into Damon's waiting carriage, she handed it to the driver along with orders to take her to the dispensary before he went home.

Catherine hoped she would be home by eight o'clock.

Her hopes notwithstanding, it was ten o'clock by the time the streetcar brought her home.

After disembarking on the corner and walking down the street, she stopped stock-still in her tracks. The house that she had left in darkness was now ablaze with light shining from the downstairs windows.

Someone was in her house. It couldn't be Molly, because she was in Brooklyn spending the holidays with relatives.

Catherine swallowed hard, her mouth dry, as she pondered what to do. She shivered as she looked around for a policeman, but this side of the square was deserted this late on Christmas

Eve. Most of her neighbors were also abed, their houses dark and silent as their children awaited St. Nicholas.

To Catherine's surprise, her front door opened. A familiar tall, broad-shouldered form stood silhouetted against the flood of light from the hallway.

"Damon, is that you?"

His amused voice replied, "Who else would be insane enough to break into your house on Christmas Eve?"

Catherine hurried up the front steps, her weariness falling away the closer she came to him. When she reached the stoop, she saw he was still dressed for dinner. She knew she must look like a washerwoman, with her hair coming loose from its pins and her shirtwaist and skirt spattered with dirt and blood.

"What are you doing here?" she asked breathlessly, as he drew her into the warm foyer and closed the door on the cold night air swirling about her skirt's hem. She sniffed the tantalizing aromas of roasting meat and spices. "And who's in my kitchen? It can't be Molly—she's gone for the holidays."

His gray eyes danced with pleasure as he kissed her quickly in greeting. "Since you couldn't come to my house for Christmas Eve, I thought I would bring the festivities to you. My chef Bernard is in your kitchen preparing a repast fit for the gods."

As Damon plucked her wool hat off, Catherine felt the rest of her hair come free and tumble past her shoulders. "You must excuse me," she said hurriedly, unwinding her wool scarf. "I must go upstairs and change. I'm a sight."

"A sight for sore eyes."

Catherine ignored the look that leaped into his eyes as he stared at her unbound hair. "I'll be right back," she said, and hurried up the stairs to her bedchamber.

In the bathroom, she quickly undressed, washed her face and hands with Sybilla's gardenia-scented soap, then put on her new velvet teagown. After brushing her hair and arranging it in a simple chignon, she went back downstairs to find Damon still waiting patiently at the foot of the stairs.

His winter gaze swept over her as she came down. "I liked you better with your hair down, but the gown is a vast improvement. That blue color becomes you."

Catherine felt her cheeks grow warm. "Thank you." She hesitated. "How did you get in?"

"I told you. I picked the lock on your back door and broke

in.'' He grinned. ''It's one of the many hidden talents I acquired during my misspent youth. You don't mind, do you?''

''I'm astonished you would risk being caught.''

''I was very careful. Besides, I was desperate to spend Christmas Eve with you.''

''You're annoyed that I had to send my regrets at the last minute.''

For one second, something like anger flared deep within his eyes, but then it disappeared so quickly that Catherine thought she had imagined it.

He chucked her under the chin. ''It did disappoint me at first, but you're a doctor, and your first responsibility is to your patients.''

A lump formed in Catherine's throat. He truly understood.

Damon released her, tucked her arm through his, and escorted her to the dining room. ''I couldn't tolerate the thought of you spending Christmas Eve alone, so I decided to bring the festivities to you.''

Catherine gasped when she saw the dining room's transformation. White candles burning in a pair of elegant silver candelabra, their branches entwined with festive mistletoe, cast a mellow glow on the table set for two with Damon's own snowy linen and Wedgwood bone china. Gleaming Tiffany flatware and sparkling Irish crystal caught the light.

When Catherine thought of all Damon must have gone through to transport his chef, food, and table setting to her house, she shook her head in wonder.

''It's beautiful.''

''Bernard should be finished,'' Damon said, pulling out her chair, ''so if you'll sit down, I'll serve you.''

While Catherine sat at one end of the table and relaxed, Damon poured the champagne, then disappeared for a moment. He returned with his chef, both carrying various dishes that they set on the table. First came the soup, a clear consommé, followed by lobster in cream sauce, peas, cold asparagus in vinaigrette, and small new potatoes. Finally Bernard carried in a roast goose that made Catherine's mouth water.

When they were alone, Damon held up his champagne glass in a toast. ''To dreams.''

Catherine raised her glass. ''To dreams.''

Then Damon served her, filling her plate with so much food

that Catherine laughingly told him to stop. Finally, he sat down
and they dined.

"What called you away tonight?" Damon asked.

"An old tenement's roof collapsed, trapping people inside,"
Catherine explained. "The Women's Dispensary was the nearest
medical facility, so they sent the victims there." She shook her
head at the memory of the steady stream of broken, mangled
bodies, the bone-aching work to save them.

"On Christmas Eve of all nights," Damon said. "What a
shame. Were any children injured?"

"Several, but not badly, thank God." She looked over at him.
"Let's talk about something else, shall we? This is one night I'd
like to forget about pain and suffering for a few hours."

"Your wish is my command."

Catherine fell silent, opening her senses to this celebration
Damon had created just for her. She ate slowly, savoring each
unique aroma and flavor. Every melodious clink of silver against
china sounded like soothing music. The table linens felt as
smooth as silk beneath her fingers, the silverware richly heavy.
Dancing candle flames framed Damon's saturnine features in
softly glowing light.

Catherine sighed in contentment. After taking care of others,
it was a pleasure to sit back and let someone take care of her.
But she mustn't get too used to it.

She looked across at Damon and noticed that the bruise had
disappeared from his cheekbone. "Has the Rollins scandal finally died down?"

He nodded. "Irate citizens don't gather outside my house or
throw snowballs."

"I'm glad."

Damon sipped his champagne. "I wonder how Nevada is
faring with Sybilla's family."

"They'll adore him just as Sybilla does." She sat back, feeling as stuffed as the goose. "The meal was delicious. My compliments to Bernard. And thank you, Damon. This is the nicest
Christmas gift anyone has ever given me."

He rose and came around to her chair. "Ah, but there is more
to come."

"More?" Catherine rose. "But you've done far too much
already."

"I can never do too much for you, Catherine," he said softly.
"Now, come with me into your parlor."

When Catherine walked into the parlor, she immediately noticed the large box sitting on the reading table. She prayed it was nothing too personal or extravagant that she would be compelled to refuse.

While Damon went to get the box wrapped in marbleized paper and a huge green ribbon, Catherine went to the small Christmas tree in the corner and found his gift among the parcels there.

Catherine sat down on the divan and Damon handed her the box. ''Merry Christmas, Catherine.''

''Thank you, Damon.'' She handed him his gift. ''Merry Christmas. Open yours first.''

He tore open the package, and when he saw the appointment book bound in fine moroccan leather, his face lit up with delight. ''This is perfect.'' He leaned over and brushed her cheek with his lips. ''Thank you.''

''I didn't know what to give you that you didn't already have,'' she said, hoping her simple gift was adequate for a millionaire.

He caressed the rich leather. ''A clean appointment book for a new year . . . Now open your gift.''

Catherine's hands trembled as she unwrapped the box. When she lifted the lid and saw what was inside, she gasped. ''Oh, Damon . . .''

He had given her a beautiful silver desk set consisting of an inkwell, pen and blotter—extravagant, but not offensively personal.

''They're lovely, and perfect for my office. Thank you.''

Damon pointed to the inkwell. ''There is a place for engraving your initials, but I decided to wait because I'm hoping your initials will change.''

Catherine frowned in puzzlement. ''Change?''

''From C.S. to C.S.D.—Catherine Stone Delancy.''

She stared at him in disbelief as he reached into a pocket.

''Catherine, I love you and want to marry you.'' He held out a ring set with three large, brilliant diamonds that could have only come from Tiffany's. ''Will you do me the honor of becoming my wife?''

For a moment, Catherine thought she was going deaf. ''What did you say?''

''I want to marry you.''

''You want to marry me?'' she squeaked.

''If you'll have me.''

Catherine felt as though Star was running away with her again, the same breathless, out-of-control feeling, of events happening too fast. She set aside the box and jumped to her feet.

"But why me? I'm not some society belle like Francine Ballard, who will tend your home while you're out conquering the world."

"That's true. But life would never be boring with you, Catherine. You're also intelligent, beautiful—" his gaze flicked over her "—and you have a passionate nature that I would enjoy awakening along with that sense of reckless abandon."

She caught her breath. "This—this is so sudden, Damon."

"Not really. I've been thinking about it for the last several months."

"I had no idea you were entertaining thoughts of marriage."

He raised a sardonic brow. "No? Not even the times I kissed you?" He rose, filling the room with his powerful presence. "I won't sling you over my shoulder and cart you off to prove it, but believe me when I say that I love you, Catherine." Damon studied her. "I'm not asking you to return that love yet, just consider my proposal."

"I—I will."

"Will you at least try on the ring?"

Catherine held out her shaking left hand and watched as Damon slipped the ring on her third finger, claiming her as his own. She swallowed hard, still dumbfounded that this man wanted her.

He said, "It looks as though it belongs there."

"It's beautiful." Catherine had always thought her stepmother's diamonds were cold and glittering, but these stones shimmered warmly.

"Keep it somewhere safe while you decide. Wear it when you're ready." Then he smiled gently. "I think I should be going. You'll need some time alone to think, since you are never reckless."

She nodded, still dazed. "Yes. Yes, I will."

"But don't take too long. I am not a patient man." He hesitated. "I chose diamonds because they reminded me of the frozen pond in Central Park, where we first met so inauspiciously."

A meeting he hadn't remembered at first, Catherine reminded herself. But that didn't matter now. "That's very romantic."

He smiled wryly. "Who would believe such a ruthless, calculating man could be romantic?"

"Anyone who knows you."

Catherine turned and showed him to the door, her mind still reeling.

Damon stopped at the door and turned, his eyes as dark as smoke by gaslight. He took her face in his hands and sought to possess her mouth with his own. The moment Catherine melted against him, he tangled his fingers in her hair, freeing it from its pins. Even as she held him close to her yielding, uncorseted body, she felt her hair fall heavily down her back.

When they parted, Damon reached out, drew a handful of her hair over her shoulder and rubbed it against his cheek while his gaze burned into her. The deliberately sensual movements made Catherine feel so giddy, she thought she would collapse in a swoon to put Francine to shame.

"So soft," he murmured thickly, "like silk."

When he released her, he rested his forehead against hers and whispered, "I won't know a moment's peace until I have your decision, Catherine. And if you refuse me, I won't know a moment's peace for the rest of my life." Then he reluctantly drew away from her and put on his coat and top hat, his winter-gray eyes never leaving her.

As Damon stepped out into the cold night air, he paused. "Listen."

She heard the clangor of church bells pealing joyously across the city. It was as though they rang for her and Damon.

"It's Christmas day," Damon said. "Merry Christmas, Catherine." He grinned roguishly. "Sleep well and dream of me."

"Merry Christmas, Damon. I shall."

She watched as he got into his waiting carriage, waved, and drove off. Then she went inside and closed the door.

Catherine walked through the foyer as though she were sleepwalking, the ring weighing heavily on her hand. Already the house seemed empty without him, especially when she passed by the dining room and saw that Damon's servants had discreetly cleared the table and stripped it of its magic. It was as though the enchanted late-night supper had never happened.

She shivered and rubbed her arms, wishing Sybilla were here to talk to, but perhaps it was better that she was not. This was one decision Catherine had to make on her own.

She went upstairs and put the ring away with her cameo necklace, so it wouldn't influence her.

She returned to the parlor and thought until the ashes grew

cold in the fireplace and the sky turned gray with morning light. Exhausted, she finally went to bed, only to have Damon haunt her dreams.

Catherine thought of possibilities and consequences from sunrise to moonrise, and two days later, she knew what she had to do.

Catherine found Damon in his study, seated at his desk strewn with papers.

When she entered, he rose and growled, ''These last two days have been a living hell for me, so I hope you're here to accept my proposal.''

''Before I do that, we have to talk.''

''So we are to discuss marriage as though it were a business arrangement? You disappoint me, Catherine. I had thought you would throw caution to the winds just this once and let life come what may.''

''It's not in my nature to enter into marriage lightly, Damon. There's too much at stake.''

''Of course you can't.'' He rounded his desk and indicated she should take a seat on the sofa. When he sat down beside her, he asked, ''What do you wish to discuss?''

Catherine organized her terms mentally. ''If we marry, you wouldn't expect me to give up my medical practice.''

''Of course not.''

His ready compliance did not ease her fears. ''You will accept my late hours, interrupted dinners, missed social events? You will accept that my life will always go against the wind?''

''Yes. Why are you so reluctant to believe me?''

She shrugged and looked away. ''It's hard for me to believe any man would accept such terms. Women have so little say about their lives in our society.''

''I'm rather an exceptional fellow and resent being considered 'any man.' You should know that by now.'' Damon regarded her in wry amusement. ''Any other conditions or terms to this merger?''

''I won't be able to take trips to Paris to buy Worth gowns like the other women, so my wardrobe won't be a credit to you.''

He gave her a look that plainly said he thought that objection trivial. ''There are capable dressmakers here in New York. Besides, you would be a credit to me no matter what you wore. What else?''

"I won't have time to make afternoon calls on the wives of your friends and business associates."

Catherine knew that most society wives spent every afternoon calling upon one another according to the rigid rules of etiquette.

"Of course you won't," Damon said. "You'll be tending to your patients. And we can always hire a woman to handle your social obligations. Anything else?"

Catherine had been saving her most serious term for last, and she was sure he would never agree to it. She took a deep breath and plunged right in. "I intend to practice anticonception as well, because I don't want children right away."

The look of stunned surprise on Damon's face would have been comical if their discussion weren't so serious. "You intend to what?"

"Practice anticonception. That's—"

"I know what it is." He raised one brow. "And I'm to have no say in this?"

"Not at first."

As he took in her words, Catherine could almost hear him thinking and searching for a way to negotiate. "I hope you're not saying that you never want children at all, because that is unacceptable to me and not subject to negotiation."

"I would like to have children someday," she admitted, "but not right away. And only two or three, not one every year like some broodmare."

He exhaled sharply. "You scared the hell out of me for a minute. I'll meet those terms."

Now that surprised her. "You will?"

"Yes. You sound surprised. You can trust me, you know. I'm not trying to trap you or force you to do anything you don't want to do."

Catherine felt her cheeks grow warm in embarrassment, because that's exactly what she had been thinking.

"Have we exhausted your list of terms yet?" When Catherine nodded, he said, "Well, I have one or two of my own that I will expect you to comply with."

She hadn't expected this. "What are they?"

Damon draped his arm across the back of the sofa and leaned so close to Catherine that their cheeks almost touched. "I know purity is a highly prized commodity in a wife," he began, his voice low and silky, "but I'm a man of—shall we say?—lusty appetites. So there will be no separate bedrooms for us. We will share one. Agreed?"

Catherine thought of waking up every day with Damon lying beside her and she felt weak. "Agreed."

He leaned closer. "And I'll expect you to send your maid away and disrobe in front of me every night, because it excites me to watch a woman undress. Agreed?"

That startled her. Hadn't Ruth told her that disrobing before one's husband was simply not done?

When she didn't answer right away, Damon persisted. "You're very quiet, Catherine. Do you agree to this term or not?"

"I agree."

"Also," he murmured, his eyes darkening as his fingers traced the line of her jaw, "I will make love to you wherever and whenever I please."

She knew he was purposely trying to shock her, so she didn't pull away in fear or disgust. She said calmly, "And will you allow me the same privilege?"

Damon burst out laughing at that and sat back. "Touché, my love, touché." Then he pulled Catherine into his arms and kissed her soundly. When they parted, he nuzzled her ear, murmuring, "Of course I'll allow you the same privilege, with pleasure. Shall we start now, here in my study, or wait until we wed?"

She thought of Sybilla's bustle and pushed away. "I think we should wait until we're wed."

"A pity. As I said, I'm not a patient man."

For the first time, Catherine allowed herself to admit she loved and wanted him. "Are you sure you want to marry me, Damon?" She thought of the Peachtrees' ball, when she had overheard those women discussing her unsuitability for Kim. Wouldn't that apply to Damon as well? "What if society doesn't accept me?"

"Then hang them all."

Catherine reached into her skirt pocket, took out her handkerchief and unwrapped it to reveal Damon's ring. "Then I would be proud to be your wife." And she gave him the ring to slip on her finger.

He hesitated and regarded it solemnly. "Do you mind keeping our betrothal a secret for a while?"

Panic and mistrust rose in Catherine's heart. "Of course I don't, if you'll tell me why."

"Because I couldn't endure the torture of a long betrothal. I want us to wed as quickly as possible, preferably as soon as Nevada and Sybilla return from Washington.'' He hesitated. ''Unless, of course, you've got your heart set on a long betrothal, followed by a huge society wedding.''

Convention demanded that couples be betrothed for at least a year before marrying, but when Catherine thought of waiting that long to become Damon's wife, she couldn't bear it either. And as for a society wedding complete with a Worth wedding gown, twelve attendants, and hundreds of newspaper reporters printing the details of her every sneeze, she blanched.

She took off the ring and wrapped it back in her handkerchief. ''Please, Damon, anything but that.''

He smiled and kissed her hand. ''Your wish is my command. There's a lovely little church in Hyde Park. We'll marry there, forgo the bridal tour for now, and stay at Coppermine, then return to the city.''

''It sounds perfect.''

Damon rose and drew her into his arms. ''Oh, Catherine, we are going to have such a wonderful life together.''

Her arms slid around his narrow waist, and she pressed her cheek to his. ''I do love you so, Damon, and I'm as happy as I was when I graduated from medical school.''

''That is high praise, indeed,'' he teased as he released her.

Catherine said, ''I should be going. Molly is due back today, and my patients will be wondering what's happened to me.''

''Go, then. I don't mind sharing you.''

Damon strode toward the study door. Just as he reached it, Catherine grabbed his hand, yanked, and spun him around. Before the startled man could recover, Catherine pulled down his head and kissed him until she felt him laughing against her mouth.

She pulled away. ''*That* is what I call reckless abandon.''

Then she opened the door and left with the roar of Damon's laughter following her down the hall.

◆ CHAPTER ◆

ELEVEN

CATHERINE shivered, more from excitement than from the chilly church vestibule.

"I can't believe you're going through with this," Sybilla said.

Catherine shot her friend an astonished look. "But I thought you liked Damon."

"Sweet sutures, I didn't mean that! I think you and Damon are perfect for each other. I meant running off to get married in secret, in this tiny church, in the middle of winter, when you could have had the kind of wedding people would talk about for years to come."

Catherine caressed the double strand of pearls Damon had given her as a wedding gift along with matching earbobs. "You know I didn't want that kind of wedding."

"Well, that's the sort of wedding I'm going to have," Sybilla declared, "with a magnificent satin beaded wedding gown—not that your gown isn't lovely," she amended hastily.

Catherine loved her simple wedding dress of soft ivory velvet rimmed with ecru lace. And she was glad she wore a hat instead of the flowing lace-trimmed veil Sybilla suggested.

She said, "This is exactly the kind of wedding I've always wanted." Catherine suddenly felt overwhelmed by sadness. "I just wish both my parents were here. I'd even be happy to see Ruth and Jervis."

Sybilla hugged her in wordless understanding.

When they parted, Catherine said, "When are you and the cowboy getting married?"

Sybilla shrugged. "Who's to say? After what happened to me in Paris, I'm in no hurry. Neither is Nevada."

That puzzled Catherine, but she had no time to ponder

Sybilla's contradictory behavior. It was time for her to marry Damon.

Catherine took a deep breath to calm her quivering insides and adjusted her bouquet of white hothouse roses and orange blossoms. "Shall we?"

Sybilla opened the doors, organ music echoed hollowly through the deserted church, and bridesmaid and bride started down the aisle.

Catherine's heart pounded faster when she saw Damon waiting for her by the altar with his groomsman Nevada at his side.

I can't believe it, she thought. *I'm really getting married, and to a wonderful man like Damon.*

As Catherine drew closer, she could see that he was looking at her the way she had always dreamed a man would look at her, as if she were the only woman in the world. Such blatant desire filled Damon's gray eyes that it took her breath away.

The moment Catherine joined him at the altar, Damon took her hand and drew it to his lips in silent tribute, before turning to face the beaming minister.

Before Catherine knew it, she was saying her vows in a clear, confident voice, especially, "I do." The moment Damon slipped the plain gold band on her finger, Catherine felt that she truly belonged to him.

When the minister intoned, "I now pronounce you man and wife," Damon pulled his bride into his arms and kissed her without waiting for permission.

Nevada, who had left off his spurs for the occasion, stepped forward to pound Damon on the back and offer his congratulations, while a bright-eyed Sybilla hugged Catherine.

After Nevada kissed Catherine on the cheek, he murmured, "He'll take some tamin', doc."

Catherine looked at her handsome husband pressing his cheek to Sybilla's and her heart constricted. "I think I prefer him wild."

Nevada grinned. "Smart woman."

Damon went to Catherine's side and drew her arm through his. "Well, Mrs. Delancy, shall we go?"

"Mrs. Delancy . . . I do like the sound of that."

His eyes danced. "Good, because it's your name from now on."

When the wedding party returned to Coppermine, they found

that Bernard had prepared a sumptuous wedding breakfast for them, complete with a small iced wedding cake.

As the champagne and laughter flowed freely, Catherine decided her wedding was perfect. She was here with the three people who meant the most to her. Once Sybilla and Nevada left to return to New York, she would be alone with her husband in this quiet, secluded house.

Two hours later, Catherine stood by Damon's side on the front steps, watching as the carriage which would carry Sybilla and Nevada to the train station moved down the drive and disappeared through the gates.

When Catherine started shivering, her husband drew her back inside.

"I didn't expect Sybilla to burst into tears like that," Damon said. "She was acting as though she'd never see you again."

Even though Catherine would be living in Damon's Fifth Avenue mansion now, she fully intended to keep her joint practice with Sybilla in the Washington Square brownstone.

"Sybilla can be sentimental at times," she said as they strolled through the foyer. "We've been close friends for a long time, and we've shared much together. It's natural for her to be emotional at a time like this."

Damon turned to her. "Well, you're mine now, so she'll have to get used to sharing."

Catherine stood on tiptoes and entwined her arms behind his neck. "Oh, I think she understands that."

He slid his hands around her waist, lowered his head and kissed her slowly.

When they parted, Catherine said, "There's something I'm going to have to get used to as well."

"And what is that?"

"Being able to hold you and kiss you whenever I want."

Damon caught his breath. "Brazen wench." He nuzzled the sensitive part of her neck just below her right ear. "Have I told you what a beautiful bride you are, Catherine Stone Delancy, in your wedding dress?"

She shivered at the sensations he aroused so skillfully. "No, you haven't."

"How remiss of me. But that's because I think you'll be even more beautiful out of it."

He released her, his intent plain as he captured her hand with his own and started for the stairs.

Catherine's heart stopped and started with a rush, leaving her lightheaded. "Damon, it—it's only one o'clock in the afternoon."

He stopped in the atrium and turned, one corner of his mouth raised in a smile. "I seem to recall that one of my terms was that I will make love to you whenever and wherever I wish."

His implacable tone and the reality of their agreement made Catherine tremble inside.

Damon groaned and drew her to him. "Don't look at me as though I've suddenly turned into a monster. Regardless of our agreement, I would never force myself on you, Catherine—never." He set her at arm's length. "You do believe me?"

Catherine searched the depths of his eyes.

She sighed. "Of course I believe you. I should be ashamed of myself. I'm a doctor, not some witless seventeen-year-old."

"All brides are nervous on their wedding day, so I'm told. But I hope you'll take pity on me, because I don't think I could survive until this evening." His hungry gaze roamed over her. "Not with you looking the way you do."

"When you look at me that way, I don't think I'll survive until evening either."

He grinned and started for the stairs again, and this time, there were no protestations from Catherine.

When they reached Damon's bedchamber, he scooped her up in his arms and carried her over the threshold, setting her down gently on the other side.

Damon closed the door, then returned to her side.

"I don't want you to be afraid, Catherine," he whispered.

Her gaze slid away. "My only fear is that I won't please you."

He caught her chin, forcing her to look at him. "Don't worry about that. I'll teach you how." Then he brushed his lips against her mouth. "Shall I undress you, my love?"

Catherine could feel the blood pounding in her ears. "If you wish."

"I do wish to. Very much. Turn around."

When she did as he bade her, she felt his fingers work the dozens of tiny covered buttons running down the back of her wedding gown, then felt the bodice loosen as they became undone. She instinctively brought her arms to her sides to hold it up.

"That will never do," Damon whispered in her ear as he slid his fingers between the fabric and her shoulders. "Let it fall."

Catherine let her arms relax and the gown slid into a soft puddle of velvet at her feet.

"Oh, Catherine . . ." he murmured, his breath warm on the nape of her neck.

Damon turned her around and undressed her slowly, piece by piece, until Catherine was standing in nothing but her lacy chemise and pantalettes, her unbound hair falling past her shoulders.

"Get into bed," he rasped. "I'll join you in a moment."

Catherine crossed the room to the large mahogany four-poster bed that a servant had already turned down, slid across the smooth, lavender-scented sheets, and propped herself up against the pillows while her husband undressed himself more quickly than he had her.

Catherine had seen Damon half-naked when she set his fractured collarbone, but even that hadn't fully prepared her for the rest of him. He was a big man, but perfectly proportioned and pleasing to the eye, from his broad shoulders to his lean hips, where his desire for her was all too evident.

Damon walked toward the bed slowly, with the litheness and grace of a stalking cat, giving her time to get used to him. Dancing flames from the nearby fireplace turned his body into warm sculpted gold.

"Do I please you?" he asked softly when he reached the edge of the bed.

Catherine looked up at him, then let her gaze travel down. "The dissecting room never prepared me for this."

Damon laughed as he slid in beside her. "But those men were dead. I am very much alive. There is a difference."

"A considerable difference," she agreed, blushing.

He propped himself up on one elbow, and stroked her cheek with his free hand. "I know most ladies—even lady doctors, I expect—are brought up to view their husband's advances as something to be tolerated, not enjoyed. But there is no shame in enjoying what we are about to share, Catherine."

As she looked into his eyes, Catherine relinquished rational thought and instead surrendered to her senses. She became aware of the warmth of Damon's body and its pleasant masculine scent, the insistent feel of his arousal against her thigh. Her nervousness vanished, replaced by growing desire.

She curled her hand around the nape of his neck. "I think the time for talk is past, my love."

Damon grinned and slid closer to her, lowering his head for a kiss.

Catherine closed her eyes, savoring the feel of his lips as they traveled from her forehead, down her eyelids, across her cheek to her mouth. As she parted her lips and accepted the invasion of his tongue, she felt his fingers deftly undoing the buttons on her chemise.

Her eyes flew open when Damon brushed the thin material aside, baring her breasts. He fondled one, then the other, and raised his head so he could watch her reaction as he grasped one swollen nipple between thumb and forefinger and gently tugged at it.

Catherine gasped at the shuddering jolt of white-hot pleasure that possessed her. Her response must have pleased him, for he drew the other nipple into his mouth and suckled it.

She caught her breath at the sweet torture, her fingers tangling in his hair as she pressed him closer. "Harder."

Damon chuckled, then complied.

Catherine groaned as her passion flared out of control. She hooked her thumbs in the waistband of her pantalettes and drew them down over her hips. Damon released her and pulled the garment off impatiently, his free hand making the return trip up along the inside of her calf and thigh.

She parted her thighs for him in blatant invitation, and Damon didn't resist, deftly covering her body with his own. He entered her slowly at first, to let Catherine accustom herself to the length and breadth of him. He felt hot and smooth and so large she feared accommodating him. Catherine lay still until she could bear it no longer.

"Now, Damon. Please."

When he thrust deeply into her, Catherine cried out at the pain she knew was necessary before she could experience full satisfaction.

"I'm sorry," Damon gasped. "I would have spared you this."

Her gentle smile was forgiving as she grasped his shoulders and moved against him. Soon they were moving together, Catherine rising to meet his every thrust, her passion rising and building until she thought she would die of it. When her climax came, she felt as though she were bursting into a thousand tiny pieces.

Just as she floated back to earth, Damon moaned and increased the tempo of his thrusts until he shuddered, then sprawled atop her, gasping for breath.

"Sweet Catherine . . ." he mumbled against her shoulder.

Despite the languor spreading like honey through her limbs, Catherine sighed in relief that she had protected herself with one of Sybilla's smuggled pessaries.

They dozed.

Later, when they woke, Damon encircled her waist with one arm and drew her against him. "You're everything I've ever wanted in a wife."

"And you're everything I've ever wanted in a husband." She hesitated. "Damon?"

"Yes?"

"You treated me as you would a—a virgin. How did you know that Kim and I were never lovers?"

"You would have told me."

His trust delighted her.

"Besides," he added, "you two didn't look at each other the way lovers do."

She ran her fingers across the scar on his shoulder. "And how do lovers look at each other?"

He caught her hand and kissed her fingertips. "Ah, I can see there is much I still have to teach you. Lovers, my dear wife, look at each other with desire and anticipation in their eyes. You and Flanders never looked at each other that way, that's how I knew."

Catherine hesitated, suddenly unsure of herself. "I know you have had lovers."

He sighed. "A man doesn't reach the ripe old age of thirty without sleeping with a woman, Catherine." He turned her so that she faced him. "Does that upset you?"

She tossed her head, flipping her hair back. "No, because I know you'll never have another, now that we are wed."

"Isn't it a little late to try to dictate additional terms of this marriage to me?"

Catherine could tell by his suppressed smile that he was only teasing. "Oh, this is one term I know you'll agree to."

"And how do you know that?"

Catherine let her gaze drift down his body and stop. "Because lady doctors are very skillful with a scalpel."

Damon stared at her in astonishment, then let out a whoop of laughter, gathered Catherine into his arms and kissed her soundly.

When he released her, he said, "What makes you think I'd ever want to leave your bed?"

"You might grow tired of me. I'm sure you've known other women who are more . . . skilled at this."

He kissed the hollow of her throat. "I love you, that's the difference. Besides, skill comes with practice."

She smiled seductively at him. "I'll just have to become such a skilled lover that you will never leave." She trailed one fingertip down his ribs. "So I'll have to practice. Often."

"Agreed."

They practiced for the rest of the afternoon and the following day. On Sunday, they had to return to New York.

Damon looked out the window as the carriage pulled up to the door of his Fifth Avenue mansion. *Their* Fifth Avenue mansion, he corrected himself. It was Catherine's home now, too, as well as Nevada's.

When he saw what was awaiting them, he swore softly under his breath. "Damn!"

"What is it?" Catherine asked.

"Newspaper reporters on the doorstep. They must have gotten wind of our wedding."

"Newspaper reporters?" she echoed in alarm. "Won't a simple wedding announcement suffice?"

"Not in my case, I'm afraid." He reached over and squeezed her hand. "Bear with me, Catherine. It'll all be over in a second."

He could see that she was nervous and a little frightened, especially when the footman opened the carriage door and a dozen men pressed forward, their cheeks and ears red from waiting so long in the cold. They fired questions, each one louder than the last as they jockeyed for position and fought to be heard.

"Is it true you got married, Delancy?"

"Is this your bride?"

"What's her name and where's she from?"

Damon motioned Catherine back and stepped out of the carriage to face the reporters crowded around.

"Good afternoon, gentlemen. It is true. I did get married in Hyde Park on Friday."

''Why the secrecy?'' someone asked. ''You got something to hide?''

Some snickered at the implication, but most didn't dare.

Damon smiled smoothly, even as he fought down the impulse to punch the man in the jaw. ''You know me, gentlemen. I'm not a patient man. When I finally met the woman I wanted to marry, I wanted to marry her right away.''

Another asked, ''Who is she? One of the Astors? Consuelo Vanderbilt?''

Damon and the rest of New York society knew that Alva Vanderbilt had her eye on a duke for her eldest daughter. No American millionaire, no matter how wealthy, had a chance with the dark-haired beauty.

He turned and extended his hand to Catherine, who was sitting there, dazed by all the attention. But she squared her shoulders, placed her hand in his, and gave him a look that plainly said, ''We're in this together, and I won't disappoint you.''

As Damon assisted her out of the carriage, he said, ''Gentlemen, this is my wife, Catherine Delancy.''

Her smile was warm and captivating as if she had been facing these wolves all her life, and his heart swelled with pride.

The reporters had the decency not to rush her, but stood quietly or shuffled their feet while they scrutinized her and scribbled their notes.

Suddenly a man Damon recognized as Liam Flynn of the *Sun* stepped forward and stared at Catherine. ''I know you,'' he said. ''You're one of the doctors who works at the Women's Dispensary.''

Catherine smiled in recognition. ''Yes, I am. I've seen you there reporting on accidents.''

''Dr. Stone, isn't it?''

''Was. I'm Dr. Delancy now.''

Another reporter hooted, ''You married a lady doctor, Delancy?''

Damon grasped Catherine's gloved hand tightly even as he shrugged. ''Why not? If I'm ever sick, she can take care of me.''

Deciding he had had enough, Damon placed a protective arm around Catherine's shoulders and started for the front door. ''Now if you'll excuse us, gentlemen, that's enough for today.''

One of the reporters pushed forward. ''Mrs. Delancy—''

''Dr. Delancy,'' Catherine corrected him as she kept walking.

"Dr. Delancy, are you still going to practice medicine now that you're married to one of the wealthiest men in New York?"

"Of course."

Flynn trotted alongside Damon. "What do you have to say about that, Delancy?"

"Exactly what my wife told you."

The door loomed before them and Damon ushered Catherine inside to safety.

He took her wrap and grasped her trembling hands. "I'm sorry. That's not exactly the kind of welcome I had planned for us."

She looked back over his shoulder. "Do newspaper reporters often hound you like that?"

"Only when I do something newsworthy, like get married."

"Or someone shoots himself in your foyer."

He nodded. "That, too."

Catherine sighed. "As your wife, I suppose I had better get used to it."

"I'm afraid so." Damon looked past her. "Now, if you'll just turn around, Winslow has assembled the household staff for you to meet."

Evidently meeting the household staff was not as intimidating as facing a gang of reporters, for Catherine turned and smiled as the dignified, gray-haired butler came forward.

"The staff joins me in welcoming you, madam," Winslow said. "We hope you live a long and happy life within these walls, and we are here to serve you."

"Thank you, Winslow."

"If you'll follow me, madam, I shall introduce you to your staff."

Damon watched as Catherine met everyone from the housekeeper to the shy little scullery maid whose name he could never remember. Catherine, however, was trying to remember everyone's name, judging by her frown of concentration.

He had chosen well, he decided. Even though Catherine had insisted that she was not the type of woman who would tend his home while he was out conquering the world, he suspected she would succeed on the domestic front as well.

When the introductions were over and the servants went back to their work, Damon whispered, "There's one room in the house I would particularly like to show you."

Catherine raised her brows. "Your bedroom?"

"Our bedroom. We will be sharing it, remember?"

She smiled. "How could I forget?"

He extended his hand and led her upstairs.

When they entered the spacious bedchamber, Damon locked the door behind him and leaned against it, watching Catherine for her reaction. To his dismay, she barely glanced at the half-tester bed or the luxurious new Turkish carpet he thought she would like. She merely stripped off her gloves without a word.

"Catherine, what's wrong?" He crossed the room to her side. "This is your home now. I was hoping you'd look pleased, not troubled."

She unpinned her velvet hat and looked around helplessly. "This is all rather . . . daunting."

"Daunting? I don't understand."

"In Cleveland, the only servants my stepmother had were two housemaids. Sybilla and I have only one, Molly Cavanaugh. Here, there is a butler, a housekeeper, a chef, six housemaids, four footmen . . ." Her voice trailed off. "I find it rather intimidating."

Damon stared at her in disbelief. "You cut people open, set broken bones, deliver babies, and you're intimidated by running a household?"

She closed her eyes and nodded.

He put his hands on her shoulders. "Catherine, listen to me. Winslow and the housekeeper have been running this house without any help from me, and I'm sure they'll do the same for you. You are the mistress of the house, and you can control as much or as little as you like. Even if you don't, meals will be served and the furniture will get dusted, believe me."

She smiled sheepishly. "I had visions of rushing off to deliver a baby while the housekeeper chases me down the street, demanding to know what I want her to serve for dinner and if she should dismiss the upstairs maid."

Damon chuckled at that, then grew serious as he pulled her into his arms and held her. "You must never be afraid to talk to me when something troubles you. I like to think I'm a fair man."

When his wife looked up at him, her lovely face glowing with trust, Damon felt the familiar tightness of arousal begin to build. Visions of her lying naked in his arms, her long ivory limbs entwined around him, almost unmanned him.

As he brushed the backs of his fingers along her soft cheek, he could see she divined his intent by the way her pale blue eyes changed, turning darker and more slumbrous. She was learning the unspoken language of passion well.

"It's time you learned how to undress me," he murmured.

A small smile of anticipation touched her mouth, and Damon couldn't resist kissing her.

Catherine applied herself to the task at hand with the same precision she used in her doctoring. She untied his tie first, letting it drop to the floor. His coat fell into the pile next, topped by his shirt.

As Catherine undid his trousers' buttons, Damon thought he would explode. But he forced himself to remain still, letting her move at her own pace. And it was excruciatingly slow, for she was also learning how to torment and tantalize him.

When he was finally naked, he helped Catherine undress and they slipped between the sheets.

"Love me," he whispered against her hair.

She explored him with her fingertips, lips, and tongue, stroking, clutching, weighing, until Damon felt delirious with excitement. When he could stand no more and pulled her down on top of him, he found that she was so ready for him, she cried his name and shuddered just as he found his own release.

Later, as Damon held his wife against him in love's afterglow, he thought fleetingly of Francine and how fortunate he was not to have married a woman like her.

The following morning, Catherine walked into the Washington Square house and breathed a sigh of relief. Patients filled the waiting room. Her surgery was just as she had left it. Nothing had changed just because she was married.

A door opened and Sybilla came out, took one look at Catherine and stopped. "What are you doing here?"

"I'm seeing my patients," she replied, taking off her coat.

"But—but you just got married two days ago, and you've just moved into a new house. Don't you and Damon want to have some time alone together?"

Catherine smiled. "He went to his Wall Street office this morning, so I thought I would come to mine. Besides, the house will run just fine without me." She drew Sybilla into her surgery. "I'm sorry you couldn't come to dinner last night, but Nevada said you were called away."

Sybilla nodded. "I wanted to, but your Mrs. Gunther had twins." Then she added, "And how do you like married life?"

Catherine thought of how Damon had awakened her this morning, and she smiled. "It's wonderful."

Sybilla grinned. "I've never seen you quite so glowing. How are the domestic arrangements?"

"This morning, Damon told me what my quarterly allowance would be. I nearly fainted. It's more than I've made practicing medicine in the last year."

"Your husband is extremely wealthy, Cat."

"I just never realized how wealthy." She shook her head. "Goodness, what will I do with it all?"

"Find a dressmaker immediately. Have your measurements taken and buy clothes by the trunkload. I'll advise you."

Catherine looked down at her brown wool skirt. "I suppose I should."

"You must," Sybilla insisted. "A wealthy man like Damon doesn't want his wife running around looking like a washerwoman. You have his reputation to uphold."

"Very well. You find a suitable dressmaker, and I'll go." She hesitated. "Since I have so much money now and you're my best friend, why don't we order you some gowns as well?"

Sybilla's face lit up. "I'm not proud. I will accept them gladly. By the way, who's taking care of the house?"

"I'm leaving it in the housekeeper's capable hands. Damon has also suggested that I hire a social secretary. Evidently there are young women out there who make a living guiding the socially inept such as myself. She will have her work cut out for her, I'm afraid."

"Well, Damon knew he wasn't getting a Francine Ballard when he married you."

"That's true enough."

But even as she agreed with Sybilla, Catherine had a niggling doubt. Damon had agreed that she would still practice medicine, but what if her refusal to play by society's rules was detrimental to him in some way? She put the thought out of her mind.

"I wonder what Francine will do when she hears about your wedding?" Sybilla mused. "She'll probably lapse into a coma. Nevada told me she thought she had Damon 'roped and branded.'"

Before Catherine could comment, there came a knock at the door and Kim burst into the surgery. "Sybilla, she's gone and married—"

He stopped short when he saw Catherine standing there.

Her heart went out to him when she saw the utter devastation in his eyes. "Good morning, Kim. Damon and I were married Friday. I hope you'll wish me well."

Sybilla murmured a greeting to Kim and slipped out.

He stared at her, his patrician features haggard. "You know I would never wish you ill, Catherine. But I feel you've made a grave mistake."

"Damon and I love each other."

Kim winced as though that admission were a spear piercing his heart. "Love is never enough for a man like that. He craves money and power. The only people who can give those to him are the very people you profess to disdain."

Catherine glared at him. "That's not true! Damon realizes I'm not Francine Ballard or Genevra Graham."

"He says that now, but you just wait. There will come the day when he urges you to call on the wives of business associates he wants to court. He'll want you to give a ball for someone he wants to impress. He'll be furious when you're late for an important dinner."

"I've heard enough. I think you had better leave."

"I know these people, Catherine. I'm one of them. Mark my words, they're going to destroy you, and your precious husband is going to help them do it."

His eyes burned into Catherine as though committing her to memory, then he whirled on his heel and left.

Catherine just stood there, shaking with rage. No matter what Kim said, Damon would never go back on his word. Never.

The door opened and Sybilla peered in. "Pus and gangrene! I could hear him shouting all the way down the hall."

"Kim is not taking my marriage very well."

"You can't blame him. He loves you, and I think he's finally realized that he's lost you."

"I didn't mean to hurt him, Syb. We were just never meant to be." Catherine sighed. "Perhaps the hurt will fade, and someday we'll be able to be friends again."

"Perhaps."

Catherine straightened her shoulders. "Well, I believe I have patients waiting to see me, so let's get to work."

Catherine tried to keep her mind on medicine, but Kim's words continued to haunt her, especially when she returned home late that afternoon and found what was waiting for her.

• • •

Catherine stared down in dismay at the silver salver covered with cards left by women who had called to satisfy their curiosity about Damon Delancy's new bride.

"Winslow, how many callers did I have today?" she asked, rifling through the small pieces of pasteboard and glancing at the names printed there. Bella Peachtree's was the only one she recognized.

"A dozen, madam."

"And what did you tell them?"

"That you were not receiving callers."

"In the future, tell them the truth, that I am not at home."

If the butler disapproved, he hid it well. "Very good, madam. I have also put the wedding gifts in the drawing room."

Wedding gifts? Catherine hadn't even thought of those.

"Have we received many today?" she asked.

"By the wagonload, madam."

Each one of them would require an acknowledgment. Catherine could see herself spending what little time she had during the day writing thank-you notes for silver coffeepots and trays.

She thanked Winslow and headed for the drawing room. Inside, it was just as she feared. Beribboned boxes were piled high on every available flat surface, each gift demanding her attention.

Catherine pursed her lips defiantly. Kim was wrong. These people were not going to destroy her. She wasn't going to let them.

She and Damon were going to discuss this as soon as he came home.

Catherine was waiting for him in the foyer the moment he walked through the door an hour later. But the moment she saw the familiar desire leap into his eyes, all thoughts of callers and coffeepots vanished from her mind in her eagerness to embrace him.

"I missed you so much today," he murmured as he pulled her against him.

She wrapped her arms around his neck. "And I missed you."

He kissed her, his mouth so heavy and sweet. "Do we have time to dally before dinner?"

Catherine smiled lazily. "I was hoping you'd suggest it."

Later, as Catherine lay curled against her husband's chest, she mentioned the callers and wedding gifts and asked him what she should do about them. Damon urged her to hire a social secretary just before he started to arouse her again.

Catherine's last coherent thought was that Kim was wrong about Damon after all.

CHAPTER

TWELVE

CATHERINE made a heroic effort to adjust to her new life, but as the days went by, she felt herself pulled in two different directions. Even though she had servants and a social secretary, she found the callers kept coming and leaving cards, and the stack of invitations kept growing, all vying with her medical practice for precious time. Social obligations always lost the battle, much to her secretary's chagrin.

One day, a month after Catherine's wedding, she was just about to sail out the door when Miss Schuyler, her secretary, stopped her.

"Mrs. Delancy, may I speak to you for a moment?"

Catherine tugged on her gloves. "Can it wait until this evening? I must get to my office at once."

"This is very important, madam."

"Very well. What is it?"

Her voice shook with excitement as she handed Catherine a heavy square of ivory vellum. "You and Mr. Delancy have been invited to Caroline Astor's."

"When?"

"Next Monday evening. Everyone knows that Monday is her night for dances and soirees."

"We can't possibly attend. I shall probably be working late that evening. Kindly send our regrets."

Miss Schuyler turned white and sputtered, "Mrs. Delancy, I'm afraid you don't realize the magnitude of this invitation. True, it's not as prestigious as being invited to her annual ball that was held two weeks ago, but everyone knows that Caroline Astor doesn't invite just anyone to her soirees. You and Mr. Delancy cannot refuse to go. It would be a terrible social *faux pas*."

"*Faux pas* or not, I just don't have time to attend," Catherine said. "Now if you'll excuse me, I have patients waiting."

Catherine left thinking the matter was closed. But she discovered it was far from closed when she returned home at eleven o'clock that evening to find Damon waiting up for her.

The moment Catherine stepped into the dimly lit foyer, Damon appeared in the parlor doorway and crossed the marble floor in his long, quiet stride.

She smiled when she saw him, and set down her medical bag. "You shouldn't have waited up for me. It's late." To her surprise, Damon didn't rush to embrace her. He stood there with his arms by his sides, his expression cool and remote. She stepped forward in alarm. "What's wrong?"

"We have to talk, Catherine." He extended his arm toward the parlor door.

He's furious with me for being late again, she thought as she preceded him into the parlor where a fire still burned in the grate.

Damon closed the doors behind him. "Please sit down."

Catherine took a deep breath. "If we're going to argue, I'd prefer to stand."

"What makes you think I wish to argue?"

"Because you're angry with me about something, and when you're angry, you tend to become as sweet as vinegar. And since I will not suffer your outbursts meekly, we are sure to argue."

A shadow of a smile flitted across his mouth, then vanished. "This is the third night in a row that you've come in late."

"I had medical emergencies that demanded my attention."

"Sybilla couldn't have seen to them?"

"They were my patients."

Damon walked toward her. "This is the third time I've had to eat dinner alone, and I hope it will be the last."

His preemptory tone made Catherine bristle. "When a woman is in the middle of having a baby, I just can't stop and say, 'I'm so sorry that I can't deliver your baby, but my husband expects me home for dinner.' " She rubbed her forehead where a headache was beginning to form. "Damon, you knew before you married me that I would often come home late and miss dinner."

A muscle worked in his jaw showing that he was on the verge of losing his temper. "Yes, I knew that, but almost every night?"

She shrugged. "I can't help it."

"But you can, if you are willing."

"I refuse to give up my medical practice!"

"I'm not asking you to give it up, merely let Sybilla take over once in a while." Damon moved closer, his gray eyes beseeching. "I'm not making this request just to be difficult, Catherine. You're my wife and I enjoy spending time with you. When I come home from Wall Street, I look forward to sitting across from you at the dinner table and talking. You soothe away my battle wounds. When you're not there, those wounds have no chance to heal."

Catherine turned away, her thoughts in turmoil. If Damon had railed at her like any other husband, or demanded that she not keep such late hours treating patients, she would have fought back just as stubbornly. But all he had done was ask her calmly and rationally to compromise, to spend more time with him. And since she missed spending more time with him as well, how could she refuse?

She turned and extended her hands. "All right, Damon. I will try to be home for dinner more often."

He smiled as he took her hands and raised them to his lips. "Admit it, Catherine. Eating dinner with me soothes your battle wounds, too."

Catherine thought of her lukewarm suppers in the quiet, cavernous kitchen with only the copper pots for company, and she sighed. "Yes, it does."

"Then let's not make it a practice of eating alone, shall we? We didn't get married to eat alone."

"I'll do my best." She pulled away to stifle a yawn. "It's been a long day. Shall we go to bed?"

"Shortly. There's another matter we have to discuss."

Catherine sensed his change in mood at once and was instantly alert. "Oh?"

"Miss Schuyler informed me that we had received an invitation to one of Caroline Astor's dances, and that you said we would not be attending."

"Yes, I did. The invitation was for a Monday night, and those nights are especially hectic. The working men who live in the tenements get paid on Friday. They get drunk, get into fights, and often beat their wives and children half to death all weekend long. The dispensary needs every doctor it can get on Mondays, that's why I refused Mrs. Astor's invitation."

Damon's gray eyes grew chilly again. "Regardless of that, I told Miss Schuyler to accept."

Catherine became very still. "May I ask why?"

"Because it's very important to me. Caroline Astor is the reigning queen of New York society, and for all my wealth and accomplishments since arriving here, she has never invited me to anything. Until now."

"I don't understand why you want to curry this woman's favor."

"There will be many influential people there. Bankers who can lend me money. Buyers for what I have to sell. It would be very advantageous for me to get to know them—that's why we are going."

Catherine took a deep breath to quell her rising temper. "Do you remember the agreement we made before I accepted your proposal of marriage? I distinctly remember asking you if you could accept my late hours, interrupted dinners, and missed social events such as this one, and you said that you could. Were you lying to me, Damon?"

His heavy brows came together in a scowl, and his mouth was tight with barely suppressed rage. "Damn it, when I agreed to those terms, I did not infer that you would be late *every* night of the week, that you would interrupt *every* dinner, and that we would miss *every* social event for the rest of our lives." His voice rose. "Is that what you intended, Catherine, to cut us off from my world entirely?"

"Of course not, but—"

"Because you're not being fair to me. I can no more cut myself off from society than you can from medicine." He whirled on his heel and stalked off to the fireplace, where he grasped the mantel so hard his knuckles turned white.

As Catherine studied her husband's broad back, so tense with anger, she tried to maintain her own self-righteousness, but found she couldn't.

She walked up to him and placed her hands on his shoulders. "You're right. I'm not being fair to you. I'll try my best to attend the Astors' dance, but if someone needs doctoring, I may be late."

He turned around. "Fair enough."

Catherine wrapped her arms around his waist and rested her head against his shoulder. "I do detest arguing with you, Damon."

He rested his cheek against the top of her head. "Then don't. Merely acquiesce to my wishes."

She looked up and saw the corners of his mouth twitching in a smile. "I prefer it when you acquiesce to mine," she said.

"I know. But as I once told you, we can't have everything we want in life." He hesitated. "I have another reason for wanting you to attend this dance."

"And what is that?"

"I enjoy seeing you dressed in your finery, outshining every woman there, and I do so yearn to dance the One-Armed Waltz with you again."

Catherine laughed when she recalled the first time they had ever danced with each other. "Oh, my dear husband. Whatever am I to do with you?"

"Love me," he whispered.

"With pleasure."

Damon swung her into his arms and carried her upstairs to their bedroom, where their lovemaking was all the sweeter coming in the wake of their disagreement.

Later, as Catherine lay with Damon's arm heavy across her waist, she thought of the troubling words they had exchanged tonight. Was Damon doing an about-face now that they were married? Was he going to make more and more demands on her, until she had nothing left to give to medicine?

Not if I have any say in the matter, she thought just before falling asleep to dream of Caroline Astor's dance.

Damon stood in the entrance hall of the Astors' Fifth Avenue and 34th Street brownstone, and smiled.

When he was a child of seven or eight, living on the streets, doing anything short of selling his body to survive, he had often looked up enviously at these brightly lit houses, wondering what it would be like for the inhabitants to welcome him inside instead of chasing him away like a mangy dog. Now, each time he stepped through the doors of a house like this, he felt as though he were entering one for the first time. He never tired of the recognition, the welcoming smiles, the respect.

He even saw respect in Mrs. Astor's eyes when it was his turn to greet his hostess.

Damon found it difficult to believe that this short, stout woman wielded so much power. She stood beneath a too-flattering portrait of herself as regally as a queen, in her beaded white satin gown. The woman was so encrusted with diamonds, from the tiara perched on her black wig to the high choker around her thick neck, that Damon wondered if she could walk unaided. She had even reversed several necklaces so diamonds cascaded down her back in a sparkling shower.

I can't wait to hear what Catherine has to say about you, Damon thought as his hostess said a few words of welcome and he moved on to the ballroom.

No sooner did he step into the room than Gordon Graham hailed him.

"So how does it feel to be an old married man, Delancy?" the big man asked, shaking Damon's hand.

"There's nothing like it," he replied, grinning as he took a glass of champagne from a passing footman. "I'd recommend the state to anyone."

Gordon looked around. "Where is the new Mrs. Delancy?"

"She had some patients to tend to, so she'll be late."

Damon had been annoyed when Catherine telephoned to tell him that she couldn't possibly get away from the Women's Dispensary any sooner, but he decided to reserve his wrath for later, if she didn't show up at all. But she was trying hard to please him. After all, she had come home for dinner almost every night since their little discussion a week ago.

Gordon sipped his champagne and shook his leonine head. "I don't know how you do it, Delancy, married to a lady doctor. Do you ever get to see her?"

Damon recalled dining alone and felt a flash of irritation. "Of course I do."

"Don't you worry about her wandering around the city at night? There are legions of violent men out there. A defenseless woman can get hurt."

"The women go out in pairs," Damon explained with exaggerated patience. "Catherine used to have a policeman escort her home, but now that she's my wife, she has a carriage."

"Still, I wouldn't want that for my Gen."

Damon knew that if this line of conversation continued, he would undoubtedly lose his temper, so he offered, "I haven't seen much of you and your wife these days. As soon as Catherine gets settled, we'll have to have you and some others over for a dinner party."

Graham cleared his throat. "We may have to send our regrets."

"Why?"

The man looked uncomfortable. "I guess you don't know."

"Don't know what?"

"Our wives have had some sort of falling out. I don't know the circumstances—Genevra won't tell me. All I know is that Kim Flanders is back to being her doctor now, and we haven't seen hide nor hair of Catherine in months." Graham shrugged. "But you know how women are. They can start a war over the silliest thing."

"Catherine's not like that," Damon said levelly. "If she and your wife had a falling out, it was over something serious."

Gordon scowled, but before he could comment, Damon saw someone else he needed to speak to, excused himself, and left.

He wove his way around the ballroom, stopping to greet people he knew and asking for introductions to those people he needed to know.

Damon was scanning the room for any sign of Catherine when he inadvertently locked eyes with Francine Ballard.

For one second her true feelings blazed out for the world to see, then they vanished behind a veil of ladylike imperturbability. But Damon could recognize hurt and betrayal when he saw it.

He maneuvered his way to her side. "Good evening, Francine. You look lovely, as always."

"Thank you, Damon." Only the ice in her voice revealed her bitterness toward him.

He stood there awkwardly, searching for something to say. "Are you here with your parents?"

"No, Kim Flanders."

Damon's eyes widened in surprise. "Flanders?" *Wait until I tell Catherine.*

Francine nodded as she opened her fan with a dismissive flick of her wrist. "He's a most charming man. I'm enjoying his company ever so much."

"I'm happy to hear it."

"Yes, Kim Flanders knows just how to make a woman feel special. He's always so attentive and considerate of her feelings. He's a true gentleman, and as we know, a true gentleman is born, not made."

"Unlike a cad such as myself."

Francine blushed and fanned herself furiously. "I never said anything of the sort."

She was too much of a lady to be that obvious.

Damon looked around. "Is there somewhere we can go to talk in private?"

"I can't leave. Dr. Flanders will wonder where I've gone."

"Well, since I can't seem to find the good doctor anywhere, I think you could disappear for a few minutes without causing a major scandal."

"I don't wish to go anywhere with you, Damon. It wouldn't be proper, since I am with another and you are a married man."

"I don't blame you, after the shabby way I've treated you. But it's very important that I explain something to you."

"Oh, very well. Follow me."

She led the way to the Astors' empty parlor. When Damon shut the door behind them, she said, "Now, what do you wish to speak to me about?"

As if she didn't know.

"I want to apologize to you, Francine. I behaved badly toward you. I unwittingly fostered certain . . . expectations that I was unable to fulfill."

Damon waited for her to shout at him, beat his chest with her fists, slap his face—anything to demonstrate that she had once felt some deep emotion for him. But she just stood there, her beautiful face a stoic mask, her dark eyes inscrutable, as she tapped her palm with her sandalwood fan.

"I hope you and your wife will be very happy," was all she said. "Now, if you'll excuse me, I have to return to my escort."

As she brushed past him, Damon caught her arm and held her fast. "I know you must hate me."

"I don't hate you, Damon. It is true that I was expecting an offer of marriage, since we had been keeping company for so long. And I will admit that news of your sudden marriage—to a lady doctor, of all people—did come as a shock to me." She raised her chin proudly as she pulled away. "But as my mama always says, there are bigger fish in the river."

Damon smiled and bowed. "At last I know your true feelings for me. Well, I wish you good fishing, Francine."

Without another word, she turned and flounced out of the parlor. Damon followed in her wake, thanking his lucky stars that he had escaped Francine's bait.

"Damon?"

He turned and smiled in delight when he saw Catherine coming toward him. She looked stunning in a new ballgown of pale blue satin that matched her eyes, but more important, she had kept her promise to him. She was late, but at least she had come to the Astors' soiree.

"I tried to get here earlier," she said, "but I just couldn't get away from the dispensary. The husband of one of the patients went berserk and we had to call in the police."

"No one was hurt I trust?"

"No, thank goodness."

Damon took her hand and kissed it. "I'm glad you're here." He tucked her arm through his and started for the ballroom. "Tell me what you think of our hostess."

Catherine's eyes sparkled mischievously. "Poor Mrs. Astor was so weighed down with diamonds that I wondered if she could walk unassisted."

Damon laughed so loudly, several guests turned and looked in his direction, but he didn't care. At least Catherine was here, by his side, her medical practice forgotten for the moment.

"I think I hear the orchestra starting to play the One-Armed Waltz," he said.

Her eyes sparkled as they entered the ballroom. "Shall we dance, Mr. Delancy?"

"What a fine idea, Mrs. Delancy."

They scandalized everyone by dancing every dance with each other, and later, when they went home and Damon held Catherine tightly in his arms, he thought of what Gordon Graham had said, and wished he could keep his wife safe forever.

As Catherine stared up at the tenement building, she shivered with a sense of foreboding she couldn't shake. Perhaps Hilda Steuben's warning had something to do with her uneasiness.

"Watch out for Maeve's husband, Tom Derry," Hilda had said as Catherine rushed out the dispensary door. "He's a bad one. He's always drunk and he hates us like the plague because we usurp his authority with his family."

Catherine looked down at Seamus, the little boy sent to fetch her. "Is your father home now?"

Seamus cringed. "No, ma'am. My da wasn't there when I left." He looked up at the building. "You'd best hurry. My ma said the baby's going to come at any minute."

Catherine smiled and patted him on the shoulder. "Then we'd best hurry."

She followed Seamus into the building and her eyes automatically adjusted to the dim light of a filthy hallway. The odors of dirt, day-old cooking, and urine nearly choked her, but she hiked her long skirt up expertly with one hand and held her breath until she thought her corset would burst. Luckily, she only had to climb two flights of stairs.

"This is where I live," he said with a pitiful touch of pride, stopping before a door and turning the knob.

Inside, Catherine found the conditions just as deplorable as every other tenement flat she had ever seen. She was used to cockroaches scurrying away at her approach and all the dirty, raggedy children huddled in a corner helplessly. And there was their mother lying on a pile of rags and groaning as she prepared to bring yet another child into the world. But what Catherine hadn't expected was Tom Derry.

Seamus trembled at her side. "Mother Mary. It's my da. And he's mad, he is."

Derry slouched at a rickety table on the only chair in the room. His arms fell slack at his sides, and his bleary eyes glittered with a mixture of malevolence and alcohol as they locked onto Catherine.

"Who're you?" he demanded, hauling himself to his feet where he stood surprisingly steady.

"My name is Dr. Catherine Delancy and I'm here to deliver your wife's baby," she said contemptuously. "Kindly step aside."

His eyes narrowed as he glared at her silently. Then he reached for a knife lying on the table, and before Catherine could blink, he rose and lumbered toward her.

"Da, no!" Seamus cried, rushing forward to try to stop him.

His father backhanded him, sending him flying across the room toward the other children. Then he kept coming at Catherine, the knife glinting.

He's going to kill me, she thought.

Mrs. Derry roused herself. "Tom, for the love of God, leave the doctor alone! She don't mean no harm."

"Quiet, woman, or ye'll regret it!" he roared.

Cowed, Mrs. Derry fell silent.

Catherine backed away, her heart pounding and every sense as sharp as the knife Derry held. He may have been taller and stronger, but his drunken state had slowed down his reflexes. Catherine hoped that this advantage could at least get her out of the building without harm.

She almost reached the door when he lunged. Catherine swung her medical bag and the knife ripped hard leather instead of soft skin.

Derry swore and swayed where he stood.

Catherine ran out the door and fled down the hall, fear goading her on even as her long skirts hampered her and her steel corset stays squeezed her lungs with every deep breath she took. When she glanced back over her shoulder, she saw Derry not far behind, surprisingly fast for an inebriated man.

"Help me!" Catherine cried, desperately pounding on closed doors as she ran for her life.

When she reached the head of the stairs, she knew if she started down, Derry would be on her in seconds and stab her in the back. Instead, she went to the corner, whirled around and swung her medical bag at him with all her might.

The bag struck him in the chest, but he must have been expecting the blow, for he merely wavered for a moment instead of going down. But the moment's hesitation was all Catherine needed. While Derry blinked and caught his breath, Catherine dropped her bag and pushed him as hard as she could.

He lost his balance, and with a high-pitched scream, went headfirst down the stairs, the knife falling uselessly to the floor.

Gasping for breath, Catherine watched as her assailant rolled over and over, to rest silently on the landing, his body as limp as a rag doll's.

Now that the danger was past, people came rushing out of their flats to see what all the commotion was about.

Seamus fought his way to Catherine's side, stared down at his father, and back at Catherine, his eyes filled with shock and accusation. He stepped away from her. "You killed him! You killed me da."

"I'm sorry, Seamus, but your father attacked me with a knife. I had to defend myself."

"He deserves it," someone said. "Always beating his wife until her screams drive you crazy."

Catherine sighed, feeling suddenly drained. She picked up her medical bag with its long gash in the side and the knife to show the police, then she went down the stairs to see if Tom Derry was dead.

"He's alive," she said to the onlookers after she examined the unconscious man. At least the police wouldn't charge her with killing him. "Someone go for the police and have them summon an ambulance. I have a baby to deliver."

Despite the fact that she was shaking, she went back upstairs to do just that.

After delivering Mrs. Derry a daughter, a weary Catherine returned to Washington Square and told Sybilla what had happened. After a hot cup of sweet tea to restore her, Catherine began seeing patients in her surgery.

Two hours later, she was just about to finish for the day and go home when the door burst open.

Damon stood there, but a Damon Catherine barely recognized—a wild-eyed man with flaring nostrils and flushed face.

"Why, Damon," she said, smiling as she rose from her desk.

He slammed the door shut and strode toward her. "Are you all right?"

She realized at once that he had somehow learned about Tom Derry and that it would be pointless to pretend otherwise. "I'm fine."

When he reached her, he pulled her into his arms and hugged her so hard that Catherine thought her ribs would break. Then he stood back and his eyes roved over every inch of her, from the top of her head down to the hem of her skirt, as if he had to see for himself that she was really alive and safe and standing before him.

Then he cupped her face in his hands and kissed her with fierce desperation.

When he released her, he said, "When Flynn called and told me what happened, I—" Words failed him.

Catherine watched as his gray eyes ignited with a desire born of fear for her and she knew instinctively that he was going to take her right here, right now.

"No, Damon, please."

But he was too far gone to listen to entreaties. He went to lock the door, divesting himself of his coat and flinging it on the floor as he strode back to her. Then he cradled the nape of her neck in one hand while he plundered her mouth with his tongue and deftly undid her shirtwaist so he could pull one breast free of the confining corset.

Catherine felt the familiar fire ignite at his skilled touch, fanned by the realization that she had come close to losing Damon through her own death. With a whimper of surrender, she ran her hands along his shirtfront to excite him further, then down to undo the buttons of his trousers.

Suddenly Damon stopped and looked around. Then he swept Catherine into his arms, carried her over to the padded leather examining table, and set her on the edge. She leaned back and lifted her legs as he raised her skirts out of the way.

Catherine gasped as his questing fingers found their mark and he continued to arouse her ruthlessly, as if punishing her for almost dying. Just when she thought she'd die of the exquisite torment, he positioned himself above her and buried himself in her welcoming softness, their mutual hunger so great, they reached the pinnacle of mutual ecstasy within seconds.

His weight resting on his arms, Damon sagged against her, his anger and frustration finally spent as well. Catherine stroked his black silky hair, gentling him.

When he pulled away, he panted, "We had better get dressed before someone comes looking for you."

Once Catherine straightened her skirts and buttoned up her shirtwaist, removing all traces of their wanton interlude, she said, "So Liam Flynn told you what happened?"

"Yes." He dragged his hand through his hair. "Damn it, Catherine, you could have been killed!"

"Tom Derry wasn't really a threat. He was drunk out of his mind, Damon, and couldn't see straight, never mind stab me. Besides, when I pushed him down the stairs, he broke an arm and several ribs. He's lucky to be alive."

"Did the police arrest him?"

"Yes. He'll spend some time in jail."

"I'll see to it that he never gets out."

"Please don't. Without the meager support he provides his family, they'll be worse off than before. He's more pathetic than dangerous. He's just poor and bitter that he can't rise above his poverty."

"All men like Derry are dangerous. I should know because I was one of them once." Damon hesitated. "You have to promise me you'll never go into the tenements again."

She stared at him, aghast. "Never go into the tenements again? I can't promise that! Those poor people depend on me to deliver their babies, and for medical care they otherwise wouldn't get. They—"

"It's too dangerous. Let the other doctors do it. Let the midwives deliver babies."

Catherine balled her hands into fists at her sides. "I won't agree to this."

Damon's hands shot out and he grasped her arms. "Damn it, Catherine, yes you will! You were almost killed, you little fool! Doesn't that mean anything to you?"

"Of course it does, but it's one of the risks of my profession."

He released her. "A risk I'm not willing to take, even if you are. I insist that you stop going there."

"I will not!"

Damon went to the door, unlocked it, and held it open for her. "It's not open for discussion. I don't want you going into the tenements any more, and that's final. Now, shall we go home?"

"Damon, I—"

"Damn it, Catherine, don't push me! Our carriage is waiting, so kindly stop arguing and let's leave."

Resenting Damon's high-handedness, Catherine demonstrated her displeasure by sitting in stony silence during the carriage ride home. When they arrived, she said she wasn't hungry and locked herself in the library, flinging herself down in one of the leather wing chairs and lacing her fingers together to keep them from shaking, she was so furious with him.

She sat there in the comforting silence and thought. Wisely, Damon left her alone.

He intended to take it all away from her, bit by bit. She had been blind not to see it before. He began by insisting that she not be late for dinner, thus cutting back the time she volunteered to the Women's Dispensary. Now he wanted her to keep out of the tenements altogether. What was next, giving up medicine entirely?

"Never," she swore aloud.

That night, Catherine went to bed before Damon and slept with her back to him. He made no overtures of any kind, but she could feel the weight of his eyes on her. The following morning, she rose while he was still sleeping and went to Washington Square, where she had breakfast with a surprised Sybilla and Molly.

As the day wore on, she grew even more miserable, and by the time it was time for her to return home, she knew she had to do something to break the hostilities between them, because she loved Damon too much to endure it any longer. And she had an idea that just might accomplish it.

• • •

When she arrived, she found Damon in his study, seated behind his desk, staring moodily out the window. He looked up when she entered, and said nothing, but his unhappy expression told her everything she wanted to know.

"You're home early," she said.

"I'm the boss. I can leave when I please."

Catherine hesitated, not knowing quite how to start. Finally, she just plunged in. "I don't like this war between us, Damon."

"Neither do I, but neither of us wants to surrender."

"I think I have a way that both of us can get what we want."

He raised his brows. "I don't see how."

"I don't want to stop practicing in the tenements. Despite the dangers, I get great satisfaction out of helping the poor." She sighed. "But I'll agree to your terms, if you'll agree to mine."

"And what are your terms?"

"Let me open an office here in this house."

He stared at her as if she had gone mad. "Here? In our home?"

"Yes. I'll convert the front parlor into a surgery. All I'll need is a desk, an examining table, and a medicine cabinet."

Damon rose, scowling. "But this is our home. I don't want strangers traipsing through it day and night."

"They wouldn't be strangers, and they wouldn't be traipsing through the whole house, only the foyer and the front parlor." She went to him. "Patients usually go to their neighborhood doctor. Who lives in this neighborhood? The wealthy. They would be my patients."

Catherine paused before hitting him with her most compelling argument. "Besides, having an office in our home would allow me to spend more time here, out of danger. Many doctors practice out of their homes. Kim Flanders does."

His eyes narrowed in speculation. "What about your Washington Square practice?"

"I wouldn't give it up entirely because Sybilla needs my help, but I wouldn't spend as much time there, and I wouldn't go into the tenements at all."

"I'll have to think about this."

"Take all the time you need."

"What if I don't agree?"

"I think you will because you love me and want to see me happy. Not practicing medicine would make me very unhappy."

His stern expression softened. "I don't want that, Catherine. But I also don't want you dead."

She headed for the door. When she reached it, she stopped and turned. "You may have to give up some of your privacy and your front parlor to do this, Damon, but I will give up far more by agreeing not to go into the tenements. As a businessman, you are getting the better deal."

"Wait," he said. As he came up to Catherine, he extended his hand to run his thumb down her cheek. "You may turn the front parlor into a surgery."

Catherine sighed and slipped her arms around his waist, relieved that the tension between them had vanished. "Thank you, Damon."

He lifted her chin so he could look into her eyes. "You drive a hard bargain, Mrs. Delancy."

"It will work out. You'll see."

If it didn't, there was no hope for their marriage.

Two weeks later, Sybilla just finished saying goodbye to her last patient of the morning when Catherine walked in the door.

Sybilla stared at her friend in disbelief. Catherine wore a crisp blue-striped shirtwaist with a slight puff at the shoulder and a fashionably wide skirt that made her belted waist seem even smaller. Someone had trimmed her upswept hair so that flattering curls now framed her face.

Sybilla turned to Bonette the skeleton and said, "Did you think you'd ever live to see the day when our Catherine would become a fashion plate?"

Catherine made a face, obviously uncomfortable in the role. "Disgusting, isn't it? Damon insists that I wear something new every day, and my maid—can you believe that I have my own maid?—won't let me out of the house without putting up my hair."

Sybilla sighed. "Thank God the days of your brown dresses and coronet braid are long gone. Now you look like a millionaire's wife." She sat down at her desk and studied her friend for a moment. "How is your home office working out?"

Catherine sat down. "Wonderfully. Damon spared no expense converting the front parlor into a surgery, and he even agreed to hang a sign outside the house."

Sybilla could tell from her friend's preoccupied air that something was still on her mind. "But you're not quite satisfied with the arrangements, are you, Cat?"

Catherine smiled ruefully. "I never could keep anything from you." She hesitated. "It's my patients. They're all society women, and I feel as though I'm turning into Kim Flanders." She rose and slowly paced the room. "I know the wealthy get sick just like everyone else, but I miss the satisfaction of working in the tenements."

"What did Hilda Steuben say when you told her that you wouldn't be working there any more?"

"You know Hilda. All she said was, 'Too bad. You could've been a great doctor.' "

"Hilda never was the epitome of tact."

Catherine stopped. "What else could I do, Syb? After Derry tried to kill me, Damon was adamant. This was the only acceptable compromise." She sighed as she sat back down. "If there's one thing I've learned since being married, it's the art of compromise." She hesitated. "And speaking of marriage, when is Nevada going to make an honest woman of you?"

Sybilla started. "Mother of surgeons. How did you know we were lovers?"

"You never could keep anything from me either. You just act like a woman who has a lover. I'm a little hurt that you didn't trust me enough to tell me."

She rose, suddenly overcome with guilt. "I—I meant to, Cat, really. And as for marrying Nevada . . ." She shrugged. "After my affair with Jean-Claude ended so badly, I just want to be very sure before I go marrying anyone, even Nevada."

"He loves you, Sybilla. I'm sure he's not anything like this Jean-Claude."

"I know. But I sometimes wonder if I have the same ability to compromise that you do."

A smile played about Catherine's mouth. "That is true. You do like getting your own way, and so does Nevada."

Sybilla tossed her head. "It's a Wolcott trait."

Catherine chuckled at that. Then she rose. "Well, I must be on my way. I should have patients waiting."

"Will you be here on Thursday?" Sybilla asked, for her friend maintained her practice here every Thursday.

Catherine nodded. "Of course. I can't let Damon have his own way in everything."

"We can't ever let the men get away with too much," Sybilla agreed.

After Catherine left, Sybilla sat at her desk and stared moodily into space, momentarily alone with her thoughts.

She couldn't believe the astonishing change in Catherine since marrying Damon. The old Catherine would have no more stopped working in the tenements than she would let a man dictate her dress. But since marrying Damon, she had done both—and willingly. Damon, on the other hand, had given up little as far as Sybilla could see.

"She must love him very much, Bonette," she mused aloud, pushing up her spectacles. "But I wonder what she would do if he ever asked her to give up medicine entirely?"

Sybilla knew what she would do, but then for all her femininity, she was made of sterner stuff than Catherine.

Still, she was grateful to Damon for keeping Catherine away from the Washington Square practice for most of the week. Catherine's absence allowed her to distribute anticonception information and devices to select patients, even though she knew her friend would be furious if she found out.

A pang of remorse shot through Sybilla at having to deceive Catherine, but it vanished when she thought of the women she was helping.

Still, she didn't want to think about what would happen if Catherine learned her secret.

CHAPTER

THIRTEEN

CATHERINE stood at a tall window and frowned as she watched the sign with her name on it sway in the brisk October breeze.

Her safe, lucrative practice bored her.

She sighed, turned and walked back to her desk. She missed the deep satisfaction of working in the tenements, the knowledge that someone depended on her for medical care they couldn't get anywhere else.

"Oh, Catherine, stop complaining," she muttered to herself. "Since you stopped going to the tenements, Damon has been the best of husbands."

She smiled fondly as she regarded the silver desk set, now engraved with her initials, and the Christmas Eve Damon had given it to her. And he had spared no expense to convert the parlor into her surgery, complete with a padded leather examining table and huge medical cabinet stocked with more drugs than a pharmacy. Yes, the first ten months of their marriage had been blissful indeed.

A knock on the door interrupted her thoughts and revealed her medical assistant Rebecca.

"Excuse me, Dr. Delancy," she said. "A Mrs. Talmadge just called and wanted to know if you would go to her house right away."

Dahlia Talmadge, the banker's wife. The ravishing beauty with the empty eyes. Catherine remembered her all too well from that weekend at Coppermine.

"Did she say what was wrong?"

"All she said was that she is feeling poorly," Rebecca replied.

"Do I have any other patients scheduled this afternoon?"

"Just one at three o'clock."

"Then I shall call on Mrs. Talmadge."

When Catherine arrived at the Talmadges' modest mansion on Madison Avenue, she was shown into a drawing room, three of its four walls covered from floor to ceiling with paintings in ornate gold frames. Since the butler asked her to wait while he announced her, Catherine strolled around the room and studied the banker's impressive collection.

She was not an art connoisseur, having neither the time nor inclination, but she enjoyed looking at restful scenes of fields and scudding clouds now and then. Mr. Talmadge's art collection, however, was far from restful. As Catherine moved from one painting to the other, she felt a niggling uneasiness grow into a shudder of revulsion.

Some were exotic oriental scenes of voluptuous naked women lounging on tasseled cushions in a harem, or being inspected by turbaned bedouins in a slave market. Others depicted leering barbarians abducting voluptuous naked women, their terrified expressions so real that Catherine could almost hear their screams. A third type of painting purported to educate and morally elevate the viewer, since it illustrated biblical scenes of Christian martyrdom, featuring yet more voluptuous naked women suffering unspeakable indignities for their faith.

While seemingly different, each painting shared a common theme, that of women in various states of enslavement and submission.

She wondered what kind of man would collect such distasteful paintings, and what type of wife would allow him to display them in her home.

Catherine turned her back on the paintings and waited until the butler returned and told her that Mrs. Talmadge would see her now.

She found Dahlia Talmadge upstairs in her bedchamber, a curiously dark, austere room, devoid of the ruffles and feminine touches most women preferred.

"Good afternoon, Mrs. Talmadge." Catherine smiled at the woman propped up against several pillows in the large four-poster bed. "I understand you're not feeling well."

Though Dahlia Talmadge's complexion was white, her dusky hair falling in a loose braid over her left shoulder, she was still one of the most beautiful women Catherine had ever seen.

"Good afternoon, Dr. Delancy," Mrs. Talmadge said in a

flat husky voice. "Thank you for coming." Her eyes showed no gratitude, or even relief.

"It's a beautiful autumn day, isn't it?" Catherine said cheerfully as she pulled up a chair and set her medical bag down beside it.

"I wouldn't know. I haven't been out."

Catherine sat down and took out her stethoscope. "Well, we'll have to make you well so you can get out. Now, Mrs. Talmadge, what precisely is wrong with you?"

"I have terrible pains here." Her right hand slid down the coverlet and stopped in the vicinity of her pelvis. "And my stomach is getting so fat, my clothes don't fit."

"Perhaps you're with child."

For the first time Catherine had known her, Dahlia Talmadge's eyes exhibited an emotion: stark fear. "I can't be."

"I'll have to examine you to be certain," Catherine said soothingly. "Now, if you'll just draw back the coverlet and remove your pantelets, please."

"Must you examine me?"

Catherine felt a rush of sympathy for the woman's excessive modesty. "Yes, I must in order to make a proper diagnosis," she said gently. "You needn't be embarrassed, Mrs. Talmadge, as we are both women."

After Mrs. Talmadge did as she was told, Catherine listened to her heart and lungs, then lifted her nightgown to examine the pelvis.

Catherine stared in shock and disbelief. Narrow faded red welts striped Dahlia Talmadge's white hips and thighs. She had been whipped.

"Who did this to you?"

The woman averted her face, her ivory cheeks crimson with mortification. "Don't ask me any questions, doctor, I beg of you. Pretend you never saw them and continue with your examination."

"I can't do that. You are my patient and I'm concerned for all aspects of your welfare." She paused. "Your husband must have done this to you."

"If you persist with your questions, it will only be worse for me."

Catherine removed her stethoscope and turned to her medical bag. "I'm sorry, Mrs. Talmadge. If you can't confide in me, I would suggest you find another doctor.'' She picked up her bag and turned to leave.

''Wait!''

Catherine turned and waited.

''You won't tell anyone else about this?''

''Of course not. Everything you tell me will be held in strictest confidence,'' Catherine assured her.

''Very well.''

Catherine set down her bag and sat down.

Dahlia Talmadge took a deep breath as if to gather her courage, and didn't look directly at Catherine. ''He can't . . . perform his husbandly duties unless he whips me. Sometimes he ties me down to the bed, and sometimes he makes me stand and ties my wrists to one of the posts.''

Catherine's gaze went to one of the bed's four posts, and she noticed scratch marks near the top made by the woman's nails on the polished mahogany surface. If Mr. Talmadge had been in the room, she would have taken a whip to him herself.

''That's appalling!''

''Oh, but when it's over, he weeps and tells me he's sorry,'' as if that excused his behavior. ''The next day, he always gives me an expensive piece of jewelry.''

Now the significance of August Talmadge's art collection became all too apparent. ''If he's so sorry, why doesn't he stop? Or why doesn't he go to a brothel and spare you such an outrage? Those women get paid for enduring a man's base desires.''

When Dahlia didn't answer, Catherine asked, ''Why don't you leave him?''

Fear widened her dark eyes and she clawed at the sheet, bunching and twisting it. ''I couldn't! I have no money and nowhere to go. And the terrible scandal . . .'' She shuddered. ''I'd be an outcast with nothing but the clothes on my back.''

''Mrs. Talmadge,'' Catherine said softly, clasping her hand, ''you can't allow him to do this to you.''

''There's nothing I can do. Mr. Talmadge is my husband. When I married him, I promised to love and obey him, in sickness and in health.'' A small smile flickered across her mouth, then vanished. ''Otherwise, he is a wonderful husband and a good provider. I have clothes, jewels, and a respected place in society.''

But at the cost of your soul, Catherine added to herself.

She wanted to shake some sense into Dahlia, but she knew

that the woman merely echoed the sentiments of most of her sex. Women could endure much, as long as a husband was a good provider. They had no other choice.

Catherine sighed. "Very well, Mrs. Talmadge, if that's the way you feel, what you and your husband do behind closed doors is none of my concern. I'll prescribe an ointment for those welts."

"Thank you, doctor. I knew you would understand."

Catherine regarded her coldly. "But I don't." Then she continued with the examination.

When she finished, she stood back. "You have a growth—a cyst—on your right ovary, Mrs. Talmadge. You'll have to go to the hospital and have an operation to remove it."

The older woman turned even paler, and for a moment, Catherine feared she might faint. "A—an operation? Can't you give me some medicine to make it go away?"

"I'm sorry, but medicine won't help. The cyst is large, about the size of an orange, and only surgery can remove it. There's no other way."

Her hands shook as she lay there in stunned silence. When she spoke, she said, "Am I going to die?"

"I won't sugar-coat the truth, Mrs. Talmadge. All surgery entails risk. But I see no reason why you couldn't survive the operation."

"I can't. I simply can't go to the hospital."

"If you don't have that cyst removed," Catherine said firmly, "then you surely will die."

"You don't understand. If I have an operation, people will see what my husband does to me. Everyone will know our secret."

"Surely your husband could control himself until the marks disappear," Catherine snapped, her patience worn out at last. "Then when you're well, he can go back to beating you to his heart's content."

Dahlia cringed, and tears filled her eyes as she shook her head.

"Then I shall have a little discussion with him concerning this matter," Catherine said crisply.

"No, you mustn't! He—he would be furious with me."

"But surely other doctors have examined you and know what your husband does to you."

"I haven't seen a doctor since the day I married Mr. Talmadge, four years ago. And I wouldn't have seen you if I hadn't been in such excruciating pain.''

So that explained why the ovarian cyst had gone untreated for so long, and allowed to grow unchecked.

Catherine softened with pity. "My colleague Sybilla Wolcott is a surgeon. I will ask her if she will perform the operation for you, and I will assist her. We will make sure that you have a private room at the hospital and that no one else sees you.''

"Would you?" Dahlia grabbed her hand and held it. "I—I don't know how to thank you.''

"I wish I could do more," Catherine said, her implication quite clear.

Dahlia's beautiful dark eyes became remote once again. "There is nothing else you can do for me.''

That, Mrs. Talmadge, Catherine said to herself, *is where you are wrong.*

As Catherine sat in her carriage, she wondered why Dahlia Talmadge's plight enraged her so. She knew that most married women shared it to some degree because they were economically dependent on their husbands and subject to their domination. But most women didn't have husbands who whipped them. That's what prostitutes were for.

Just the thought of August Talmadge made her blood boil. A respected banker, invited to all the best homes—including the Delancys'—hid his vice so well from the world that not even Catherine had suspected. But now that she knew, she doubted if she could even be in the same room with him without wanting to expose him for the animal he was.

And the man was one of Damon's bankers.

Catherine decided that the patient coming at three o'clock would just have to wait. She knocked on the roof of the carriage and told the driver to take her to her husband's Wall Street office, assuming the driver knew the address, since in the ten months since her marriage Catherine had never once been to Damon's office.

When she arrived at the large building, she had to ask someone the location of Delancy and LaRouche. It was on the third floor, and the faint staccato click of typewriting machines guided her like a siren song.

"Won't Damon be surprised to see me," she muttered to herself as she opened the door and went inside.

The moment she entered, the typewriting ceased. Two young women she knew were called "typewriters" sat at their big black machines and stared at her.

Catherine smiled at them. "I am Catherine Delancy and I am here to see my husband. Is he in?"

One of the young women replied, "He's in a meeting, ma'am."

"Thank you." Catherine marched up to the door with Damon's name on it.

The young woman jumped to her feet. "Mrs. Delancy, you mustn't go in there!"

Her warning came too late. Catherine opened the door and went inside. She found Damon seated at a wide mahogany desk with three other men she didn't recognize seated across from him.

She smiled brightly at the men. "Good afternoon, gentlemen." Then her gaze sought out her husband, who looked annoyed. "Please excuse me for the interruption, but there's something important I must discuss with you."

All the men rose to their feet, obviously disconcerted by the interruption, and by one of their wives, no less.

"Can't this wait?" Damon asked with strained civility. "I'm in the middle of a meeting."

Still fuming over August Talmadge, Catherine was in no mood to acquiesce to any man, even her beloved husband. "I realize that, but this is very important and cannot wait."

Damon hesitated, as if he couldn't decide whether to accede to her wishes and interrupt his meeting, or ally himself with his colleagues and have her wait.

"Gentlemen, if you'll excuse us," he said to the two men in a tone that brooked no argument. "We'll continue this meeting later." After the men filed out and the door closed behind them, Damon glowered at her. "I don't appreciate having my meeting interrupted, Catherine."

Her temper flared. "So, you may come to my office and interrupt me any time you like, but I cannot do the same?"

Her retort left him speechless, but only momentarily. "Forgive me for snapping at you. I can see that you're upset about something." He crossed the room, took her hands, and kissed her lightly on the mouth in apology. "You know I'm always happy to see you. Now, what is this important matter you wish to discuss?"

She took a deep breath. Patient confidentiality or not, she had to help Dahlia. "I want you to sever all ties with August Talmadge."

Damon dropped her hands and took a step back, regarding her as if she had asked him to give away his fortune. "May I ask why?"

"Because he's a monster who should be locked up in an insane asylum."

As Catherine told him what she had discovered about the banker and his beautiful remote wife, she watched her husband's face for his reaction. First his eyes widened in shock and disbelief, then his lip curled in revulsion.

Coming to the end of the sordid tale, Catherine added, "The poor woman is so ashamed she's even been avoiding getting the medical care she needs, because she's so petrified someone will learn their dirty little secret. And if she doesn't have an operation, she will die."

Damon just shook his head. "August Talmadge . . . it's hard to believe he's capable of such monstrous behavior."

"You'd be stunned to know the number of 'respectable' men who hide vile little secrets from the world," Catherine said. "But their wives know, and they confide in me."

Damon shook his head again. "August Talmadge . . ."

"But do you know what's really sick? The woman makes excuses for him and defends him! I had all I could do to keep from spiriting her away to a place where she would be free of that horrible man."

She looked over at Damon. "But since that would create a scandal, I thought of a better way to punish our Mr. Talmadge. And that would be to deny his bank your patronage."

Damon ran his hand along his jaw and began pacing his office. He stopped. "What good would that do?"

"What good would it do? It just might persuade him to stop beating his wife!"

"I doubt it."

Catherine stared at him in shock. "What are you saying, Damon, that you're not going to do this for me, that you're on his side?"

His face twisted in anger. "Of course I'm not on his side. But I'm a businessman, Catherine. Talmadge may be a monster to his wife, but his bank has lent me unlimited funds at an attractive interest rate."

"So you won't withdraw your company's patronage from his bank."

"I'd be a fool if I did."

His betrayal cut her to the heart. She was so dumbfounded that all she could do was stand there in silence.

Damon smiled and placed his hand on her shoulder. "I'll have a long talk with Talmadge and explain the alternatives to beating his wife. The threat of exposure is sure to bring him around."

Catherine shrugged his hand off and whirled away, pleased to see the startled look on his face. "So you think that a woman's life is worth less than unlimited funds at an attractive interest rate?"

Damon's dark brows came together in a scowl, and his eyes blazed with anger. "As I once explained to you, I am a businessman, not a social reformer. You know nothing about commerce, Catherine."

His comment stung. "I see." She fought to control her temper, but failed. "Since commerce is not my sphere, I have no say in how you conduct your business. Then what gives you the right to meddle in my sphere, which is medicine?"

Before Damon could answer, Catherine plunged on heedlessly. "And you have meddled. You insisted that I come home for dinner every evening, no matter that patients might need me. You forced me to stop working in the tenements because of one incident. Yet when I ask this one favor of you, you warn me to stay out of your sphere. What gives you the right?"

"My right as your husband," he growled, his anger dwarfing her own. He strode over to her, his arms stiff at his sides, and Catherine knew he itched to shake her but restrained himself. "I forbade you to work in the tenements for your own good, because you were in danger. I have the right to protect my own wife. What you're asking me to do will not protect Dahlia Talmadge from her husband."

"Perhaps not. But it might cause him to think twice about beating her again."

Damon ran his hand through his hair in frustration. "Damn it, Catherine, you're too emotionally involved to think this through clearly."

"Perhaps. But at least I'm trying to do something to help that poor woman. Unlike you." She swallowed hard, thankful that her white-hot anger prevented her from crying. "Words can't express how you've disappointed me, Damon."

A dull red flush spread across his lean face, and a muscle worked in his jaw. "I'm sorry I can't live up to your high expectations."

Catherine walked to the door. "I won't keep you any longer," she said coldly. "I know you have more important matters to attend to that I can't possibly understand."

When she reached the door, she stopped and turned, the desire strong to wound him. "By the way, I'll be working late tonight. So late, in fact, that I may not be home at all."

"Damn it, Catherine—"

She was out the door before he could stop her. She knew he would never follow her and drag her back into his office, not in front of those two curious young women and his colleagues waiting to resume their meeting.

When she left the office, she managed to keep her emotions under tight control, but once she was safe in the carriage, she let the tears come.

The tears stopped by the time she arrived at the Washington Square house, and she was relieved to find Sybilla alone in her surgery, the last of her patients gone.

Sybilla took one look at Catherine's swollen eyes and said, "What's wrong?"

Catherine sat down, and in a tired, trembling voice told her friend all about Dahlia Talmadge.

Sybilla leaned back in her swivel chair and let out an unladylike whistle. "Mother of surgeons. I knew there was something wrong with that woman the moment I laid eyes on her."

"Her husband is what's wrong with her."

"The man's a scrofulous swine of the first order," Sybilla agreed.

"But that's not the worst of it."

"What could be worse?"

Catherine told her all about going to Damon's office to demand he sever his ties with Talmadge's bank, and how he had refused.

She rose and walked around the room, knotting her fingers together to control her inner turmoil. "I thought Damon and I would surely agree. I thought he would be willing to help me do something about this—this animal."

"And he wasn't?" Sybilla's voice rose incredulously. "That doesn't sound like Damon. Nevada once told me that both he and Damon don't hold with beating women."

"Oh, he said something about showing Talmadge an alternative to beating his wife, but that he would not stop doing business with his bank." Catherine rubbed her forehead. "We had a terrible row about it, Syb. Damon was just so damned arrogant and patronizing, acting as though I, a mere woman, couldn't know anything about commerce."

"But he's right. You don't. You're a doctor."

"Well thank you very much, Dr. Wolcott. Damon doesn't know any more about medicine than I do about commerce, yet he doesn't hesitate to interfere with my sphere."

Sybilla sighed. "That is so typical of a man, isn't it?"

"Still, I thought Damon was different."

"Actually, he is. He—and Nevada, of course—are more enlightened than most. But even so, they're not above trying to impress us with their masculine strength now and then."

"He certainly did that with me this afternoon, and I am furious with him."

Sybilla rose and went to her friend. "I'm sure this will all work out. Once you go home and—"

"I'm not going home tonight," Catherine said. "I want to stay here."

Sybilla's green eyes widened and she started. "Catherine Stone Delancy, are you out of your mind? Do you know what you're doing?"

"I assure you that I'm perfectly sane, and yes, I do know what I'm doing."

"You're—you're leaving your husband!" Sybilla sputtered.

"Only for tonight. I'll go back to the Fifth Avenue house tomorrow morning, but right now, I need time away from Damon to think, and to give him time to think as well. I'm sure once I have time to calm down, I'll be in a more rational mood."

"You're playing with fire," Sybilla warned her. "A man like Damon isn't going to take too kindly to this. He may not sling you over his shoulder and abduct you the way Nevada did me, but underneath, he's still as possessive as they come."

"I'm not afraid of him, Syb," Catherine declared stubbornly.

"I would be." Sybilla placed a reassuring hand on Catherine's arm. "There's still time to go home. I'm sure Damon's there waiting to reconcile now."

Catherine squared her shoulders. "I'm not going anywhere. If Damon wants me, he knows where to find me. Now, what is Molly serving for supper? It smells like a roast, and I'm starving."

Sybilla threw up her hands in defeat. "Don't say I didn't warn you."

They went off to the kitchen together. After dinner, Molly asked no questions as she readied a room for Catherine, though anyone could tell she was burning with curiosity. Catherine didn't enlighten her. She just got ready to spend a night away from her husband for the first time since her marriage.

Her bed was so lonely without Damon.

Half-asleep, Catherine rolled over on her side and reached out for him, expecting to encounter his warm, hard body lying next to hers, but there was nothing except an endless expanse of cold, empty bed. That realization brought her fully to her senses, and she opened her eyes to a dark, unfamiliar room.

Momentarily disoriented, she sat up, her heart pounding in panic. Then it all came back to her: she had argued with Damon and hadn't gone home.

She was right, she reminded herself stubbornly. Then her resolve wavered. If she were right, why did her victory make her feel so hollow inside?

Catherine rose, the floor cold beneath her bare feet as she padded noiselessly over to the window. She pushed aside the curtain and looked down into the street below. No familiar carriage stood parked at the curbside.

"He's not coming after you," she muttered in disappointment as she let the curtain fall.

She returned to bed and dozed. Minutes—hours?—later, she heard her bedroom door open, followed by a flash of blinding light. When her eyes became accustomed to the sudden brightness, she saw Damon filling the doorway, a lamp in his hand.

He dominated her room with his masculine presence, his eyes smoldering with a primitive desire for conquest as they locked with Catherine's across the room and held.

As soon as he closed the door, tension crackled in the air between them. "Why didn't you come home?"

Catherine sat up and drew her knees to her chest. "I was angry with you and needed to be alone, to think."

"You couldn't think in our home?"

"You can be quite distracting, as you know."

"And you can drive a man to despair with your willfulness."

She raised her chin. "I am only willful when I know I'm right."

Damon crossed the room soundlessly, set his lamp on a nearby table, then eased himself into a chair. "I went to Talmadge's house this evening," he said conversationally, "and had a private talk with him."

"You did?"

He nodded. "Why does that surprise you?"

Catherine looked away. "After our . . . discussion in your office, I didn't think you would."

"I must admit I was annoyed with you," he said softly, "but you can be very persuasive, madam."

She couldn't resist a peek at him. "What did you and Mr. Talmadge talk about?"

"I told him that I knew he beat his wife, and if he didn't stop, not only would I withdraw my patronage from his bank, but also persuade others to do the same until I ruined him."

Catherine's eyes widened in astonishment. She hadn't expected him to go this far. "You could do that?"

"Oh, yes." Damon grinned with ruthless satisfaction. "All I would have to do is call in a few favors, and Talmadge knows it."

"And did he agree?"

"Wouldn't you, under those circumstances?"

She nodded, awed once again by her husband's power to control lives, as if they were nothing more than pawns in a chess game.

"Once the initial shock of his exposure wore off, Talmadge promised to frequent those establishments that cater to his particular vice," he said with a grimace of distaste, "so his wife will be spared."

"I'm so glad. I could just imagine what the poor woman went through, living in fear day after day like that."

As she looked at her husband, she felt the hurt and bitterness melt away, replaced by a love so fierce and powerful, she could have wept.

"You know, Damon," Catherine said almost shyly, "when you do something as—as kind and generous as this, I find myself falling in love with you all over again."

He started, his sharp intake of breath revealing how deeply

her words stirred him. "Then it was worth it." He extended one hand, his entire body straining to keep from going to her. "Come here."

Catherine flung back the covers and went to him gladly, unbuttoning the top of her flannel nightgown so that it fell loose around her shoulders and bared the gentle swell of her breasts to entice him. When Damon pulled her onto his lap with a wordless growl of triumph, she melted against him, savoring the hardness of taut muscle and bone beneath cloth as she sought his mouth with the hunger of a starving woman. His lips were as sweet and demanding as she remembered, and soon their anger dissipated in the face of their mutual need.

When they parted, he stared deeply into her eyes. "Is this how you're going to bring me to my knees, by leaving me each time I won't do your bidding?"

"Bring you to your knees?" Catherine drew back, appalled that he could misunderstand her motives. "It wasn't my intention to humble you, Damon. I needed to be alone."

He grasped her shoulders. "Then you must never ever do this to me again, Catherine."

"Never," she agreed, her voice trembling. "I can't bear it when we're angry with each other. I feel so—so lost, so empty inside."

"I waited and waited, and when you didn't come home tonight, I—" Choked with emotion, he closed his eyes and just held her.

When he released her, he shook his head. "I never thought I'd see the day when any woman had such power over me. No man likes being a slave."

She touched his face tenderly, sensing how much it had cost him to make such an admission. "You're no one's slave, Damon. The only power I have over you is whatever you choose to give me."

"Then I am doomed." He reached up and pulled the front of her nightgown down, fully freeing her breasts so he could kiss one, then the other with tantalizing slowness. "Let's go home, Mrs. Delancy."

Catherine slid off his lap, her heart singing. "It will only take me a moment to dress."

"I don't think I can wait that long." Damon rose. "Throw a coat over your nightgown, and let's go home."

Once Catherine and Damon were back home in their own bed,

their passion consumed them like wildfire, as though this would be their last night together. Much later, when they had feasted their fill and lay panting and sated, Catherine shivered.

"Cold?" Damon asked, pulling the sheet over their damp bodies.

Catherine shook her head as she curled against him. "I was thinking of Dahlia." She ran her hand over her husband's chest. "I can't imagine what it must be like to have to make love to a man who has just beaten you."

"What Talmadge did to her wasn't love. It's sickness."

"And you stopped him. I'm very proud of you."

"It was worth it to bring you to my arms again."

He smiled as he drew her to him, this time in gentleness rather than passion, and they slept.

The next time Catherine saw the Talmadges was at a dinner another society hostess was giving to honor some visiting Austrian nobleman and his wife.

Dahlia was still as remote as ever, her eyes just as devoid of emotion, making Catherine wonder if she had done the woman any good at all. But when she caught August Talmadge staring at his wife when he thought she wasn't looking, Catherine knew by the resentment in his eyes that Dahlia had nothing to fear from her husband any more.

♋ CHAPTER ♋

FOURTEEN

April 1892

SYBILLA showed her last patient of the day out the door and smiled to herself in anticipation. She couldn't wait to tell Nevada that she was going to make an honest man of him at last.

"Molly," she said as the maid went to tidy up the surgery, "if any other patients come to the door, send them to the Women's Dispensary unless they're dying. Mr. LaRouche will be here at seven-thirty to take me to Catherine's dinner party, and I don't want any interruptions while I get ready."

"Yes, Dr. Sybilla."

But no sooner did Sybilla finish dressing in her newest black silk gown than Molly appeared in the doorway.

"Sorry to interrupt you, doctor, but there's a little girl downstairs asking for Dr. Delancy. She says her ma needs a doctor real bad."

Sybilla grimaced. "Mother of surgeons, I knew this was going to happen." As she swept down the upstairs hall, she muttered, "This had better be a matter of life and death, that's all I can say."

She found a raggedy child of about seven standing uneasily in the downstairs foyer. When she saw Sybilla gliding down the stairs, she stared as though she were looking at an angel descending from the heavens.

"Good evening, little girl. What's your name?" Sybilla asked.

"Gerta." The urchin pushed an unwashed lock of hair out of her eyes. "You Dr. Delancy?"

"I'm not Dr. Delancy, but I am a doctor."

"I'm supposed to give this to Dr. Delancy." She held a dirty piece of paper tightly as though reluctant to part with it.

239

"Dr. Delancy isn't here," Sybilla explained, "but I'm just as good as she is. If your mother needs a doctor, I'm afraid I'll just have to do."

By the confused look on the child's face, Sybilla suspected she had been given specific instructions to bring Dr. Delancy and did not want to deviate from those orders lest she be punished.

She smiled. "It will be all right, I promise. No one will hurt you if I take Dr. Delancy's place just this once."

The girl hesitated, then surrendered the paper to Sybilla. "My mama's real sick. That's where we live."

She took the paper gingerly and read the address written there. "That's not far from here. Just let me get my wrap and bag and we'll help your mama get all better."

After Sybilla concealed her gown beneath a lightweight evening cloak, she handed the paper to Molly. "This is where I'll be in case I'm not back before Mr. LaRouche calls. Tell him I had to see a patient, and I'll be back as soon as I can."

Molly pursed her lips in disapproval. Ever since Catherine had been attacked, Molly feared for her doctors' safety. "You shouldn't be going out alone at night, Dr. Sybilla. The night's as black as a peat bog, and there's no telling what's out there."

"Don't worry, Molly, no one is going to harm me."

"Still, you'd best be careful. Take a policeman with you."

Molly's warning echoed through Sybilla's mind half an hour later when the hansom cab pulled to a stop at a corner and the driver announced that he would go no farther because this was too dangerous a neighborhood.

Sybilla hesitated. Every fiber of her being told her to tell the driver to take her back to Washington Square, but when she looked down at Gerta's worried face, she knew that as a doctor, she would never forgive herself if something happened to the child's mother.

Sybilla paid the driver and got out with Gerta.

They started walking down the dimly lit street, their footsteps echoing eerily. Sybilla was conscious of furtive eyes watching their every move from doorways and windows, but no one accosted them.

Finally Gerta stopped and pointed. "My mama lives down there, in the house at the end."

Sybilla found herself looking down an alley so narrow, a wagon could barely squeeze through it without scraping its sides, and so long and dark, she couldn't even see Gerta's house at the end.

Suddenly Sybilla wished she had never come, patient or no patient.

Gerta must have sensed her change of heart, for she looked up at Sybilla with appeal in her eyes. "You are coming with me, aren't you?"

The sooner you get this over with, Sybilla said to herself, *the sooner you'll be with Nevada.*

"I'm going to try," she said to Gerta with an optimism she didn't feel. "Let's go, shall we?"

As soon as Sybilla started into the alley, she felt as though she were entering a tunnel. Her eyes strained through her spectacles to adjust to the blinding blackness as she felt her way along one wall. The only sounds she heard were the tapping of footsteps, the soft swish of silk, and the thudding of her own heart.

Sybilla had walked almost halfway down the alley when she sensed another presence besides Gerta. Something warned her to drop her medical bag, turn and run, but it was too late.

She felt something fall over her head. One second later it tightened around her neck like a hangman's noose, stopping her in her tracks. She clawed at the leather strap to stop the crushing pressure, but she couldn't dislodge it.

No! Her scream was nothing more than a choked gasp as she struggled and fought for air.

She had to hurt whoever was doing this to her, and she had to hurt him badly enough to make him stop long enough for her get away. She kicked back savagely, hoping her heel would break the bastard's shin or kneecap, but all it did was rip through the taffeta of her petticoat. Ignoring the burning in her bursting lungs and the lights dancing before her eyes, she summoned one last burst of strength and reached back in an attempt to gouge her assailant's hands with her nails.

When her desperate fingers clawed thick leather gloves, Sybilla knew that Nevada was not to be her destiny after all.

Her strength gone, her arms fell to her sides in acceptance of her fate and she sagged forward.

Damn it, Catherine! Is medicine worth dying for?

Through the pain, Sybilla envisioned Nevada's face and held it in her mind until the image faded into blackness and the pain finally stopped.

• • •

"What could be keeping Sybilla?" Catherine asked Damon
in annoyance as she took him aside so they could speak privately.

She looked around the parlor at the dozen people chatting in
little groups, and she could tell her guests were getting impatient
to dine.

"Nevada went after her well over an hour ago. They should've
been back here by now."

Damon winked suggestively at her. "Perhaps they've been
. . . unavoidably detained."

Catherine couldn't accept his suggestion that Sybilla and Nevada were off trysting somewhere when people were expecting
them for dinner. She shook her head. "Sybilla wouldn't be so
inconsiderate. No, something's wrong."

Just then the butler appeared and whispered something in Damon's ear.

"Excuse me," he said to Catherine. "Nevada's on the study
telephone." He smiled reassuringly. "I'm sure he's just calling
to tell us that everything's all right and they're on their way.
Why don't you return to our guests?" And he left to talk to
Nevada.

But when Damon returned, Catherine could tell at once from
his solemn expression that everything was not all right.

"Where are they?" she asked, rising and going to him. "What
did he say?"

"He wants us to come to Washington Square right away."
Damon grasped her hands and held them tightly. "He says Sybilla has disappeared."

By now the other guests realized something was amiss and
conversation in the room ceased.

"Disappeared?" Catherine echoed, feeling suddenly lightheaded.

"That's what Nevada said." Damon turned and addressed his
guests. "My friends, I'm afraid Catherine and I are going to
have to be terrible hosts and leave our own party, but something
has happened to Dr. Wolcott."

Collective expressions of shock rippled through the parlor.

"You're all invited to stay for dinner, of course," he added,
"but we must leave you at once."

Thankfully, all the guests chose to leave, so after saying their
goodbyes, Catherine and Damon left for Washington Square.

When they arrived, they were greeted by a bitterly weeping Molly.

"Oh, Dr. Catherine, it's all my fault," she wailed. "I warned her not to go out tonight, but she wouldn't listen. I should have stopped her. I should have sent for you sooner."

Catherine patted her on the back. "Hush, Molly. Why don't you come into the parlor and tell us what happened?" She looked around the empty foyer. "Where is Mr. LaRouche?"

"He's in Dr. Sybilla's surgery," Molly replied with a watery sniff. "He's looking real queer, he is."

Catherine exchanged glances with Damon. "Then let's go in there."

They found Nevada seated at Sybilla's desk and staring at Bonette. He looked up when they entered, and the hardness in his eyes made Catherine shiver.

Damon went to his friend's side at once. "What happened?"

Nevada's wary eyes sought Molly. "Better let her start." And he turned them back on Bonette as if the skeleton brought him solace.

They all sat down and Molly told them about the little girl who had come for Dr. Delancy to tend to her sick mother.

Damon scowled. "The girl asked for Catherine?"

Molly nodded as she wiped her eyes. "But I know Dr. Sybilla feels she is just as good a doctor, and she went instead."

Catherine didn't have to look at her husband to know he was thinking that if she had been here tonight, she would be the one missing, not Sybilla.

"Do you know where they went?" Damon asked.

"I do," Nevada said. He rose, crossed the room, and handed Damon a grimy piece of paper. "They went to this address. I went there, thinking I'd find Sybilla. It's just an empty house at the end of a mean canyon of an alley."

Catherine felt cold with fear. "No sick mother?"

Nevada shook his head.

"Did you find anything in the alley," Damon asked, "any sign that she had even been there?"

"Just this in the dirt." He handed the object to Catherine.

"Sybilla's spectacles," she said, her heart sinking.

Damon swore under his breath.

Catherine said, "Did you go to the police?"

"First thing," Nevada replied. "They couldn't tell me anything."

Catherine rose, and in a voice amazingly calm, said, "I don't want to alarm anyone, but I would suggest we check the morgue."

The 26th Street morgue was colder than death.

Please don't let Sybilla be here, Catherine prayed silently as they walked up to the inquiry desk, where the attendant stared at their fancy evening clothes.

After Catherine described Sybilla to him, the attendant said, "We have several women answering to that description. One was shot, another drowned, and the third was strangled."

Catherine swallowed hard. She had seen strangling victims with their tongues protruding through their blue lips and hands clenched helplessly in frustration, and she prayed her friend had not met such an end.

As they followed the attendant down a long, cold corridor, Catherine hung on Damon's arm, grateful both for his strength and Nevada's.

What am I doing here? she asked herself. *Sybilla can't be dead. She just can't be.*

The attendant hesitated before a closed door and said to Damon, "Perhaps the lady would prefer to wait out here."

Catherine bristled. "The lady is a doctor, and she most certainly does not want to wait out here!"

Damon squeezed her hand resting in the crook of his arm. "Catherine, you don't have to do this."

"But I do." She turned to Nevada. "Perhaps you should wait out here."

Nevada silently shook his head.

The attendant opened the door and the three of them went inside.

They were shown into a small, hushed room of soul-numbing cold that made Catherine shiver uncontrollably. Three narrow tables stood in a row, the nameless corpses resting there discreetly shrouded with white sheets to conceal the shock of gray, lifeless flesh from those who had come to claim them. Catherine stared at those still forms, willing them to show any sign of life, but they remained ghostly and unmoving.

Footsteps, the swishing of skirts, even the soft exhalation of breath seemed out of place in this room that reeked of death.

She didn't dare look at Damon or Nevada, because they would only remind her that she was a woman and Sybilla's friend. She concentrated on the bodies beneath the sheets—she needed to be a doctor now.

"Won't you look at the clothes first?" the attendant suggested. "It might make identification easier."

Catherine studied the clothes hanging on the wall. The black silk gown looked like something Sybilla would wear, but she had mentioned wearing a yellow brocade gown to dinner tonight, not black silk.

"Those don't help at all," she said to the attendant. "I'll have to look at their faces."

Taking a deep breath, Catherine walked over to the first table and lifted the covering.

When she saw that it was Sybilla, Catherine the woman went dead inside, but the doctor part of her calmly let the sheet fall, turned to her companions and said, "It's Sybilla. She's been strangled."

Damon stood there in shock and disbelief, but Nevada started forward, his eyes wild with denial.

"Keep him away!" Catherine snapped. "He mustn't see her like this."

Damon sprang to life and grabbed his friend's arm, restraining him. Nevada stopped and just looked at him. "Take your hands off me, Delancy."

Damon dropped Nevada's arm and reluctantly stepped aside.

Catherine moaned, "Nevada, don't. Please remember Sybilla the way she was."

His voice shook as he said, "Step aside, doc, and let me have a few minutes alone with her."

Damon put his arm around Catherine and they staggered out, saying nothing as they waited outside the door for Nevada. Minutes later, he came out, shuffling like an old man tired of living. He stopped and looked around, a bewildered expression on his face.

"I loved her," he said. "I wanted to marry her and spend the rest of my life with her." He closed his eyes and swallowed hard, his brow furrowed with anguish. "But it's too late now."

Later, when they sat in the carriage heading home, Catherine said to Nevada, "I wish you hadn't put yourself through that."

His calm reply was, "I wanted to see what that sidewinder did to her so I can pay him back in kind."

Catherine started crying and couldn't stop.

• • •

During the next several days, Catherine didn't know what she would have done without Damon.

While she floated in a thick fog of grief, he broke the news to Sybilla's family, who wanted her body returned to Washington, D.C. for burial. Then he made all funeral arrangements, handled the police inquiries, and fended off the newspaper reporters swarming around their front door like vultures. When she wanted to talk about Sybilla, Damon was there to listen, and when she woke up sobbing in the middle of the night, he was there to comfort her.

Catherine managed to endure the funeral, strengthened by the sight of so many people—Sybilla's friends and patients alike. Back at the house for the funeral meats, sharing her sorrow with Kim Flanders and a forgiving Genevra Graham helped to ease Catherine's loss.

But once the last mourner walked out the door, Catherine finally realized Sybilla was gone and never coming back.

She looked up at Damon standing by her side. "I can't believe she's gone."

He kissed the top of her head. "I can't either."

She took a deep breath and looked around. "Where's Nevada? I haven't seen him since the funeral."

"I suspect he's out in the stables, currying the horses." At Catherine's startled look, he added, "It's what he does when he needs time alone to think."

"How sad." Catherine fought back fresh tears. "I'll try the stables, then."

She found Nevada just as Damon said, in the stables, brushing Cheyenne, his black-and-white painted pony, with long, sure strokes. His blue eyes were dry, his face composed, but Catherine suspected that inside, he was in agony.

Catherine stepped up to the stall. "If you brush that horse any more, you'll wear out his hide."

He didn't stop or even look at her. "It's good for this old Cayuse. And me."

Catherine could see why. The stables were dark, peaceful, and quiet, save for the soft sounds of the horses shifting in their stalls and blowing through their nostrils in equine contentment. The sweet scent of fresh hay and the pungent odor of horse offered a simple, bucolic sort of comfort.

She reached out and let Cheyenne nuzzle her palm. "Nevada, there's something I've got to tell you."

He still didn't stop. "I'm listening."

"Sybilla was going to have your baby."

He stopped and grew very still, staring over Cheyenne's back. "I didn't know."

"I don't think she knew herself, because surely she would have told one of us. The coroner told me yesterday. I couldn't bring myself to tell you until just now."

He said nothing.

Catherine hesitated. "I'm so sorry."

Tears filled his eyes and slid down his cheeks without him so much as whimpering.

Whether Nevada wanted her comfort or not, Catherine entered the stall, took the brush from his unresisting hand, and put her arms around him. He responded, clinging to her and crying his heartbreaking, silent tears.

Two weeks passed before Catherine could bring herself to go to Washington Square.

The moment she walked through the door, memories rushed up to overwhelm her. She remembered Sybilla surprising her the day she returned from Paris, the excitement in her eyes when she first met Nevada, her indignation when Nevada slung her over his shoulder and carried her off.

Someday the memories would be pleasant, but right now, they just hurt.

"Sweet sutures, Dr. Wolcott," she muttered through her tears, "why did you have to go and die like that?"

Catherine wiped her eyes, squared her shoulders, and went into Sybilla's surgery fully intending to be brave, but when she saw Bonette sitting there, her good intentions dissolved in the onslaught of earlier memories.

She closed her eyes and bit her lower lip to keep it from trembling. She saw Sybilla confronting Jervis with that rolling pin. She remembered the day when Sybilla said goodbye and left for Paris.

Now Catherine had to say goodbye again, this time forever.

Just then, Molly appeared in the doorway, her eyes red and swollen from crying. Catherine rose and gave her a hug.

Molly drew away. "I packed Dr. Sybilla's clothes, just like you wanted me to."

"Thank you for sparing me that task, Molly. I know it couldn't have been easy for you."

"It wasn't." The maid frowned. "I thought I should tell you that I found some peculiar things in her closet."

Of course. The bustle full of pessaries.

"Don't concern yourself, Molly, I'll take care of them."

Up in Sybilla's room, with boxes of clothes piled off to one side, Catherine was startled to find not only the bustle with its depleted supply, but boxes of other anticonception devices.

She rocked back on her heels. This could mean only one thing: Sybilla had been distributing them to patients all along.

She couldn't bring herself to be angry with Sybilla. Since working in the tenements and seeing firsthand how too many children placed an impossible economic burden on their poor parents, Catherine herself had come to believe they should have access to anticonception devices, Anthony Comstock or no Anthony Comstock.

She only wished she had said something to Sybilla sooner.

Unable to remain in the house for another second, Catherine left for home.

When she arrived, she found Damon waiting for her, looking even more saturnine in the unrelieved black of mourning. She flew into his arms and hugged him. "I miss her so much."

"I know. But time will ease the pain."

She nodded as she drew away from him.

He tucked her hand in his arm and led her to the parlor. "Catherine, we have to discuss Sybilla's murder."

She sighed. "Must we?"

"We've put it off too long as it is."

"Very well." She entered the room and sat down on the sofa. "I know what you're going to say, that I was the intended victim, not Sybilla."

He strolled over to the cold fireplace. "Molly said the little girl asked for you specifically. She was probably paid to lead you to your death, only in the darkness of the alley, the murderer couldn't see who he was killing. His victim was a woman with a medical bag, so to him she must have been Dr. Delancy."

"But why didn't the child warn the murderer that he had the wrong woman?"

"Perhaps she feared losing the money she was paid. Perhaps she didn't know the man's intentions. We won't know until the police find her."

Catherine shuddered. "To use a child that way . . ."

"That child knows who killed Sybilla," he said coldly. "She

probably witnessed it, so the police are eager to find her. They also want to question you, but I've been putting them off.''

''Thank you, Damon. I don't think I could have faced them so soon after Sybilla's death.''

''They want to know who would want to kill you. I told them about that Tom Derry fellow who tried to stab you, and they investigated him. Unfortunately, he had an alibi.''

''Why would he want to kill me? All I did was deliver his wife's baby.''

Damon shrugged. ''Who knows what possesses a man like that?'' He walked over to one of the windows and looked out at the sunny spring weather. ''There's a murderer walking around out there, Catherine. By now he surely knows he killed the wrong woman.'' He turned, his gray eyes cold. ''He may try again.''

Catherine rose and dismissed his concerns with a wave of her hand. ''I'll be very careful.'' Now was as good a time as any to tell him. ''Damon, I've decided to spend more time at the Washington Square practice. With Sybilla gone now, her patients will need another doctor.''

''No. It's too dangerous, especially now. There are other doctors in the area.''

''But they're not women.''

''That's not my concern.''

She felt the heat rise to her cheeks. ''But their welfare is my concern!''

His eyes narrowed into angry slits. ''I don't want you practicing medicine in that part of the city.''

''But Damon, I—''

''In fact, I don't want you practicing medicine at all.''

Catherine stared at him. ''What did you say?''

''You heard me. Some madman is trying to kill you, Catherine. If you're running around the city tending patients, you'll be the perfect target.''

She smiled soothingly. ''I'm touched that you're so protective of me, but forcing me to give up medicine isn't the answer.''

''Damn it, Catherine, I don't want to lose you!'' His booming voice reverberated through the parlor. ''I don't want to have to go to the morgue someday and find you lying on a table with a sheet over your face.''

She went to him, placed her hand on his arm and felt it harden with anger. ''You're not going to lose me. I promise I'll be careful.''

"I can't take the risk."

Her hand fell away. "Why are you being so unreasonable?"

"If wanting to keep my wife safe is unreasonable, then I will be the most unreasonable man in this city." He paused, his voice softening. "Especially since I want her to bear our child."

Catherine stepped back, dazed by his abrupt shift in conversation. "A child?"

"Why not? We've been married for over a year." Those winter eyes were implacable. "Before we were married, you did agree to have children. Well, it's time."

"But I'm not ready."

"Well, I am," he snapped.

Her temper exploded. "You don't want a child. You want to use a child to bend me to your will, and I'll not have it."

He arched one brow. "Oh, no? Do you remember the favor you owe me for saving Dahlia Talmadge from her husband?"

Catherine remembered all too well the night Damon had come for her, held her on his lap and gave her Dahlia's freedom.

"I remember it well," she said. "I also remember that night as a time of forgiveness and compromise and love for both of us, virtues you seem to have lost."

Her words had no effect. His hand shot out and grasped her wrist. "Are you refusing to honor your debt?"

"Yes. Your price is too high."

"You push me too far, Catherine."

She placed her free hand against his cheek in an attempt to reach him. "Damon, please don't do this to me." But when she looked into his eyes, she saw only a stranger.

Wrenching her wrist free, Catherine turned and fled from the parlor.

She found a bedroom far away from the one she shared with Damon, locked the door behind her and leaned against it heavily, her heart pounding.

What had happened to the reasonable man she married, a man who claimed to be not like other men, a man willing to accept the challenge of an unconventional wife? He had turned into a stranger—an overbearing, domineering man like Jervis.

Catherine staggered over to the half-tester bed and lay down, resting her arm against her aching forehead. She knew with bitter certainty that unlike the other times, this time Damon would not compromise. He wanted her to give up medicine, have a child, and become a woman like the very ones he professed to disdain, the Genevra Grahams, the Francine Ballards.

"I won't give up medicine," she declared stoutly, "and he can't force me."

But as Catherine was soon to discover, he could try.

That evening, Catherine did not go downstairs to join Damon and Nevada for dinner, but had a tray sent up to her room and had her maid bring some nightclothes. Later that night, she did not return to the room she shared with Damon.

She was determined to sleep alone.

Catherine lay wide awake in the darkness, listening to the house creak and groan as it settled down for the night, for even as she knew sleep wouldn't come to her, she knew her husband would.

The clock on the mantel just finished chiming eleven when Catherine heard the doorknob turn and the door open. She sensed, rather than saw, Damon standing there in the darkness. She sat up, lit the small lamp on her bedside table, and waited for him to make the first move.

Damon wore his black silk robe loosely belted so that it gaped open artfully, revealing his bare chest and legs as he approached the bed with the litheness of a prowling cat. His tousled hair begged to be mussed some more, and his eyes looked as black with desire as the night he had come to Washington Square to claim her.

But there was one difference. She could tell her power over him was gone, overwhelmed by his greater need to dominate her.

He stopped at the foot of the bed and looked down at her. "This is foolishness."

"Is it?" She forced her gaze away from his compelling physical presence and kept it on the coverlet. "You may think it foolish of me to want to be a doctor, but I certainly don't."

He sat down on the edge of the bed. "Catherine, look at me."

The moment she looked into his eyes, she felt the old mesmerizing pull, but she steeled herself against it. She mustn't let him seduce her, for that, she knew, was his intention.

"I'm sorry we quarreled," he said softly, "but I'm hurt that you don't want my child."

She ran her hands through her hair in frustration. "I do want your child, Damon, but I don't want an innocent life conceived as a pawn to keep me from practicing medicine.''

''Is that what you think I want?'' His astonishment sounded so genuine that, for a moment, Catherine almost believed him.

''Don't you?''

A muscle twitched in his jaw. ''I want an heir, Catherine.''

''Not when there is so much anger and bitterness between us.''

He smiled lazily as he grasped her shoulders. ''Anger? Bitterness? I think not.''

She let him draw her to him, and just as their lips almost touched, she whispered, ''If you insist on this, I'll see to it that any child conceived of such a union is never born.''

Her threat appalled him, as she knew it would, for he released her at once and rose, rage emanating from him in palpable waves. He glared down at her for what seemed like an eternity, then he whirled on his heel and strode out without another word, slamming the door shut behind him.

Catherine extinguished the lamp and lay back in the darkness, wondering why her victory left her feeling so sad.

In the weeks to come, Catherine and Damon drifted farther and farther apart, separated by a wall of anger and obstinacy. Neither would surrender.

Every morning Catherine would go to her office and Damon to his, each seeking solace in his work. Every evening they dined together in cold, stony silence, more like enemies than lovers. They slept in separate rooms, and with every morning they awoke alone, they loved each other a little less.

One rainy afternoon in early June, Catherine was sitting at her desk in the Washington Square office when the familiar sound of leisurely footsteps and jingling spurs caused her look up and see Nevada standing in the doorway, his black Stetson in hand.

''Mind if we sit a spell and talk, doc?''

She smiled wanly. ''I wouldn't mind at all.'' Catherine paused. ''How are you, Nevada?''

He shrugged. ''I've got a hole in my heart. I expect I always will.'' Then he came in and eased his lanky frame into the chair across from her desk. ''You and Delancy can't keep up this feuding forever.''

Catherine sighed. ''Nevada, he wants me to give up medicine.

I've worked too long and too hard to do that.'' She looked over at Bonette. ''I wish Sybilla were here. She'd understand.''

Pain flickered in Nevada's eyes, then vanished. ''That's why she wouldn't marry me. Said she liked doctoring too much to give it up for any man.''

''And you never pressed her, did you?''

Nevada looked surprised that she had even asked. ''Of course not. It's hard to change the course of a river, you know.''

''You're a wise man, Nevada LaRouche.''

''Just blessed with common sense, I guess.''

She leaned back in her chair. ''Well Damon has been blessed with little of that, I'm afraid. He insists that I stop practicing medicine, and just won't listen to reason.''

''He can be as thick-headed as a bull sometimes.'' Nevada grinned. ''But so can you.''

''We're well-matched in that regard.'' Catherine added, ''When I was serving my internship at the New England Hospital, a very wise doctor once told me that marriage would only distract me from medicine. I didn't believe her then, but I do now.''

''I know Delancy loves you, doc, and this feud has been killing him.''

''But it hasn't been killing him enough to make him bend a little,'' she replied tartly.

''Well, one of you had better bend before it's too late.''

''Perhaps neither of us can.''

''Now that would be a real shame.'' He paused. ''You know, maybe if you bend a little now, he'll bend a little later. He's been known to.''

''And if he doesn't?''

''Might be a risk worth taking.'' Nevada rose. ''Answer me one question, doc.''

''If I can.''

''How would you feel if Damon died today?'' Before the stunned Catherine could reply, he added, ''Think about it,'' turned and left her, his spurs jingling softly.

After the door closed behind Nevada, Catherine sat there, staring at her uncluttered desk. How would she feel if Damon were dead? With a drawn-out sigh, she buried her face in her hands. That possibility was too painful to even contemplate.

A life without Damon would be a like a life without medicine—bleak, empty, impossible.

Perhaps Nevada was right. Perhaps if she bent a little now, Damon would bend a little later. She could have the child he demanded and return to her practice once the baby was born. Many women doctors did just that, working out of their homes so they could be near their families. If he agreed to her terms, perhaps they could salvage their marriage.

Smiling in jubilation, she rushed out of her office, grabbed her long rain cape, and started for home.

Damon stood at the window, staring out at the slanting sheets of falling rain and wondering when Catherine would be home.

He knew she was going to be devastated by what he had done, but he had no other choice. Perhaps in time, she would come to see the wisdom of it and forgive him.

As much as he loved her, Damon couldn't let her continue on this obstinate course that was sure to lead to her destruction. A man who let the woman he loved destroy herself was no man at all.

He turned away from the window, his heart heavy, and waited.

As Catherine stepped out of the cab and stood there in the driving rain, she realized that something was different about the house.

Then it came to her: the sign with her name on it was gone.

A sense of forboding rippled along her arms as she hurried beneath the porte-cochere to escape the pouring rain. Once inside, she received an even greater shock.

Her office had disappeared.

She stood in the doorway as though rooted to the spot. Gone was her desk, the examining table, and the medicine cabinet, as if they had never existed. The room had been turned into a parlor again, with the same rugs and furniture returned to the exact same places.

Catherine closed her eyes, hoping against hope that when she opened them again, she would see her office just as she had left it that morning. She opened her eyes and her hopes turned to dust.

She closed the door, walked over to the horsehair sofa and sat down, her hands tightly folded in her lap, her mind still reeling from his betrayal. She had been foolish to think he would ever bend. Hadn't he been powerful enough to create springtime in the middle of the winter, and turn her humble dining room into a Christmas fantasy? But what Damon granted, he could also take away just as easily as he had taken her office. He had worked his black magic again, only this time to shatter her dreams.

What was she going to do? There was no more compromising. She had to choose between Damon and medicine.

She didn't know how long she sat there in the darkness listening to the rain. Minutes? Hours? When she made up her mind, she rose and walked down the hall to Damon's study.

When she walked in, she saw him standing at the window, watching the rain. He turned and looked at her, his eyes as cold as ice.

"What have you done with my office?" she asked.

"It's become what I intended it to be—a parlor," he replied. He put his hands in his pockets and strolled over to his desk. "Since you won't be practicing medicine, you won't need an office or an assistant, so I dismissed Rebecca."

"I see."

"This has gone far enough, Catherine. I'm quite out of patience with you. It's time you were made to see reason, and if this is what it takes . . ." He shrugged.

"I still have my Washington Square office. I can practice medicine there."

"Not for very long. I intend to buy the building and evict you."

His announcement hit her with the force of a cyclone, and for one endless moment, she thought she was going to faint. When she recovered herself, she felt perversely calm and strong.

Finally Damon frowned. "Well? Don't you have anything to say?"

"There's nothing else to say because there is nothing left for us." She took a deep breath to give her courage. "I need my freedom, Damon. I've decided to leave you."

Damon's shocked expression would have been comical if it weren't so sad. He pulled his hands out of his pockets and leaned heavily on his desk. "What did you say?"

"You heard me. I said I'm leaving you. I can't live with you any more." She twisted her rings off her finger and smiled wistfully. "You know, I once thought that these diamonds cast such a warm light. Now they've become as cold as our marriage."

She stepped up to the desk to hand him the rings, but he caught her wrist instead. "You can't leave me. I won't let you."

"And what will you do to stop me?" she said wearily. "Lock me in the attic and feed me bread and water until you break my spirit? I think not."

He released her, but did not accept the rings, so Catherine placed them on the desk and turned to go.

Damon said, "There are other ways of stopping you."

She paused and turned back. "I'm sure there are. You're a powerful man. You can buy my building and evict me. You can turn my society patients against me. But I'm asking you not to."

He studied her for what seemed like hours, his saturnine face reflecting confusion, disbelief, and hurt pride. "If being married to me is so repugnant to you, I won't keep you here against your will. I have some pride left."

"What about my medical practice?"

"You can keep your damn medical practice, since it's all that matters to you. I won't buy your building."

Relieved, Catherine nodded.

"I suppose you'll want a divorce."

"I haven't thought that far ahead." Divorce was so final. "I suppose. Eventually."

"As you wish." Then he added, "Catherine, I—" And he stopped.

"Yes?"

"Never mind. It was nothing of importance."

"Then, goodbye, Damon." It seemed so inadequate after all they had shared.

"Goodbye, Catherine."

She turned and left without a backward glance.

CHAPTER

FIFTEEN

April 1893

A thin, piercing wail of outrage filled the small windowless room.

Catherine smiled at the newborn infant lying in her arms. "Happy birthday, Baby Rourke." She stroked its downy cheek with the tip of her index finger. No matter how many babies she delivered, she viewed each one with wonder. "Being born wasn't so bad, now was it?"

She glanced down at the baby's mother lying in the narrow bed, her white, haggard face still mirroring her harrowing ordeal, even in repose. The birth had been a long and agonizing one, and Catherine had come close to losing both mother and child several times during the course of the last fifteen hours. But it was over now, and would soon be forgotten once the mother held this new life she had brought into the world.

After soothing the fretful infant, Catherine turned to its mother, a dark-haired woman who once must have stolen many a heart in her Irish village before repeated childbearing had stolen her looks.

"Mrs. Rourke," Catherine said softly, "would you like to hold your son now?"

Eyelids flickered open, revealing tired eyes of a delicate blue, but their beauty was overshadowed by resentment and resignation as they rested on the tiny mewling bundle in Catherine's arms. When Mrs. Rourke made no attempt to take her son, Catherine was forced to place the baby in its mother's arms.

Now everything will be all right, Catherine thought. *Once she sees the little mite and holds him, she'll fall in love with him.*

She'll forget all she went through. They all do, rich and poor alike.

"Do you have a name for him yet?" Catherine asked.

"Me husband hasn't decided."

She waited for Mrs. Rourke's expression to soften with acceptance, for a smile of wonder to touch her mouth, but she remained stone-faced, and didn't even bother to part the blanket to see if her baby had come with just the right number of tiny fingers and toes.

Oh, dear, Catherine thought in dismay.

She knelt by the bedside. "Mrs. Rourke, don't you want this baby?"

One thin shoulder lifted in a listless shrug as she turned her face to the wall. "I already have seven others, Dr. Delancy, that I do. Holy Mother of God, what do I need another one for?"

The woman was only twenty-five years old, two years younger than Catherine, and already she had borne eight children.

"I know it's hard," Catherine said. "But just look at him. He's so small and helpless. Surely you can't blame him for being born, now can you?"

Mrs. Rourke turned her head back to glare at Catherine. "Doctor, how can ye be knowin' what I think of this baby? He'll take food from our bellies and clothes off our backs. He'll cry like a banshee and keep me poor husband up at night. He'll get sick. Holy Mother of God, I know it's a sin, but I can't pretend I'm glad to have another one of 'em, especially if himself loses his job."

She couldn't argue with the woman, because she understood her plight all too well.

"I know you're exhausted and want to sleep, but will you at least feed him?" Catherine said.

For a moment, she thought Mrs. Rourke was going to refuse even that basic request. Then she shrugged in resignation and struggled to sit up. "Aye, at least I can do that for 'im."

Catherine helped her lean back against the wall, for there were no pillows, and watched as Mrs. Rourke put the child to her swollen breast, where the child sucked greedily. But no emotional connection passed between mother and child. No bonds of closeness were forming. It was as though Mrs. Rourke were physically providing nourishment, but nothing more.

"Mrs. Rourke," she said gently, "where is your husband?

I'll send someone to fetch him. He should be with you at a time like this.''

He should be, but he wasn't. The moment Mr. Rourke had come home from work to find his wife in labor, he turned on his heel and disappeared without so much as a word of encouragement to her, and hadn't returned all night.

His wife shrugged. ''I expect himself is havin' a jar somewhere. Oh, he likes the gettin' of children well enough, my Padraic, and he's the quick one to come to me bed, but he's a coward to see the results o' his deed. Now isn't that just like a man fer ye?''

Catherine thought of Damon. No, there were some men who wouldn't desert their woman at such a time.

''And where are your other children?'' she asked.

''With a neighbor downstairs.''

''Would you like me to send for them so they can meet their new baby brother?''

Again resentment flared in those tired eyes. ''If ye don't mind, doctor, I'd rather a wee bit of time to meself.''

Catherine could well understand that. There wasn't much privacy or rest to be had when a two-room flat was shared by seven children—now eight—and two adults.

She looked around the tiny room. Aside from the bed, the floor was littered with dirty, bare mattresses where she supposed the children slept. At least it was better than the streets.

''Mrs. Rourke, where will the baby sleep?''

''Wherever he can find a bit of room.''

A baby deserves a proper cradle, Catherine said to herself. To the mother, she merely nodded. She knew that arguing would be futile.

Stifling a yawn, Catherine looked at the lapel watch she had pinned to the bodice of her shirtwaist and saw that it was five o'clock in the morning. She had been here all night, and now it was time for her to go home. At least she would be able to get a few hours sleep before the first of her patients arrived.

''I've got to go,'' she said.

Just as Catherine turned to collect her new leather medical bag and leave, Mrs. Rourke reached out her hand and said, ''Dr. Dee, wait!''

Catherine looked down. ''Yes?''

The woman grabbed her hand and pulled her close as if wishing to confide a secret. ''I know it's a sin, but I don't want to have any more children,'' she said, her voice fierce with determination, ''not ever. Can ye . . . give me something to keep it from happenin' again? I know the Protestants have a way.''

Catherine patted her hand and nodded. ''When you've recovered, we'll discuss it.''

''Oh, thank ye, Dr. Dee, thank ye, and God bless ye.''

Catherine wished mother and child good day and left.

When she stepped out of the tenement onto Mulberry Street, Catherine hesitated and looked around. The sky was a light, pre-dawn gray over the rooftops of lower New York City, illuminating the street just enough. It was empty except for a man sleeping in a doorway with a box over his feet, and another man who ducked behind a corner the moment she looked his way.

She had seen the second man too often for coincidence. She suspected Damon had hired him to follow her and see that she didn't share Sybilla's fate.

Catherine rubbed her stiff neck in consternation. She and Damon had been separated for almost a year now, and he still treated her like a possession to be guarded. Yet as much as she resented Damon's interference, she grudgingly admitted that her ''shadow'' made her feel safer when she was out alone.

She started down the street, eager to get home.

When Catherine arrived at her townhouse, Molly accosted her the moment she walked in the door.

''There you are, Dr. Catherine,'' she said, taking the medical bag. ''I was beginning to worry about you.''

''Dear Molly. After being in my employ for as long as you have, you should know that a baby comes in its own sweet time.''

''I do, but I still can't help worrying about you all alone in those dangerous places, especially after what happened to—'' Her eyes filled with tears, and to hide them, Molly disappeared briefly to put the bag in the surgery, and when she returned, she said, ''You look exhausted, Dr. Catherine, and I'll bet you're hungry. Would you like some breakfast?''

''Just a cup of cocoa for now. I'll have breakfast after I take a nap.''

''I'll have it ready for you.'' Molly bustled off toward the kitchen.

Catherine went upstairs, and once she was in her bedroom, she removed her shirtwaist, loosened her corset, and went to lie down for a well-deserved nap. But while her body craved rest, her mind refused to cooperate.

She couldn't stop thinking of Damon.

When she had left him last June, she had been devastated, even though she knew it was for the best. As the weeks went by and she threw herself into her work, she missed him less and less and the hurt eased. Even at Christmas, when he made that huge donation to the Women's Dispensary in her name, Catherine had been strong enough to maintain her resolve that their marriage was over.

But all of a sudden it was as though the year of their separation hadn't passed and she was still so deeply in love with him. She felt the overwhelming urge to see him again, to watch his pale winter eyes light up with warmth at the sight of her, feel his mouth heavy against hers and his coaxing fingers gliding along her naked skin . . .

"Stop it!" she chided herself angrily, rising and pacing the room. "You made your choice, and now you're going to have to live with it."

Well, tonight she was having dinner with Kim Flanders, so perhaps that would banish those ambivalent thoughts of Damon.

When Catherine arrived at Kim's house that evening after a long, exhausting day when nothing seemed to go right, she knew at once that the unsettling feelings plaguing her were not going to disappear.

As she stood in the foyer and watched Kim stride toward her, as nattily dressed as always, she was glad they were friends again, with all differences forgotten or forgiven. Once she had left Damon, Catherine wondered if Kim would try to resume their former relationship, but he hadn't—he had fallen in love with Francine Ballard. Now Catherine and Kim were just good friends.

Kim's gaze flicked over her, but he was too polite to comment on her pallor and the dark smudges beneath her eyes, or the way her skirt fit too loosely. "Busy day?"

Catherine nodded as she stifled a yawn. "Exhausting, but satisfying."

"You can tell me all about it in the library, while we relax with a glass of sherry before dinner."

Once in the library, seated on the sofa and sipping her sherry, Catherine found she didn't want to discuss her day.

She stared deeply into her glass. "Kim, how is Damon?"

He started, splashing several drops of sherry on his trousers, but he ignored the stain. "You surprise me. I thought you told me that you never wanted to discuss Damon, ever."

She looked over at him. "I need to know."

Kim shook his head, his blue eyes soft with compassion. "Why don't you ask LaRouche?" he said gently.

Catherine thought of Nevada and smiled wistfully. After she had left Damon, Nevada came to her to try to convince her to change her mind. But once he saw she was adamant, he kissed her on the cheek with regret and brotherly affection, and never called on her again.

"That would only raise false hopes, and I don't wish to do that to anyone." She paused. "Now, will you or won't you tell me how Damon is? I know you've seen him because you move in the same social circles."

Kim sat back in his chair. "Damon is no recluse, Catherine. His box at the opera is always full, and he dines with the Grahams and Peachtrees regularly. He dances every dance except the last one at the balls and looks as though he's enjoying himself."

Catherine smiled wryly. "It doesn't sound as though he's pining away for me, does it?" Then she asked the question she dreaded hearing the answer to: "Is he keeping company with another woman?"

"Catherine—"

"Please, Kim. I have to know."

"If he is, he's discreet. After all, he's still a married man. He always arrives and leaves alone."

She felt more relieved than she thought she would.

Kim swirled his sherry around in its glass. "Do you still love him?"

Catherine sighed. "It's foolish of me, but yes, I still do. I probably always will."

"Are you thinking of going back to him?"

"I won't lie to you. Sometimes I have fleeting moments of temptation, like the one I'm experiencing now. But when I think about all Damon would insist I give up . . ." She shrugged helplessly. "It's like running against the wind. Medicine just means too much to me."

He shook his head. "Far be it from me to say 'I told you so,' Catherine, but I did warn you about marrying a man who isn't another doctor. They just can't understand what drives us."

"You were right. Damon is also proud and possessive. He

acquires the best and treats his possessions well, but once they're his, he hates to lose them.''

Catherine paused to finish her sherry, then said, ''Is society still gossiping about us?''

She shuddered when she recalled the way certain members of the press had savaged her and Damon with speculation and innuendo when news of their separation became public knowledge, how they had waited on her doorstep to hound her. Some unscrupulous ones even tried to bribe Molly for any snippet of information.

''No,'' Kim replied. ''The main topic of conversation in society is this worsening depression. Gossip about who's the latest to lose his fortune has replaced Damon Delancy's personal life.''

Catherine looked at him in alarm. ''Damon hasn't—''

''Not yet. Unlike half the population of this city, the Wolf of Wall Street keeps getting richer.''

Catherine shuddered to think what would happen to Damon if he suddenly lost everything and was faced with the poverty he had known as a child.

Kim said, ''I even overheard him talk of building a mansion in Newport.''

''Newport? That surprises me. He's always hated the place. What about Coppermine?''

Kim shrugged. ''Perhaps he intends to sell it.''

Coppermine . . . where she and Damon had spent their wedding night. Perhaps the house no longer meant anything to him.

''I've never seen anything like this depression,'' she said. ''Everyone's suffering, the poor most of all. The dispensary is filled to capacity, and philanthropic support for the other hospitals is drying up. I don't know what the future will bring.''

''None of us does.''

Even as Catherine thought about the poor who needed her services more than ever in these terrible economic times, she felt the ambivalence lose its powerful grip on her, overwhelmed by the rightness of her decision to leave Damon.

A knock on the door revealed Kim's housekeeper to tell them that dinner was served.

Kim rose and extended his hand. ''Shall we dine?''

As Catherine joined him, she said, ''I feel better having talked with you about Damon.''

''That's what I'm here for.''

Later, when Catherine left Kim's house, she felt as though a great weight had been lifted from her shoulders. She had wrestled with her demon and vanquished it once again, but she knew that it would return when she least expected it.

Two days later, Catherine walked into her waiting area to call her next patient into the surgery and was startled to find none other than Liam Flynn, the newspaper reporter with the *Sun*, sandwiched uncomfortably between two women.

"Why, Mr. Flynn, this is an unpleasant surprise," she said coolly as he rose.

"Good afternoon. Dr. Delancy." He glanced at the two women. "I believe I'm next."

Catherine looked him up and down. "You look perfectly healthy to me."

His head fell forward and he drooped pathetically. "I'll die if I don't get medical attention."

"You'll probably die if I do give you medical attention," she retorted.

Alarm flashed across his florid features momentarily, then vanished. "What do you have against me? I'm only doing my job."

"What you do isn't work." Catherine turned on her heel and left the waiting room, followed by Flynn. Once they were in her surgery, she said, "What is it you really want, Mr. Flynn?"

He whipped out his dog-eared notebook and a worn pencil stub. "I want to know how you feel about your husband almost dying in that explosion."

Catherine felt as though she had just been hit by a train. "What did you say?"

"You know. The explosion in the stables this morning." Flynn looked up from his notebook and turned pale beneath his rusty beard. "By God, you *don't* know, do you?"

The walls teetered and the floor slid unsteadily to one side, pitching Catherine off balance. She grabbed for the edge of her desk as a sickening feeling rose up to catch her by the throat. Before she could fall, Flynn slipped his arm around her waist and lead her over to the nearest chair.

As she sat there and tried to compose herself, Nevada's words of last June echoed through her mind: "What if Damon died today? How would you feel then?"

Now she knew.

Catherine looked up at the reporter. "Is Damon dead?"

"No."

Shaking with relief, she muttered, "Thank God. What happened?"

"All I know is that he went out to the stables this morning and there was an explosion. The police suspect a bomb went off."

Catherine gaped at him. "A bomb? Who would want to do something like that?"

Flynn leaned forward, his eyes shining expectantly. "Precisely what I wanted to ask you, Dr. Delancy. A man like your husband always has enemies. Powerful enemies."

Catherine knew she had said too much already. She rose to her feet, her strength returning. "I have nothing more to say to you, Mr. Flynn. Now, if you'll excuse me . . ."

"Are you rushing to your fallen husband's side?" he asked eagerly. "If you are, I have a cab waiting. It's yours in exchange for an exclusive interview."

Catherine called Flynn a name that made the reporter blush, grabbed her medical bag and rushed off to find her own cab.

Half an hour later, her cab followed by Flynn's pulled up before the imposing mansion that Catherine had once called home.

She hesitated a moment, staring up at the magnificent house where she had known some of the happiest moments of her life. It still looked elegant and imposing.

As she disembarked, Catherine noticed a group of men loitering around the entrance, but she paid them no mind until one of them shouted, "Look! It's her, Delancy's wife!" and they all rushed at her like a swarm of locusts.

One of them said, "Dr. Delancy, can you tell us anything about your husband's condition? Will he live?"

Catherine squared her shoulders and kept walking. "If you'll excuse me—"

"If you and your husband are separated, Dr. Delancy, why have you come here?" another persisted, matching his stride to hers and practically shoving his nose in her face.

Catherine kept on walking, nearly running him down. "That, sir, is none of your affair."

When a third had the temerity to block her way and ask, "Is it true that you're considering a reconciliation?" Catherine stopped and purposely brought the heel of her shoe down on his instep, hard, causing the man to howl in pain and hop back out of her way.

Then she snapped, "No." That much she was willing to say to these vultures.

They followed her, firing their questions, but Catherine refused to answer, even when they tried baiting her into saying something imprudent. She rang the bell and was relieved when the butler Winslow answered the door. The reporters fell silent abruptly when they noticed the shotgun cradled in his arms. Catherine was sure it wasn't loaded, but she didn't tell the reporters that.

The butler's white brows rose in astonishment almost to his hairline. "Why, madam . . ."

"Good afternoon, Winslow," Catherine said. "May I come in before these vultures eat me alive?"

"Of course, madam." And he stood aside to let her pass while he glared at the reporters.

The moment Catherine entered the expansive foyer and heard the front door close behind her, shutting out those clamorous voices, she hesitated and looked around uncomfortably, feeling as though she were trespassing.

Catherine glanced into the parlor that had once been her surgery, a testimony to all that had been wrong with her marriage. Today it reminded her forcefully that her relationship with Damon hadn't changed. She mustn't succumb to sentimentality.

She turned and smiled at the butler. "Thank you, Winslow. You came just in the nick of time." She removed her cape and handed it to him. "I trust you've been well?"

"Yes, madam, very well, thank you. Until this morning, of course."

Catherine took a deep breath. "That is why I've come."

"Very kind of you, madam."

Catherine was just about to ask him how the master was when the slow, steady tapping of cowboy boots striking marble and jingling spurs caught her attention, and she turned to see Nevada's familiar lanky form come ambling toward her.

"Afternoon, doc," he said in his lilting drawl. "It's been a while."

Catherine studied him for a moment to gauge any sign of hostility or resentment toward her, but all she found was the same helpless controlled rage he had shown when Sybilla died.

"Good afternoon, Nevada. How are you?"

She noticed that his coat didn't quite conceal the worn gun holster resting low on his hips and tied to his thigh with a rawhide thong. After the attempt on his friend's life, he was taking no chances.

"Feeling ornery, thanks." His keen eyes flicked over her in blatant appraisal. "You been working too hard, doc. You need to put some meat on those bones and get some sleep." He grinned disarmingly. "You still look right pretty, though."

She thanked him for the compliment, adding, "And you haven't changed at all."

He reached out and grasped her hands. "I'm surprised to see you here."

"No, you're not," Catherine replied. "You knew I'd come. Why didn't you send for me yourself?"

"Seeing as how you and Damon aren't living as man and wife no more . . ." He shrugged. "Didn't seem much point."

She glared at him indignantly. "That doesn't mean I would refuse to see him if he were hurt, which he obviously is, according to one Liam Flynn." Catherine took a step forward. "Is he in our—his bedroom?"

Nevada nodded.

"I'd like to see him now, if you don't mind."

"Why should I mind? You're still his wife." He stepped aside. "You remember the way, doc?"

"I think I can manage." Catherine strode past him and started up the sweeping staircase. As Nevada fell into step beside her, she said, "Was his head injured, or any bones broken?"

"No. He's mighty bruised, though."

"Who attended him?"

"Stryker, Van Wormer, and Halsey."

Catherine stopped on the stairs, panic ripping through her. "Carter Halsey?"

"That's the one."

"He's an ophthalmologist." Her voice rose. "Dear God, was Damon blinded in the explosion?"

Nevada placed a reassuring hand on her arm. "Easy, doc. Don't go fainting on me. They don't know. That Halsey feller spent a couple of hours picking lord-only-knows-what out of Delancy's eyelids. Then they put some ointment on 'em and bandaged him up."

Catherine clutched at the banister for support as she felt light-headed again.

"You feel up to this?" Nevada asked.

She nodded.

Nevada released her and stepped aside. "You know me and him go back a long way, doc. Been through some tough times together. I'd hate to see anything happen to him, not now."

"Neither would I."

Nevada gave her an odd look, but said nothing as they started down the long upstairs corridor. They walked in silence and finally stopped in front of a closed door.

"You have someone watching over him, I trust?" Catherine asked.

"A nurse." Nevada knocked softly at the door, opened it, and motioned to the nurse who was seated in a chair by Damon's bedside. When the woman reached the door, Nevada whispered, "The doc here wants to be alone with her husband."

The nurse gave Catherine a startled look, but said nothing as she joined Nevada.

The door closed behind her, and Catherine was standing in the bedchamber she had once shared with Damon.

She stood there for a moment and took a deep breath to compose herself as the vivid memory of the first time she had entered this room flashed unbidden in her mind.

Stop it!'' she admonished herself to banish the potent image, then walked toward the half-tester bed.

Her footsteps slowed and her heart went out to Damon when she saw him lying there so still, his face blotched beneath its slick, shiny coating of ointment, his eyes bandaged. Powder burns . . . Catherine prayed his eyes' corneas hadn't been damaged by the blast.

"Oh, my poor Damon . . ."

In the months that had passed since Catherine and Damon separated, she had often wondered how she would feel when she saw him again. Now she knew. As she stood beside his bed and looked down at him lying there so helplessly, she was totally unprepared to be so drawn to him all over again, to experience dangerous, gut-wrenching emotions of yearning and tenderness she thought she had long put behind her. She had the absurd urge to cradle his head against her shoulder, to hold and comfort and protect him.

She smiled dryly at that. There had been times during the last months of her marriage when she could have cheerfully murdered him herself.

"Stop letting your emotions get the best of you and start be-having like a doctor," she muttered to herself as she set down her bag and prepared to examine him.

After gently pulling the covers back partway, Catherine no-ticed that Damon's bruised and battered torso was bandaged as well. She scowled in frustration, wishing she could examine him more thoroughly, but there was only just so much she could do. She would just have to ask the other doctors for a report on the extent of his injuries.

They were right about one thing: he would live. That gratified her. Much as she and Damon had been at each other's throats during those last few months, she didn't wish him harm.

In an unconscious gesture, Catherine reached out and tenderly brushed a lock of dark hair off Damon's forehead.

"Fight, Damon," she whispered, resting her palm against his cheek.

For a moment, Catherine thought she sensed an almost im-perceptible change in him, an awareness that she was here beside him, but when he didn't stir, she thought she must have imag-ined it.

She drew the covers back over him and straightened.

"You'll be fine, Damon," she said softly, then turned and left the room.

She found Nevada and the nurse waiting outside in the cor-ridor.

When the nurse went back to her patient and closed the door behind her, Nevada turned to Catherine and said, "Well, doc?"

"They were right. He'll live."

Nevada's tense shoulders relaxed. "That's the best news I've had all week." As he and Catherine started walking back down the corridor, he said, "You look plumb tuckered out. Want some grub before you go?"

"I'll settle for a shot of bourbon rather than the—er, grub, if you don't mind."

Nevada flashed her a wide white smile of approval. "Just follow me."

Once they were downstairs and seated in Nevada's private study just down the hall from Damon's, he opened a drawer in his wide oak desk and took out two small glasses and a half-empty bottle of bourbon. He filled the glasses with a hand that shook ever so slightly and handed one to Catherine.

"To Damon," Nevada said.

Catherine raised her glass, then swallowed down the liquor in one gulp, letting it sear her throat and bring tears to her eyes.

"All right," she said, setting her glass down and leaning forward. "Now tell me exactly what happened."

Nevada leaned back in his swivel chair and laced his fingers behind his head, his languid posture belying the steel thread of tension and anger Catherine detected in his voice.

"Some low-down sidewinder put a bomb in the stables. If Damon had gone in there at nine o'clock, as usual, he'd be dead by now. But he was late, so he was outside the building when the bomb went off. The force of the explosion threw him halfway to California. For a while there, the doctors thought he went deaf."

Catherine felt the blood drain from her face. "What about the grooms?"

Nevada said, "Sam Tucker died. Most of the horses, too." He swallowed hard and his eyes became hard and bright. "Cheyenne was one of 'em."

Catherine's heart went out to him. She still remembered that day she had gone out to the stables to tell Nevada that Sybilla was pregnant when she died, and there he was currying the hide off his painted pony.

"I'm sorry, Nevada," she said gently.

His voice trembled. "I loved that old Cayuse, doc." He regained control of himself and leaned forward in his chair. "But at least Damon was spared."

"Thank God for that. I take it the police are investigating?"

"Yes, but they haven't been able to come up with anything yet. They know about as much as I do, which is nothing."

"So they don't have any idea who did this?"

"Not a clue, doc. But in the meantime, I'm not taking any chances on this sidewinder striking again. I've hired some men to keep an eye on the house and grounds."

"I know Damon is in good hands." Catherine hesitated. "And how are you, Nevada?"

"I still miss her, and I suspect I always will. But at least the pain is easier to bear now."

Catherine nodded. "I miss her, too. Sybilla was one woman in a million."

"She was the finest—one of the finest—women I've ever known. I just wish . . ." His voice trailed off.

She fought back tears as she rose. "Regrets are useless, I'm afraid. There are many things I wish I had said to her while she was alive and I still had the chance. But the opportunity is gone now.''

Catherine extended her hand. ''Well, it's been a pleasure seeing you again, Nevada, and I thank you for your hospitality, but I have other patients to attend to today, so I'll be on my way.''

He rose as well, a hopeful expression on his face. ''Thanks for coming, doc. You going to come by tomorrow?''

She shook her head. ''That won't be necessary. I've seen for myself that Damon will live.''

''He's been as ornery as a wildcat with a thorn in its paw ever since you left.''

Catherine gave him an exasperated look. ''Don't try to make me feel guilty, Nevada. A reconciliation with Damon would be futile. We're both too stubborn and headstrong to get along with each other. You know that as well as anyone.''

Nevada said nothing.

Catherine took her bag and headed for the door. When she reached it, she stopped and turned. ''Oh, don't be so despondent. He's an attractive, wealthy man. He'll have no trouble finding someone else someday.''

Nevada looked up, his eyes burning with indignation. ''Both you and Sybilla are one in a million, doc. He'll never find another woman like you. Heard him say so himself many a time.''

Catherine could think of no response to that, so she bade Nevada goodbye, turned and walked out the door.

Damon awoke to excruciating pain.

His body was as sore as if it had been stretched on the rack, every muscle screaming in agony at the slightest movement. The fire consuming his eyes and face told him he must have died and gone to hell.

But he was alive.

Blackness surrounded him, and he scowled. He was disoriented and confused, and he fought to clear the heaviness weighing down his thoughts.

Then it all came back to him. He remembered hearing the ear-splitting ''boom'' seconds before the world exploded in a flash of orange light, even as it lifted him off his feet and flung him into the air as though he were a piece of discarded paper. When he hit the ground, the world had disappeared into a black void.

Damon tried to open his burning eyes, but couldn't. Something weighed his eyelids down. He reached up and felt bandages. His hand fell back.

He immediately thought of Catherine and felt a deep abiding calm inside. He had no way of knowing, but he sensed that she had been here with him, soothing him like a ministering angel with her gentle voice and touch. There had been no animosity about her this time, just tender concern for his welfare.

Damon swallowed hard as he pictured her in his mind. He could see her sweet, lovely face as clearly as if she were leaning over him. Her pale blue eyes were serene instead of glittering with self-righteous anger, her full rosy lips smiling instead of pursed in an obstinate line. Her hands smelled faintly of idoform, as they always did.

God, he missed her.

Catherine . . . he had to see her. She was a doctor. She would examine him and tell him he would soon be well.

"Nevada!" he called, unmindful of the jarring pain that vibrated through his skull.

Nevada would find Catherine and bring her to him.

❧ CHAPTER ❧

SIXTEEN

———

"HE'S been asking for you, doc."

Catherine shuffled the papers on her desk. "I have a waiting room full of other patients to see today. Damon has three of New York City's finest doctors caring for him. He doesn't need me, Nevada."

"That's where you're wrong. He wants to see you. He sent me to bring you back, and I will if I have to carry you myself."

Catherine rose and glowered at him. "That may have worked with Sybilla, but it will not work with me."

The cowboy regarded her as though she had turned into a rattlesnake right before his very eyes. "You refusing to come with me?"

"I—"

"What happened between you two when you were married— you're not still holding that against him, are you?"

"Of course not."

"Then why are you refusing to help him when he needs you so bad?"

"Damon's not a part of my life any more, and I prefer to keep it that way."

The cowboy stroked his mustache in consternation. "I'm not asking you to move back in with him. I'm just asking you to see him."

How could she explain to him that she feared falling under Damon's powerful spell again?

"Nevada, I—"

"Please, doc." He came around the desk and grasped her hands desperately. "You've got to come with me. I'll give you everything I have in the world. I'll get down on my knees and beg, if you want, but you've got to come. He won't let on, but he's scared. I never seen him this scared before. You're the only one he trusts.''

Catherine sighed. ''All right, I'll go with you. But don't think it changes anything.''

Nevada's grin almost split his face as he released her hands. ''Thanks, doc. I knew you wouldn't let us down. The carriage is right out front.''

Once inside, Catherine sat there in silence, nervously plucking at her skirt as she worried about the outcome of her visit to Damon. She prayed he wouldn't take advantage of his injuries to ensnare her sympathies. He was ruthless enough to do anything to get what he wanted.

Remorse overshadowed her suspicions. Nevada had said Damon was scared and fighting not to show it. Anyone would be terrified of going blind. He wanted her with him to stave off the fear. She could at least provide that.

The moment Catherine arrived, she left Nevada and headed for Damon's room.

When she reached the door, she paused for a moment to take several deep calming breaths. She had to radiate confidence and strength for Damon's sake, and she couldn't let him affect her as he had yesterday. She opened the door and went in.

''You may leave us now,'' she said to the nurse sitting there.

The moment Damon heard her voice, he called out, ''Catherine?''

Suddenly, it was as though their year apart was nothing more than a day. ''I'm here.''

As she approached his bed, her professional appraisal found him looking better today. He was propped against pillows rather than lying flat on his back, and his skin had lost yesterday's paste-gray pallor.

''I didn't think you'd come,'' he said, his deep voice stronger than she would have expected. But then, Damon had always been a fighter.

''I wasn't going to,'' she replied honestly, ''but Nevada wouldn't take no for an answer, so I thought it prudent to come.''

He smiled at that. ''I'm glad he was able to persuade you.''

She set down her medical bag and seated herself in the chair near his bed. When he fumbled for her hand, she took his in both of hers and held it wordlessly, trying to share her own strength. His clasp was warm and desperate, nearly crushing her fingers, and for a moment, Catherine felt her insides quiver at the remembered pleasure of his touch.

"Nevada told me what happened. How are you feeling?"

"As Nevada would say, I feel like a herd of longhorns just stampeded over my body."

She smiled at that even though he couldn't see her expression. "At least you're alive. Be thankful for that."

A muscle twitched in his jaw. "Why are my eyes bandaged?"

"I understand they were injured in the explosion."

"How badly?"

"They'll know when they take the bandages off."

Damon's whole body tensed. "Will I be blind?" When Catherine hesitated, he snapped, "You've always been honest with me, Catherine, so kindly have the decency to be honest with me now."

She laced her fingers through his. "I don't know."

Since his eyes were bandaged, she couldn't tell what he was feeling. The shock apparently left him speechless.

"Damon, listen to me." She dislodged her hand and touched his face. "You mustn't panic. It's too soon to know if the explosion caused any permanent damage."

"Don't panic?" he muttered bitterly. "I may never see again, and you're advising me not to panic?"

"I don't know what else to say." She hesitated. "Perhaps I should be on my way. You need your rest."

His hand shot out and he grasped her arm with surprising accuracy. "Don't go just yet. Stay with me a while. Please."

She was just about to protest that she had other patients to attend to, but the raw despair in Damon's voice halted her. "As you wish."

He released her. "Your company will do more good for me than rest."

An awkward silence descended. Catherine didn't know what to say to comfort him.

"Have you missed me?"

She started, thrown off balance again by the seductiveness of his tone, for after their embattled last weeks together, she had assumed Damon wanted nothing more to do with her.

"As I explained to you, I came here reluctantly, and only because Nevada begged and threatened me. I'm here as a doctor, not as your former wife."

"Estranged wife. We're not divorced. And you haven't answered my question.'' He reached out, found her hand again and ran his fingertips over the back of it in a gentle caress. ''Do you ever miss me, Catherine?''

Yes, she missed him sometimes. She missed the endless conversations they would have late at night before the drawing room fire, when the servants were abed and the house was hushed and still; dancing the One-Armed Waltz with him, the sheer pleasure of his holding her tightly, gliding over the dance floor as though they were one; and lying naked with him in this very bed, pleasuring each other endlessly until they both became delirious with ecstasy.

But just because she missed him didn't mean they could get along and build a life together.

Catherine pulled her hand away, disconcerted by his touch, as always. ''I miss what was good about our marriage,'' she admitted, ''but I would have missed practicing medicine more.''

Her answer didn't please him, for the corners of his mouth turned down in a scowl and he became fretful.

''I think you should rest now, Damon,'' Catherine said. ''Would you like me to give you something to help you sleep?''

''Why should I sleep? I may soon be living in darkness for the rest of my life.''

Catherine couldn't think of anything reassuring to say, so she just patted his hand and rose. ''Goodbye, Damon.''

''Catherine, wait.'' When she hesitated, he said, ''I want to go to Coppermine to recuperate. Will you come with me?''

The eagerness in his voice wrenched at her heart, but she reminded herself that he was a master at playing on her emotions. ''I don't think that would be wise.''

''Why not? Are you afraid I'll seduce you away from your precious medicine?''

''No. But we've said all there is to be said between us, and if you'll recall, much of it wasn't pleasant on either side.''

''Much was said in the heat of the moment. Catherine, all I'm asking is a few days of your time.''

''Must I constantly remind everyone that I do have other patients?'' she snapped.

''Your friend Flanders can take care of them.''

''Can he? He's got patients of his own.''

''Damn it, woman! Why are you being so stubborn? I'm only asking for a few days. Surely you can spare me that.''

How could she be so petty and churlish as to refuse a sick

man her company for a few days? These were special circumstances.

Damon swallowed convulsively. "You know I'd rather die than beg anyone for anything. But I'm begging you to come with me. I need you by my side when these bandages come off. After that, we can go our separate ways again."

To see such a proud man humbled was Catherine's undoing. "All right. I'll go with you to Coppermine, but only until you are well again." She refused to consider what the future would hold if Damon were blind. "Are you sure you feel strong enough to travel?" Catherine asked.

"I'll get there if it kills me. I need the solitude. Besides, it will give you a chance to escape newspaper reporters."

"Now that's a benefit I hadn't considered. When do you want me to be ready?"

"Early tomorrow morning. We'll go by train, in my private car. Tell Nevada. He'll know what to do."

Catherine hesitated. "I just want to warn you that our marriage is over, Damon. This won't change anything between us. Once you're well, we'll go our separate ways again. I hope you understand that."

He made no comment. All he did was avert his face.

Catherine turned and went in search of Nevada to make arrangements for their trip up the Hudson River Valley.

Catherine sat in Damon's private railroad car and watched the gray Hudson River and the blossoming trees from her window.

She shook her head in wonder. She still couldn't believe they had managed to spirit Damon away in a furniture dray to Grand Central Station without arousing undue curiosity or the attention of newspaper reporters. But they had, and now the two of them were on their way to Coppermine.

Catherine looked away from the scenery and focused on Damon lying in the bed at the end of the car. He wore trousers and a loose-fitting white shirt in deference to his injuries, his dark head outlined against the white pillow, the bandages a stark reminder of the explosion that almost claimed his life. After she had left Damon's house yesterday, she had consulted with his ophthalmologist Dr. Halsey, and he had told her to remove those bandages in three days.

In three days, they would know Damon's fate.

"Catherine?"

She rose and went to sit beside his bed. It was easier to talk to him without looking into his eyes. "How do you feel?"

He grimaced. "Still sore." Then he ran his hand over his jaw dark with stubble. "I can see—" His hand fell back. "Poor choice of words."

"Perhaps your valet can shave you once we arrive," she said.

Damon fumbled for her hand. "What have you been doing since we . . . separated?"

"You should know, you've had a man following me. And don't try to deny it, because I've seen him."

"If you've seen him, he hasn't been doing his job properly." Damon hesitated. "He's only there to make sure you're safe. I don't want you murdered like Sybilla."

As much as Catherine wanted to tell him that she resented his interference, she decided this was neither the time nor the place to argue. "I appreciate your concern."

"How is your practice? I know you still go to the tenements."

"I do. Helping the poor gives me a great deal of satisfaction, but I also have other patients. Paying patients."

"I've heard that most of the society ladies have stopped going to you since our separation."

"I expected that to happen, since I moved my practice out of their neighborhood," Catherine admitted, "but I am managing quite nicely in spite of it. Molly and I live comfortably."

"You're the kind of woman who should live in luxury," he said softly, "not just comfort."

Again Catherine bit back the retort that was on the tip of her tongue. Damon was hurt. She mustn't agitate him. She would wait until he was well before reopening those old arguments.

Instead she asked him, "And what about you? I've heard you've been very successful financially in spite of the depression."

He smiled bitterly. "That seems to be the one constant in my life."

"I've also heard you plan to build a mansion in Newport."

"I had been considering it."

"Why? I thought you hated the place."

"I used to, but lately I've found it quite amusing."

That saddened Catherine, for the man she had married always disdained following society's more pretentious crowd.

Damon touched her hand. "I'm sorry the police never discovered who killed Sybilla."

She felt the old sorrow claw at her heart. "Oh, I'm sure they tried their best. But there are thousands of children in the tenements. How could they expect to find one little girl among them?"

"And no one has made another attempt on your life?"

"No. But since Sybilla died, I've been extremely careful. And of course, there is my shadow," she added dryly.

"Your shadow?"

"That's what I call the man you hired to follow me." She looked down at him. "And what about you? Do you have any idea who could've planted the bomb in your stables?"

"I have many enemies, Catherine. A successful man usually does. It could have been a disgruntled employee, a competitor— who knows? Especially with this depression turning even rational men desperate."

"I'm sure the police will do their best."

Damon grew very quiet and thoughtful. Without warning, he reached out blindly, splayed fingers groping at the air.

"What is it?" Catherine asked, reaching for his hand with her own.

"I'd like to touch your face," he said. "Isn't it ironic? Even though it's the first time I've seen you in a year, I can't really 'see' you."

His request startled her, and for a moment, she hesitated. Then she decided she could comply with such a simple request. It wasn't as though Damon wanted to make love to her.

Catherine leaned forward and guided his hands to her face. Damon slid his fingertips lightly across her forehead, down her nose, across her cheek, and along her jawline, his touch awakening such powerful memories of the intimacies they had shared. Catherine held herself very still, refusing to succumb to the shudder of delight building within her, but when his fingertips passed over her lips, she kissed them involuntarily, then drew back, shocked by what she had done.

"Closer," Damon whispered. "I want to feel if your hair is as soft as I remember it."

What could be the harm? She leaned closer, her face just a foot away from his.

Suddenly Damon's hand slid behind her neck and with surprising strength, he pulled her toward him. Catherine saw at once that he intended to kiss her, and she braced her arm against the bed and averted her face just in time.

She pulled away and glared down at him. "If you try that again, I shall have this train put me off at the next stop and you can go to Coppermine by yourself."

He clenched his fist in frustration. "Have you no compassion for me?"

Guilt sliced through Catherine, but she steeled herself against it. "I'm sorry you were injured, but that doesn't change our situation."

"You're a hard woman, Catherine."

"Only when I need to be." She paused. "Get some rest. I'm going to return to my seat by the window."

As Catherine sat there, she watched Damon lying so still and she marveled at his stoicism. That he could face the possibility of blindness with such equanimity was a testament to his strength. If he was terrified, he didn't show it.

She imagined how she would feel if she were blind, and she shuddered. To never practice medicine again, to never see the faces of loved ones or the miracle of a sunrise . . . It was just too horrible to contemplate.

Yet that horror might soon be Damon's reality.

Catherine looked out the window at the hills rising from the river's edge, clasped her hands together tightly and prayed that wouldn't happen, for both their sakes.

Later, when the train came to a shuddering halt, Catherine rose and said, "We're here."

To her surprise, Damon swung his legs over the side of the bed and sat there clutching the edge.

She hurried to his side. "You mustn't exert yourself. The men will be here in a moment with a stretcher."

He looked in her direction. "Send them away," he snarled. "I'll be damned if I'm going to be carried out of here like some invalid."

His tone took Catherine aback. "But your injuries—"

"They seem to bother you more than they do me." He reached out. "If you will take my hand and guide me, I'll be fine."

Catherine took his hand and he grasped it as he rose unsteadily. Damon stood there for a moment, and when he regained his balance, he took a tentative shuffling step.

"Shall we go?" he said.

Catherine slipped his arm through hers and started slowly toward the door, taking great care to keep Damon away from seats and objects that might bump or trip him. He held his head high, his jaw tight with pride and determination.

When they reached the door leading to the platform, Catherine said, "Perhaps I should go first and you follow."

Damon nodded curtly as she opened the door.

She grasped the hand rail and stepped down, then she turned and looked up at him standing there so awkwardly. She reached up and guided his left hand to the rail. Then Damon took his first step. When his foot found that step, he felt for another.

"One more to go," Catherine said, taking his right hand to balance him, "and then it's the platform."

As Damon stepped down, the longer length between the last step and the platform fooled him, and he stiffened, then stumbled uncertainly. Catherine caught him before he could fall to his knees.

He pushed away from her, his cheeks flaming with embarrassment. "Are there any other people on this platform?" he snapped.

"The men with the stretcher and several passengers getting on the train at the other end," Catherine replied.

"Are they laughing at me?"

Her heart went out to him. "No, they're not even looking at you."

"Don't lie to me," he muttered between clenched teeth.

She bit back her retort and waved away the men with the stretcher before taking his arm. "The carriage is waiting for us."

On the drive to Coppermine, Damon sat in his corner of the carriage in brooding silence, locked in his own world. Catherine turned her attention to the passing scenery, the budding ash and elm trees and wildflowers by the roadside.

When they arrived at the house, Catherine assisted him out of the carriage and guided him up the front steps. With Damon's every step, she watched his frustration mount. When he accidentally bumped his shoulder against the doorjamb, his face turned dark crimson with impotent rage.

By the time they reached the foyer, Catherine felt both drained and exultant that they had navigated the course with only one minor mishap.

The housekeeper greeted them as though nothing untoward had happened to the master, but Catherine could see the pitying look in the woman's eyes, and she knew Damon sensed it.

"I'm tired," he announced. "I want to go to my room and lie down for a while."

"Of course," Catherine said.

She guided him to the stairs, told him where the banister was, and they climbed the stairs as slowly and deliberately as if Damon were an old man of ninety.

When they reached his bedroom, he flopped down on the bed with an exhausted, relieved sigh.

"It's like fighting a battle," he muttered. "Suddenly everything I once took for granted—doorjambs, walls, steps—have become damned obstacles."

She placed a comforting hand on his shoulder. "I can imagine. Just rest now."

He turned his head in the direction of her voice. "When can these bandages come off?"

"Soon. Dr. Halsey told me to take them off the day after tomorrow."

"Soon," Damon echoed.

Catherine expected him to explode, to rail against the possibility that he would be blind, but he didn't. He just lay there in moody, contemplative silence.

Then he said, "Where will you be staying?"

"In the adjoining bedroom."

"You used to stay here with me."

"We were married then."

"We still are."

She looked down at him. "This conversation is pointless, and you know why."

"I won't beg you to share my bed. I'm not that desperate for intimacy. It would just be comforting to have you there, lying beside me in the night."

Even if you could resist me, she said to herself, *I don't know if I could resist you.*

Aloud, she said, "Under the circumstances, I can only offer you spiritual comfort."

"I'll accept whatever you offer."

She walked over to the window nearest the bed and looked down at the sweeping lawn still shaggy from the winter. "You should rest, Damon. Shall I have a tray sent to you for luncheon?"

"I'm not hungry. But I will be down for dinner, and I'll have you know that I'm perfectly able to feed myself."

She looked at him in surprise, then admiration at his determination to present a courageous facade in the face of possible tragedy.

"I'm going out for a walk," she said, "I'll see you at dinner."

He raised his hand fretfully. "You'll be close by if I should need you?"

"Just pull the bell by your bed, and the servants will find me."

He sighed deeply and averted his face, indicating that he wanted to sleep, so Catherine left him alone.

She knew she had to get as far away from the house as possible, so she went down to the stables, had one of the grooms saddle Star and another horse for himself, so he could follow at a distance, and she cantered away from the house without once looking back.

Catherine didn't slow down until she reached a narrow dirt road running through the woods. Then she slowed Star to a walk and forced herself to confront her own feelings about Damon's condition.

Like Damon, she had been ignoring the possibility that when the bandages came off the day after tomorrow, he could be blind. Suddenly that realization, and all it entailed, hit her with the force of a fist, causing her to gasp aloud.

She was still Damon's wife. She would be morally responsible to return to him. She knew without a second's hesitation that she would do so willingly, but she dreaded the possibility nonetheless.

She thought of a once-vital man forced to live such a constricted life, and she shuddered. She would hate to see Damon become querulous and bitter, making all those around him as miserable as he.

Catherine turned her horse around on the narrow path and signaled for the groom to return to the house. She and Damon were going to have a long talk about the future at dinner, whether he wanted to or not.

Catherine had dinner served early at six o'clock.

She dressed formally as a symbolic gesture that life would go on no matter what the status of Damon's eyesight. She also ordered the dining room table set with a full complement of silver and crystal for the same reason.

When Catherine went to Damon's room to escort him to dinner, she was both pleased and dismayed to see that his valet had dressed him in white tie for dinner as well.

"Doesn't it hurt to wear such constricting clothes?" she asked, concerned about his injuries from the explosion.

"I'm sore in one or two places, but I always dress for dinner." Then he added, "What are you wearing?"

"My pale blue silk gown."

"My favorite. I remember how lovely you look in it."

Catherine took his arm and led him downstairs without mishap and into the dining room. Once Damon was shown his chair, he seated himself and used his fingertips to determine the location of plates, cutlery, and crystal stemware.

Catherine watched him carefully for any sign of rage or frustration, but if Damon were feeling such emotions, he kept them tightly under control.

"What's on the menu?" he asked.

"We're starting with a clear beef consommé," she replied, signaling the footman to serve the soup.

Catherine was on pins and needles as Damon began eating, but to her relief, he moved slowly and deliberately, taking his time. Sometimes the spoon would miss his mouth and he colored in embarrassment, but he merely set down the spoon and dabbed at his chin or cheek with the napkin.

When he managed to finish the lobster in creamed sherry sauce easily, Catherine relaxed. But then the main course was served, and her false sense of security vanished.

"What's on my plate?" He breathed deeply. "It smells like spring lamb."

"It is, and it's on your left. New potatoes are on the right, and green beans are below them."

Damon managed to spear the potatoes with his fork, followed by the beans, but when he reached too quickly for a wine glass, that was his undoing. He knocked it over, sending red wine spilling and splashing on the tablecloth like a widening bloodstain.

Before Catherine could even gasp in surprise, Damon was on his feet, his face crimson with uncontrolled rage. Uttering an oath, he drew up his right arm and sent it sweeping across the table, causing china, crystal and silverware to fall crashing and tinkling to the floor.

Catherine jumped up so fast she sent her chair toppling backwards. Just as she reached Damon's side, his arm went up again, and this time when it came down, it caught Catherine full in the chest.

She was too stunned to cry out. Just as Catherine started falling, Damon realized what he had done and bellowed her name. But her main concern was saving herself, so she reached out to break her fall. As her hands landed in the shards of broken glass scattered on the floor, Catherine screamed in agony.

Damon swore and staggered toward her. As Catherine sat up and looked at her bleeding palms in stupefaction, he found her. He knelt down, unmindful of the broken glass, and gathered her into his arms, his cheek pressed to the top of her head.

"Dear God, Catherine, I'm sorry." He crushed her to him. "I didn't mean to hit you like that. I didn't mean it."

Even in her shock and pain, her first thought was for him. She twisted in his arms so she could look at him. "I'm fine. You didn't hurt me."

"Then why did you scream? Don't lie to me."

"I cut my hands a little, that's all."

He swore again. "Damn these bandages!"

When he reached up as if to claw them off his eyes, Catherine grasped his wrists to restrain him, embedding the glass deeper into her soft flesh. "No, Damon, you mustn't."

She struggled to her feet and pulled him up after her. "Everything's going to be fine," she said softly, holding him.

"Is it?"

"You mustn't give up hope. Whatever tomorrow brings, you will face it with your customary courage."

She waited, hoping he would release his pent-up bitterness and frustration in a stream of invectives, but all he did was shudder uncontrollably as he fought to maintain an iron control of his emotions.

When he stopped trembling and collected himself, he said, "You should have the housekeeper tend to your hands."

"I'll do that right now."

"Will you show me to the study first? I'd like to be alone for a while."

"Of course."

Once Catherine showed Damon to the study, she went to the kitchen and endured with a stoicism of her own while the housekeeper fussed over her, washing her hands in warm water and carefully picking out pieces of glass. Then Catherine put some healing ointment on her palms and instructed the housekeeper how to bandage them. When that was done, she went to the study to look in on Damon.

She was glad she left the door open, for she had a chance to observe him silently. He sat very still in a chair, his brooding silence filling the room.

Catherine wished he would stop being so brave and confide his fears to her. But she knew he wouldn't. Damon prided himself on being strong. Only a weak man would wallow in self-pity or confess his innermost fears to a woman.

But Catherine knew that even the strongest of men had a breaking point, and whenever Damon's came, she would be ready.

The clock had just finished chiming one in the morning when a noise awakened Catherine.

She sat up in bed and looked around her bedroom, but all she saw were the indistinct shapes of furniture partially illuminated by moonlight through the windows. She listened. And then she heard it again, the low moaning coming through the open connecting door from Damon's room.

Catherine ignored the burning in her hands to fling back the covers and fumble for matches to light the small lamp by her bedside. Without bothering to slip a wrap over her nightgown, she hurried into his room even as the moaning grew louder and more urgent.

She could see he was having a nightmare. Damon lay in the center of his bed, his face and bare torso drenched in sweat, the covers twisted and tangled around him as he jerked and thrashed about, groaning and muttering.

Catherine set down the lamp. "Damon, wake up."

He didn't hear her, for he continued to toss his head from side to side, his body twitching with the terrors of his soul.

She reached out and shook his shoulder while calling his name.

He started, cried out, "No!" and sat bolt upright.

"Don't fret," Catherine murmured as she slid into bed beside him. "You were having a nightmare."

When Damon realized where he was, he cradled his head in his hands, his breath coming in ragged gasps.

Catherine smoothed back the damp, dark hair from his brow,

the acrid odor of cold sweat strong in her nostrils. "Hush. It's all right."

He sagged against her. "I'm frightened."

Moved by his admission, she drew his head against her shoulder. "I know. So am I."

"I have to face the fact that I may never see again, and I don't know if I can."

Catherine groped for something to say, but everything she thought of sounded too facile or patronizing. Instead, she just held him as tightly as she could.

She had been sitting there and holding him for about ten minutes when she sensed the change in him. Damon's breathing slowed, becoming more regular, and he gradually regained that iron control.

By the time Catherine realized she was in danger, it was too late.

"Love me, Catherine," he whispered. "Tomorrow my life may change forever, but while it's still the same, will you give me one last night?"

By the soft light of the lamp, he looked as desirable as he had on their wedding night, his black hair tousled from sleep, his shoulders tense with restraint. Catherine felt the old familiar pull of desire weakening her own resolve not to succumb to him.

One last time, she said to herself. *What could be the harm?*

Consequences flitted through her thoughts, but this time, the pull of her heart was stronger.

She leaned forward and touched his lips tentatively with her own and was startled by her own body's violent response, the surge of pleasure heightening her senses.

Damon eased her down onto the pillows, his rapacious mouth following her descent, teasing her lips with his own. After almost a year of being apart, his deep kisses robbed her of breath and made her head spin.

"I may not be able to see you," he said, his breath soft against her face, "but I can love you with all my other senses."

He buried his face in her hair and inhaled deeply. "Your hair smells like you washed it in rain water, and your skin is as sweet as primroses." His left hand lifted her nightgown and came down in a swift, startling caress between her thighs. "And I know your feminine essence smells spicy."

Even as Catherine gasped in shock at his bold, evocative words, she quivered deep inside. She sat up and pulled off her nightgown in one swift motion and flung it away, her bare skin tingling with anticipation.

"I can hear you," Damon went on relentlessly. "Every catch in your breath, every passionate moan, every movement of your lovely body."

"Damon, I—"

"Hush." He fondled one breast. "Your skin is so soft, but this part—" his thumb circled the aureole "—is like satin, and this part—" he caught the nipple and teased it into hardness.

Catherine groaned helplessly as every nerve burst into flames of pleasure. Her breasts had gone without his tender ministrations far too long, and she wanted more.

She pulled his head down. "Not another word."

He chuckled, for he knew he had won.

Catherine stretched her arms above her head and abandoned herself to the sweet sensual onslaught as Damon began feasting on one breast, then the other, while his warm fingers explored the rest of her.

He raised his head to grin wickedly and murmur, "Tight," when his explorations became the most intimate of all.

Catherine gasped, reached down and retaliated with remorseless caresses of her own, exulting in her feminine power to enslave such a man.

Finally, Damon lay back. "Help me!" he rasped.

Catherine straddled him, easing down slowly so her body could accommodate him comfortably after such a long abstinence. When the tightness eased and she was able to possess him completely, she splayed her fingers across his chest to balance herself, and then began moving her hips with tantalizing slowness.

As Damon writhed helplessly beneath her, begging her to end his torment, Catherine felt her own excitement rising and building. Finally, her tortured body exploded and she cried out Damon's name just as he shouted hers and spent within her.

Panting and gasping, Catherine slowly drifted down to earth. When she fell against him, he drew her into his arms and cradled her against his side.

Drifting off to sleep, Catherine decided that their last night together had been the most memorable of her life.

❧ CHAPTER ❧

SEVENTEEN

WHEN Damon woke he reached for Catherine, but his quest-ing hand encountered only rumpled sheets. The rest of the bed was empty.

Annoyance warred with disappointment as he passed his hand over his stubbled jaw and lay back against the pillows. Then he recalled last night and grinned.

He had never spent a more remarkable or fulfilling night with a woman in his life. Even his frequent sessions with Danse to ease his randiness faded into mere gymnastic exercises.

Damon felt himself grow hard just thinking of the ways Cath-erine had used her body to please him, and like a child greedy for sweets, he wanted more. But all he had asked for, and she had promised him, was one last night.

He swore aloud.

"Ah, you're awake."

He turned his head in the direction of Catherine's voice com-ing from the vicinity of the connecting door. He longed to see if her expression was soft with satisfaction and if a secret smile of feminine contentment played about her mouth. But he couldn't. And her voice maddeningly betrayed nothing.

"Good morning," he said, sitting up. "I trust you . . . slept well."

"I don't believe either of us slept much."

He strained his ears, but heard no telltale sound of her moving closer. She remained in the doorway, keeping her distance.

"Then why did you leave my bed?" he asked.

"I thought it best, under the circumstances."

He extended his hand. "Catherine, come here. Please."

Still from the doorway, she replied, "I gave you your last night. Don't ask anything more of me."

"All I want to do is thank you properly for that wonderful night."

"Consider your thanks given and accepted."

His patience worn out at last, Damon flung back the covers, swung his legs over the side of the bed, and stood there, naked. Then he lumbered toward that disembodied voice coming from the connecting door.

He heard her walk toward him, her voice coming closer and closer as she said, "Get back into bed before you trip over something and hurt yourself."

He stopped as he sensed her standing right before him, a tantalizing physical presence he couldn't see. Before she could evade him, he reached out and that presence suddenly took form in his arms.

As he crushed her to him, his touch told him that she wore no corset beneath what felt like a silk dressing gown, and even though her body was stiff and unyielding with protest, Catherine still felt as though she belonged there.

Damon buried his face in her sweet-scented hair. "Come back to bed."

"If you don't release me this instant, you'll have a far more serious injury to worry about."

Realizing his nakedness left him particularly vulnerable, Damon stopped. "You wouldn't."

"I would." Her voice told him she wasn't making an idle threat.

He stepped back and raked his hand through his hair in frustration. "Damn it, Catherine, why not? You were willing enough last night."

"You were very persuasive. But after it happened, I realized that I shouldn't have gone to bed with you. It creates false expectations." She hesitated. "And judging by your behavior this morning, I can see that I was right."

"You are a hard woman, Catherine Delancy."

"Why? Because I am ruled by my intellect rather than pleasures of the flesh?" She sounded amused rather than insulted.

He reached out and boldly squeezed her breast, noting with satisfaction that she gasped and the nipple hardened through the silk of the dressing gown.

As Catherine knocked his hand away, Damon chuckled. "Your intellect is formidable, my dear, but so is your capacity for passion. And someday you're going to realize that and come back to me, where you belong."

He turned away from her and started fumbling his way back to the bed. "Can my bandages come off today?"

"Tomorrow."

"I want them off right now."

"Damon, I—"

"What difference can a day make?"

Catherine mumbled something under her breath.

His knees hit the edge of the bed and he slid in. "I want them off now. Unless, of course, there's some reason to wait." As he sat there, he sensed her doubt and hesitation. "Is something wrong?"

"No, nothing's wrong. Let me get my medical bag."

But as he listened to her walk out of the room, Damon knew that the prospect of his permanent blindness terrified Catherine as much as it did him. In a few minutes they would know.

While he waited for her, he thought about the possibility that he would never see again, and he knew bone-shaking fear. But he also knew he would survive, as he always had. He had amassed more than enough money to keep himself in the lap of luxury for the rest of his life, even if he never did another day's work for as long as he lived.

And if he were blind, Catherine would return to him without hesitation.

He heard her cross the room and set her medical bag down on the nightstand near the bed.

"Ready?"

Her voice may have been strong and steady, but Damon could sense that she feared for her own future as well as his.

He took a deep breath. "I'm as ready as I'll ever be."

He could smell the faint, familiar scent of idoform on Catherine's hands as she reached to undo the bandages wound around his head. He heard a snip-snip as she cut them, then he felt the gossamer weight of the bandages disappear as she unwound them, leaving his head feeling bare and exposed. Once the bandages were gone, all Damon felt were two pads against his eyelids and the beads of sweat on his brow.

"I'm going to take these off now," Catherine said, her voice calm and soothing. "When I do, don't open your eyes right away. Give them time to adjust to the light."

"Assuming I'll be able to see light."

"Let's hope for the best."

The pads came off.

Damon kept his eyes closed. He thought he could detect light through the lids.

He held his breath and waited. Catherine must have been holding her breath as well, for he couldn't hear her soft rhythmic breathing. But he did feel her own bandaged hand grasp his tightly.

Slowly, ever so slowly, he opened his eyes.

At first, all he saw were indistinct shapes of dark and light, all blurred and fuzzy. He couldn't tell if he was looking at a bureau or Catherine sitting at his bedside.

If this were all he could see, he might as well be blind.

"Well?" Catherine asked anxiously, her nails digging into his palms.

Damon closed his eyes again. This time, when he opened them, the world suddenly came into sharp focus.

He turned his head and looked at Catherine. "You're just as beautiful as I remember."

A look of wonder and relief flitted across her face. "You can see."

He could indeed see the face he had feared he would never see again. He drank in her soft brown hair flowing freely down her shoulders, her pale blue eyes filled with some strong emotion he couldn't name, the slender body that had pleased him so much last night.

Suddenly Catherine's lips trembled and she rose hurriedly, turning away from him.

He caught her wrist and drew her back. "Why are you crying?"

She looked down at him, silent tears sliding down her cheeks. "I'm glad you're not blind."

"So am I."

Catherine wiped her eyes with the back of her hand. "I—I should dress now. It's almost noon." And she turned to go.

"Tell me something," Damon said. When she turned, an inquiring look on her face, he added, "If I had been blind, would you have come back to me?"

"Without hesitation."

"Know this, then: If I had gone blind, I wouldn't have taken you back."

She stood there in astonished silence at his unexpected declaration. Then she nodded, turned, and disappeared into the adjoining room.

With the restoration of his sight, Damon gained a new appreciation for the beauty of the world around him. Colors captured his attention, from the muted green of his bedroom wallpaper to the soft gray marble fireplace mantel. And it was a wonder to see things again, not just touch them. Even his own reflection startled him, especially the coldness in his eyes.

Later, after he bathed and his valet helped him dress, he went to the connecting bedroom door and knocked.

"Come in," Catherine answered.

When he walked in, he saw a maid there as well, folding Catherine's clothes and packing them in a valise.

Damon dismissed the maid with a curt nod toward the door, and when he was alone with Catherine, he said, "Are you leaving?"

"Of course," she replied, inserting a last hairpin into her chignon and standing back to judge the results in the mirror. "I thought I'd return to New York this afternoon."

He scowled. "We just arrived here yesterday. It's so pointless to leave right away. Won't you stay for at least another day?"

She turned to face him. "Don't you ever tire of trying to coerce me into doing your bidding?"

He raised his brows in mock astonishment. "Coerce you? Catherine, I doubt if anyone has ever made you do anything you didn't want to do."

She suppressed a smile. "Still, there is no reason for my staying, and you know it."

"Isn't there?" He went over to the window. "There is this beautiful spring day to enjoy, and the solitude of the countryside. Surely those are compelling enough reasons." When she didn't respond, he added, "Besides, you look as though you never get enough rest or food."

Catherine raised her head indignantly. "I'll have you know I work very hard."

"Too hard, if you ask me. Surely your patients wouldn't begrudge you one day of relaxation and pampering, to celebrate my restored eyesight."

She sighed as she went to the other window and looked outside. "I'm tempted. It is so beautiful here."

"Then you'll stay?"

She looked at him. "On one condition."

He smiled wryly, for he knew what she wanted. "That I don't try to seduce you tonight?"

"Exactly."

He held up his hands in surrender. "You have nothing to fear from me. Merely lock your door. I promise I won't try to break it down."

"Then I'll stay."

He walked over to her and took her left hand in his, turning it palm up so he could examine the bandage that crisscrossed it. "The glass didn't damage your hands permanently, I trust?"

"Just a few lacerations," she replied, flexing her fingers. "They'll be stiff for a while, but it won't keep me from practicing medicine."

He brought her palm to his lips for a light kiss. "I'm sorry I struck you."

She touched his face hesitantly. "Don't blame yourself. You didn't mean to do it."

"Of course I didn't. But that doesn't excuse what I did."

"Forget it, Damon. I have." Then she smiled. "Shall we go down to luncheon? Afterward I would like to go riding."

He grinned as he crooked his arm. "Your wish is my command."

Later, after they enjoyed an amicable luncheon devoid of pressure or innuendo, they went out riding.

As Catherine rode through the fields beside Damon, she found herself questioning the wisdom of staying here for even one more day. After being separated from him for almost a year, she had thought herself immune to his considerable charm, but it had taken last night to show her how wrong she was.

Riding down the narrow path with tall oaks nearly meeting overhead, Catherine wished last night hadn't happened. While Damon's lovemaking had been glorious, the cold, sobering reality was that Catherine had succumbed to his sweet seduction without the usual protection of an anticonception device.

She mentally cursed her own stupidity for letting herself get swept away on passion's tide. Even now she could be pregnant with Damon's child.

The raucous jeering of crows overhead seemed to mock her. Intelligent, level-headed Catherine who was never reckless. . . .

She wouldn't even contemplate the disastrous consequences

until she knew for certain. She would concentrate on enjoying her respite in the country before returning to New York City.

"How was the country, Dr. Catherine?" Molly asked the moment Catherine walked in the door two days later.

"Just wonderful," Catherine replied as Damon's driver set down her valise in the foyer, tipped his hat, and left.

The extra days had been wonderful. Damon was the perfect gentleman and host the entire time, insisting that she sleep late, eat hearty meals and take long, leisurely afternoon walks. Not once did he try to persuade her to return to him. By the time Catherine boarded his private railway car for the trip back to the city, she felt truly well-rested.

"The best news of all," she said to Molly, "is that Mr. Delancy has regained his eyesight."

Molly clasped her hands together. "Oh, doctor, that is wonderful news. I was so worried about him."

Catherine pulled her hatpin from her bonnet and smoothed her hair. "So was I. But luckily, the explosion didn't damage his eyes at all."

Molly picked up the valise and started for the stairs. "I can't imagine being blind. It must be a frightening feeling."

Catherine headed for her office, then stopped at the door. "How were matters here, Molly?"

The maid stopped and shrugged. "You had more patients than usual, but I told them you were away and sent them over to the Women's Dispensary."

"I hope none were seriously ill," she muttered fretfully as she disappeared into her office to resume her work.

No sooner did she finish reading the mail on her desk than Molly appeared at the door. "Excuse me, but Dr. Flanders is here to see you."

Then she stood aside to admit Kim, as dapper and well-dressed as always.

The moment he walked into the surgery and closed the door behind him, he got right to the point: "Is Damon going to be blind?"

Catherine shook her head. "He's fine. The bandages came off the day before yesterday, and he can see."

Kim looked relieved. "I'm glad to hear it. I wouldn't wish blindness on anyone, even Damon." He studied her for a moment. "You look as though the country air agrees with you."

She rose and leaned against the edge of her desk. "I must admit that the respite did me good."

"And how was Damon?"

"The perfect gentleman."

Something like disbelief flickered in Kim's blue eyes, then disappeared. "All society is agog with the bombing."

Catherine leaned forward. "Does anyone have any idea who might have done such a thing?"

Kim shook his head. "The general consensus seems to be that it was a disgruntled former employee, someone who used to work for one of Damon's companies before being dismissed."

"It's possible."

"There's also a lot of speculation about you and Damon."

That took Catherine aback. "Such as . . . ?"

"That you might reconcile."

She moved away from her desk. "That's preposterous. I only went to Coppermine because Damon needed someone with him when the bandages came off, nothing more."

Nothing more? She thought of their lovemaking and shivered.

"You can't blame them for thinking that," Kim said. "After all, you've been separated for almost a year and still aren't divorced."

Catherine said nothing, just went to the window, parted the curtain and stared into the street.

"I know it's none of my concern, Catherine, but have you and Damon discussed divorce?"

"No, we haven't."

Kim's ensuing silence spoke volumes.

Catherine turned and smiled apologetically. "I've been so busy, I haven't thought about divorce. And Damon hasn't mentioned it, either."

"That's because he's still in love with you," Kim said quietly.

"You're wrong. Damon doesn't love me any more."

"Then why won't he ask you for a divorce? It's not the scandal it once was, and you both could be free to marry someone else."

"I'm in no hurry to marry again, Kim. Doctors make terrible wives, as I've learned only too well."

"Not now, but perhaps someday." He hesitated. "Speaking of marriage, I want you to be the first to know. I've asked Francine Ballard to marry me, and she's accepted."

Catherine smiled in delight and went to him, her hands extended. "Oh, Kim, I'm so happy for you. Francine will make you a wonderful wife."

Kim needed someone like Francine, who would devote herself to his career and use her social connections to her husband's advantage.

He clasped Catherine's hands tightly. "I think we will suit each other admirably."

As Catherine leaned forward to give him a congratulatory kiss on the cheek, she sensed a wistfulness about him, and she wondered if he was recalling those first days of their relationship, when they were on the verge of falling in love.

Kim took a deep breath. "Catherine, I want you to know that I'll always have a special place for you in my heart."

She smiled. "And I for you, Kim."

A troubled frown marred his brow. "I just wish things could have been different for us."

"So do I, but it was never meant to be."

"Still, I sometimes wonder—"

"Don't," she said, placing her hand on his arm. "Give Francine all of your love unconditionally. Never let doubt cloud your life."

He smiled and nodded. "I'll try."

"When is the wedding?"

"Next spring. Either April or May."

"What a lovely time for a wedding."

Kim took his timepiece out of his waistcoat pocket. "Well, I have to be going. I only stopped by to see how your trip to Coppermine was, and to tell you my news."

"Thank you for coming. And congratulations again."

He kissed her lightly on the cheek. "What are friends for?"

Catherine escorted him to the door, and just as she was about to open it, the doorbell rang. When she answered it, she was astounded to see a messenger boy holding a long white box tied with a red ribbon.

"Mrs. Delancy?" the boy asked. When Catherine nodded, he thrust the box into her hands. "These are for you." And he left.

She gave Kim an inquiring look.

"Open it," he said.

When she did so, she gasped in surprise at the dozen red American Beauty roses nestled in the box.

Kim pushed a lock of fair hair off his brow and brushed an

imaginary speck of lint off his sleeve. "I'll bet I know who sent them."

Catherine knew, too, but she read the enclosed card anyway. It was Damon's, and on the back he had scrawled, "Thank you."

Kim raised one wry brow. "If he doesn't still love you, he has a strange way of showing it."

"He's merely being polite."

"If you say so." Kim smiled, wished her good day, and left her standing there cradling her roses.

Catherine put the roses in a vase and forgot about them as patients began trickling in. She was forcibly reminded of his gift the following day when another dozen red roses arrived, and another dozen the day after that. When even more roses arrived on the fourth day, Catherine reached her breaking point and decided to put a stop to Damon's badgering once and for all.

Catherine threw the roses down on Damon's desk. "I want a divorce."

The gray eyes that had once been hidden behind bandages widened in affronted innocence. "Why? For sending you roses every day that we're apart?"

She glared at him. "This estrangement isn't working. I want a clean break from you."

He rose with predatory grace and sat on the edge of his desk. "But I don't want to give you a divorce."

Hot, fierce anger raged through her. "Surely you can't be happy in this sham of a marriage? We haven't lived as husband and wife for nearly a year."

"We can remedy that situation quite easily."

"I don't want to remedy it. I want my freedom. I want to put the past behind me and move on."

"Do you now?" His gaze roved boldly over her. "After the night we spent together at Coppermine—"

"You asked for one night, and I gave it to you. Believe me, I've regretted it ever since."

His smile was maddening. "Have you?"

Catherine made a strangled sound as she threw up her hands in exasperation. "Damon, what do you want from me?"

He looked perplexed. "What I've wanted all along. I want you to come to your senses and return to me."

"Why? You don't love me."

Damon's expression softened. "But I do."

"If you loved me, you wouldn't have insisted that I give up medicine. No—you see me as a possession, as something that belongs to you. You lost it, and now you want it back. Your motives are quite transparent."

Her accusation must have rankled him, for his eyes narrowed. "That's not true. It's because I love you that I want to protect you."

Catherine shook her head, all patience gone. "If you don't stop sending me flowers, I'll throw them in the street to rot."

He glanced down at the roses on his desk, then up at her. "And what will you do to me if I don't give you a divorce?"

"Take a lover and flaunt him right under your nose. Cause a scandal the likes of which society has never seen."

If she sought to provoke him, she failed. Damon merely shook his head pityingly. "You'll lose patients if you're the center of a scandal." Before Catherine could comment, he said, "Are you and Flanders lovers? Is that why you want a divorce?"

"Don't be absurd," she snapped. "Kim Flanders has just become betrothed to Francine Ballard."

"So Francine has snared the good doctor," Damon mused. "She always did consider him quite eligible. I've never seen two people more suited to each other." Then he said, "Is that why you're so furious with me, because you've lost Flanders to another woman?"

"I won't even dignify that comment with a reply," she said with a disdainful sniff.

Damon grinned. "Good, because Flanders isn't worth it."

"And I suppose you are?"

"You know I am, if you'd just come to your senses and admit it to yourself."

Catherine balled her hands into fists. "If you won't divorce me, then I'll divorce you."

"On what grounds? That I send you flowers every day? Some would call it the height of consideration. Adultery? I dare you to prove it. Desertion? If I recall correctly, you left me." He shook his head. "You're in for a long, expensive fight, Catherine, one I don't think you can afford."

She stood there helplessly, feeling as though she were standing on quicksand and sinking fast. "Let me go, Damon. Please. Just let me go."

"Never."

Catherine whirled on her heel, but before she could storm out of the study in righteous indignation, she felt Damon's hand capture her wrist to detain her.

She spun back to face him, her heart racing out of control as he caught her other wrist and held her fast.

He smiled. "Why do you keep trying to run away from me, Catherine? You know I'm going to have you in the end."

"You arrogant—"

"Bastard. Yes, I know I am. But you're still my wife and we belong together."

She wouldn't lower herself to struggle against his superior strength. She just stared up at him coolly, ignoring his smoldering eyes and the sardonic curve of his lips.

"Damon, let me go."

"I don't know why my gifts enrage you so. Could it be because you still care for me?" He released her. "Think about it." And he returned to his desk.

Without a word, Catherine turned and fled from his study.

Once she was safely ensconced in a hansom heading back to Washington Square, Catherine rested her head back against the worn leather squabs and closed her eyes. Gradually the trembling in her limbs subsided, and she was able to think rationally again.

She sighed dismally, wishing Sybilla were here to talk to. But Catherine knew what she would say if she were: "Mother of surgeons, the man sent you flowers, that's all, and you go tearing at him like some harpy."

Catherine rubbed her forehead where a headache was beginning to form. "You know why, Syb," she whispered as though her friend were sitting right there beside her.

She did not fear Damon, she feared herself.

Damon was her weakness. When he left her alone, she was strong, but when he exerted himself to woo and win her, Catherine found her resolve weakening. That night at Coppermine forcibly reminded her of her own vulnerability.

She closed her eyes again and took a deep breath. She had to find some way to end their relationship once and for all, or she would be at his mercy forever.

The roses stopped coming the following day. When a week passed without any sign of them, Catherine's spirits lifted and she breathed a sigh of relief. But not for long.

She realized her jubilation was premature when she walked

into the Women's Dispensary and found the dour Hilda Steuben actually smiling as she rolled bandages.

"You're a godsend, Dr. Delancy," she said, pounding Catherine on the back, "a veritable godsend."

Catherine stared at her as if she had gone mad. "I don't understand. What have I done?"

"I'm assuming you're responsible for persuading your hus— er, Mr. Delancy to make that contribution to the dispensary."

She stiffened. "Contribution?"

"It was more in the nature of a bequest."

"How large a bequest?"

Hilda stopped and squinted at her. "You don't know?"

"No, since my husband and I are estranged. Please enlighten me."

"One hundred thousand dollars."

Catherine's jaw dropped. "That's a small fortune!"

Hilda nodded. "Large fortune, small fortune, we're not fussy. We're delighted to have anything, especially in these terrible economic times, with so many out of work. Oh, the good we can do with that money!"

Catherine didn't have to be told. She saw the economic devastation firsthand. She knew the dispensary desperately needed money, especially since many of the city's philanthropists were cutting back on their contributions to charities as their own fortunes dwindled or disappeared.

All except Damon.

She smiled dryly. One hundred thousand dollars was far from the seventy dollars she had tried to coerce out of him when they first met.

Still, she knew that behind Damon's act of generosity lay yet another attempt to bend her to his will, to wear her down until she could no longer fight him.

But those who worked in and ran the dispensary didn't know of his ulterior motives, so Catherine had to endure their profuse thanks for her husband's generosity.

As she examined patients, she realized she would have to thank Damon—perhaps she could use the opportunity to convince him that he had no hold on her after all.

When she returned home, she sent him a message inviting him to dinner the following evening.

She wore his favorite gown, the blue satin, not so much to please him as to emphasize her command of the situation. He would see her in the gown, be drawn to her, and she would resist him.

When Damon arrived, looking as dashing as always in white tie and evening attire, with a premature gleam of triumph in his eyes, he surprised Catherine by proffering a solitary white long-stemmed rose.

"Why, thank you," she said, sniffing its delicate fragrance. "It's lovely."

"I had a florist in New Jersey name it after you," he said. "From now on, this rose will be known as the 'Dr. Delancy' rose."

Instead of rounding on him for trying to buy her with such an extravagant tribute that must have cost thousands of dollars, Catherine kept her temper in check and smiled sweetly. "What a lovely gesture. I'm probably the only doctor in the United States to have a flower named after her."

Her response must have surprised him, for he regarded her strangely. "I'm sure you are."

"I'll have Molly put this in water, and then we'll dine."

As she turned, Damon caught her arm. "You're not angry at me for being so extravagant?"

"It's your money. You may do with it what you please."

He scowled. "What game are you playing, Catherine?"

"No game," she said. "I just realized I'm being silly for refusing your generous gifts." Then she started for the dining room.

After handing over the rose to Molly, Catherine sat down at the dining room table, set simply in contrast to the Christmas when Damon had proposed to her. As she opened her napkin she could see that this abrupt change in her bewildered him. Good. She had succeeded in throwing him off balance.

As Molly served the soup, Catherine said, "Damon, I just want to thank you for your generous bequest to the Women's Dispensary."

He smiled across the table. "What's money for if not to do good?"

"It will certainly do that. We'll be able to buy badly needed supplies and equipment and care for more people. With so many out of work . . ." She shrugged. "Thank you again."

"I feared that you would refuse my bequest."

"Now why would I do that?"

A flicker of annoyance passed across his stern features.

"Come now, Catherine, don't play the innocent with me. You know you haven't exactly accepted my gifts graciously in the past."

"A bequest to the dispensary is quite different," she replied. "I am not averse to your spending your money for philanthropic purposes. Just don't expect anything more of me other than my gratitude." She smiled. "I wouldn't return to you if you gave the dispensary a million dollars."

"You would be worth it," he said softly.

She was glad the length of the table was between them as she fought to keep her tone light and noncommittal. "Philanthropy should be its own reward."

He leaned back in his chair and dabbed at his lips with his napkin. "Just why did you ask me to dinner tonight?"

"Why, to thank you for your bequest to the dispensary, nothing more." She laughed. "Why, you didn't think I asked you here to reconcile, did you?"

"Of course not." But his disappointed expression betrayed him.

"Good." Catherine added, "This is delicious soup, isn't it?"

"Delicious," Damon muttered.

When they finished and Molly began serving a roast chicken redolent of rosemary, Catherine said, "Will you be spending your weekends at Coppermine, or in Newport this year?"

"Perhaps both." He sipped his wine, his cold gray eyes warming. "Why do you ask? Do you wish to join me?"

"You're not blind anymore, so it would be most improper, since we are separated."

Catherine could see that he didn't know quite what to make of her confounding new attitude, for a line of frustration formed between his brows. If he mistakenly equated anger with interest, her calm, collected demeanor indicated a blatant lack of it.

She smiled. "I hope you have wonderful weekends, wherever you spend them this summer."

"You should get away yourself," he said. "New York in the summer is downright unhealthy."

"You know I can't," she replied evenly. "I have responsibilities here. The cholera infantum epidemic is sure to be even greater this summer, and the dispensary will need all the doctors it can get."

"If you should change your mind—"

"I won't."

As the meal progressed, their conversation became more restrained and polite, as though they were merely two friends sharing a companionable meal rather than former lovers. Catherine soon felt a distance growing between them that was longer than the length of the table.

Finally, when dinner was over, Damon made no attempt to linger this time. He made some excuses about having to rise early the following morning and got ready to take his leave.

At the door, he didn't try to kiss her, merely took her hand and bowed stiffly over it. When he raised his head, Catherine could see both pain and resignation in the depths of his eyes.

"Goodbye, Catherine," he said softly.

"Goodbye," she replied, knowing their friendship and marriage was over at last.

He stepped through the door and trotted down the steps without a backward glance.

Catherine didn't even linger in the doorway to see him get into his carriage, because her vision became so blurry that she couldn't see.

She couldn't understand why she was crying. After all, she had finally gotten what she wanted. Damon was gone.

CHAPTER

EIGHTEEN

THE cool morning air wafted in through Catherine's bedroom window, causing the sheer white curtains to billow away from the sill.

After the sweltering July night had robbed her of refreshing sleep, Catherine could have slept all morning, but she had patients to see today. As she sat up and swung her legs over the side of the bed, she caught a whiff of some fetid city odor that caused her stomach to clench in protest.

Clapping her hand over her mouth, she bolted for the bathroom, where she retched until she was almost too weak to stand. When she was done, she wet a washcloth from the tap and returned to her bed, where, after shutting the window, she lay down, closed her eyes, and placed the cool compress across her forehead.

She was pregnant.

When she had missed her first menses in late May, the familiar "ceasing-to-be-unwell," she attributed it to the emotional upheaval in her personal life. Later, she dismissed the nausea as being caused by the city's noxious summertime odors. But she couldn't ignore her second missed menses in June, and all the other subtle and obvious physical signs she noticed so astutely in other pregnant women day after day.

"I'm going to have Damon's child," she said aloud, as if speaking the words would help her accept the reality of her situation.

"One night," she muttered bitterly, "one damn night."

In her mind, she heard Sybilla's voice. *Sweet sutures, Cat, one night is all it takes. You're a doctor. You know that.*

"But I didn't expect anything to happen at Coppermine," she retorted. "That's why I didn't take any pessaries with me."

And now you're paying the price, Sybilla's spirit said.

"Don't remind me."

When Catherine felt stronger, she rose, ignored the shooting pains in her breasts, and went to run her bath.

What was she going to do?

She was separated from Damon. In fact, since the night two months ago when she invited him to dinner, he had vanished from her life. There were no more roses, no more bequests to the dispensary. All calls and invitations stopped. Even her "shadow" was nowhere to be seen anymore. It was as though her husband had finally lost patience with trying to win her back and was washing his hands of her.

Catherine sighed as she slipped off her sweat-soaked nightgown and stepped into the tub. She had the demands of her medical practice to consider. She couldn't have a baby now.

She looked down at her abdomen, still deceptively flat. "Like it or not, I am pregnant, and I have to decide what to do about it."

Did she even want this baby at all? As she had once threatened Damon when he wanted—no, demanded—a child to bind her closer to him, she knew how to get rid of it. A squirt of ergot and warm water into the uterus would be enough to induce a miscarriage. Catherine would solve the problem without Damon even knowing she had been pregnant with his child. Her medical practice would be unaffected. Her life would go on as she had planned it from those early days in medical school, without inconvenience or interruption.

But this was Damon's child as well.

Catherine finished washing and stepped out of the tub. As she dried herself slowly, she thought of a child with Damon's winter eyes and shock of black hair, and she knew in that instant that she couldn't abort the results of their union. She had always believed in the sanctity of life, and motherhood as a woman's ultimate destiny.

As she dressed, her conviction grew stronger. Yes, she would keep this baby, even if it meant temporarily giving up her medical practice and having to return to Damon.

A niggling doubt gnawed at her: what if he no longer wanted her? She hadn't heard from him in weeks. True, he hadn't filed for a divorce yet, but what if he had fallen in love with someone else? Even the society columns Catherine read occasionally were mute on that point.

In spite of the warm morning, Catherine shivered just once, then her resolve strengthened. If Damon was out of her life forever, she would raise this baby herself. Before it became obvious she was pregnant, she would quietly retire to the country for a rest until the baby was born. Then she would return to New York with some tale of it being her orphaned niece or nephew.

After dressing, Catherine went to her office. Now that she had reached a decision concerning this child, she had things to do and plans to make.

Catherine seated herself behind her desk and rubbed her throbbing head.

Once again, Damon wasn't home. He wasn't at his office either, for she had just come from there and everyone claimed they didn't know where he was. Catherine almost lost her temper. She was sure the two women typewriters were lying, but she maintained her dignity and left with her head held high.

On her way home, she stopped at the tobacconist's, where she telephoned Damon's house. Winslow told her that both the master and Mr. LaRouche had gone to Newport and had not said when they would return.

Damon was trying to avoid her purposely. Not that she could blame him. She had scorned his gifts and made it clear she wanted nothing more to do with him. But circumstances were different now.

She rested her forehead against the heels of her hands and closed her eyes. Fatigue left her so drained these days, even though she was no longer seeing patients in the morning. She wasn't even helping with the cholera infantum epidemic this August, because she feared inadvertently harming her unborn child in some way. Already the waistband on her skirts was becoming snug. In a month or two she wouldn't be able to wear them at all.

She looked at Bonette ruefully. "The fashionable hourglass figure is not suited for concealing my condition, I'm afraid."

This time the skeleton's fixed grin seemed reproachful.

Just then there came a knock at the door, and Molly appeared carrying a medium-sized box that she set on Catherine's desk, then left.

Catherine knew the box contained such anticonception devices as rubber condoms and womb veils. As she stared at it, she recalled the afternoon that Sybilla had returned from Paris, her wire bustle filled with smuggled pessaries. At the time, Catherine had refused to help her distribute them, but during her work in the tenements, she had come to understand the necessity of it.

As Catherine put the box in her desk drawer, the irony of her situation hit her with full force. Here she was secretly distributing such items to her patients and lecturing them about family limitation, when she herself had failed to take her own advice.

She burst into irrational tears.

When the tears subsided, Catherine pulled a handkerchief out of her skirt pocket and dabbed at her eyes as she fought to bring her emotions under control, something that was so difficult to do these days.

"Well, Sybilla," she said to the empty room, "what am I going to do now?"

You've got to tell Damon, a familiar voice seemed to say.

"And what if he doesn't want to reconcile? What if he's fallen in love with someone else? He has been avoiding me."

Sweet sutures! Then you just go to his house and march right in. Make him see you.

Catherine shook her head and smiled. "You're right. That's exactly what I will do."

At half past five that evening, Catherine took a cab to the Fifth Avenue mansion. Just as she arrived, she noticed that an open victoria coming in the opposite direction suddenly swung into Damon's short drive and came to a stop beneath the porte-cochere.

Inside the carriage seated side by side were Damon and a beautiful woman.

Catherine signaled her driver to stop and he pulled up the hansom just before the drive. She had a clear view, so she sat there and watched in shocked silence.

Damon was too absorbed in his lovely companion to pay attention to a cab parked a little down the street from his house. A footman opened the victoria's door on Damon's side and he stepped down, never taking his eyes from the woman's face. Then he extended his hand, she took it and stepped down daintily, managing to stumble on the last step so he would have to catch her gallantly around the waist and swing her down. Of course he held her for a second longer than propriety dictated.

The moment Damon drew the woman's hand to his lips, Catherine felt an unexpected surge of pure, primitive jealousy, the likes of which she had never experienced before. And when her husband offered the woman his arm and they disappeared inside, jealousy was replaced by an overwhelming sense of betrayal.

They had all lied. Damon wasn't in Newport after all. He was cavorting around New York City with another woman.

Catherine pounded on the cab's roof. When the trap door slid open and the driver's face appeared, she said, "Take me back to Washington Square. At once!"

When she arrived, she felt drained and defeated, so she ignored Molly's curious look, went right upstairs, locked herself in her bedroom, and flung herself down on the bed.

Her marriage was over. She had rejected Damon once too often. Now she knew exactly how he had felt—the pain, the longing, the desolation—when she rejected him, and it devastated her.

She had gotten exactly what she deserved. She had her medical practice, but she was pregnant and alone.

Two weeks later, Kim returned from Newport and invited her to his house for dinner.

"I can see the fresh salt air of Newport agrees with you," she said as she joined him in the drawing room. "Or perhaps it's Francine who is making you look so happy and content."

"Both, I think." Kim's blue eyes roved over her, hesitating at her midsection for just a heartbeat before returning to her face. "And how have you been, Catherine? I've seen so little of you this summer."

"Don't apologize," she said. "You have much to keep you occupied these days, Dr. Flanders."

"Between my practice and Francine . . ." Kim's lighthearted mood vanished and he wore a puzzled expression as he glanced at Catherine's waistline again. "Would you like a sherry before dinner?"

Catherine ran her hand along the back of the Chesterfield sofa. "I might as well come right out with it." She looked over at him. "Kim, I'm going to have a baby."

His hand fell away from the sherry decanter and he turned to her, regret in his eyes. "I can see that." Then he blinked several times as though trying to gather his scattered wits. "Damon?"

She nodded as she sat down. "It happened after the bombing, when I went to Coppermine with him."

Kim crossed the room slowly, as if he were sleepwalking, and sat beside her. "Do you want this baby?"

She knew at once what he was implying. "You know that if I wanted an abortion, I have the knowledge and the means to do it myself."

"Damon doesn't know about the child, does he?"

Catherine shook her head. "I haven't seen Damon all summer. He's been avoiding me. I suspect there is another woman in his life."

Kim's gaze slid away and he rose, hurrying over to one of the windows facing the street.

Catherine said, "I can tell that you know something, but you're reluctant to tell me."

He bowed his head but still wouldn't turn to look at her. "You don't want to know. It would only hurt you too much."

As the late afternoon sun gilded Kim's perfect profile, Catherine felt moved by his concern for her. She rose and went to him.

Placing her hand on his arm, she said, "You needn't worry about hurting me. I'm quite beyond it. You will be doing me a great kindness if you tell me what you know."

A troubled frown appeared between his fair brows. "He doesn't go to social functions alone any more. And his name has been coupled with not one, but several women."

"I've suspected as much."

"There is also a rumor that he's going to file for a divorce soon."

She felt her heart constrict in pain, but she tried to maintain a brave front. "Then our marriage is over."

Kim turned to her, blue eyes flashing. "But he can't divorce you. Not when you're carrying his child."

Feeling suddenly weary, Catherine returned to the sofa and sat down. "If he doesn't want me, I won't force myself on him, child or no child."

"If he doesn't want you back, what will you do?"

She told him about her contingency plan. "In any case, I'm perfectly capable of supporting a child by myself."

"Lies have a way of coming back to haunt you, Catherine.

Trying to pass off your own child as a niece or nephew can only lead to heartache for both you and the child.''

''I know, but I have no choice.''

He crossed the room to sit beside her and take her hand, his fingers warm and reassuring. ''Lord knows there's no love lost between Delancy and I, but I know how I would feel if my wife tried to keep something like this from me. You have to tell him about his child, Catherine. He has a right to know.''

''I will. When I'm ready.''

''What do you think his reaction will be?''

''Once, it would have been elation, but now . . .'' Catherine shrugged.

Kim shook his head in wonder. ''You have to be the bravest woman I've ever known.''

''I don't feel very brave. At the moment, I feel afraid of what the future holds for myself and my child.''

''Whatever you decide, I want you to know that you can always count on me if you need help. I may love Francine, but I can still be your friend.''

Tears of gratitude stung her eyes. ''You always will be, Kim.''

''Who's going to deliver it?''

Catherine looked away. ''I was thinking of asking Hilda Steuben.''

If he was offended that she hadn't asked him, Kim didn't show it. ''Hilda may be an old crab, but she's an excellent doctor,'' he said.

''So are you,'' Catherine said, ''but I'd just feel more comfortable having a woman tend to me at a time like this.''

''I understand.''

Just then the housekeeper appeared and announced that dinner was served. Kim rose, extended his hand, and escorted Catherine into the dining room.

As they dined, Kim tried to buoy Catherine's spirits with society gossip, and she pretended to be interested to give him the satisfaction of helping her. But when he began talking about the Talmadges, he truly captured her attention.

''He's ruined,'' Kim said.

Catherine stared at him, her fork halfway to her lips. ''Ruined?''

''Yes. It's this damned depression. Talmadge's bank has failed.''

She thought of the beautiful Dahlia and her terrible secret, and she shuddered. "What are they going to do now?"

"I've heard they're going to have to sell their house. Perhaps they'll move to another city and try for a fresh start."

Catherine felt ill. The only deterrent keeping August Talmadge from beating his wife was Damon's threat to ruin him financially. Now that Talmadge was ruined through no fault of Damon's, what was to keep him from resuming his abuse of his wife?

As much as Catherine wished she could help the poor woman, she realized she couldn't force her to accept that help, so she tried to put Dahlia out of her mind by concentrating on dinner and Kim's company.

But when she returned home later that evening, she found her thoughts straying to Damon and how she was going to break the news to him about their child.

A week passed and Catherine still hadn't tried to contact Damon.

Whenever she was on the verge of going to his house again, she recalled the strange woman in the victoria—one of many, according to Kim—and her resolve evaporated. Catherine was just as proud as Damon, and the thought of forcing herself on someone who didn't want her was too shameful to contemplate.

But as she was putting away medicines on this warm Friday evening, Catherine realized wryly that she would have to confront him sometime before the baby's birth.

There came a knock on the door, and when it swung open, there was Molly, dressed to go to the theater tonight.

"I'll be on my way, Dr. Catherine," she said. "Are you sure you won't need me this evening?"

"No, Molly. Go and enjoy yourself."

She returned to her task at hand, and soon the silence of the empty house enveloped her. Catherine paused and listened. She was so used to the sounds of the front door opening, slow footsteps in the hall, the strained voices of people nervous or in pain that the utter quiet of her house this evening was restful.

She continued to inventory the medicines until she noticed that the September twilight was fast turning into darkness, so she rose and lit the gaslight on the wall.

Beneath the soft hiss of gas, she thought she heard the sound of a door opening and closing somewhere in the house, and she paused to listen. Nothing. Catherine dismissed it as her imagination and returned to her desk.

She opened the medicine cabinet and was just putting a bottle of chloroform on a shelf when she thought she heard footsteps. She froze, her hand poised in midair as her eyes darted to the open door. Again, there was nothing.

Closing the medicine cabinet door, she rounded her desk and went out to the hall. She looked up and down, but there was no intruder lurking in the shadows. The hallway and the staircase were empty.

"You're hearing things," she muttered to herself as she crossed the room and returned to finish her work.

When Catherine had shelved the last bottle, she closed the cabinet door. There, reflected in the glass almost as clearly as a mirror, was a man.

Catherine gasped and whirled around, her heart pounding in fear, for she recognized the man standing in the doorway as none other than August Talmadge.

To say that the banker had changed was an understatement. Aside from his dark hair slicked back with too much macassar oil, Talmadge had the slapdash look of a man whose disheveled appearance reflected a disordered mental state. Now that he had lost everything, there was no need to even try to hide the bright, insane glitter in his eyes.

The moment Catherine noticed the thick gloves he was wearing on such a warm evening, she knew that he wasn't here for medical advice or a social call.

"Why, Mr. Talmadge," she said, her voice surprisingly strong and clear.

He took a step into her office, his eyes holding her. "I've waited a long time to get you alone. A long time."

Catherine fought down rising panic. "If you're here to see me about a medical problem—"

"I wouldn't let a lady doctor touch me if I was dying," he sneered. "I'm here to get even with your husband."

Fear skittered along her arms. "What are you talking about?" But she already knew.

Talmadge took another step toward her. "The both of you meddled. You had no right to come between me and my Dahlia. No right!"

Catherine grasped the back of her swivel chair. "And you had no right to whip her like—like an animal!"

"I had every right. She's my wife. Besides, she enjoyed it." His thick lips parted in a smile. "She didn't tell you that, did she?"

A picture of the fearful Dahlia, her ivory flesh scored with red welts, sprang vividly into Catherine's mind, infuriating her. "I think you had best leave, Mr. Talmadge," she said coldly, "before you do something you'll regret for the rest of your life."

"Who do you think you are, giving me orders? Just because you're married to that rich bastard doesn't give you the right to give me orders."

Catherine grew very still and watchful as the man took another step toward her.

"He had no right to ruin me."

"He didn't ruin you. Many have lost their fortunes in this depression," Catherine said.

"He shouldn't have come between us. Dahlia and I were happy until you two started meddling. But I swore I'd make Delancy pay someday. I was sure that bomb would kill him, but he's got more lives than a cat."

Catherine stared at him. "You did that?"

He licked his thick lips. "Let's just say a friend of mine did." His lecherous eyes roved over Catherine as if envisioning her bound and at his mercy. "But if I can't kill him, you'll do."

Panic scattered Catherine's thoughts, but she fought it down ruthlessly. She had to think clearly. Her life and her baby's depended on it.

She swallowed hard. "You'll never get away with it."

"I got away with killing your friend, didn't I?"

Catherine was so stunned she couldn't breathe. She dug her fingers into the chair's back. "*You* killed Sybilla?"

Talmadge took another step closer. "That alley was dark and I didn't realize I had the wrong woman. It was all that stupid girl's fault. She was supposed to bring you to me, but she brought your friend instead."

Sybilla had died for her. Catherine felt as though she had been turned to stone. But she couldn't allow herself the luxury of paralyzing shock. She had to concentrate on her own immediate survival.

She said, "But it was me you wanted to kill all along."

Talmadge nodded. "An eye for an eye, to repay Delancy for

taking my wife." He scowled. "No one suspected me, of course, not a man of my stature and standing in the community. Then he had that man watch you. I had to bide my time. And I did."

As Talmadge boasted of his cleverness, Catherine's thoughts leaped ahead. She needed a weapon, something she could use to defend herself. Her desk top was clean. Her scalpels and other medical instruments were locked away in drawers, caustic medicines in the cabinet behind her, so close, yet miles away. By the time she reached them, Talmadge would be on her.

Out of the corner of her eye, she saw Bonette sitting in her chair, and a plan sprang into Catherine's mind.

Talmadge reached into his pocket and took out a short length of rope, stretching the garrote taut between his hands. "Your death won't be painless, but it will be quick."

He lunged for her with the swiftness of a striking cobra.

Catherine feinted to the left to make Talmadge think she was going to bolt around the desk and head for the door. When he moved to intercept her, she ran to the right, grabbed Bonette off the chair and held the skeleton in front of her. Talmadge swore and flung down the rope, coming at Catherine with his hands open like claws.

She screamed as she threw Bonette into his open arms, and dashed for the open office door. Behind her, she heard the rattle of bones and Talmadge's curse. Just as she reached the door, she felt desperate iron fingers stab into her shoulder and pull her back inside.

Catherine did the unexpected as she whirled around—she attacked him. Her nails raked his cheek, startling him.

"You bitch!" he bellowed.

Her defiance infuriated him. Before Catherine could get away, Talmadge hit her across the face with the back of his hand.

She cried out as excruciating pain shot through her jaw and skull, and the force of the blow brought her to her knees. When she looked up through the red mist gathering before her eyes and saw Talmadge draw back his foot to kick her savagely, her only thought was for her baby. She fell to the floor, sheltering her abdomen with her arms and drawing up her knees in expectation of pain.

"Don't hurt my baby!" she cried.

The sounds of hurried footsteps in the hall beyond didn't register until the anticipated blow never fell.

"Catherine!"

Upon hearing Damon's voice, she opened her eyes to find him kneeling on one knee beside her, his gentle hands drawing her against him.

"Damon," she gasped, shuddering with relief. She allowed herself to accept several seconds of his strength and comfort, then she drew away from him, her frantic gaze searching the room for Talmadge.

She found him cringing on the floor before Nevada.

"He strangled Sybilla," Catherine cried, fighting to rise. "He told me so himself, just before he tried to kill me."

Nevada's head jerked toward Catherine in stunned surprise.

"She's crazy," Talmadge said, wiping blood from the corner of his mouth where Nevada must have struck him.

She grasped Damon's arm. "He intended to kill me to get back at you for Dahlia, but the little girl brought Sybilla instead, so he killed her. And—and he's the one who bombed the stables."

Damon's eyes turned as cold as ice and he exchanged looks with Nevada.

A flush of rage crept up the cowboy's cheeks. He drawled, "Why don't you take the doc upstairs?"

As Damon slipped his arm around Catherine's waist, Talmadge's eyes widened in terror and he scrambled to his feet. "He's going to kill me!" he shrieked. "Call the police!"

Without so much as a backward glance, Catherine allowed Damon to lead her out of her office, and it was she who closed the door behind them.

She almost wavered when she heard Talmadge's inhuman scream followed by a crash, but Damon swept her effortlessly into his arms and carried her upstairs to her bedchamber, where he laid her on the bed and lit the gaslight.

She couldn't tear her eyes away from him. The dark shock of black hair falling onto his forehead, the enigmatic winter eyes, the strength radiating from him, all made her realize how much she had missed him.

Catherine grasped his hand. It hurt her to speak, but she managed to utter, "Why did you come?"

Damon smoothed the hair from her brow. "Let me get a cold compress for your jaw, and then we'll talk."

She released him reluctantly as he went to her bathroom.

When he returned, he had a wet cloth that he pressed gently to her aching jaw.

He said, "I could kill him myself for hurting you."

"Why did you come tonight?" she asked again.

Damon drew up a chair and sat down by her bedside. He smiled ruefully. "Nevada made me."

Catherine frowned and reached for his hand again, needing the reassurance of his touch. "I don't understand."

His fingers tightened on hers. "Have you noticed that you haven't seen much of me this summer?"

She thought of the woman she had seen disembarking from Damon's carriage and she looked away. "I've noticed."

"I've been avoiding you deliberately."

"Why?"

"Simple. I wanted to hurt you as much as you hurt me."

Catherine's startled gaze riveted on him.

He shifted uncomfortably in his seat. "I wanted you to feel the same agony that I felt when you left me. I wanted to pay you back in kind."

And he had. When Catherine recalled how she had suffered when he rejected her, she couldn't blame him.

"I'm not proud of what I did, Catherine," he said softly, staring down at her hand. "Today Nevada thought I had gone far enough. He could see that I was miserable without you. He said that if I didn't go to you and resolve matters between us, he would dissolve our partnership and go back west."

Damon ran his hand through his hair. "He insisted that we come here tonight, and I thank the good Lord that he did. As we were climbing the steps, we heard you scream. When we rushed in, we found you on the floor, and Talmadge about to kick you."

Catherine closed her eyes. "After he failed to kill you, he decided to try for me. He blamed you for the collapse of his bank and the estrangement of his wife." She shuddered as tears filled her eyes. "That bastard killed Sybilla!"

"Hush," Damon crooned, patting her shoulder. "He'll pay. Nevada will see to that." He hesitated for a moment, his face taut with tension. "You're with child, aren't you?"

So, he had heard her plea to spare her baby. "Yes."

Damon disengaged his hand from her grasp, rose and went to the window, where he parted the curtain and stared out into the night. "Is it Flanders' child?"

She sat up. "Damon Delancy, how can you even think that?"

"Why shouldn't I? We've been separated for over a year. You are a desirable woman. You could have taken several lovers, for all I know."

"I don't know if I should be flattered or insulted," she murmured wryly. "But rest assured, I've had no other lovers."

He whirled around, pride warming his eyes and delight written plainly on his face. "So it is mine."

"It must have been conceived that night we spent together at Coppermine."

Damon crossed the room and dropped down onto the chair. "My child . . ."

"You're pleased?"

"Pleased? You even have to ask?" He drew her hand to his lips, then said, "But why didn't you tell me sooner?"

"I went to see you once, but you were in a carriage with another woman. I watched you help her out of the carriage and escort her into your house." She stared down at her clenched hand. "I didn't think you'd appreciate being interrupted, so I turned around and went home."

Damon bowed his head. "I thought I recognized you in the cab. I knew you were watching, so I tried to make you jealous by lavishing attention on my . . . companion."

"You knew I was there and you let me believe that woman was your lover?" Catherine's voice rose incredulously.

"I know I'm a ruthless bastard, and I wouldn't blame you if you never forgive me for what I've done. But you gave me no other choice. A desperate man resorts to desperate measures."

"So all those rumors about other women—"

"Are nothing but rumors I started."

"But you were seen with other women at social gatherings."

"They were acquaintances, nothing more."

Slow, weary footsteps punctuated by the light jingling of spurs heralded Nevada's approach, and both Catherine and Damon fell silent and turned toward the open door.

There stood a Nevada who froze Catherine's blood. The cowboy's face was grim and implacable, and his blue eyes dark with savage blood-lust.

"Talmadge is dead," Nevada said. "I broke his neck. I'm going to get the police and turn myself in."

As Nevada turned to go, Damon said, "But you didn't intend to kill him. He tried to escape. You tried to stop him and accidentally broke his neck.'' He looked at Catherine. ''Isn't that how it happened?''

''Yes. We were there. We're witnesses.''

Nevada looked from one to the other. ''You don't have to do this for me. If I have to pay, I'll pay.''

Catherine swung her legs over the side of the bed and went to Nevada. In spite of her aching jaw, she said, ''He was going to kill me and you saved my life. No one in the world can blame you for that, my friend.''

Nevada's gaze hardened as he studied her bruised cheek.

''We have to stick together,'' Damon added, ''otherwise our stories won't match and all three of us will wind up in trouble.''

Nevada stroked his mustache, a frown of deliberation between his brows. Finally he nodded. ''I'll agree to that.''

Then he nodded at Catherine and went back downstairs to summon the police.

Catherine turned back to Damon. ''Poor Nevada. My heart aches for him.''

''Now that Sybilla's killer has been brought to justice, perhaps he can allow himself to heal.''

''I know some claim that vengeance is hollow,'' she said, ''but I'm glad Talmadge is dead. Glad!'' Her eyes filled with tears. ''I still miss Sybilla so much.''

Damon reached for her, and Catherine went willingly into his arms. ''We all do.''

She squeezed her eyes shut and rested her head against his shoulder, grateful for the comfort he offered.

After a few minutes had passed, Damon released her and stepped away, his expression guarded. ''What are you going to do now, Catherine?''

She knew he was referring to her situation now altered irrevocably by the child growing inside her. She paused, waiting for Damon to tell her what she was going to do, but he merely regarded her in polite silence.

When the silence dragged on far too long, Catherine turned away. ''I—I don't know yet.''

''Oh, but I think you do. You always know exactly what you're going to do in any given situation.''

Catherine thought of their passionate union that night at Coppermine. ''Not every situation.'' Then she added, ''I thought of raising the child myself.''

She heard Damon sigh behind her, then she felt his hands rest lightly on her shoulders. "Let's stop dancing around each other, Catherine," he said wearily. "You know I can't allow you to do that, not while you're still my wife."

"You could always divorce me."

"Not now. Not ever."

As always when dealing with Damon, Catherine felt pulled in two directions. While she was delighted that there were no other women in his life and he had no intention of divorcing her, she knew the issue of her practicing medicine was still unresolved. If Damon thought that a child would make her tractable on that issue, he was sadly mistaken.

She turned to face him. "I don't have any choice, do I? I have to go back to you."

Damon's face darkened in anger. "You make it sound as though you're going to prison and I'm your jailer."

"In some ways, you are," she said softly. "A kind, loving jailer, but my jailer nonetheless."

"Sometimes life deals us an unfair hand," Damon said brutally, "and we just have to make the best of it. I didn't want to be an orphan any more than Nevada wanted to lose Sybilla, but we've both learned to accept and adapt. I would suggest you do the same."

Catherine was spared replying when the doorbell rang downstairs.

"The police must be here," Damon said. "Shall we go? I'm sure they'll want to talk to you. And then I'm going to have a doctor look at your jaw."

Catherine nodded.

He added, "After all that has happened, you shouldn't be left alone tonight."

"Molly's here. I'll be fine."

"I'll sleep in Sybilla's old room," Damon said sternly.

Catherine took one look at his determined face and knew it was pointless to argue. Together they went to join Nevada.

Catherine's office looked as though a hurricane had swept through it, with overturned chairs, a broken lamp scattering glass on the carpet, and Bonette lying in a heap of broken bones. Talmadge was lying face down, one arm extended toward the door as if he had been crawling to escape.

The police spent an hour questioning them, but when all three told the same story, no charges were brought against Nevada. The following morning, Damon consulted with members of the press who agreed to attribute Talmadge's death to a fall. Later in the week, Catherine received an unsigned note with only the words "Thank you" written inside, just before Dahlia Talmadge left New York City for parts unknown.

❧ CHAPTER ❧

NINETEEN

ON a chilly, overcast early autumn afternoon, Damon's mansion looked as withdrawn and unwelcoming as its owner.

"It's rather an elegant prison, don't you think?" Damon said.

Catherine paused on the carriage's top step and looked down at him. Ever since the night of Talmadge's death two weeks ago, when Catherine had appeared less than eager to resume their marriage, Damon had been distinctly cool toward her.

"Very elegant," she retorted, placing her hand in his so he could help her disembark.

As his fingers tightened around hers, Catherine felt an unexpected jolt at his touch, but when she looked into his eyes to determine if he felt anything in return, she was disappointed to see no companion spark in those cold gray depths.

Damon drew her arm through his and escorted her into the foyer, where Winslow was waiting.

The butler bowed gravely. "Welcome home, madam."

She glanced wistfully at the parlor that had once been her office, then smiled. "Thank you, Winslow."

Damon said, "Have Mrs. Delancy's bags brought up to the Blue Room at once."

So they would not be sharing a bedchamber. Under the circumstances, it was for the best.

As the butler headed for the door, Catherine said, "I think I'll go upstairs and rest for a while. I'm feeling fatigued."

Damon became solicitous at once. "Do you want a tray sent up, or a maid to attend you?"

"No, thank you. I'm not hungry, just tired. Women in my condition usually are."

"I see." Damon offered her his arm. "I'll show you to the Blue Room."

"No need. I know where it is." At the opposite end of the hall and around a corner, far from the room they used to share.

As Catherine started up the stairs, Damon said, "When you've rested, come down to my study. There are matters we need to discuss."

"I quite agree." And she proceeded up the stairs, conscious of his eyes following her.

The Blue Room was a guest room tastefully decorated in shades of its namesake color, but because no one person dwelt in it for any length of time, it lacked the individual personal touches that would have given it character.

The moment Catherine stepped in the door, she felt more like a guest than the mistress of the house. If it was Damon's intention to make her feel awkward and uncomfortable here, he had succeeded.

She pulled out a hatpin, removed her bonnet, and set it down on a nearby bureau.

"What do you expect of the man?" she said aloud. "You made it quite clear that you're only returning to him because of the baby."

But was she? As she lay down on the bed for a nap, Catherine recalled the uncontrollable jealousy she had felt when she saw him with that other woman, and the fear that stabbed her heart when Kim told her Damon was going to file for a divorce.

No, she couldn't deny that she still loved him. But as always, medicine came between them—an obstacle as high and insurmountable as a stone wall. And as always, he refused to compromise.

Catherine closed her eyes and slept. When she awoke an hour later, she straightened her clothes and went downstairs to Damon's study.

He was seated at his desk studying some papers, but set them aside and rose the moment she entered. "Is the Blue Room to your liking?"

"It's very comfortable," she replied as she sat down.

"If you'd prefer another—"

"No, it's fine."

Damon jammed his hands into his pockets. "I realize this is an awkward situation for you, but you are still my wife and the mistress of this house. I hope you'll accept the responsibility of running the household as you did before we . . . parted company."

Managing the servants, planning dinner parties until her condition became too apparent for entertaining . . . Catherine could feel the stultifying boredom weighing her down already.

"I suppose it will help to fill my days, since I won't be able to practice medicine."

Kim had agreed to see Catherine's patients in the Washington Square office, so there would always be someone there. Damon had mentioned letting another doctor take over her practice completely, but when Catherine had threatened not to return to him under those circumstances, he dropped the suggestion.

"It wouldn't be seemly for you to practice medicine in your condition," he said.

"It's not seemly for a woman in my condition to do much of anything, I'm afraid." No exhausting walks through the tenements, no horseback riding in Central Park, no dancing the One-Armed Waltz.

"And with good reason. You wouldn't want to harm yourself or the child."

Was he thinking of the time she had threatened to abort any child of his conceived by force? she wondered.

Her hand strayed to her abdomen protectively. "If I didn't want this child, I would have done something about it months ago, and you never would have even known of its existence."

Damon made no comment, his stony expression revealing nothing. Then he said, "We should let our friends know that we've apparently reconciled. Perhaps a small dinner party. We could invite the Grahams, the Peachtrees, Flanders and Francine, a few other people . . ."

Apparently reconciled, he had said. The distinction was not lost on Catherine.

She smiled and forced herself to be as polite and distant as he. "That sounds pleasant. Shall I make the arrangements?"

"You have carte blanche. Just don't tire yourself. That's what servants are for. Your social secretary Miss Schuyler left our employ, but I'll hire you another, if you like."

"That won't be necessary." Catherine rose. "I'll consult with Winslow and the housekeeper. Shall the invitations be for a week from Friday?"

"Fine."

"If I'm to resume my duties as mistress of the house, I'll need my escritoire moved to the Blue Room sitting room." Her desk presently occupied a corner of the sitting room off Damon's bedchamber.

"I'll see that it's done right away."

She thanked him, and added, "I'll see you tonight at dinner then."

"I'm afraid not. I have to go out with Nevada on business."

"I see." Catherine saw all too well. "Well, have a profitable meeting." And she turned and walked out of the study without another word.

When the door closed behind her, Catherine squared her shoulders resolutely. Their estrangement wasn't her fault. If Damon would have agreed to her practicing medicine, she never would have left him, so she would be damned if she was going to make all the concessions to reconcile now.

She went in search of the butler.

"Good morning, madam," Winslow said the following day, when Catherine seated herself at the dining room table for breakfast. "I've just finished ironing the newspapers, if you'd like to read them."

"No, thank you, Winslow." After a restless night alone in her bed and an exhausting bout with morning sickness when she rose, Catherine didn't feel like reading. "Has Mr. Delancy left yet?"

"Yes, madam," the butler replied, pouring her a cup of tea. "Both he and Mr. LaRouche left the house quite early for Wall Street."

Catherine felt irrationally disappointed. It would have been considerate of Damon to spend the day with her.

She tried to nibble on a toast point, but the odor of bacon coming from a covered dish on the sideboard caused her sensitive stomach to cramp in protest. Catherine rose, flung down her napkin and said to Winslow, "Please come into the study. We can discuss plans for next week's dinner party."

"But, madam, your breakfast . . ."

"I'm not hungry."

Once Catherine was inside the study and seated at Damon's desk, the butler began. "What would you like on the menu, madam?"

She realized that she didn't care. "Have Bernard make up several menus and submit them to me for my approval. I trust his good judgment."

"Very good, madam. Now, what about the table decorations? Would you like pyramids of pears set at each end? Favors from Tiffany's for the ladies?"

Will the world end if I don't have pyramids of pears on the table? Catherine wondered.

"Pears will be fine," she said.

"And what of the flowers, madam? Do you prefer red Gloire de Paris roses, or something more seasonal, like marigolds or chrysanthemums?"

She thought of all the babies who had died in this summer's cholera infantum epidemic, and here she was, discussing which flowers to have at a dinner party.

Catherine sighed as she rose. "Winslow, I think we had better not have this dinner party after all. In fact, I don't think Mr. Delancy and I will be entertaining very much in the coming months." The servants would all know why soon enough.

"Very good, madam." The butler hesitated. "Will you be at home to callers today?"

"No."

He nodded and left her alone.

Catherine placed her elbows on the desk and cradled her head in her hands. After saving lives every day, how was she ever going to get used to the trivial life of a society wife? Pyramids of pears, favors from Tiffany's . . . these were not life-and-death decisions.

She felt as though a black cloud was settling about her shoulders, weighing her down with hopelessness and despair. With a sigh of resignation, she rose and went to sit in the parlor and watch the outside world pass by her window.

Catherine was still sitting there hours later, when the men returned from Wall Street.

Sitting in semi-darkness, she watched as the carriage stopped at the front door and Damon and Nevada got out. Both men had a look of triumph about them and a swagger to their step, as if they had just conquered the world. Catherine felt a twinge of envy.

Through the closed parlor door, she heard Damon laugh and say, "With only a fifty-thousand-dollar investment, we'll triple our earnings in a year."

Nevada made some reply and the men passed by, leaving Catherine to her solitude and thoughts turning progressively darker. She was not alone for long. The parlor door swung open to reveal Damon.

"There you are. What are you doing sitting all alone in the dark?" he chided as he lit the gaslight on the wall.

Catherine shrugged listlessly as light flooded the room. "I just wanted to watch the world pass by."

Damon slowly approached her chair, a worried frown between his heavy brows. "I noticed all the calling cards on the hall table. Word must have gotten out that you've moved back here." When Catherine made no comment, he said, "Did you have an enjoyable afternoon visiting with your friends?"

"I didn't feel like seeing anyone, so I was not at home to them."

"You can't be a hermit, Catherine," he said softly.

"But I can," she replied, keeping her attention focused on a smart brougham speeding down Fifth Avenue. "I am *enceinte*, subject to strange whims and fancies that I'm afraid you'll have to indulge. Right now, I crave solitude." She looked up at him. "I crave it so much that I don't wish to have a dinner party next Friday night."

Surprisingly, Damon just said, "As you wish."

So he was not going to argue with her this time.

He said, "Will I have the pleasure of your company at dinner tonight?"

She decided to test him. "I thought I'd have a tray sent to my room." She yawned as she rose stiffly from her chair. "I'm feeling quite fatigued."

A flicker of anger passed across his features, but he repressed it quickly. "Do what you feel is best for the child."

Catherine suddenly felt her power over Damon return, but it was not of a sexual nature. Because she was bearing his child—his heir—he would not risk upsetting her by arguing.

"Oh, I will," she assured him as she walked out of the parlor.

Later, alone in her room, Catherine took her medical bag out of the armoire, opened it, and dumped its contents on her bed. She handled the familiar instruments with a growing feeling of melancholy, wondering if she would ever use them again. She thought of lucky Kim tending to her patients and Hilda Steuben at the dispensary, and she felt herself plunge even deeper into a bottomless black pit of depression.

She wondered if she would ever climb out.

• • •

Damon paced in his study like a caged panther as he waited for Dr. Steuben to finish examining Catherine.

He was worried sick about his wife.

Ever since Catherine returned to him three weeks ago, she had undergone a change so profound it was as though a total stranger had entered their midst. She was moody and withdrawn, moving silently through the house like a ghost. She would sit in the parlor for hours, staring listlessly out the window, taking no interest in her surroundings. Whenever Damon spoke to her, she had a faraway look as distant as the moon.

Even Nevada couldn't get through to her by reminiscing about Sybilla. Tears always filled Catherine's eyes but never fell.

Damon stopped before a window and ran his hands through his hair in helpless frustration. He was losing her again. This time, it would be forever.

"Catherine," he whispered, "come back to me. You can practice medicine again, just please come back to me."

The knock on the door sent him whirling around. "Come in."

The door opened and Dr. Steuben strode in, her plain features revealing only a thinly disguised hostility. Damon suspected this gruff, mannish woman had little use for men.

"How is she?" he demanded.

"Terrible."

Stunned, he tried to speak, but no words came out.

Seeing his stricken expression, the doctor said, "I don't mean she's unhealthy—physically, Catherine's as healthy as a horse. So is her baby. But her mind . . ." The woman set down her medical bag and sat down without being invited. "Well now, that's another story."

Damon felt numb inside. "You mean she's going mad?"

"Some women do, you know, but it's usually after the baby is born. Puerperal insanity, it's called. But I'm getting ahead of myself. No, Catherine isn't going mad."

"Thank heaven for that." Relief left him weak-kneed and he sunk into his chair.

"But she is miserable."

"What do you mean?"

"Just what I said. Catherine's a doctor, trained to recognize symptoms. Now she's trying to diagnose herself and is worrying herself half to death." Dr. Steuben shook her grizzled head. "She's especially concerned about eclampsia, and—"

"What's that?" Damon asked.

"Those are fatal convulsions during labor," Dr. Steuben explained.

Damon felt the blood drain from his face. "She doesn't have that, does she?"

"I don't see any signs of it yet, but one never knows," she replied. "But aside from that, Catherine misses practicing medicine."

Damon's eyes narrowed. "She can't do that now. She's going to have a baby."

"And after the baby is born?"

"I can't have the mother of my child exposing herself to danger and disease."

Dr. Steuben snorted in derision. "Mr. Delancy, your wife has a greater risk of dying in childbirth than she does practicing medicine."

That fact did not cheer Damon. "What about Tom Derry? He almost killed her."

She shrugged. "I was almost run down by a cab as I tried to cross the street yesterday morning. You were almost blown up by a bomb."

Damon didn't know how to answer that.

The doctor regarded him with the same piercing, assessing stare his Aunt Hattie used to give him when he skipped church on Sunday to go fishing. "You don't really love Catherine, you just want to have your own way. You want to control her."

"Who in the hell do you think you are to tell me what I want? I love my wife, and don't want to see her come to harm."

The doctor hesitated. "I'm a tough old bird, Mr. Delancy, so tough you could make a pair of boots out of my hide. I don't believe in sugar pills. I speak my mind no matter who it hurts."

"I admire plain speaking."

"Good. Then maybe you'll listen to what I have to say and take it to heart." She leaned forward in her chair. "Catherine needs to be a doctor as much as she needs food and water. By denying her that, you're going to kill her."

Damon reared back in his chair. "I would never do anything to harm her."

Dr. Steuben's eyes flashed. "What do you think you're doing to her right now?"

"I'm an excellent provider. She wants for nothing."

"But this house is a prison," she snapped. "It's nothing but a gilded cage to a woman like Catherine."

"Once the baby comes—"

"She'll learn to love her prison, is that it?" The doctor's voice dripped with sarcasm. "Of all the stupid, selfish— But what else can one expect from a man?"

Rage heated Damon's face. "If you weren't a woman, I'd ask you to step outside."

She raised her brows mockingly. "Can't take the truth?" Before he could respond, she rose and leaned over his desk. "Do you think Catherine is one of your useless society wives who does nothing more taxing than choose which dress to wear to the theater? No, she's a doctor, damn you! She cures the sick. She keeps people from dying. You should be proud of her. But no. You want to assert your dominance by turning her into some—some simpering idiot!" Dr. Steuben's lip curled in disgust. "And she'll probably let you do it because she loves you, Lord only knows why."

The doctor grabbed her bag and headed for the study door. When she reached it, she turned. "Think about what I've said. I'll be back to examine Catherine next week, and I hope to God her disposition has improved, or both of their lives may be in danger."

Without so much as a "good day," Hilda Steuben stormed out and slammed the door behind her.

Damon jumped up and glared at the closed door. "Old hag," he muttered under his breath. Her brutal accusations still smarted like the lash of Talmadge's whip.

Moments later, Damon's anger at Dr. Steuben dissipated, replaced by rational calm. He sank back into his chair and leaned back, rubbing his chin thoughtfully.

Was the old virago right? Was he nothing more than a selfish man who wanted to turn his wife into some "simpering idiot"?

But he loved her. Surely no one could blame a husband for wanting to shelter and protect his wife.

Yet Damon knew Catherine was unhappy. One only had to compare the woman he had first met—laughing, vital, exciting—to the listless, unreachable shadow she had become, to know that something was terribly wrong.

Much as it galled him to admit it, Damon knew he was to blame. Hadn't his insistence that she give up medicine driven her away in the first place?

He sighed deeply. Perhaps it was time he accepted the fact that Catherine had to follow her own path in life—to go against the wind, as she had said to him so long ago—no matter what the risk.

The crusty Dr. Steuben's words flitted through his mind: *You don't love Catherine, you just want to have your own way.*

He felt overwhelmed with guilt because he knew that part of what she had said was true. He was a strong-willed man who liked to get his own way. But he also did love Catherine.

Damon still had a lot of thinking to do. He rose and called for his carriage.

Catherine watched as the carriage passed beneath her bedroom window, and she wondered where Damon was going so late in the afternoon. She thought he would have at least come up to see her after Hilda's examination.

She let the curtain fall. Her cheeks still felt warm from Hilda's tongue-lashing.

"What do you think you're doing to yourself, not to mention your baby?" Hilda had ranted. "If I didn't know you better, I'd swear you were trying to kill it, losing weight the way you are, looking at me as though you've lost your mind."

Then she shook her. "You're acting like a spoiled, self-indulgent child, not the intelligent woman you are."

Catherine suspected Sybilla would have agreed.

She absently touched her rounded abdomen as she drifted into the sitting room. How could she have been so selfish? In her bitterness and resentment over what fate had handed her, she was punishing her innocent unborn child. Damon's child.

She had to set aside her own desires and consider the child's welfare. He deserved a happy home filled with love. And it was up to Catherine to provide it.

She knew what she had to do.

That evening, she dined alone in her room and when she finished, she read her long-neglected medical journals until the clock struck eleven. Then she took her lamp, went to Damon's room and opened the door carefully. His bed was turned down but empty.

With a satisfied smile, Catherine closed the door behind her and set the lamp down on the bedside table. Then she disrobed, leaving her nightshift in a puddle of pale blue silk on the floor where Damon was sure to notice it the minute he walked in.

She shivered, but more from anticipation than the chilly autumn night. After checking the looking glass to make sure her unbound hair flowed to her shoulders, she slid between the sheets and waited.

She dozed off several times, only to be startled awake by a creaking floorboard in the hall or hoofbeats and clattering wheels in the street below. Just when she feared Damon wasn't coming home at all, she heard the unmistakable sound of the doorknob turning.

Heart hammering, Catherine propped herself up on one elbow, making sure to cover her bare breasts with the sheet.

What if he won't forgive me? she thought nervously. *What if I'm making a fool of myself?*

The door swung open. Damon stepped inside then stopped abruptly when he noticed Catherine's crumpled nightshift lying on the floor.

Her heart began to beat faster when she watched his searching gaze move from the floor to the bed. When he saw her, his eyes widened in astonishment and involuntarily betrayed him by warming with suppressed passion. Then they turned cold again as he brought his emotions under control and walked toward the bed.

He stopped at the edge and looked down at her. "I went to your room, but you weren't there. I never dreamed I'd find you in my bed."

"I'm tired of sleeping alone, Damon."

"I thought that's what you wanted."

"Not any more."

He paused. "I've been worried sick about you."

She looked away, suddenly ashamed. "I know. I could see it in your eyes every time you looked at me."

"I wanted to help you, but you wouldn't let me. I couldn't reach you. It was as though you had gone away to some secret place where no one else could follow."

"I wanted to escape. I didn't want to become pregnant. It's made me angry and resentful, and I'm afraid I've taken it out on you." She looked at him. "I'm sorry."

He said nothing, his expression unreadable.

Catherine took a deep breath and continued. "If you can't forgive me, I'll move away, because I won't endure a cold, empty marriage, even for the sake of my child."

Damon sat down on the edge of the bed and reached out to place his hand on her shoulder. "I didn't want you to return to me because you had to, Catherine. I wanted you to return to me because you wanted to. When you compared me to a jailer, it was more than I could stand.'' He took a deep breath. ''I thought you would be happy to bear my child.''

''I am. Now.''

''Are you sure?''

''I'm sure.'' She reached for his hand and kissed it. ''We've both said and done far too many hurtful things to each other. It's time to forgive and get on with our lives.''

She waited for Damon to draw her into his arms, but to her astonishment, he rose and turned his back to her. ''Damon, what is it?''

''Perhaps you should return to the Blue Room.''

Catherine felt as though he had struck her. So, he wasn't going to forgive her after all. ''If that's what you want,'' she said coldly, flinging off the sheets.

Damon whirled around. ''It's not what I want,'' he cried in an anguished voice. His gaze roved over her naked body with the avidity of a monk being beset by temptation and doing his best to resist. ''I just don't want to harm the baby.''

She was so relieved she almost laughed out loud, but one look at Damon's tormented face erased that impulse. ''You won't.''

''You're sure?'' At her exasperated look, he smiled sheepishly. ''You're a doctor. Of course you're sure.''

He rose again, stripping off his clothes eagerly. When he was naked, he just stood there, letting Catherine drink her fill. Then he slid into bed beside her, pulled her so her back and bottom fit perfectly. Then he buried his face in her hair, murmuring, ''My sweet Catherine has come back to me.''

She closed her eyes with a contented sigh, but they flew open at Damon's next words.

''After the baby comes and once you've recuperated, I'll have no objections to your practicing medicine.''

''I didn't hear you. What did you say?''

''You heard me well enough.''

Catherine wriggled around until she faced him. ''You won't try to stop me from practicing medicine?''

''I still have my reservations, but I won't stand in your way this time.''

''Damon, I—'' She shook her head in bewilderment. ''What made you change your mind?''

''Dr. Steuben reminded me that if you love someone, you

want them to be happy.'' He leaned forward to nuzzle her neck.
''I want my wife to be happy.''

Catherine stared at him, still unable to comprehend the change
in him. But her heart soared with happiness. Just when she
thought she would have to choose between medicine and her
husband, Damon had learned to compromise.

''Your wife is happy,'' she said, her eyes misting with tears
as she drew his head down to her waiting mouth.

As Damon loved her tenderly and with restraint that night,
Catherine thought that her life couldn't be more perfect.

The weeks flew by, and before Catherine knew it, the golden
days of autumn gave way to the white days of winter.

She delighted in the child growing larger inside her womb
every day, relishing the experience she had guided so many other
women through.

Damon was never more attentive and loving, even as Catherine's once-slender figure became shapeless and cumbersome.
But Catherine often caught a worried look deep in his eyes when
he thought she wasn't looking. She knew why: women died in
childbirth.

She noticed that his fear increased as her time of confinement
drew closer. No matter how hard both she and Hilda tried to
reassure him that it looked as though she was going to have a
normal delivery, they could not still Damon's fears.

And with good cause.

Catherine was dozing before the fire in her sitting room when
a grinding pain awakened her.

She listened to the whistling of the wind and the scratching
of sleet against the windowpanes on this cold February afternoon, and thought, what a terrible day for a baby to be born.

Without warning, her waters broke, saturating her thighs and
petticoat.

''It's time,'' she said with a calmness she was far from feeling.

She lumbered over to the window and with her right hand
pressed into her lower back to ease the ache, looked out in dismay. Sleet had been falling since late last night, coating the
world with a thick layer of ice that sent carriages skidding across
the street and brought horses to their knees.

Catherine shivered. She remembered it had been just as cold

in Philadelphia six years ago when she had gone to deliver Lucy Hunter's first baby. Now she would be the one waiting for a doctor as all her patients had waited for her.

She rang for her maid to help her change. While she waited, Catherine tried to remain calm. She was a doctor who had delivered countless babies. She knew what to expect.

Yet her best intentions soon flew out the window. She was a woman about to give birth and she was suddenly beset with the same age-old fears. Would she be able to endure the pain? Would she die in childbirth like her own mother?

Catherine swallowed hard and shivered.

When her maid appeared and Catherine changed, she said, "Tell Mr. Delancy I have to see him at once. He didn't go to work today, so he should be in his study or the library."

The maid left, and two minutes later, Damon appeared.

"I've gone into labor," Catherine said. "Send for Hilda."

Damon's reaction was almost comical to behold. His face fell and his voice rose in panic. "You're having the baby now? There's an ice storm raging out there, for God's sake! How will Hilda ever get through?" Damon began pacing back and forth. "I'll send the cutter for her."

Despite her own mounting discomfort, Catherine placed a reassuring hand on his arm. "Don't worry. The baby won't come for hours yet. Hilda has plenty of time to get here."

Damon's hands trembled as he took her hands and held them to his face. His cheeks felt so cold.

He looked deeply into her eyes. "I love you."

She wished he weren't so frightened for her. "And I love you. Now, go find Hilda. I'll be fine."

"You're sure?"

She nodded and shooed him away.

But five minutes later, Damon was back. "Hilda went out to deliver another baby. Nobody knows when she'll be back."

"Try her again in a few hours." She managed a tremulous smile for her anxious husband. "I'm sure Hilda will be here in plenty of time."

Damon's worried glance at the storm outside told Catherine that he wasn't so sure.

As the afternoon wore on and the sky darkened from gray to black with approaching evening, Catherine's labor pains increased in intensity and duration. As she had advised so many other women, she resisted the urge to bear down, for this would retard her labor, not hasten it.

Damon kept her company, stroking her hand, letting her lean on him as she lumbered around the room. While Catherine usually banished husbands from the lying-in room, she found her own husband's presence comforting and soothing, even if he did scowl at the clock every two seconds.

It was now eight o'clock and the storm showed no signs of abating. Catherine had been in labor for six hours.

Suddenly she felt the character of her pains change from grinding to bearing down.

She looked at Damon. "You had better find Hilda."

He blanched. "If she's not here by now . . ."

"Then send Nevada for Kim. His house is closer."

At the mention of his former rival's name, Damon tensed, and Catherine suspected the thought of Kim being with her in such an intimate setting did not sit well with her husband.

"But he's not your doctor," Damon said.

"He can deliver a baby just as well as Hilda."

"I'll telephone him, then send Nevada to bring him back."

Catherine waited until Damon was out the door before she groaned and staggered over to the chair. She was sweating profusely and her back ached so badly it felt as though someone kept driving an axe into it.

As she sat there, counting every interminable second, she wondered what she would do if Damon couldn't find a doctor to deliver her baby.

She smiled wanly. Then Damon would just have to bring his own child into the world.

Luckily, Damon was spared.

An hour later, Kim rushed into the sitting room, his cheeks ruddy with the cold, and melted sleet clinging to his fair hair.

Damon jumped to his feet, relief plainly written on his face, and extended his hand to Kim. "Thank you for coming."

Kim shook Damon's hand like the gentleman he was, all animosity forgotten. "Don't thank me. It was LaRouche who got me here. I've never seen such driving in all my born days." His eyes went to Catherine. "How are you bearing up, doctor?"

She grimaced as another contraction turned her words into a groan.

Kim set down his medical bag and stripped off his coat. "I think we had better get you into bed."

"What can I do to help?" Damon asked, smoothing Catherine's damp hair off her forehead.

"Nothing," Catherine said. "It's all up to me now."

"Actually, you can have someone boil water," Kim said. "Gallons of it."

Damon squeezed Catherine's hand, brushed his mouth across her parched lips, and left to do Kim's bidding, pausing in the doorway to mouth the words, "I love you."

Kim rolled up his shirtsleeves, then helped her out of the chair and into the bedchamber where her bed had been made with clean linens and a puller attached to one of the posts.

"Now," Kim said, "let's deliver this baby."

"He should be here soon," Catherine said.

Intent on scrubbing his hands, Kim didn't respond.

The next few hours seemed like an eternity to Catherine. Her existence was limned by ceaseless pain and Kim exorting her to "Push! Push!" She even welcomed the temporary release of chloroform when he offered it.

Finally, when Catherine thought she could endure not another second, Kim said, "I can see his head!"

She pushed with all her strength and screamed.

"I've got him!" Kim crowed.

Panting and exhausted, Catherine lay back against the damp pillows, her eyes half-closed as she watched Kim hold her squalling infant. Suddenly she saw his eyes widen in horror and heard him swear from far away.

"What is it?" she demanded before a dreadful weakness sapped what little strength she had left and the room faded into silent darkness.

Catherine dreamed she was in a dark, empty room, a room without furniture, walls, or people. She felt cold and alone.

"Damon?" she called. "Where are you?"

He didn't come, but Sybilla did, materializing out of shards of dancing light, her golden hair floating about her shoulders, her green eyes clear and wise.

Catherine smiled. "You're alive."

"Go back, Cat. It's not your time."

Not your time. Not your time.

Catherine opened her eyes and the dark, empty room was suddenly full. Sybilla had vanished, but Damon was there, sitting beside her bed, his elbows propped on his knees, his dark head bowed.

Catherine felt so drained, she could barely speak. "Damon?"

His head jerked up. The change in him appalled her. His eyes were swollen and red-rimmed, and his cheeks were streaked with tears. Odd, because Damon never cried.

He smiled wanly and grasped her hand. "You're awake."

"Baby?"

He understood what she needed to know, for his eyes shone brightly with pride. "We have a son, Catherine. The most beautiful baby boy you've ever seen."

"Healthy?"

"Of course he's healthy. His mama is a doctor."

With superhuman effort, she managed a weak smile. "Me?"

"You're going to be fine. But Flanders says you have to rest."

"Sleepy."

"Sleep then. Your son will be here when you wake up."

She closed her eyes and slept.

When Catherine next opened her eyes, Kim sat by her bedside. Their gazes locked in mutual comprehension.

Catherine said, "I almost died, didn't I?"

Kim took a deep, shuddering breath and nodded. "Postpartum hemorrhage."

She shivered. She didn't need Kim telling her that she had almost bled to death. Her own mother had died that way, but fortunately for her daughter, the doctor attending her had cared enough to fight.

"Thank you for saving my life," she said, reaching for his hand.

"For a minute I thought I had lost you, but I managed to stop the bleeding." His voice trembled. "Catherine, if you had died—" Kim shrugged helplessly as words failed him.

"But I didn't, thanks to you." She looked around. "Where is my baby?"

"With his nurse in the nursery. Damon didn't want him to disturb you."

As if her own child would. "Will you find Damon and have him bring him to me?"

"Of course."

"I want to see if he was worth the agony."

Kim grinned. "Oh, he is a little charmer. He's got a head full of dark hair already, and the biggest blue eyes you've ever seen. Even LaRouche can't take his eyes off him.'' Kim paused at the door and turned. ''By the way, what have you decided to name him?''

''William. Bill for short. It's the closest we could come to Sybilla for a boy.''

Kim nodded and went to get Damon.

Catherine agreed with Kim's assessment when Damon placed the tiny bundle in her arms and she parted the blanket to see her son's face for the first time. He looked like all the infants Catherine had ever delivered, but because she was his mother, she thought there was no other baby in the world like him.

''Oh, Damon,'' she murmured, as he sat beside her on the edge of the bed. ''I never thought I'd be a doting mama, but I must say that this little lad is perfect. He looks exactly like his papa.''

''But he's got your eyes.'' He reached out and stroked the baby's cheek with his forefinger. ''I'm just glad he's still got a mama.''

Catherine looked at him, realizing for the first time how much Damon must have suffered right along with her.

She smiled at Damon as the baby fussed and screwed up his face to let out a lusty wail. ''That's over and done with. Let's not think about what could have happened,'' she said.

He nodded, but she could tell he would never forget the night he had almost lost her forever.

CHAPTER

TWENTY

AFTER William's birth, the spring and summer of 1894 were anticlimactic to Catherine, despite resuming her medical practice with Damon's approval and Kim's elaborate society wedding to Francine Ballard.

Yet the pleasant lull in her life came to an abrupt and shattering end one September afternoon.

On that day, with the last of her patients gone, Catherine paused to stand at her Washington Square office window, idly watching the many passing carriages now filling the streets since the hot, hazy days of summer were over. As she let the curtain fall and returned to her desk, she smiled in contentment.

She had never been so satisfied with her life as she was at this moment. William was the best baby that a mother could wish for, and Damon had finally accepted her need to practice medicine, tearing down the last barrier between them. She would never stop missing Sybilla, but now time had even dulled the ache of that loss.

Catherine glanced at the clock on her desk, and when she noticed that it was four o'clock, she decided to leave early. Unfortunately, no sooner did she put on her hat and step into the hall than the front door opened to reveal a short, wiry man.

Catherine hid her dismay behind a smile. "Good afternoon. May I help you?"

The man whipped off his bowler hat and held it to his chest. "Are you Dr. Delancy?"

"Yes, I am." She stepped forward and extended her hand. "How may I help you, Mr.—?"

"Baggins." He wiped his palm across his trousers and extended his hand. "That is to say, Homer Baggins."

Mr. Baggins' palm was hot and damp, his handshake weak

to Catherine's firm grip, his watery blue gaze elusive. Catherine guessed his age as middle thirties, and judging by his frayed collars and cuffs, he worked in an office.

She smiled. "I must tell you that I am primarily a woman's doctor, Mr. Baggins, but if you have no objections to a woman examining you, I can treat whatever ails you as well as any man."

His restless eyes darted around the hallway, never lighting on Catherine. "My problem is female in nature. That is to say, my problem concerns my wife, and we are hoping you may help us."

Catherine wondered fleetingly why Mr. Baggins hadn't brought his wife with him. "Step inside my office."

Once she sat at her desk and the nervous patient across from her, Catherine said, "Now, what is your wife's problem?"

The man stared at his hands still clutching the rim of his bowler as it rested on his knees. "I am a clerk by profession. That is to say, I am not a wealthy man. Five years ago, just when I despaired of ever finding someone to share my humble life, I met a wonderful woman who wanted to marry me."

"That's wonderful, Mr. Baggins."

"It is." He looked up at Catherine, his gaze focusing somewhere to the left of her eyes. "That is to say, it was until the little ones started coming."

"How many children do you have?"

"Three, and another on the way."

Catherine certainly didn't envy Mrs. Baggins with three children all under the age of five.

"I wish you had brought your wife with you," she said. "If she is having medical problems due to repeated childbearing, I must examine her."

"There is nothing wrong with her." Mr. Baggins looked down at his hands. "That is to say, everything would be all right if only she didn't keep having a babe every year."

And then Catherine understood. Mr. Baggins was here to learn how he and his wife could keep from having so many children so quickly.

"I don't make much money," he went on, "and with so many mouths to feed, what little I make doesn't stretch far enough. That is to say, we just can't make ends meet." For the first time since he had come into Catherine's office, Mr. Baggins looked her in the eye. "I've heard that doctors know ways to keep a woman from having babies."

Catherine was just about to open her desk drawer and take out one of the anticonception pamphlets she kept there, when a niggling doubt stayed her hand. There was just something about Mr. Baggins that made her uneasy. Perhaps it was his reluctance to look her straight in the eye that made her suspicious. Or perhaps he lacked the air of true desperation and despair that characterized so many of her patients in similar circumstances.

She leaned back in her chair and studied him. There was an air of sly watchfulness about him now, as though he was just waiting for her to do something.

Catherine sighed. "I'm afraid there's nothing I can suggest to you except abstinence, Mr. Baggins. That is to say, if you don't wish any more children, you'll have to avoid marital relations with your wife."

Chagrin passed across his features. "But I can't do that, doctor!" He swallowed hard and leaned forward. "You must know of ways my wife can keep from having a baby."

"I do, but if I supply such information to you, I'll be breaking the law. It's a serious offense. If I'm caught, I'll go to jail. I'm a married woman, Mr. Baggins, with a child of my own to consider."

"I won't tell a soul. You have my word."

Catherine smiled regretfully. "I'm sorry, but I can't. My hands are tied."

"Please! You must help me." His watery blue eyes became wetter. "Think of my poor wife and my poor little ones without enough food to eat, with only rags to wear. You're a mother. How would you feel if your little one never had enough to eat?"

His piteous plea would have swayed Catherine if her suspicions weren't so strong. "I'm sorry, Mr. Baggins. The law is the law." She rose. "Good day."

As Homer Baggins rose, his downtrodden air suddenly vanished. He glared at Catherine resentfully, then jammed his bowler hat on his head and stormed out of the office without another word.

Catherine stood there in silence, listening as his footsteps disappeared down the hall, followed by the opening and slamming shut of the front door. Then she hurried over to the window and parted the curtain so she could watch Mr. Baggins' progress unobserved.

He hurried across the street, where he joined another man who appeared to be waiting for him. This man was as portly as Mr. Baggins was wiry, with a huge paunch hanging over his belt and legs like tree trunks. Huge white mutton-chop whiskers framed his face, and although he wore a bowler, Catherine knew he was bald beneath it.

She spit out his name as though it were poison: "Anthony Comstock."

As Catherine watched, Homer Baggins shrugged and gesticulated defensively, while Comstock turned fiery red with indignation before the two men stalked off.

She let the curtain fall, turned and walked slowly back to her desk.

So Anthony Comstock, the self-appointed guardian of the public's morals, had sent one of his henchmen with a piteous tale to try to trap her into giving him anticonception information.

Catherine propped her elbows on her desk and rested her cold cheeks in her hands, her whole body shaking with relief at the narrowness of her escape.

She knew no one could expect mercy from Comstock. Sixteen years ago, his entrapment tactics had caused Carrie Restell, the notorious abortionist "Madame Restell," to slit her throat in her bath rather than serve a prison sentence.

Upon learning of Restell's suicide, Comstock's only comment was, "A bloody ending to a bloody life."

And now he had Catherine under his scrutiny.

She rose. She had to talk to someone she could trust, someone who would understand the seriousness of her situation. Slipping her wrap over her shoulders, she left the office and hailed a cab.

The moment Catherine arrived at Kim's house, the housekeeper showed her into the library, the only room in the house that Francine hadn't usurped since becoming Mrs. Kimbel Flanders four months ago.

Catherine stalked around the cozy, book-lined room, knotting and unknotting her fingers. After what seemed like hours, the door opened and Kim appeared looking as dapper as if he had just come from the theater instead of his surgery.

His eyes widened in surprise, for he had just seen Catherine last week, when he and Francine had gone to the Delancys' for dinner to welcome her back from summering in Newport.

"Catherine, this is a surprise," he said. Then he frowned in puzzlement. "Is something wrong?"

She grasped his hands and glanced uneasily at the door. "Can we talk here without someone interrupting us?"

"Of course. Francine is shopping and visiting her mother this afternoon. I don't expect her home until dinner." He hesitated. "What is it? You're obviously upset."

She took a deep, shuddering breath. "Anthony Comstock is after me."

Kim blanched. "What?"

"He sent one of his henchmen to trap me into giving him anticonception information."

"That bastard." He placed his hand beneath her elbow and directed her to the sofa. "Come sit down and tell me what happened."

While Kim listened attentively, Catherine told him all about her visit from Homer Baggins.

"I almost gave him a copy of *A Married Woman's Secret*," she said, "but a little voice inside my head stopped me just in time."

"Good thing," Kim replied. "How did you know he was one of Comstock's men?"

"When he left, I looked out the window. Comstock was waiting for him."

"How did you know it was Comstock?"

"I've seen his likeness often enough in the newspapers to recognize his paunch and white sidewhiskers."

Kim shook his head. "That man infuriates me. He claims to be doing the Lord's work, but he's nothing more than a pompous, self-righteous hypocrite. And yet he's a powerful man. People have feared him for over twenty years, and with justification."

"That's because we let him have power over us."

"I'd be careful, Catherine, because the old buzzard delights in persecuting women. Did you know he's responsible for fifteen people committing suicide?"

Catherine's jaw dropped. "Fifteen? Suicide?"

Kim nodded. "Men and women who couldn't face the thought of a long prison term."

"I wouldn't give Comstock the satisfaction."

"Still, I'd like to think Comstock isn't as powerful as he once was. People are beginning to see him for what he is—a prudish hypocrite determined to force his own beliefs on everyone else whether they want them or not. One day he'll be a laughing-stock, and I'll be at the front of the line, laughing the loudest.''

"I fail to see the humor in causing so much misery and fear.''

"I quite agree. The next thing he'll be doing is arresting new mothers because they gave birth to a nude child.''

"How absurd.''

Kim leaned back. ''The man is absurd, but that doesn't make him any less dangerous. He's chosen you as his next target, so what do you intend to do about it?''

Catherine rose and went to the window. ''Sybilla was a staunch advocate of anticonception. Did you know that when she returned from Paris she smuggled a bustle full of pessaries past Customs?''

Kim chuckled. ''I can see Sybilla doing something like that. She was a woman of conviction.''

"We had so many discussions about it. I, of course, being the timid one, refused to have anything to do with giving anything to my patients because it was illegal. Sybilla was ready to flood the East Side with them and damn the consequences. In her own way, she was just like Anthony Comstock, only his opposite.'' Catherine paused. ''Later, of course, I came to agree with her and began distributing anticonception pamphlets and devices to those patients who requested them and who I could trust not to betray me.''

"What made you change your mind?'' Kim asked softly.

"My own marriage. Loving my husband as I do, I wanted to enjoy the—the physical side of marriage, yet being a doctor, I didn't want the burden of a yearly pregnancy.'' Catherine gave him a defiant look. ''And despite what the religious zealots claim, I don't believe conjugal loving is solely for procreation.''

Kim grinned. ''Now you sound like Victoria Woodhull and her free-love advocates.'' His smile died. ''But are you still going to distribute pamphlets and devices with Comstock watching you so closely?''

Catherine sighed. ''Yes, I am.''

He rose and went to her, concern written on his handsome face. ''Catherine, do you dare? You've got little William to consider now.''

"Oddly enough, it's because of William that I feel I must continue.''

Kim scowled in puzzlement. ''I don't understand.''

"Before I became a mother myself, I could sympathize with my patients, but I didn't really understand their plight. Now I do." Catherine's voice hardened. "A baby is so helpless. It depends on us for its food, shelter and well-being. Yet how can a poor family provide a good life if they keep having a baby year after year?"

"They can't."

"I have the means to help women give their children better lives."

"You're taking a big risk, Catherine."

She smiled wanly. "So do you."

"Because I perform the occasional abortion?"

She nodded. "And you have a wife to consider."

He looked sheepish. "She doesn't know about that part of my profession, and she doesn't care."

Ah, yes, Catherine thought. *Unlike me, Francine is the perfect wife for Kim—deaf, dumb and blind.*

Kim added, "Even if they found me out and arrested me, I'd probably get off with a stiff fine. But the penalties for distributing so-called obscene publications and devices are much harsher, Catherine. You could spend years in prison if you're convicted."

Privately, Catherine couldn't understand why preventing the conception of a child was considered more reprehensible than aborting one.

She sighed. "I feel like I'm being pulled in two different directions. I have a responsibility to my patients, yet I also have a responsibility to my husband and child."

Kim placed his hand on her arm. "There's something else you've got to consider."

"And what's that?"

"Damon would kill Comstock before he let that buzzard harm you."

Catherine's expression clouded. "I know he would. Damon is very protective of me."

"Justifiably so."

She looked at the mummy-case clock on the wall. "Gracious, it's getting late and I have to go. Damon will wonder what's happened to me."

Kim drifted toward the door. "I'm glad you came to discuss this with me."

"You're a fellow doctor. You understand."

He raised a surprised brow. "Are you implying that Damon wouldn't?"

A flush of disloyalty heated Catherine's cheeks. "Of course he would."

When they reached the door, Kim opened it and paused. "Remember what I said. Think carefully."

She smiled and squeezed his hand. "I shall."

Just at that moment, Francine came sweeping down the hall toward them. She must have just come in from her afternoon of shopping, for she was still attired in a dramatic short cape of Buffalo red velvet dripping with jet bead passementerie that shivered and danced with every step. A matching velvet hat with a spotted veil drawn over her face lent her a dramatic air.

The old animosity flared briefly in Francine's eyes, then disappeared behind her ladylike mask of polite interest. "Why, Catherine," she murmured with a smile, "how good of you to call." Then she lifted her veil and offered her smooth ivory cheek to her husband for a kiss.

Kim complied. "Did you have a pleasant day, darling?"

"Yes," she replied, focusing her attention solely on her husband to exclude Catherine from the conversation. "I'm afraid I was very naughty and bought out Madame Dumont's."

He smiled indulgently. "I'm sure you'll look lovely in every gown you bought. And how is your mama?"

"Just wonderful. She wants us to accompany her to the opera tonight."

Feeling the intruder, Catherine said, "I must be going."

Francine feigned dismay like the perfect lady she was. "Are you sure you won't stay for dinner?"

"Thank you, but no. Damon is expecting me."

The three of them walked to the front door and lingered.

Kim said, "I'll have my carriage take you home."

Catherine thanked him, said a polite goodbye to Francine, and got into the Flanders' carriage.

As the carriage started off, she waved out the window. Kim was standing on the front steps with Francine beside him, her arm around his waist possessively as if to warn Catherine off.

"I am not a threat, Francine," Catherine murmured to herself, "no matter what you may think."

Then she sat back against the soft leather squabs. She never would have made Kim a good wife, she decided. They may have shared the same profession, but underneath, Kim was a conventional man who needed a conventional wife.

And despite all the stormy weather and rocky roads she and Damon had endured, she was glad she had married him. If she hadn't, she never would have known the joy of having such a precious child as William.

Alone in the carriage with disturbing thoughts she didn't want to acknowledge, Catherine sighed. Could she risk her happiness with Damon for her principles? The prospect of being caught and sent to prison, the thought of being separated from her husband and child for years made her shudder.

But when she thought of how Anthony Comstock had tried to entrap her today, and the poor women he had persecuted in his zeal to impose his prudish beliefs on a society hovering on the edge of a new enlightened century, Catherine felt her blood boil.

"It's just not right," she muttered.

Perhaps she would tell Damon about Comstock and discuss the alternatives with him.

But when she arrived home and found Damon waiting to sweep her into his arms for a passionate embrace, her courage deserted her. This would have to be one secret she kept from her husband.

Two days later, she discovered that her husband had a secret of his own.

At seven o'clock at night, Catherine disembarked from the hansom cab, paid the driver, and stared up at the grand, dark house she had been summoned to just twenty minutes ago.

Without a second thought, she skipped up the steps and rang the bell. If the lady of the house was having a miscarriage as the distraught maid claimed to Molly, then Catherine didn't have a moment to waste.

Seconds later, the door swung open to reveal a striking blond woman in a white flounced and lace-trimmed gown that was much too youthful for her forty-some-odd years.

"Are you the lady doctor?" the woman asked, shrewd eyes raking Catherine from head to hem as if calculating her worth in dollars and cents.

"I am Dr. Delancy," she replied, a sudden feeling of uneasiness skittering down her spine. "I was told someone was suffering a miscarriage and required a doctor."

The woman stepped aside. "Come in. We've been expecting you."

The moment Catherine stepped inside the foyer that smelled faintly of perfume and strongly of cigars, the door shut behind her with a deep, ominous thud, and she had the unmistakable sensation of walking into a trap. Beyond the foyer, she could hear the rumble of masculine voices and the trill of feminine laughter underscoring the energetic tinkling of a piano.

"What is this place?" Catherine demanded with a suspicious scowl.

"Ivory's," the woman replied. "It's named after me."

And then Catherine knew she had been summoned to one of the most discreet and exclusive brothels in the city, a place gentlemen whispered about over port and cigars and ladies like Francine didn't suspect existed.

Despite the flush of embarrassment rising to her cheeks, Catherine said, "Where is the woman who sent for me?"

Surprise filled the madam's eyes. "I thought you'd turn up your pretty little respectable nose and run out of here."

"I'm not a judge, I'm a doctor. Now, where is my patient?"

"She's upstairs. Follow me."

As Catherine followed Ivory up the curving staircase, she prayed she would be spared the humiliation and disillusionment of meeting any men she knew. The thought of seeing a friend's husband, a man she had thought of as happily married, sporting with one of Ivory's harlots, was almost too much for Catherine to bear. Yet she suspected half the men in society had frequented these rooms.

But the upstairs corridors were blessedly empty and quiet save for the occasional startled cry coming from behind a closed door.

Finally, they stopped before one of the doors, Ivory knocked, and ushered Catherine inside.

"Danse, honey, the doctor's here."

The room was not at all what Catherine expected. The decor was tasteful and sumptuous rather than garish, done in restful shades of green. The varied fabrics were sensual, from the soft brocade of the draperies to the plush velvets and slubbed silks of upholstered chairs that invited dalliance.

As she followed Ivory silently across the thick, deep carpet toward the elaborately carved bed, Catherine forgot her surroundings and instead concentrated on the woman who needed her medical skills.

The young woman lying on her side, her knees drawn up to her chest, was as beautiful as the exotic name she bore. Her unbound hair spread out on the pillows like a black thunder-cloud, and her features had a vivid, sultry beauty.

"I'm Dr. Delancy," she said, setting her bag down on a nearby chair and opening it. "I understand you're with child."

Slanted obsidian eyes stared at her in shrewd appraisal as she slowly nodded. Her voice was sultry. "I've got these awful pains. I think I'm losing my baby."

"We'll see." She glanced at Ivory. "Would you please leave us so I can examine Miss, er—Danse in private?"

The madam nodded curtly, turned and left.

Catherine examined her patient with her customary thorough-ness, then stood back and looked down at her coldly. "You're not having a miscarriage at all, are you."

A fleeting look of guilt passed across her features. "No, but I thought if I told you that, you'd . . . do something so I wouldn't have the baby."

Catherine pulled off her stethoscope and stuffed it into her medical bag. "You're asking me to perform an abortion," she said angrily. "I don't perform abortions."

The young prostitute sat up. "I thought you might if you knew it's Damon's baby."

Catherine froze. Damon? Her mind went blank. She couldn't think a coherent thought.

"Damon Delancy is your husband, isn't he?" Before Catherine could reply, the sultry voice gloated, "He's been coming here to me for years. I'm the only one of Ivory's girls he comes to. He doesn't keep me, but one could say that I'm his mistress."

Catherine stared at her in disbelief and finally choked out, "You're lying."

She smiled smugly. "If I'm lying, how do I know he's got the scar from a bullet right—" she pointed to exactly the correct spot on her own arm "—here?"

She would have had to have seen Damon shirtless to know that.

"I can tell you other things about him. Intimate things. Things only a mistress would know."

Suddenly hundreds of doubts screamed through Catherine's mind, and she fought to banish them.

"The baby's his," Danse insisted. "We'll all be happier if you just get rid of it."

"I don't believe it," Catherine said. "You're four months

pregnant. Damon and I have never been happier since the birth of our son seven months ago.'' She snapped her medical bag shut with an angry ''click.'' ''Good evening, Miss Danse. I'm afraid your little attempt at blackmail hasn't worked.''

Her eyes widened in desperation. ''It is his, I tell you!''

Catherine walked out of the room without a backward glance.

As she marched down the long corridor, her shock and disbelief turned to white-hot anger. The woman had to be lying. She didn't know Damon. She had read about him in the newspapers, and when she learned his wife was a doctor, hoped to blackmail her into performing an abortion.

Catherine's steps slowed. But if that were true, how did Danse learn about the scar? And why would she be so stupid as to make such an easily verifiable accusation unless there was some truth to it?

Catherine stopped at the head of the stairs, suddenly feeling lightheaded. It was fortunate that she did, for Ivory was in the foyer below, welcoming another patron.

''Evening, Miss Ivory,'' came a familiar drawl, followed by the soft jingle of spurs.

Catherine's heart nearly leaped out of her chest as Nevada smiled and offered his arm to the madam with the air of an old and valued customer. He lowered his head to catch something Ivory whispered to him, then he chuckled as he stroked his drooping mustache. Finally, the two strolled off down the hall where the girls waited.

If Nevada frequented Ivory's, then Damon did, too.

Grasping the banister so she wouldn't fall, Catherine staggered down the stairs as fast as her trembling legs could carry her. When she reached the door, she didn't look back, just opened it and rushed out into the cool, welcoming night before Nevada could see her.

She was so intent on hailing a cab that she paid no mind to the silent figure standing in a doorway across the street, watching the comings and goings with keen interest. Her only thought was to get away.

Sitting inside the cab, Catherine started shaking, and not from the chilly night air. Fresh doubts about Damon assailed her, leaving her feeling sick inside. If Danse was four months pregnant, that meant Damon had gone to her three months after William's birth—a time he claimed was the happiest of his life.

Oh, Damon . . .

She closed her eyes and swallowed hard, her mind in turmoil. When she thought of Damon lying naked with that woman, sharing intimacies that should have been Catherine's exclusively, primitive jealousy shook her to the core.

"It can't be true," she murmured over and over, heartsick.

She would confront Damon as soon as she returned home.

When she walked into the foyer, Winslow was waiting to take her wrap.

"Where is Mr. Delancy?" she asked, trying to keep her voice steady.

"In the parlor, madam, with Master William," the butler replied.

That surprised Catherine. It was way past the baby's bedtime. His nurse always took him back to the nursery when his parents were through playing with him before dinner.

She marched to the parlor door, opened it, and stepped inside. "Damon, there's something I—" She stopped at the touching sight that greeted her.

Damon dozed in a chair by the fire, his long legs stretched out on a hassock. William was dozing as well, against his father's broad chest.

Catherine closed the door behind her and quietly came into the room. As she looked down at the two men she loved most in the world, she felt a lump form in her throat and tears fill her eyes. William's head snuggled against his father's shoulder, and Damon's large hand lay protectively on his son's back.

Suddenly, as if sensing a strange presence, Damon's eyes flew open and he stared at Catherine. Then he smiled, stifled a yawn, and glanced down at his son with a proud paternal gleam in his eyes.

"We were having a little man-to-man discussion when he fell asleep on me," he whispered, careful not to jostle the baby. "I didn't have the heart to wake him."

Watching Damon handle such a small, fragile baby with such gentleness and tenderness always touched Catherine's heart, but especially tonight, when she was beset with such appalling doubts about his love and loyalty.

She stepped forward and lifted the sleeping baby, who fussed and wriggled in his sleep, then settled against his mother's shoulder with a contented sigh, one small fist in his mouth.

"I'm sending him back to the nursery," Catherine whispered. "It's mama's turn to have papa all to herself."

"Hurry back." Damon grinned wickedly as he stretched, oblivious to what awaited him.

After handing William over to his nurse, Catherine returned to the parlor. The moment she walked through the door, Damon drew her into his arms, and his mouth came down on hers with a fierceness that left her breathless.

"I missed you today," he whispered, his gray eyes as soft as morning fog. Then he kissed her again.

He loves only me, not her, Catherine told herself as she pressed herself against him, trying to burn away all doubts in the fire of his passion. But Danse's words survived the flames as if made of steel.

Catherine drew away.

Damon sensed her reluctance at once. He scowled. "What's wrong?"

She took a deep breath. "There's something we must talk about."

He hesitated, his eyes searching her face. "This is something serious, isn't it?"

"I'm afraid so."

Catherine went to stand before the fireplace, hoping the warmth would ease the chill in her heart. Damon followed and stood a few paces away, his hands in his pockets, a puzzled expression on his face.

"Tonight I received a summons from a woman having a miscarriage," she began. "When I arrived, I discovered that what I had thought was a private home was none other than a bordello."

The admission that she, a lady, had dared to enter such a house didn't disturb Damon, for he knew her work took her into places a lady didn't belong, and it gratified her that he could be so accepting now. He just looked impatient for her to proceed.

"I was shown to a young prostitute's room. After I examined her, I discovered she wasn't having a miscarriage at all. She was four months pregnant and hoped to trick me into performing an abortion."

Damon's eyes narrowed. "Why are you telling me this, Catherine?" he asked softly.

"Because her name is Danse and she claims that the child is yours."

Catherine yearned to see him so stunned with shock that she would have no doubt of his innocence, but to her horror, Damon didn't look surprised at all. His expression remained controlled and inscrutable.

"Do you believe her?"

"I don't want to!" she cried. "But she knows so many damning things about you, intimate details that only a lover would know." She began shaking. "And then as I was leaving, I saw Nevada coming in. He and the madam seemed to be old friends."

Damon shook his head sadly. "Guilt by association, I see."

Catherine whirled away, sick with betrayal. "So you're not denying that you've been to Ivory's."

"Yes, I have been to Ivory's."

His admission was a dagger slicing into her heart. With hot tears stinging her eyes, she turned to escape, but ran blindly into Damon, who had come up behind her. She tried to go around him, but his hands came up to grasp her arms, holding her fast.

Trying to push him away was like trying to budge a mountain. "Let me go, damn you!"

His grip tightened. "Not until you listen to me."

She stared at him, her breath coming in shuddering gasps.

"Please." And he led her over to the chair he had shared with William, and once she sat down, he seated himself on the hassock, his elbows resting lightly on his knees as he leaned forward without attempting to touch her.

"Do you remember on our wedding night, when you said that you knew I had had other lovers?"

"Yes."

"Danse was one of them."

Catherine vision suddenly blurred.

Damon reached out and grasped her hands. "But never when you and I were together, Catherine, so that child can't be mine." His voice shook. "I love you too much to ever do that to you."

She studied him for what seemed like an eternity, then drew his hand to her tear-stained cheek. "I'm sorry I ever doubted you."

"I don't blame you. I'm not a saint, and Danse can be very persuasive." His gaze hardened. "She can also be spiteful and vengeful. She didn't accept our last parting graciously."

"I don't want to talk about her anymore," Catherine said resolutely, rising.

Damon rose with her, a question darkening his eyes. "What do you want to do?"

"I want to go to bed," she whispered.

Damon grinned as his hands slid around her waist. "Then let's go upstairs."

Much later, as Damon lay in bed with Catherine curled against him, he smiled to himself in contentment.

He should have been furious with her for doubting him, but instead he felt absurdly pleased. There had been times in their stormy relationship when he had despaired of her ever loving him as much as he loved her, but her jealousy of another woman proved otherwise.

"What are you grinning about?" Catherine asked sleepily. "You should be furious with me for believing that terrible woman."

He kissed the top of her head. "Any man would be flattered to be fought over."

"I did want to claw her eyes out."

Damon grew serious. "I'm happier than I've ever been in my life. I have a wife I adore, and a son who means more to me than life itself. I'd never do anything to jeopardize that."

"Neither would I," Catherine said sleepily.

Later, her words would return to haunt him.

✌ CHAPTER ✌

TWENTY-ONE

DESPITE foiling Homer Baggins' attempt to entrap her, Catherine wasn't foolish enough to believe she had confounded Comstock permanently. She knew he would bide his time, then strike again like the viper he was.

She didn't have long to wait. Two weeks after Baggins' visit, Catherine's patients in the tenements reported being visited by a portly man flashing an official-looking badge, demanding to know if their doctor had told them sinful ways of not having children. All of her patients insisted Catherine had done no such thing, enraging the man.

As much as Catherine wanted to stop distributing anticonception information, all it took was a tearful plea from a woman with twelve raggedy children clinging to her skirts to weaken her resolve. She risked much, but how could she deny anyone the means of bettering their own lives?

She had to trust her patients not to betray her. If Comstock couldn't get evidence against her, perhaps he would leave her alone.

But she underestimated the man's tenacity.

One cool October morning, Genevra Graham walked into Catherine's office, her pale cheeks flushed from more than the brisk autumn air, and her hazel eyes indignant.

"What's wrong?" Catherine demanded, rising from behind her desk. "Nothing is wrong with little Stone, is there?"

"My son is fine," Genevra replied, removing her chocolate brown velvet cape, "but there is the most horrid man outside your door, asking your patients—" her color deepened "—the most embarrassing personal questions."

Catherine walked over to the window and peered out from

behind the curtain. There stood Anthony Comstock, confronting anyone who approached her stoop.

She swore under her breath.

Genevra joined her. "Who is he?"

"Anthony Comstock."

"Comstock!" Genevra's eyes widened. "What's he doing here, harassing your patients?"

Catherine stepped back. "He has singled me out for persecution." Then she scowled. "I was beginning to wonder why I haven't seen a single patient since I opened this morning. He's been scaring them away."

Genevra, who had benefited from the very type of information Comstock sought to suppress, turned white. "Oh, Catherine, does this mean he's going to arrest you?"

"I'm sure he would like nothing better, but he doesn't have any evidence against me. At least, not yet."

"This is so—so frightening. What are you going to do?"

She took a deep breath to quell her indignation, but it didn't help. "First, I'm going to make him stop harassing my patients."

As Catherine marched out the door, Genevra called out fretfully, "Oh, do be careful, won't you?"

Catherine opened the front door and started down the stairs. There was Comstock trying to intimidate young Mrs. Pleasance, a society newlywed who had come to Catherine before she married to avail herself of anticonception information.

". . . and you must think of our innocent young people, contaminated by the obscene filth this so-called doctor distributes!" Comstock said, towering over his diminutive victim and blocking her way.

But Mrs. Pleasance refused to be intimidated. "Let me pass, you pompous buffoon, or I'll kick you in the shins."

Comstock turned purple. "Do you know who I *am*?" he roared. "*I* am Anthony Comstock!"

"And I am shaking in my shoes," Mrs. Pleasance snapped, elbowing her way past him and starting up the stairs.

For one moment, it looked as though Comstock would drag the woman back, so Catherine started down the stairs.

"I'll thank you to stop harassing my patients," she demanded.

Comstock looked up, his eyes shining with fervor and hatred

as they locked on Catherine. "Ah, another rogue and devil who would keep me from the work of God," he jeered.

Catherine walked down the rest of the steps and stood before him. "If you don't leave my patients alone, I'll have you arrested for depriving me of my livelihood."

The thought of someone daring to do to him what he had done to countless others shook his massive frame with apoplectic rage. "How dare you speak to me that way, you smut-dealer who calls herself a doctor!"

The man so incensed Catherine that she wanted to punch him in his huge stomach, but she knew that was what he was counting on. Then he would have her arrested for assault and she would have accomplished nothing. So she just glared at him coldly, and started back up the stairs.

For such a large man Comstock was surprisingly agile, blocking Catherine's way with his great bulk before she could take another step, looming over her like a vulture about to swoop down and devour her.

"You should hang your head in shame, you evil woman!" he roared, a blue vein standing out in his left temple. "You dare to sully the purity and beauty of womanhood with your vile, disgusting publications and devices."

Catherine stood her ground, fighting to remain calm and controlled. "Let me pass."

"I'll stand here all day to keep you from Satan's work!"

When Catherine looked over Comstock's shoulder and saw Molly hovering in the open doorway, she said, "Molly, call the police."

The moment Comstock turned to glare at Molly, Catherine stepped around him. She didn't take two steps when she felt a hot, moist hand encircle her wrist like a manacle.

Comstock's boldness enraged her. She was just about to send her free hand crashing into his smug, self-righteous face when a low, menacing growl came from behind them: "Take your hands off my wife."

Comstock released her wrist as if it had turned white-hot, and Catherine turned to see Damon standing at the foot of the stairs with murder in his eyes.

"Go inside," Damon said to her, his gaze never leaving Comstock.

As Catherine started up the stairs, she heard Comstock say, "You can't stop me from doing the Lord's work, Delancy. Your wife is a handmaid of Satan, and you're just as sinful for defending her. I'll fight her with my last breath.''

"If you don't leave her alone, you'll be taking that last breath sooner than you think," Damon said.

Comstock just smiled as he walked down the bottom two steps. "All the money in the world won't protect you from the law and God's wrath."

Damon held his ground with feet planted in a threatening stance, forcing the big man to sidle around him, then he looked up at Catherine. "Are you all right?"

She nodded and held out her hand to him. He took the steps in one stride and grasped her hand, his strong fingers warm and reassuring. They walked up the steps in silence. Once in the foyer, Catherine told Molly to have Genevra and Mrs. Pleasance wait while she collected her shattered nerves and spoke to her husband privately.

Inside her office with the door closed, she turned to him with a tremulous smile. "You came just in time. How did you know what was happening?"

Hatless and coatless, Damon looked as though he had bolted out of his office without a thought to his attire. "My old friend Liam Flynn was passing by your office this morning and saw that Comstock had camped outside your door. He told me what was happening, and I got here as soon as I could."

Catherine placed her palms against his chest and sighed. "Thank the Lord for Liam Flynn and his flapping tongue."

"He told me Comstock had Flynn's sister arrested because she once left a naked wax dummy in her dress shop window. He claimed naked dummies inspired lustful thoughts."

Catherine rolled her eyes. "The man goes too far."

Damon's gaze held hers. "Catherine, what is going on? Why has Comstock singled you out?"

"He's trying to find evidence that I've been distributing anticonception literature and devices to my patients."

"And have you?"

"I won't lie to you. Yes, I have."

He looked as though she had just confessed to having a lover. "Why didn't you tell me? Don't you know this is against the law?"

"Yes, I do."

"Then why do you do it?"

"Because they're starved for this kind of information."

Damon studied her. "You're taking a great risk, Catherine. You could go to prison."

She moved away from him. "I'm very careful. I only give it to patients I can trust not to betray me."

"How can you be so sure they won't?"

"No one has yet," she said.

He dragged his hand through his hair. "I don't want to lose you, not after we've found each other again. And there's William to consider as well."

She shrugged helplessly. "But I'm a doctor. I have to do what's right."

"You're also my wife and William's mother." His gray eyes flashed with anger. "Don't we mean more to you than your patients?"

"Of course you do!"

He swept her into his arms and hugged her, his hard cheek pressed desperately against hers. "I know you're idealistic and you want what's best for your patients, but I'm begging you to give this up, at least for now."

Catherine stepped back. "I have tried, but it may be too late. Comstock has singled me out for persecution, and is determined to find evidence against me."

"I'll do anything in my power to protect you, but you've got to help me by desisting for a while." He hesitated. "Please, Catherine. Promise me." Then he held his breath while waiting for her answer.

"I promise."

He closed his eyes as he let out the breath he had been holding. "Good. Now if you'll excuse me, I've got to see about putting some pressure on Comstock to leave you alone."

Catherine raised her brows. "What do you intend to do?"

Damon grinned wickedly. "Unleash the power of the press." He kissed her quickly, then strode out the door, leaving Catherine to wonder just what mischief he had up his sleeve.

She found out two days later when the *Sun*, the *Herald*, and almost every other New York newspaper carried scathing articles or satirical cartoons denouncing Anthony Comstock's methods and holding him up to public ridicule.

While Damon leaned back in his swivel chair and chuckled maliciously as he went through the pile of newspapers on his desk, Catherine didn't share his optimism that public censure would send Comstock scurrying back into his burrow. The man was a zealot, and like all zealots, single-minded and thick-skinned.

But at least Comstock disappeared from her doorstep, allowing her patients to come and go without harassment. Still, Catherine was careful, regretfully telling even her most trusted patients that she couldn't obtain any more devices for them. And she couldn't shake the feeling that when Anthony Comstock finally reappeared, catastrophe would follow in his wake.

In the days ahead, Catherine's worries about Comstock were overshadowed by her preparations for a ball Damon wanted to give. By the time the gala Saturday night arrived, her only worry was that her guests wouldn't enjoy themselves.

The evening started out well. From the moment Catherine came gliding down the stairs in her new gown of burgundy stamped velvet to find her dashing husband in the foyer, following her descent with approval and desire in his eyes, she glowed with happiness and contentment. Standing by Damon's side, greeting their guests, Catherine felt truly at home.

Later, after a sumptuous buffet supper, the dancing began.

As the melodic strains of the first waltz filled the ballroom, and Catherine joined Damon on the dance floor, she smiled up at him.

"Why are you smiling?" he murmured, taking her into his arms.

"I was just thinking how happy I am. I have a handsome, loving husband, a wonderful son, and a thriving medical practice." She glanced at all their guests as they glided around the room. "And I'm finding that I actually enjoy life in high society."

Damon started, his dark brows rising. "Did I just hear you say that you are enjoying all this?"

"As long as it doesn't detract from my practice," Catherine amended.

He grinned. "For a moment, I thought you were turning into Francine."

"You needn't worry about that."

Damon glanced around at the other dancers whirling past. "Speaking of Kim and Francine, I don't see them here tonight."

"They had to send their regrets. Francine's father took ill about a week ago, and they've been spending every evening with him."

When Damon made no comment, Catherine looked up and found him with a preoccupied scowl on his face, his attention directed toward the ballroom's entrance.

Catherine followed his gaze, and when she saw who was filling the doorway, her heart sank to her shoes.

Damon growled, "What in hell is Comstock doing in our house?"

Conversation ceased. Dancers stopped. The music faltered, then died.

Damon started forward, his jaw clenched, his winter eyes pale with murderous rage as he crossed the ballroom. Nevada stepped out of the crowd and joined him, his expression deceptively mild. Catherine followed, feeling as though the grim reaper himself had come for her.

Her enemy stood there, smiling smugly. Three uniformed policemen stood several steps behind him.

Damon stopped not three feet away, his hands balled into fists. "Get out of my house before I throw you out."

"I am here to do the Lord's work," Comstock said, pulling out his badge and holding it up so it caught the light and glinted like Gabriel's sword. "I have a warrant for the arrest of the smut-dealer and abortionist, Dr. Catherine Delancy, and I'm not leaving without her."

A buzz of outrage rippled through the room.

Catherine stood there, paralyzed with shock, but anger soon revived her. "That is a lie!" she cried, taking a step forward. "I have never performed an abortion in my life!"

Comstock whipped the warrant out of his pocket and waved it in the air for all to see. "Not according to Miss Virginia Knott."

"I have no patient by that name," Catherine retorted.

"She is a fallen woman who has seen the error of her ways and repented," Comstock said. "But when she wallowed in degradation, she seduced God-fearing men by another heathen name—Danse."

Aghast, Catherine bristled. "I never—"

"Protestations are useless," Comstock said. "We have a witness who saw you leave the house of ill repute after performing the sinful act. I am here merely as the instrument of the Lord, to bring you to justice."

As Comstock stepped forward to take Catherine into custody, Damon blocked his path. "I told you once before, touch my wife and I'll—"

"Whoa there, Delancy," Nevada said, placing a restraining hand on his friend's shoulder as the policemen tensed and fingered their billyclubs. "This isn't the place for a shoot-out. You won't do the doc any good."

"You'd best listen to him," Gordon Graham said, stepping forward to stand by Damon's side, "or you'll wind up in jail as well."

"They're right, Damon," Catherine said softly. "I have to go with them. You can help me by having one of your lawyers arrange bail as quickly as possible."

Damon's lean face was tight with resistance. "But this is a Saturday night. I won't be able to post bail until Monday morning. You'll have to spend two nights and a day in the Tombs."

Catherine's courage flagged at the mention of the Tombs, a cavernous jail built on what had once been a swamp. She put the horrendous tales out of her mind, for she had to be brave for Damon.

"I'll be fine," she said with more courage than she felt, "as long as I know you won't do anything rash."

"Catherine, I—"

"Please don't make this any harder than it already is! I can face anything if I know you're not going to jeopardize your own freedom."

He capitulated with a resigned nod. "Don't worry about me. I'll handle this legally and aboveboard."

Catherine turned to her tormentor, conscious of the sea of sympathetic faces watching her. "I wish to change into more appropriate attire."

"And give you a chance to escape?" Comstock sneered. "Not a chance."

"Let her change!" someone shouted, and others joined in to chant, "Let her change! Let her change!"

Comstock finally agreed, and Catherine went upstairs to change out of her ballgown and into a serviceable shirtwaist and skirt. When she was finished, she returned to the foyer, her head raised regally as she glided down the stairs.

Winslow brought her velvet wrap, and after Damon placed it

lovingly about her shoulders, he pulled her into his arms for a passionate, defiant kiss.

"Enough of that!" Comstock blustered, stepping forward to separate them.

"Aw, let 'em be," one of the policemen muttered.

Comstock turned to glare at him, and by the time he turned back to Catherine and Damon, they had parted.

"I'll not have my wife carted off to jail in a paddywagon like some common criminal," Damon said, eyes flashing. "She'll go in our carriage."

Another policeman stepped forward and nodded respectfully, for he knew Damon Delancy had powerful friends in the department. "That will be fine, sir." Ignoring Comstock's glare, he said, "If you'll have your carriage brought around, sir, we'll be on our way."

Inside the carriage, Catherine clung to Damon, still unable to grasp the fact that she was going to jail.

"I knew Danse was a spiteful little bitch," Damon said, "but I didn't think she'd go so far as to accuse you of performing an abortion."

"I went to Ivory's that night because I thought she was having a miscarriage. One of Comstock's men must have seen me."

"I'd like to wring her neck."

Catherine didn't say what she'd like to do to her.

Damon turned to her. "You will go free, Catherine. I promise you."

She closed her eyes and nodded.

Her arrival at the Tombs and her heart-wrenching parting from her husband passed like a bad dream. Catherine remained detached, as though she stood outside herself, watching someone else experience the humiliation of incarceration.

Later, when she lay in her dark cell, trying not to listen to the desperate sobs and incoherent mutterings of the doomed women around her, the sobering reality of her situation hit her. She wondered what it would be like to spend months—years—in such a cell. Never to be free. Never to see Damon and William except on visiting days. Never to practice medicine.

And she understood why fifteen of Comstock's victims had preferred suicide.

But even bars and prison walls couldn't confine her dreams,

and when Catherine finally fell into an exhausted sleep, she dreamed of Damon and their next meeting.

As it turned out, she saw Damon sooner than she expected.

The following afternoon was a Sunday, and Catherine paced her cell in an attempt to alleviate the excruciating boredom when she heard heavy, hurried footsteps coming down the hall. She nearly fainted when she saw Damon accompanying the matron.

Impotent rage heated his cold gray eyes as they darted around her cell. "Get her out of that rathole at once!"

The minute the matron had the cell door open, Catherine flew into Damon's arms, not caring that the other prisoners began jeering. Just the feel of his hard arms around her gave her strength and courage.

When they parted, she regarded him in bewilderment. "What are you doing here? I thought I wouldn't be released on bail until tomorrow."

Damon put her velvet wrap around her shoulders. "The charges against you have been dropped."

"Dropped? But—"

"I'll explain when we're out of here," he said, slipping his arm around her waist and ushering her along. "I just want to get you home where you belong."

Once they were alone in the carriage, leaving the Tombs behind them, Catherine reached for her husband and kissed him with a ferocity that left both of them breathless. He reciprocated, his hungry mouth roaming over her face while he held her clasped against him.

When they finally parted, Catherine said, "Now, tell me why the charges were dropped. Danse—Virginia—claimed I performed an abortion on her. Did she change her story?"

Damon shook his head. "Oh, she had an abortion, but someone else did it. Being the vengeful little bitch that she is, she thought she could pin the blame on you without anyone being the wiser. But she didn't count on that other person coming forward with the truth."

Catherine felt cold all over as the truth dawned on her. "Oh, Damon, it wasn't—"

"Kim Flanders." Seeing her stunned look, he took her hand. "When he heard what had happened to you and who had brought charges, he knew that Danse was trying to ruin you."

Catherine leaned back against the squabs. "Dear God."

"He came to see me this morning and said he couldn't let you take the blame for something he did. He went to the police and turned himself in. Danse, of course, insisted that you were the guilty party, but Flanders was pretty convincing."

"Where is Kim now?"

"In jail. I told him that I would put up his bail tomorrow and get him the best lawyer money can buy."

Catherine shook her head. "Poor Francine. Once this scandal hits society, she'll be devastated. She never knew Kim performed abortions."

"I never had much use for Flanders," Damon admitted. "I always thought success came too easily to him. But the man has a core of steel, I'll say that for him. He didn't have to come forward the way he did. He could have left you to take the blame, and no one would have been the wiser."

"He never would have done that to me."

Damon looked at her. "I agree. That's because he loves you almost as much as I do. Enough to risk a prison term."

"I did love him once," she admitted, "before I met you. But I thought that once he married Francine, he would stop loving me."

Damon smiled. "It's very difficult to stop loving you, Mrs. Delancy."

"As long as you don't stop." Then she said, "I hope Kim won't have to serve a prison term. He once told me that the judges are very lenient with doctors who perform abortions, much to Comstock's chagrin. They usually get a fine and a suspended sentence. But what this will do to Kim's reputation and career . . ."

"I'm just glad you're out of there."

"So am I."

Suddenly Catherine began shaking uncontrollably.

"Cold?" Damon asked, drawing her closer to his side to share his warmth.

She snuggled against him. "When I was in that cell, I had to face hard reality. Imprisonment was the price I was going to have to pay for trying to help my patients. And it scared me to death."

"Idealism can exact a high price."

"But to be separated from you and William for months or even years?" Catherine's voice shook. "I'm not that idealistic. I realize that now."

Damon brushed his lips against the top of her head, but said nothing.

Catherine looked up at him. "What did our guests have to say about my arrest?"

"Most of them were incensed that Comstock dared arrest you in such a public fashion, in front of half of New York City society. But it's one of his favorite tactics. He enjoys arresting his victims personally, especially on a Saturday night when they can't post bail until Monday. He likes them to cool their heels in jail for another day to ponder their sins."

"Loathsome man."

He looked at her. "Let's not waste any more time discussing Comstock."

"I agree. I just want to go home and see my son, and then I want to find some way of helping Kim and Francine."

Damon nodded solemnly. "I owe Flanders a debt I can never repay."

"We'll find a way."

The following afternoon, after reading the sensational front-page newspaper accounts of her own arrest and Kim Flanders' coming forward to take the blame, Catherine went to his house to comfort Francine. But Francine was in no mood to be comforted.

Catherine fought her way through the throng of newspaper reporters camped on Kim's doorstep. But the moment she walked in the door and was greeted by Kim's housekeeper, she knew something was terribly wrong.

"I've come to see Mrs. Flanders," Catherine said, handing her wrap to the housekeeper. "I don't suspect she is receiving callers today, but perhaps she'll make an exception."

Worry strained the housekeeper's face. "Oh, Dr. Delancy, I don't know what to do. The mistress has been acting so strangely ever since the master was arrested."

"How strange?"

"She's taken to her bed and refuses to get up. She won't eat. She won't see anyone. She won't stop crying."

"I'd better talk to her," Catherine said, heading for the stairs.

The housekeeper called after her, "It's as though her mind has snapped."

Catherine hurried upstairs, and when she found Francine's

room, she knocked on the door. "Francine? It's Catherine. May I come in?"

"Go away."

Catherine opened the door anyway and entered the bedchamber. She was startled to find Francine sitting up in bed, her dark hair dull and matted as it flowed past her shoulders, her eyes puffy and red from crying.

"Get out of here!" she shrieked.

Catherine approached the bed cautiously. "I want to help you."

"Liar! It's your fault that my husband is in jail." Her face crumbled and her shoulders shook. "We were so happy. Our life was perfect." She glared at Catherine. "And then he felt honor-bound to take the blame for something you did!"

"I'm not going to argue with you, Francine," Catherine said soothingly. "This is a matter you'll have to discuss with Kim."

"Oh, he insisted he had done it, but I don't believe him. I know he still loves you and wants to protect you." Her voice rose. "He's always loved you more than me, damn you!"

"That's not true. You're the one he married. Kim loves you," Catherine said.

The words came haltingly between sobs. "If he loved me, he'd put my welfare first. He'd make me happy." Francine looked up at Catherine. "How will I ever be able to hold my head up in society again? How will I be able to endure the pitying looks, the whispers behind my back? I'll be cut in the street. I'll never be invited to any more parties or dinners."

Catherine stiffened with impatience. "Is that all you can think about—your silly parties and balls? Your husband needs you to be strong for him, to stand by him, and here you are, lying in your bed and blubbering like a child." She glared down at her. "Where is your backbone, Francine Flanders?"

"How dare you speak to me that way!"

"Someone has to," Catherine retorted. "You've always had it so easy. You've always gotten whatever you wanted. You've never known real hardship or even unpleasantness. And now that you're experiencing some adversity, you don't have the strength of character to fight it, do you?"

Francine turned scarlet, reaching toward the nightstand and grabbing a silver-framed photograph. "Get out!" she screamed, flinging it at Catherine.

Catherine sidestepped it neatly, and it crashed to the floor in an ineffectual tinkling of glass. Marching to the door, Catherine turned for one parting shot. "It's time to start acting like a grown woman, Francine, not a spoiled little rich girl."

A howl of rage followed Catherine out the door.

When Catherine reached the foyer, the housekeeper stood there with an anxious look on her face. "Is Mrs. Flanders losing her mind?"

"Mrs. Flanders' mind is fine. She's merely indulging in a fit of temper. I'm sure she'll recover once her husband comes home."

But as she got into her carriage and headed home, Catherine wondered if Francine would ever recover from the scandal of her husband's arrest. She hoped that what she had said today would shock some sense into her, but somehow she doubted it.

"Poor Kim," she muttered to herself. "Just when he needs his wife to be strong for him, she's more concerned with losing her place in society."

Catherine thought of Damon during the last few days, and how he had been a tower of strength for her during this terrible ordeal. Because he loved her, he had learned to compromise—something Francine would never do for Kim.

Catherine sighed. She prayed Francine would somehow gain an inner strength and be able to stand beside her husband.

Francine was not present when Kim posted bail, though Catherine and Damon were. In the carriage on the way back to Kim's house, Catherine tried to make excuses for Francine, blaming her absence on her delicate nature, but she could see from the bleakness in Kim's eyes that he didn't believe her.

In the days to come, Catherine thought it best not to interfere, and stayed away from the Flanders. But all she had to do was pick up any newspaper to know that the scandal was rocking New York City society.

In spite of her arrest, Catherine's practice didn't suffer. In fact, she gained new patients. But now she adamantly refused to dispense anticonception devices, no matter how piteous the pleas. Memories of her chilly, cramped cell in the Tombs was a powerful incentive.

During Kim's trial, which Francine did not attend, he was found guilty; but as he predicted, the sympathetic judge ignored

Comstock's rantings, and gave Kim nothing more than a small fine and a suspended sentence.

While Kim's victory was sweet, it was short-lived.

The moment Catherine walked into Kim's foyer and saw the housekeeper dabbing at her eyes with her apron, she knew that something was dreadfully wrong.

"Has something happened to Dr. Flanders?" she demanded.

"Mrs. Flanders," the housekeeper replied in a shaking voice before bursting into tears.

"Dear God . . ." Had Francine's mind finally snapped? "Where is the doctor?"

"In—in the library."

Catherine ran down the hall as fast as her long skirt would allow, and threw open the library door without knocking. She gasped in shock when she saw the normally fastidious Kim sprawled across the Chesterfield sofa, a drink in hand, his pale gold hair disheveled, and his clothes so crumpled he must have slept in them.

"Kim, what on earth happened?" she asked, going to him.

Bleary-eyed with misery, he looked up at her. "Francine's left me."

Catherine rocked back on her heels in disbelief. "She what?"

"She packed her bags and went back to her mama and papa like a good little girl. She said she doesn't want to be married to me anymore."

Catherine sat down next to him. "Give her time. Once she realizes how much she loves you and can't live without you, she'll be back."

He patted her hand. "You don't believe that any more than I do, but thank you for saying it anyway."

"Perhaps if you go to her—"

Kim's mouth tightened. "It's too late."

Catherine rose and turned away. "I feel responsible. If you hadn't stepped forward to challenge Danse's accusation—"

"But you didn't perform that abortion," he said indignantly. "What kind of man would I be to let you take the blame for something I did?" He rose and refilled his glass with something stronger than his usual sherry. "I accept the consequences of my actions, even if it means losing my wife."

Catherine turned to him. "You know, I always thought you were a society doctor, more concerned with treating wealthy patients than doing what's right. But I was wrong. You have more integrity than most men.''

Kim smiled wryly as he sat back down. ''The cost has been very high, Catherine. But I couldn't let that bastard Comstock get away with sending you to prison.''

''Has the scandal hurt your practice?''

''It's only hurt Francine. Several of her so-called friends weren't at home to her when she called. Invitations stopped coming. She couldn't bear the ostracism.''

Shallow, foolish woman, Catherine thought. *You're not worthy to lick Kim's boots.*

Kim sipped his drink. ''I wish you were my wife. I know you wouldn't desert me at a time like this.''

Catherine's heart went out to him. ''Let's not dwell on might-have-beens. I may not be your wife, but you know that both Damon and I are your friends.''

Tears filled his eyes. ''I think I'd like to be alone now, if you don't mind.''

''Of course not,'' Catherine murmured, rising. She patted him on the shoulder and smiled. ''Everything will turn out for the best. You'll see.''

''One can only hope.''

Then Catherine left him staring moodily into his glass.

The housekeeper had stopped crying by the time Catherine was ready to leave, and helped her with her wrap. ''The house seems so empty without the mistress,'' the older woman sniffed.

Catherine thought of the day she had been here when Francine returned from shopping—so vivacious, her dark eyes sparkling with happiness. She had stood with her arm around her husband's waist, the very picture of a loving wife, as Catherine's carriage drove away. Francine and Kim had been so happy then.

''Perhaps she'll come back one day,'' Catherine said.

''Perhaps.'' But the housekeeper didn't sound convinced.

After saying goodbye, Catherine left Kim's house. She didn't pay any attention to the carriage parked behind hers until its door swung open and a too-familiar stout figure with white sidewhiskers came rolling out.

Catherine stopped and curled her lip in disgust. ''Leave Kim Flanders alone. Haven't you caused him enough misery?''

Anthony Comstock looked like a dog salivating over a ham

bone. "I'm not here for Flanders this time. I've got a warrant for your arrest, Dr. Delancy."

Catherine felt the blood drain from her face, but she stood her ground. "What are you talking about? Those charges against me were dropped."

"These are new charges," he said, gloating. "I've just come from searching your offices. And what I've found there will put you behind bars for a long, long time."

CHAPTER

TWENTY-TWO

"YOU'RE in serious trouble, Dr. Delancy."

Catherine squeezed Damon's hand harder as they sat across from his lawyer, a crafty courtroom campaigner with a deceptively guileless face. Since her arrest and jailing early that afternoon, Catherine's day had been a nightmare until Damon posted bail, insisting that his lawyer consult with them, even though it was now seven o'clock at night.

Catherine cleared her throat. "How serious, Mr. Ledyard?"

He studied the police report in front of him, then rubbed his bloodshot eyes. "According to this list of charges, you could be facing a prison term of five to ten years."

Five to ten years in a place like the Tombs.

Catherine swayed as she felt the office tilt to one side, then right itself. "Five to ten years?" Her voice sounded hollow, as though she were speaking through a tunnel.

"I'm afraid so."

Seated beside her, Damon had turned as gray as his eyes. Suddenly he jumped to his feet. "That's unacceptable, Ledyard. For what I'm paying you, I want you to make damn sure my wife goes free."

Annoyance flashed across the lawyer's tired face. "I'm the best lawyer in New York City, perhaps on the East Coast. But even with my considerable expertise, there's only so much I can do. Comstock has a damning case against your wife. So damning, that if you weren't such an old and valued client, I'd refuse to defend her."

Damon glared at the lawyer. "If that bastard Comstock hadn't sneaked into my wife's office when she wasn't there . . ."

He wouldn't have searched her desk drawers and found the pessaries and copies of *A Married Woman's Secret* that Catherine had stupidly not destroyed as soon as she was released from jail that first time. But in all the excitement surrounding Kim's arrest and trial, she had never dreamed that Comstock would obtain a warrant to search her office.

Ledyard said patiently, "He obtained that warrant on the suspicion that Dr. Delancy possessed and distributed so-called 'obscene' literature that had been sent through the mails, violating the Comstock Law. And he found it in its original wrappings with postage affixed."

Catherine shook her head, perilously close to tears. "How could I have been so stupid?"

"It's not your fault," Damon said. "Your office is private property and that bastard had no right to trespass."

Ledyard said, "That warrant gave him the right."

Damon's nostrils flared as he fought to bring himself under control. When he appeared calm and rational, he said, "What do you plan to do to defend my wife?"

"If she pleads guilty to the charges, there's a chance that the judge may give her a suspended sentence, since she is a first-time offender."

Hope surged through Catherine's veins, and she looked at Damon eagerly, grateful for any chance to end this nightmare.

He wouldn't meet her gaze and remained staring at Ledyard. "But no guarantees."

The lawyer shook his head. "Comstock is especially vengeful against those who distribute anticonception literature." His sympathetic eyes held Catherine's. "And he is going after you with a vengeance, Dr. Delancy."

Damon said, "Surely the judge or the district attorney can be bribed if enough money is offered."

"Damon!" Catherine cried, aghast.

He turned to her, a hard light in his eyes. "I would resort to anything to keep you out of prison. Anything!"

Ledyard shook his head. "I'm afraid you'd be wasting your money. This particular judge and district attorney are quite incorruptible, more's the pity."

"Catherine is the mother of an eight-month-old child," Damon said. "Could we play on the judge's sympathies about separating a mother from her child?"

"I'm afraid not. While Comstock claims to be preserving the purity of women and children, he has no compunction about separating children from their parents, and wives from their husbands."

"Damned hypocrite!" Damon spat.

Suddenly Catherine felt a bone-chilling weariness steal over her. She was so tired of fighting and arguing. She just wanted to go home, hold her baby in her arms, and let Damon hold the both of them.

She rose and faced her husband. "I've had enough. Please take me home."

"It is late."

Ledyard rose. "But we haven't discussed your defense."

Damon said, "It will have to wait. My wife can barely stand after the kind of day she's had." He ushered Catherine toward the door. "We'll talk tomorrow, Ledyard."

"As you wish, Mr. Delancy. Good evening to you both."

They left the lawyer's office in silence, their locked hands making them seem as one.

Once they were in the carriage, the velvet darkness gave Catherine the courage to utter the unthinkable.

"It's hopeless, isn't it?" she asked the silent shadow that was Damon sitting beside her.

"No!" he growled, pulling her into his arms.

Catherine burrowed against him, wanting to feel as safe and protected in the loving circle of his arms as she usually did, but for the first time that feeling of security eluded her. She could cling to him like a shipwrecked sailor hanging on to a rock, but at any moment, turbulent waves of circumstance could wash her out to sea. And even he couldn't stop it.

"We'll fight this together, Catherine," he promised, his lips against her hair. "You're not going to prison."

But as she sat there in silence, listening to his breathing and the beating of his heart beneath her cheek, she wondered how he was going to stop the inevitable. Even wealthy, ruthless Damon Delancy couldn't fight the law this time. He was powerless.

The moment Catherine entered the foyer and saw the somber-face Winslow standing there as always, she had to fight to keep back tears.

"Welcome home, madam."

"It's good to be home, Winslow." But who knows for how long?

As Damon removed her wrap, she said, without looking at him, "I'm going up to the nursery to see William."

"I'm going to my study," he said heavily. "I have to think."

Catherine watched as he stalked off down the hall without another word, his shoulders slumped and his strong step a little slower. Then she started up the steps to go to her son.

In the third-floor nursery, she found the devoted nurse sitting beside her charge's crib, ready to soothe the slightest sniffle or cry.

"I'm going to take him for a while, Ida," Catherine whispered, going to the crib.

Her son was sleeping soundly on his stomach, and for a moment, Catherine hated to disturb him. But tonight, her need to hold him, to feel his familiar weight in her arms, was greater than his need for rest.

When she lifted him and held him against her shoulder, the baby opened his huge blue eyes and stared at her, but didn't make a sound.

"You know something's wrong, don't you?" Catherine whispered, fighting back tears.

She carried him downstairs, to the parlor that had once been her office, sank down into a soft, comfortable chair and sat him in her lap. She ran her hand gently over his dark, fine hair, so silky to the touch, and tickled him in the sensitive spot just below his right ear. William squealed in delight and grinned, a rakish, lopsided smile that could break a mother's heart. Catherine inhaled deeply, savoring the sweet smell of powder and freshly bathed baby. She had to gather such memories now, while there was still time.

"You're such a big boy for eight months old, Wild Bill Delancy," she said, calling him by the nickname Nevada had given him. "You're going to be tall and strong, just like your father. And all the ladies will fall in love with you."

Her eyes watered. She rested her head back against the chair and let helpless tears slide down her cheeks while William's curious fingers worried a button on her shirtwaist.

I love you more than life itself, she thought, *and they're going to take me away from you, my little angel.*

"Catherine?"

She looked up to see Damon silhouetted in the doorway. "Yes?"

He turned on the gaslight and she could see that he was in his shirtsleeves, his waistcoat unbuttoned. "What are you doing here, sitting in the dark?"

"Just spending some time with William." *While I can,* she added to herself.

Damon strode over to her, his expression grim even when his son gurgled and extended his chubby arms up to him. "Take the baby back to the nursery. We have to talk."

Catherine hugged the baby, her hot tears falling on his head. "We've lost, Damon. We've got to resign ourselves to it."

"The hell I will," he growled, glaring at her, "and neither will you." Before Catherine could say a word, he scooped up the baby, who laughed delightedly, and walked off.

Two minutes later, he came striding back into the parlor, shut the door behind him, and faced her. Catherine sensed a renewed optimism about him, and she rose.

"Our situation isn't as hopeless as we originally thought," he said.

Catherine flung up her hands in frustration. "Of course it is! Didn't you listen to Ledyard?"

"Of course I did. He told us that our only chance is to have you plead guilty in the hopes the judge will give you a suspended sentence." He came up to her and looked down at her without attempting to touch her. "It's your life, Catherine. You have to decide if you're willing to risk it."

She stared at him in disbelief. "You do surprise me," she said softly. "The old Damon would have told me what to do."

"Tried to tell you what to do," he amended dryly. "I've learned the futility of trying to order you to do anything."

Catherine knotted her fingers together and began pacing the floor, her brow furrowed in deep thought. Then she stopped and turned to him. "But there's not just my wishes to consider. I have to think of you and William."

"My wishes are obvious. I don't want to spend a day without you, Catherine, never mind five years. And I know William wouldn't want to grow up without his mama."

"What else can we do?" she wailed.

Damon grasped her hands and held them to his chest, his winter eyes alight with hope rather than despair. "We can leave the country."

Catherine was so astounded that she rocked back on her heels. "Leave the country? Are you serious?"

"I've never been more serious about anything in my life."

She stared at him, her thoughts roiling with the ramifications of such an action. "Where would we go?"

"England. We speak the same language."

"But—but we'd be fugitives from justice. We'd never be able to go home again."

"Home is wherever you and William are. You must know that."

"But what about your business?"

He dismissed it with a shrug. "Nevada knows how to run it."

She glanced around the parlor at the familiar furnishings and bibelots. "You would give up everything you've worked so hard for? Your fortune? Your position in society?"

"I can transfer funds, so we won't be destitute. And I've made one fortune—I can make another." He squeezed her hands. "I'm not saying it will be easy. We'll be starting over in a strange country, among strangers. But at least we'd be together, and you'd be free. And you'd be able to practice medicine, Dr. Delancy."

Catherine burst into tears.

"There, there," Damon crooned, taking her into his arms. "Why are you crying?"

"You've never called me 'Dr. Delancy' before. I've always been 'Mrs. Delancy' to you."

He sighed. "You've always seemed like two different people to me, the doctor and my wife. I can accept both of you now."

"You don't know how much that means to me." She paused. "How would we get to England?"

"The *Copper Queen*," he replied, mentioning the steam yacht that had carried them up the Hudson to Coppermine. "As I once told you, she's capable of crossing the Atlantic."

Catherine raised her chin stubbornly. "But I hate running away. It's so—so cowardly."

"On the contrary, it takes great courage. Besides, how can you help your patients if you're behind bars?"

Catherine didn't know what to say to that.

"It's your decision. If you want to stay here and take your chances with a suspended sentence, I'll support you. But if you want to leave, that's what we'll do."

She stifled a yawn. "I'll have to think about it very carefully."

He stroked her cheek. "Don't take too long, my love. You go

to trial in three days, so we haven't much time." Then he took her hand. "Let's go to bed."

They made love as intensely as if it were their last time, and when both of them knew shuddering ecstasy and Damon lay sleeping, Catherine remained awake, watching the patterns of moonlight crawl across the floor.

Escape to England . . .

To leave dear friends like Nevada, Kim, and the Grahams, the success that Damon had struggled his whole life to achieve, her own patients . . . Catherine wondered if she had the courage to do it.

She closed her eyes and slept.

Catherine spent most of the following morning with Damon in Mr. Ledyard's office planning a defense, but by afternoon, she had had enough and left them to return to her office in Washington Square.

An indignant Molly gave a vivid account of Anthony Comstock's raid, telling how he had pushed her roughly aside when she tried to stop him. Catherine started seeing patients, most of whom expressed their own outrage at her arrest.

By four o'clock, just as dusk was beginning to darken the city and Catherine was about to go home, Molly told her there were two gentlemen waiting to see her.

"They're not part of Comstock's band, are they?" she demanded suspiciously.

"No, Dr. Catherine. They say their names are Mr. Featherstone and Mr. Ironside, and they wish to discuss your trial."

"Then send them in."

As the two men entered the office, Catherine thought they made a curious pair. While they didn't look alike—one was short and dark as the other tall and fair—they moved so much in concert that they acted as close as twins, even completing each other's sentences as if one read the other's mind.

"How do you do, Dr. Delancy?" the tall one said, extending his hand. "I am Hugh Featherstone, and this—"

"Is Adam Ironside, at your service."

When they were all seated, Catherine said, "What may I do for you gentlemen?"

The fair-haired Featherstone began. "We have followed your confrontations with Anthony Comstock with great interest, and—"

"—we think you're just the person to finally defeat him," the dark-haired Ironside finished.

Catherine was taken aback. "Me? Defeat him? I fail to see how."

"We represent an informal organization of free-thinking men and women dedicated to overthrowing this Puritan zealot," Ironside continued. "And we would like you, Dr. Delancy, to—"

"—challenge the Comstock Law itself," Featherstone finished.

"Gentlemen, I'm flattered. But why do you think I can accomplish this?"

Featherstone said, "There's been a great outpouring of public sympathy and support for you ever since your first arrest, when you were falsely accused. That sympathy and support has turned to—"

"—outrage since your second arrest."

Catherine looked from one to the other. "What are you suggesting that I do? My lawyer has advised me to plead guilty and hope for a suspended sentence."

Both men shook their heads in unison.

"That will never do," Featherstone said.

"Never do at all," Ironside echoed. "You must plead innocent on the grounds that the Comstock Law is unconstitutional because—"

"—it violates principles of free speech," Feathersone added.

Catherine sat back in her chair. "Gentlemen, while I consider myself a woman of high moral principle, I am not a crusader. My main concern is avoiding a prison sentence so that I can be free to live my life with my husband and baby son."

Their disappointed faces fell.

"But think of the service you will be performing for women throughout this country," Featherstone said. "They will be free to limit—"

"—the number of children they have. Those children they do have will be able to be fed, clothed and educated properly. They will never have to want."

Catherine fell silent as she considered their persuasive words. She thought of all the women in the tenements she had treated over the years, women exhausted by yearly childbearing, and their children with never enough nourishing food to eat or clothing to wear, and she knew she would like nothing better than to abolish the law that kept them enslaved. She knew the risk of going to trial and challenging the law would be great, but if she succeeded, so many unfortunate women would be helped.

Seeing her hesitation, the men leaned forward expectantly.

"You're the one who can defeat Comstock," Ironside said. "You're the ideal of American womanhood—young, and, if I may say so, beautiful and demure. The press has already come out on your side. The judges are growing tired of Comstock's arrogance in the courtroom and—"

"—his silly complaints." Featherstone added, "We must strike while the iron is hot, Dr. Delancy. We must end this— this maniac's twenty-five-year reign of terror and intimidation!"

Catherine rose. "Gentlemen, I shall have to consider this carefully. Thank you for coming."

They rose in tandem.

"When will we know your decision?" Ironside asked.

"Tomorrow," she replied.

"Very good. Thank you for your time and—"

"—good evening."

When Catherine was alone again, she remained at her desk and let the room's deepening shadows steal over her.

The men's proposal astonished her. Sybilla had always been the contentious one, the crusader—not she. Catherine could well imagine her marching into that courtroom with her green eyes blazing defiantly, daring the judge to sentence her to prison.

But Catherine wasn't Sybilla.

When it became so dark that she couldn't see, she finally rose and lit the gaslight.

Suddenly the doorbell rang, startling her.

When she answered the door, she found the tobacconist's messenger boy standing there, panting and out of breath, his round cheeks flushed.

"One of the tenements is on fire, Dr. Delancy," he said between gasps. "I'll bet this message wants you to go there right away."

Catherine looked out over his head. Fire tainted the southern sky an eerie orange.

"I'm sure you're right," she said, opening the note.

As they expected, it was from Hilda, urging her to rush to Bayard Street immediately and bring as much morphia and Vaseline as she could spare.

Before the boy could say another word, Catherine whirled around, rushed back to her office, and stuffed her medical bag with all the supplies she could. Then she prayed she could find a cab.

Catherine had to abandon the cab several blocks from the fire and proceed on foot because the streets were clogged virtually wheel-to-wheel with carriages, streetcars, and wagons. Milling, wild-eyed horses were half-crazed from the smell of smoke fouling the air. The fire engine of a hook and ladder company from another district, its snorting horses harnessed three abreast and firemen warning other drivers to let them through, slowly made headway, its bell clanging indignantly.

People were everywhere, desperate people fearing for their loved ones, concerned people seeking to help in some way, and the merely curious craning their necks to see what was going on. All of them were in Catherine's way.

"I'm-a-doctor-please-let-me-through," she chanted until her throat felt raw. "I'm-a-doctor-please-let-me-through."

Miraculously, they did.

When she arrived near the scene, she felt as though she had stepped into Hell.

Red-orange flames poured out of the tenement building's windows in a roaring swoosh, snapping greedily as they soared into the sky in search of more to devour, finding only a sprinkling of stars and the full moon hanging low. The heat hit Catherine like a blast from a furnace as police let her through their barricades, and the air was so thick with the acrid odor of burning wood that she knew she would be smelling in her sleep for weeks to come. Horses screamed. Firemen shouted. Those who had lost loved ones sobbed, and those who had managed to survive stood mute with shock.

A horse ambulance charged past. Catherine wondered how many victims were packed inside and what hospital they were going to. Then she went in search of Hilda.

She found her over with a crowd of homeless tenants huddled together on the sidewalk like a frightened herd of cattle. Hilda's stern face was streaked with sweat and soot, and her iron-gray hair escaping from its pins every which way made her look like a witch.

"It's about time you got here," she snapped with her usual brusqueness, never taking her attention off the second-degree burn she was dressing.

Catherine didn't take offense. "How did the fire start?"

"One of those social reform photographer fellows was taking pictures of the deplorable conditions in this particular building. His flash exploded and started the fire." She shook her head. "All of these pest holes will burn to the ground."

"Were many injured?"

"Dozens. The fire spread quickly. I'm sure they'll be digging out bodies for days."

"What do you want me to do?" Catherine asked.

"The ones with fourth- and fifth-degree burns have already been taken to the hospitals. Several people had broken legs and fractures, but the other doctors are seeing to them. Dress the burns and wait to see if any of the firemen need care."

Catherine nodded and moved off.

She passed a woman standing there, staring at the burning building in shock, her children huddled to her skirts. Catherine paused when she recognized one of her patients.

"Mrs. Rourke?"

The woman looked at Catherine, her eyes dull and her jaw slack with grief. "Dr. Dee, me Padraic is in there. And me Annie and Maeve and babbie Niall, Holy Mother of God."

Baby Niall was the last child Catherine had delivered for Mrs. Rourke nearly two years ago, the child its mother had resented and didn't want to accept. Now she was mourning him as though her heart would break.

"God's punishing me for my wickedness, Dr. Dee," she cried in a high, keening voice. "I defied the Lord's will, so he's taken me husband and babies from me."

Catherine grasped her shoulder, furious that she should blame her family members' deaths on her use of anticonception measures. "That's not true. God couldn't be so cruel."

"Oh, yes. He's punishing me for me wickedness, that he is."

She shook her head. Why did women always feel that all of life's catastrophes were their fault?

Hearing the low moans of others, Catherine excused herself and went to help.

As she dressed burns of both tenants and firemen alike, Catherine realized how much she would miss practicing medicine in the tenements if she and Damon fled the country. But if she challenged the Comstock Law as Featherstone and Ironside wanted her to do, she could better women's lives everywhere.

But even if it meant sacrificing her husband and son?

You must, a little voice inside her urged. *You must take the risk for a greater good.*

Hours later, the tenement was nothing more than a smoldering pile of ash and rubble. Catherine rubbed her lower back, cramped from hours of stooping and bending, and watched as workers picked through the refuse looking for charred bodies to lay out in the wet street before their trip to the morgue. She shivered, for with the fire finally out, the autumn night had turned cold again.

Hilda came striding over, glanced at the bodies burned beyond recognition and said, "They're better off."

"Hilda!"

"I'm only speaking the truth and you know it."

Catherine rubbed the back of her neck. "You're a fine doctor, but you could display a little more sensitivity now and then."

"No, I'm too old to change." Then she looked at Catherine. "When do you go to trial?"

"The day after tomorrow."

"You don't have a chance, you know."

"Hilda!"

"Don't yell at me. I'm just being realistic. And if you do get off, Comstock will just keep hounding you and hounding you until he finally gets you behind bars where he thinks you belong."

"Then someone should stop him."

Hilda sighed, suddenly looking old and tired. "I'm sure someone will someday. But it's late, and we should get home."

Catherine nodded. She had come to a decision about combating Anthony Comstock.

Damon paced the parlor, glancing at the clock on the mantel every time he passed. It was ten o'clock and Catherine still wasn't home yet. She hadn't even telephoned to tell him she'd be late, and when he called Washington Square, Molly must have gone out for the evening, for she didn't answer.

He went to one of the windows and parted the draperies. He had heard one of the tenements was on fire, and he knew that was where Catherine would be.

He scowled as resentment filled him. Catherine went to trial the day after tomorrow. The least she could have done was let someone else handle any emergencies and come home to her husband, to spend what little time they had left together.

But that was Catherine. Medicine always came first with her. He suspected it always would.

Deep inside his soul, he knew she was going to choose to stay and fight that fanatic, and the thought of losing her terrified him more than the prospect of his going blind after the bombing. He had considered kidnapping her and taking her to England by force, if necessary. But he knew he couldn't. This was Catherine's decision.

He swore under his breath. "Damn it, where is she?"

As if in answer, a hansom cab pulled up the drive, sending Damon flying out of the parlor. He ran through the foyer and out the front door before the cab came to a complete stop beneath the porte-cochere.

He opened the doors and practically pulled Catherine out of the cab. His worried gaze flickered over her, noticing her lovely face smudged with soot, and lines of exhaustion bracketing her mouth. She reeked of smoke.

"You went to the fire." He led her through the front door.

She brushed a kiss across his mouth. "Yes. I'm sorry I didn't telephone to tell you that I'd be home late, but I had to rush."

He caressed her cheek. "I'm just glad you're all right."

She looked down at her soiled shirtwaist and skirt. "I know it's late, but I've got to clean up. I feel filthy."

"You're beautiful."

"Only a loving husband would say that." She started for the stairs, then turned. "I won't be long, and then I'll tell you about the two gentlemen who came to see me today."

He caught her hand. "No, I can't wait. We'll talk while you bathe."

Fire and invitation warmed her pale blue eyes. "How scandalous, Mr. Delancy," she murmured.

But Damon didn't have seduction on his mind. He wanted to know what her decision was, yet he knew he couldn't rush her.

So while Catherine bathed in her pink marble tub, Damon listened to her tell of a Mr. Featherstone and a Mr. Ironside and their proposition. As he sat on a nearby stool and watched her scrub the soot from her face, he wished he could tell what she thought of challenging the Comstock Law, but he couldn't. His wife was keeping her feelings carefully guarded, which in itself didn't bode well for him.

"Are you going to do what they want?" he asked.

"No. I don't think I could win, and then I'd just be a martyr to their cause." She ducked her head into the water to wet her hair. "The tenement fire made me realize what I had to do."

Damon's heart was beating so loudly he was sure she could hear it.

She spoke softly while she lathered her hair. "Being a doctor is my life, Damon, even if I must live that life always fighting against the wind. The thought of never practicing medicine again . . ." She shrugged helplessly, then fell silent as she finished washing the smoke out of her hair.

Damon felt as though he were being slowly flayed alive.

Catherine rose from the water, her skin slick and glowing as she stepped out of the tub and into the towel he held for her. She looked up at him. "But I can't practice medicine while I'm in jail. And there are sick people in England." She placed her hands on his chest, letting the towel fall. "Most of all, I can't risk losing you and William."

He let out the deep breath he had been holding and closed his eyes, enfolding her in his arms. "Catherine, dear Catherine. You don't know the fright you've given me."

Her eyes filled with tears. "I had thought of going to trial and risking everything. New York City is our home. I'm dedicated to my patients. But I also love you, Damon Delancy, and our son. If you're willing to give up all that you've worked for to see that I stay free, I'd follow you to China."

He kissed her deeply and passionately, and when they parted, he said, "Let's go to bed. We have much to do tomorrow."

Anthony Comstock shivered in the cold night air, chilled to the bone in spite of his bulk. He had been standing in the shadows since seven o'clock, watching Delancy's mansion with the patience of a jackal. It was almost midnight, but he would gladly endure the cold all night to bring another smut-dealer to justice.

The Delancy woman was going to bolt.

He could feel it in his bones.

Her husband was a wealthy, powerful, and arrogant man who thought himself above the law. Such a man would think nothing of leaving the country to keep his wife out of prison, especially when he had the means to live anywhere in the world.

"Not if Anthony Comstock can stop you," he muttered.

Self-righteous anger warmed him when he realized all the times Damon Delancy had threatened him as though he were some insignificant underling. Well, he would soon see just how insignificant Anthony Comstock was.

Catherine Delancy's trial was tomorrow, and Comstock intended to see that she appeared in court to be tried and punished.

He waited.

"I hate goodbyes," Catherine said as she hugged Nevada in Damon's study, where the three of them had gathered to say their goodbyes privately.

When they parted, the cowboy drawled, "Sometimes you have to ride on to find greener pastures."

Tears stung Catherine's eyes. "Thank you for being a good friend and making Sybilla's life so happy."

His blue eyes lost their wariness for a moment. "I'll miss you, doc, and little Wild Bill."

Damon clapped him on the back. "Then you'll just have to come to London to visit."

He stroked his mustache. "I don't know about crossing an ocean, Delancy. I'm mighty partial to solid land beneath my boots."

"Just think of it as a vast prairie, only wet," Damon replied. The three of them laughed.

Damon said, "We have to go while there's still time." He extended his hand to Nevada. "Adios, partner. If Comstock comes gunning for you, you don't know anything."

Nevada nodded. "Don't worry. I can handle him."

"We thought we could," Catherine said sadly.

They left the study and walked down the hall, their footsteps slow and reluctant. Even the jingling of Nevada's spurs seemed subdued tonight. When they reached the foyer where Winslow and Ida waited with the sleeping baby, Catherine looked around for the last time and tried not to let the memories, both good and bad, overwhelm her.

As Catherine took her son in her arms and said goodbye to his nurse, Winslow said, "The carriage is ready, sir."

With tearful goodbyes echoing after them, Catherine, Damon, and their son disappeared into the night.

Comstock grinned with glee and uttered a prayer of thanks when he saw the Delancys' carriage pull up to the mansion's front door.

Just as he suspected, they were going to try to escape. But

they hadn't counted on the persistence of Anthony Comstock and the righteousness of his cause.

He hurried down the street to where a hansom cab was waiting, heaved himself in, and ordered the driver to follow the black brougham just pulling out of Delancy's drive and heading down Fifth Avenue. He decided to see where they were going before he confronted and arrested them. After all, it wasn't a crime to go for a carriage ride, even at two o'clock in the morning. But if they headed for Grand Central Station, he'd have them dead to rights.

Twenty minutes later, Comstock could barely contain his elation as Delancy's carriage turned down East 42nd Street. When it stopped in front of the train depot, Delancy got out and assisted his wife, who was dressed in an old-fashioned long hooded cloak and carrying their baby. They hurried toward the entrance.

Comstock was as excited as a bloodhound on the scent. They must have intended to escape by taking Delancy's private railroad car.

When the cab stopped, Comstock jumped out and followed them through the cavernous depot. He cursed roundly when he lost sight of them, but they soon came into view, heading for Delancy's private car parked on one of the tracks.

When they reached the car, the Delancys stopped and conferred. Comstock licked his lips in anticipation as he pulled out his badge and approached them. He wished he could see their faces when he arrested them, but Delancy's was concealed by the muffler wrapped around his neck, and his wife's hidden in the hood of her cloak.

"Catherine Delancy," Comstock began in his most authoritative voice, "I arrest you for—"

His voice failed him when the man whipped off his top hat and muffler, and the woman threw back her hood.

Kim Flanders grinned with the Devil's own satisfaction. "Looks like you're trying to arrest the wrong woman this time, Comstock. This isn't Catherine Delancy, it's Molly Cavanaugh."

"You remember me, don't you, Mr. Comstock?" the woman taunted. "I tried to stop you from breaking into Dr. Delancy's office that day when she wasn't there, and you pushed me aside."

Comstock fell back a step, sputtering incoherently in rage. When he finally regained his voice, he bellowed, "You tricked me!"

Flanders' eyes narrowed spitefully. "Just the way you've tricked so many others, you hypocritical bastard. How does it feel to be on the receiving end?"

"I'll arrest you for helping them."

The woman widened her eyes innocently. "We've broken no laws. Dr. Flanders and myself are just going to visit my poor sick mother in Brooklyn, and are taking her this." She unwrapped the "baby" in her arms to reveal a whole ham. "The Delancys kindly offered us the use of their private car."

Comstock felt his face turn scarlet with rage. "Where are they?" he snarled.

Flanders and Cavanaugh dared to laugh at him.

And then he remembered that Delancy owned a private yacht. He wheeled around and started running. If he hurried, he could still catch them.

"You're too late this time," Flanders jeered.

When Comstock arrived at the docks, Delancy's yacht was gone.

Catherine stood by Damon's side at the *Copper Queen*'s rail, watching the lights of New York City as they glided effortlessly through the harbor and toward freedom.

"I'd give anything to have seen Comstock's face when he discovered that we tricked him," Damon said.

"How did you know he would try to stop us?"

She sensed him smile in the darkness. "I put myself in his place and decided that's what I'd do. My suspicions were confirmed when Nevada saw him skulking down the street tonight."

"I'm surprised Kim volunteered to take your place."

"I'm not. He lost his wife because of Comstock. I'm sure he saw this as the perfect opportunity to exact a fitting revenge." He tightened his hold on her. "I can understand that."

Catherine rested her head against his shoulder. "Thank you for buying the Washington Square brownstone for Molly."

"It was the least I could do to reward her for her loyalty." Damon turned. "Look. The Statue of Liberty."

Catherine turned, and a lump formed in her throat as she looked up at the symbol of freedom, its torch illuminated and outlined against the night sky.

"Isn't it ironic?" she said. "So many come to this country to seek freedom, but for us to remain free, we have to leave."

Damon slipped his arms around her waist and held her tightly.

"Oh, we'll be back someday, once someone vanquishes Comstock."

"Someone stronger than I."

"Don't berate yourself. You're the strongest woman I know, Dr. Delancy."

"Strong enough to face what lies ahead for us, at least," Catherine said.

As the Statue of Liberty grew smaller and its lighted torch became one with the stars overhead, Catherine turned in the direction of England and her new life. This time, the wind was at her back.

THE TENDER TEXAN

by Jodi Thomas

Anna Meyer dared to walk into a campsite full of Texan cattlemen...and offer one hundred dollars to the man who'd help her forge a frontier homestead. Chance Wyatt accepted her offer, and agreed to settle down and build a home with the lovely stranger. They vowed to live together for one year only. But the challenges of the savage land drew them closer together and although the boy in him never considered the possibility of love, the man in him could not deny the passion . . .

___THE TENDER TEXAN 1-55773-546-8/$4.95
(August 1991)